CRAWLERS

JOHN SHIRLEY

BALLANTINE BOOKS
NEW YORK

A Del Rey® Book
Published by The Random House Publishing Group
Copyright © 2003 by John Shirley

All rights reserved under International and Pan-American Copyright Conventions.
Published in the United States by The Random House Publishing Group, a division of
Random House, Inc., New York, and simultaneously in Canada by Random House
of Canada Limited, Toronto.

Del Rey is a registered trademark and the Del Rey colophon is a trademark of
Random House, Inc.

www.delreydigital.com

Library of Congress Cataloging-in-Publication Data
Shirley, John, 1953-
    Crawlers / John Shirley. — 1st ed.
        p. cm.
    ISBN 0-345-44652-6
    I. Title.

PS3569.H558C73 2003
813'.54—dc21   2003045346

Book Design by Kris Tobiassen

Manufactured in the United States of America

First Edition: November 2003

10   9   8   7   6   5   4   3   2   1

Prais   s

"An allegory for our time, full of creepy splendor and excitement . . . *Demons* is a brave and smart book. Read it if you dare."

—*San Francisco Bay Guardian*

"*Demons* is funny, outrageous, and frightening, and, as a metaphor for our times, it works frighteningly well."

—*The Rocky Mountain News*

"John Shirley writes like a runaway train. . . . Intensely suspenseful, visionary, surreal, and every bit as gritty and immediate and believable as a police report, this book will scare you, dazzle you, and delight you."

—Tim Powers

"John [Shirley] never fails to produce work that is both relentlessly readable and truthful. His clear, vivid writing tells real stories; the fantastic elements always convey ideas of substance and observations on human nature. *Demons* is a must-read not only because the writing kicks ass, but because it matters."

—Pat Cadigan
Author of *Tea from an Empty Cup*

"Shirley dishes up enough horrific spectacle, grim humor, and suspenseful storytelling to make the novel well worth reading."

—*San Francisco Chronicle*

"Shirley succeeds in fashioning an over-the-top occult thriller solidly anchored in a bedrock of social consciousness."

—*Publishers Weekly*

SELECTED WORKS BY JOHN SHIRLEY

Novels

A Splendid Chaos

Eclipse

Eclipse Penumbra

Eclipse Corona

Wetbones

City Come A-Walkin'

The Brigade

And the Angel with Television Eyes

Spider Moon

Demons

Short Story Collections

Black Butterflies

Darkness Divided

Really, Really, Really, Really Weird Stories

Heatseeker

for Paul Mavrides
He'll get it.

When another said, "Let me first
go and bury my father," Jesus said,
"Leave the dead to bury their dead."

THE AUTHOR WISHES TO THANK

Micky Shirley,

Julian and Perry and Byron
(for special dialogue coaching),

Paula Guran,

Steve Saffel,

Ivan Stang
(for sundry revelations),

Paul Mavrides
(for appropriated anecdote),

and Q

CRAWLERS

1

Some people are not meant to be in this world very long. They know it, too, in the back of their minds. Maybe they're uncertain, shaky in the way they live life. Maybe they're fragile. Others are the opposite extreme, too reckless. Some, like Ray Burgess—

Who was only twenty-seven years old, that night, in a remote Nevada lab—

—Some are just prone to being in the wrong place at the wrong time. Death seems to know who's going to be the antelope that strays too far from the herd.

Right now, Burgess was crouched behind an overturned metal table in the break room, the table's stainless steel legs projecting away from him toward the door. The lights of the lab were still burning, out there, but here he huddled in the dark next to a soft-drink machine that made him twitch every time it hummed and clicked inside itself. A little light came from the slightly opened door and from the softly suggestive glow of the vending machine.

His right-hand thumb was clamped between his teeth, and every time he heard any kind of metallic noise or the sound of something moving, from the next room, he bit down hard to keep from yelling. It was crumpled and torn, that thumbnail. Pretty soon blood would be seeping out.

He tried to see the luminous face of his watch, but he had his glasses on, thick glasses for his severe nearsightedness, and they made it harder to see things very close. He didn't want to move enough to lift his glasses. He was afraid if he moved, he might bump the table, might make some kind of sharp noise. Did the watch say 9:10?

If it was 9:10 P.M., then he'd been crouching there for more than two hours.

He wondered if Ahmed had bled to death, in that time.

Chances were, Ahmed was pasted to the floor by a sticky puddle of his own blood by now.

He pictured a skin on the pool of Ahmed's blood, like on cooled cocoa. He had always liked Ahmed; the little guy had a sense of humor that was balanced by a kind of trusting optimism. He might still be alive.

If I could get out, get someone to take care of Ahmed.

Probably not going to happen. The damn things had of course cut the phone lines, right out of the box. They might even have incorporated the phone lines—fused them with tissue, somehow.

He'd never make it to the phone down the hall. And thanks to the Dazzling Geniuses, as Ahmed called them, in Security, they weren't allowed to have cell phones in Lab 23. It had never made sense, and now not being allowed to have cell phones made it more likely, it seemed to him, that he and Ahmed were going to die.

Optimistic Ahmed.

Ahmed is going to bleed to death, if he isn't dead already, and I . . .

Ahmed's death might be merciful, really, considering the way Kyu Kim had died. The things had picked Kyu because he was the one who opened the Development Box. He was the one who'd discovered that they had disengaged the lab's safety circuits.

The breakouts had divided Kyu's body into five parts, to use as many muscle groups as they could commandeer. Which meant Kyu's legs had begun to thrash and work themselves free from his torso, like snakes being born from eggs. And then his limbs had started moving around the room on their own. The torso, with the head still attached, went humping off in another direction.

And Ahmed had fallen in front of Kyu's reorganized body, and

Kyu's new jaws started that snap-snap-snapping like electric lawn clippers and ripped into Ahmed's side—before Ahmed had pulled the sterilizer down, onto Kyu's head ... and smashed it. Smashed Kyu's head broken and bloody.

But Kyu's body wasn't dead. Burgess could still hear it thrashing in the next room, now and then, under that big metal cabinet.

Ahmed lost blood fast, lost consciousness when the blood went, and Kyu's eyeless limbs proved to be more or less useless to them. The breakouts were always experimenting, ironically—so they'd abandoned Kyu's parts and started some other kind of "interconnected mutual e-construction." Wasn't that the term the Pentagon boys had come up with?

Something went *click-click* in the lab next door, and Burgess gnawed more deeply into his thumbnail, beginning to taste blood.

He told himself, again, that he had to sit still till morning. *Dr. Sung will have his daybreak shift at the lab. He'll put out the alert, and maybe the Secure Penetration Team will find a frequency, or set up a decoy or—something.*

Or would they just abandon him? Ahmed had said something about how they might have to firebomb the Facility, under certain conditions—as if it was a bioweapons lab. It almost *was* a bioweapons lab. But then again, it wasn't. They hadn't developed a virus or bacterium; not one.

He had to pee and it was getting worse. Could he hold it? Could he pee on the floor without the breakouts hearing? How good was their sense of smell?

He had taken the wrong road in life, the fatally wrong road, signing on for the Facility. He knew that now. But there was no excuse for it: Everyone at the National Security Agency Advanced Research Facility knew that once you were in the Facility, you were committed.

You can't just say, *I've decided to go into something else.* If you thought that Chinese scientist at Lawrence Livermore had it bad, just try walking out on the Facility. Suddenly you'd be "an enemy agent."

Not like there hadn't been warnings. There had been rumors. Things had been going wrong before he'd arrived. There'd been more than one infection. There'd been a Lab 21 and a Lab 22, dedicated to the same project, and they'd both been quarantined. But the new protocols were supposed to be more than enough. "Micro-womb integrity," they liked to say. Burgess had shown just the gift for tunneling-electron manipulation; and they had offered the two-hundred-grand-a-year starting salary he'd needed. It had seemed right.

But he'd known. He's always known that life had it in for him. He'd been pretty sure of it since his mother had joined that Christian end-times bunch. The cult had sucked her right in, like some kind of mutually incorporating program. He'd watched her drive away with those guys. Thin, underfed, faintly smiling guys in prim, cheap suits. And since Dad wouldn't have anything to do with them, he knew then he'd never see her again.

Right now, he really, seriously had to pee.

He peered at his watch, squinting. Pretty sure it said 9:12. Time was ... well, it was crawling. The breakouts were so methodical, it wouldn't be long before they came in. They'd divided things up into sectors by now, probably, and made their assignments. They'd come when it was most efficient.

Come on, man, there's hope. The Facility will get its SP Team together, and they'll break in to save you. Any second now.

Was the break-room door swinging inward, just now, a little?

It did seem that the wedge of light spilling from the lab into the darkened room was wider. Was something peering in, looking for him?

The door opened just a centimeter or two more. Not like a person opening the door. Not like someone coming to save him.

Burgess prayed it wouldn't turn on the light. He didn't think he could see one without screaming. And if he screamed, they'd know for sure he was here.

I won't go on drinking binges with Belinda anymore. I know it was wrong, I know she's married and has a little child, and I won't ever do that again.

I'll go see my dad back home, I swear. I know he's got maybe a year to live and I never go see him. But I will, I'll go see my dad.

Just don't let it turn on the light.

There was a muttering, clickety sound from the door.

And the light came on, and he couldn't help looking over the edge of the table.

And Burgess gave a short scream, distantly aware that he was wetting his pants.

They had stripped all the skin off Ahmed's skull, to be used in some other project, but they'd left the eyes, and there was no mistaking those big brown eyes. Ahmed's eyes.

The skull ratcheted up on a shiny metal improvised spinal stalk, turning slowly, like a periscope, to look right at him.

Then the thing began to crawl his way.

The breakouts climbed into some people and reorganized them, like with Kyu. Others were just . . . parts.

Which was maybe why it pushed the overturned tabletop against him, and simply crushed him against the wall.

He was *mostly* dead before his head popped off his shoulders.

Which was proof, wasn't it, that death is often merciful?

Major Henri Stanner, AF intelligence liaison to the NSA, was leaning out an open door, half hanging about eight hundred feet over the desert floor. He flicked a toggle on the binoculars to filter out the glare of the sun so the boulders and little trees and gullies were crisply outlined within a wash of blue tint. The wind brought the sharpness of sage, the mild perfume of cactus flowers. Maybe there was a faint rotten smell, too, underneath. Could be someone's steer had wandered off and died. Could be a lot of things.

Looking over Lab 23 from the air, Major Stanner said, "If you use a compound that burns hot enough, something magnesium based, I think firebombing will do the trick. That's what the Cleansing

Protocol says." He had to speak loud enough to be heard over the helicopter's engine, the thwack of its blades. The Blackhawk tilted as it curved back over the Facility. He lowered his field glasses and shook his head. "It's really not necessary to nuke it."

"We were thinking just a tactical nuke." Bentwaters scratched his nose and leaned back in the harness. He was a heavy, pale man with a blond crew cut and watery blue eyes. He looked queasy. He wasn't used to choppers. He was used to making decisions into telephones. "Possibly . . . possibly a thermobaric bomb—or two. 'Daisy cutters.' "

Bentwaters was NSA, technically a civilian, but he worked closely with military intelligence. The pale green of airsickness seemed to fit him more, at the moment, than the desert-cammie Special Forces jumpsuit he'd put on for the flight.

The copter came sharply around again, the desert rotating like a vast turntable below.

Leaning toward the open door, Bentwaters looked out, and down—and winced. He quickly drew back.

Stanner asked, "The lab is thoroughly sealed?" Bentwaters frowned and pointed at his ears. Stanner repeated the question more loudly.

Bentwaters nodded, overdoing it. "We went out of our way to do that. There are three walls between the lab and the outdoors. Earthquake-proof, the works. But there are places set up for introducing the bomb charges."

"Okay. You think they'll call this thing off now?"

"You mean, the Facility?" Bentwaters frowned, shook his head.

The chopper quivered again and sucked inertia through itself as it came about. The inertia jolted through both passengers, making Stanner grab a stanchion and Bentwaters grab his stomach. He seemed to blurt the next statement just to keep his mind on something else besides his airsickness. "There's . . . a new plan . . . a way to let it evolve without any risk of infection."

"No risk? No such thing exists!"

Bentwaters said, "They're going to—"

But he wasn't speaking loud enough, and the noise of the chopper drowned him out.

"What?"

Bentwaters shrugged. "Actually, better you don't know until you have to!" He wiped his mouth with the edge of his hand. "Let's go back to base."

Stanner nodded and leaned to catch the pilot's eye, made the "return home" hand signal. The chopper veered again, out over the Nevada desert toward the AF base.

What is it about this side of the department? Stanner wondered. *Why do they all make me feel kind of . . .*

How do I feel, around them? Guys like Bentwaters.

Then he knew. Like his skin was crawling.

He had known guys all his life who gave him that feeling. Even as a kid. People who were always lying, even when they didn't have to.

How'd he end up working for these guys?

He shrugged. He'd seen worse. Some stuff the CIA had pulled in Indonesia. All he'd done was give them some satellite imagery. But what they'd done with it . . .

But then, had it been worse, really?

Could it be worse than the things the Lab 23 cameras had shown them, or the fact they'd known that Burgess kid had been hunkered down in there alive—that they had deliberately waited till he died before they'd moved in? If he hadn't been infected, he might anyway have been traumatized enough to talk to the media. So they'd let those things pop his head off like a champagne cork.

He seemed to hear his father's voice again—as he always heard it, when he doubted his duty. "Stay on task, punk," his career-marine father would repeat to him. "Just stay on task."

Stanner closed the side door, got out of his harness, crossed over to Bentwaters, who was swaying like a drunk with the chopper's motion. Stanner held on to a strap, leaned close—something he didn't like having to do—so they could talk without shouting. Without the pilot catching any of it.

"After what we saw on the cameras," Stanner said, "you guys are really going ahead? For sure?"

Bentwaters licked his lips. "People died testing every major jet fighter prototype," he said, looking out the window, though there was nothing to see. "Astronauts died over at NASA. CIA guys die in the field, just to get a few more facts.

"This project could change everything. Give us an edge the Bad Guys'll never catch up with. The Chinese have something approaching nuclear parity; the Arab Fundies'll have it soon. We need another edge."

Stanner went back to his seat. He didn't say what he was thinking. *When does it end?*

2

Not quite three years later . . .

September 30

A balmy afternoon, the smell of pine resin; the smell of a basketball sitting in the sun.

Adair Leverton scooped up the basketball from the driveway, its rubber hot in her hands, and shot it at the hoop that leaned a little too much toward her on the portable backboard. Her mom had come out of the open garage with a flowerpot in her hand; her father glanced up from his workbench, where he was tinkering with the filter on his scuba gear. They both paused to watch Adair. The ball glanced off the backboard, rebounded into the hoop's rim, spun around twice, and popped out.

Her mom put the empty flowerpot down and caught the ball on the rebound. She said, "I taught you better than to lay up with two hands like a girl, Adair." And she jumped, laying the ball up for a basket with a flip of her right hand. Adair caught the ball as it slipped through the basket, and Mom jumped in to steal it as Dad watched, smiling with one side of his mouth, the way he did.

Mom was only half an hour back from a Saturday girls-track meet and still had her coach whistle whipping with her movements on its thong around her neck; still wore her tan shorts and white shirt and white tennies. She had narrow doelike features, long hair she called dishwater blond caught up on her head with a rawhide clasp—the residue of her hippie days.

Dad still had that little gray ponytail, though his hair was receding. His long, wind-reddened, weather-seamed face showed a hint of his youth, too, in that moment; he was working on something he loved, fine-tuning his salvage equipment, and he was with his kids on a sweet day—both kids because now Adair's older brother Cal was driving up in Dad's truck. LEVERTON SALVAGE on the truck's doors, beginning to fade.

Cal took in the scene as he walked up, tugging up his droopy pants. He walked over to his dad, swiping the rebounding basketball, passing it over Adair's head back to Mom. Adair squealed in mock outrage as Mom faked her out to the left, darted around her. "You got to be faster than that, Adair!"

"Oh, like I want to be a jock like you, Mom!" But Adair was grinning as she skillfully flicked the ball away from her mom's hand.

"What you got going on?" Cal asked, looking over the gear spread out on the worktable beside the driveway. "That filter still choking up?"

"It needs to be replaced. I've got a contract for next weekend— sunk cabin cruiser. It's only forty feet of water so they figure it might be worth it to raise her. Hull's tight, so . . ."

Adair paused, glancing at her brother.

"A contract?" Cal looked at his dad hopefully—then looked away, hiding again. That's how it seemed to Adair.

She passed the ball to her mom, who went to the imaginary free throw line to practice.

Dad had probably figured out what Cal was thinking. But Dad was in a good mood. He hadn't been drinking for a good while; he'd been taking his antidepressants. And he was over being mad: Cal had gotten puking drunk one night, a few months earlier—and next day, hungover, he ran their boat aground on a sandbar. They'd had to be towed off, which cost money, and Dad had said Cal was too irresponsible to work with. Maybe Dad's own drinking issues made him come down hard on Cal.

Cal hadn't done any binge-drinking since, that Adair knew of. He acted as if what Dad thought didn't matter to him. But she knew it mattered, big-time.

Blowing into the filter, Dad said, "You going to help me out, Cal? I'll give you eight bucks an hour, best I can do."

"Oh, God, Nick, you shouldn't have to pay him," Mom said, pausing with the ball in her hands. Catching her breath. These days, she was mostly a coach and not so much an athlete. "He lives with us. We feed him." She shot the ball, missed. Adair caught the rebound.

"Hey, he's old enough to be drafted, he's old enough to be paid," Dad said.

Adair bounced the basketball to her mom, watched her take a shot, and felt, for a moment, that maybe everything was going to be all right. She knew Mom was unhappy with her, though she'd never said so. Mom not liking Adair's computer-art obsession, her interest in sharing art files over the Internet—like she thought Adair was secretly dealing in porn, or something. She'd felt like her mom wanted her to be more into feminism and athletics. Or become a teacher. Yeah, like her.

Zilch interest from Adair in teaching, and Mom had given out a faint but perpetual air of disappointment, until yesterday—when Mom'd seen her artwork in the digital-art show at the Youth Center. It was the best stuff there, and Mom had been proud. And today they were having fun together on Mom's turf.

Cal and Dad were getting back together, and Dad was talking, and working, not in that black funk he'd been in for so long, when he'd been secretly drinking and plunking his guitar alone on his boat at two in the morning.

And she'd met a cool guy, Waylon, at school. He was a year ahead of her, a junior. He'd asked for her screen name so he could instant-message her, and they'd talked late last night on-line. Today was sunny, and birds were singing, and Mom was throwing her the ball again and smiling, and Dad was laughing at some story Cal was telling about what a spaced-out knucklehead his cousin Mason was.

And it was funny how things came together and came apart and came together again, in pulses, in patterns. But then, didn't that mean that things would have to come apart again?

Or maybe something else was coming. Something new.

And for some reason, as she paused to take her free throw, she found herself staring at the sky.

November 19

On the night the light screamed in the sky, Adair was walking with Waylon Kulick, the two of them looking at the television shine in picture windows. Two teenagers looking for something to do on an unseasonably warm evening.

But if you didn't have a car, and you lived where the mass transit was lame, you were stuck between the suburbs and the horse ranches, making it up as you went.

"What I like to do," Waylon said, "is walk around at night and try to guess what people are watching on TV, just by the lights you see in their windows."

He said it in a nervous way, like he was wondering, *Will she think I'm a geek?*

"How do you do that?" Adair asked. They were walking down Pinecrest Street, which meandered along the little defile between Pinecrest Ridge and the high, deer-trammeled grassy hills of the protected watershed.

Adair took the little glow tube out of her mouth and looked at it lighting up the palm of her hand in soft green. It was a souvenir from the rave her big brother had taken her to—glowing like the TV lights in the living room windows.

Waylon glanced at it. "That's hella weird shit, people putting glow sticks in their mouths and little blinking things in their ears at raves."

"I know. And vibrators in their pockets." She tossed the little light-stick in the air and watched him effortlessly catch it. Good hand-eye coordination.

Waylon was tall, too, and leanly muscular, but she was guessing he wasn't a team type. Too bad: the Quiebra Cougars could've used the help on the basketball court.

He was cute, all right, though it was a bit spoiled by the perpetual scowl, the harshness of a pig-shave haircut relieved only by a few Day-Glo blue spikes; just now they seemed to go with the light-stick.

He held the small light-stick up between two fingers to watch it glow against the backdrop of the night. It was the color of cemetery fox fire.

Just to see how he'd react, she said, "Ooh, yuck. It's still got my spit on it."

He permitted himself a brief grin. "Gross. Here, take it back with your, like, DNA samples all over it. That came from a rave? We didn't have any raves where I lived in New York. They got some on Long Island, I heard, over by the Sound, but we were alla way upstate."

Adair found herself looking around—unsure what she was looking for. It was like she could feel the night itself, waiting for something, and that made her wait for it, too.

Mostly she looked over her shoulder, at the sky. She could see lots of stars, out here, since there weren't really enough streetlights.

Something else is coming. She could definitely feel it.

It wasn't like she was psychic; she never really knew what was going to happen. But sometimes—maybe once or twice a year—a kind of *weight* was in the air, a feeling of bigness impending. The feelings weren't frequent. But now and then, only that much, she'd feel something she could never identify till it happened: *Oh, that's what that feeling was about.*

She'd felt something was going to happen the day before her dad had his breakdown. Sometimes—just sometimes—she could feel changes coming the way animals supposedly could feel a storm about to break.

She felt a tightening right now. It was like the night air was some-thing you could roll onto a spindle, stretch it up like a guitar string, tighter and tighter.

"What you lookin' at?" he said, following her gaze into the sky.

"Nothing." What *was* she looking for? She didn't know. "Um, you glad your mom moved to California?"

"I don't know, ask me after I've been here more'n a month." He stared off into the dark hills. Adding, "I can't see my dad much, liv-ing out here." He seemed to realize he'd exposed himself a little, and blurted a change of subject. "And I mean, fuck, *Quiebra, California*, it's sort of embarrassing—"

"Oh, thanks, my town is all embarrassing!"

"Just the name. Quiebra. It's, like, Spanish for queer-bait."

She snorted, not quite laughing. "Don't say that at school, you'll get your butt kicked."

"Ooh, I'm all scared of that. What the fuck's that mean, *Quiebra?*"

"I think it means like broken or . . . a crack in the ground or something. It has to do with they had an earthquake once, in this area, when the Spanish people were here, like before the white peo-ple, and there was a big ol' earthquake crack formed the first day they were here."

"Oh, great. Now I live in a town named after a fucking crack in the ground. What's Spanish for *butt crack?*"

She rolled her eyes. "Ex-*cuse* me? Um, shut *up?*"

"Earthquakes, huh. Hey, where's the earthquake crack?"

Adair shrugged. "Gone, I *guess*, probably. Filled up. I think it was over in the next town anyway, probably, in Pinole. Anyway, we're closer here to San Francisco than you were to New York City. We're right across the bay. San Francisco is cool."

"Yeah, right, the town of Queer-Bait across the bay from fucking *San Francisco*, home of gay parades and shit."

But he said it in a way that made her smile, because he was laugh-ing at himself as he said it. The familiar shade of irony people put on everything. You knew he was the kind of guy who could have a friend who was gay and maybe give him a little shit about it, but neither of them taking it seriously. That's why she liked him, and almost trusted him.

He was the kind of guy who'd make fun of Latino people sometimes, too—but she'd seen him be really nice to Suzie Jalesca, who was Mexican and a flagrant lesbo, and you could tell it was the way he really felt about it: Like there was an obligation to make fun of people of every kind. Make fun of them for being trailer-park whites, ghetto gangbangers, low-rider cholos, white Republican drones, knee-jerk liberals, computer nerds, football fanatics, gays, whatever. Just make fun of them all because that made them all equal. People were more the same than different, and guys like Waylon knew that.

She looked at a TV light shining, blinking web-colored onto the darkened lawn of the house they were passing. "I'd like to do some photography of that . . . just get that glow."

"You into cameras and shit?" It was a gruff way of asking, but he seemed really interested.

"Yeah, I took an after-school class, and I'm sort of hooked on it. It'd be hard to do something like colored lights from a window at night—I mean, to get it the way it really should look. I'm still learning—and I've got a kind of half-assed Canon my mom got me for Christmas last year."

"I always wanted to do that. Photography or movie cameras or something. I can play some guitar, is all."

"My brother plays guitar. Not very good, but he plays. My dad used to sing, but he gave it up." She tried to peer through the half-curtained picture window of a ranch-style house; past the small saguaro in a cactus garden and under a season flag that showed a simplified harvest cornucopia. "Huh. You can't see the actual, like, TV sets most of the time. You can really tell what they're watching from the glow?"

"Those people are watching *The Simpsons* reruns. I just saw some colors that means Bart threw something at Lisa."

"You know too much about television. You should go on that show, *Beat the Geeks.*"

"It's true," he said. "My mom . . . watching TV's about all we do together. Watch TV when she's—"

He seemed about to say something more, but broke off. Another touchy area. But she knew what it was. Maybe they had something in common.

They came to a corner, followed it around till they were walking down Birdsong toward Owlswoop Avenue.

Quiebra was right on the edge of a wilderness preserve. The coyotes were somewhere near, hoping a fat, slow old cat would get restless enough to come up into the hills that crowded the street.

There were rattlers up there, too. They'd come down from the hills and canyons to ease soundlessly through the ivy between houses. Raccoons raided garbage cans, and there were so many horned owls some nights it sounded, Adair's mom said, "like an owl convention."

Adair smiled, seeing jack-o'-lanterns still on people's porches, starting to sag like they were elderly people beginning to fall in on themselves. There was still a Halloween feeling in the air. The O'Haras still had their Halloween lawn scene up three weeks past the time. A life-size plastic skeleton hung from a noose tied to an ornamental plum tree branch, swaying and grinning. A ghost made of white polyester gently bobbed in the slightly growing breeze on a wire depending from a clothesline stretched from the roof to the tree. Rain-shredded black crepe still hung around the front door, with fake cobwebs and half a dozen rubber bats. Two big, wrinkled-up jack-o'-lanterns sat to either side of the porch step. There were gray-painted Styrofoam tombstones in the lawn, some of them knocked over. They had legends on them like, GEORGE DIED HAPPY, GEORGE DIED QUICK, TOO MUCH LIKKER'LL MAKE YOU SICK.

Pretty soon the O'Haras would take the Halloween decorations down, store them in cardboard boxes in the garage, and put up the Christmas stuff. They did everything over the top. Her mom said the garish coating of Christmas lights and props made the O'Haras' house look like a carnival midway. But Adair liked it that way.

"I like how people leave their Halloween and Christmas decorations up way too long," Adair said. "I think it's tight. I wish it was always Halloween, like that place where Jack lived in that Tim Burton movie—"

"Yeah! That's a fucking tight movie!" he said, much to her relief.

Adair and Waylon turned a corner, and the owls declared themselves. One talking to another, tree to tree. Some smaller night bird twittered and muttered and twittered again. Then fell silent.

Then the owls went quiet, too. Waylon was talking about how back home he and his friend had made some kind of Halloween explosive out of cherry bombs with confetti and wax cups and match heads, made some kind of motherhump beautiful blast. But she only half heard him. She felt the night air tighten a little more. The string might break.

Then he started talking about TV lights in windows again, and she tried to make herself listen, but it was hard, with that feeling growing on her.

He pointed at a half-curtained front room window. "It's like, that window there? You can see just see the light from the TV on the ceiling, but it's, like, pulsing real fast, and it's got a lot of red in it? See that? What kind of show you think that is?"

She shrugged. "Um, an action movie?"

"Totally. I check the listings when I get home sometimes, if my mom's not on-line and I can get on."

So he was like most of her friends: he'd almost always rather go on-line, more than anything else, at night. Maybe he was just out with her now because he couldn't get the access line.

The string was twisting tighter.

"What about that one, across the street?" she asked. "What're they watching? I'm not sure about that one, are you?"

"Oh, yeah. That blue light, and it's not flickering that much? It's a drama, or a love story. Because if the light is, like, all jumping around, it's more actiony, or at least a cop story. Yeah, it just got some soft reddish colors in it . . . a love story. Maybe that movie with Kevin Costner about the message in the bottle."

"That was so lame."

He nodded vigorously. "Really." He sang, softly, " 'I had a vision . . . there wasn't any television.' "

She remembered the lines. "The Pixies, isn't it?"

He gave Adair a look of surprised admiration that kindled a warmth in her. "Yeah. So—okay . . ." He pointed. "There's that big brown house, they're watching either an action movie or it's the action part of a movie. Look at those flashes, explosions, everything. It's like the family's having a firefight in their living room, man."

"They're all, like, shooting people in their minds," she said. She glanced at him to see if he thought she was uncool to say that. But he was nodding gravely.

Encouraged, she went on, "Look over there—you can see through the curtains, it's, like, really dark but there are little spears of light . . . science fiction shit."

"Totally. See, you got it."

It gave her a spacey, displaced feeling, looking at the TV lights in the windows; the colored shadows of media dreams.

Waylon articulated some part of her thoughts, but then he took it to extremes that seemed typical of him. "It's like you're seeing hypnosis lights. You know, like when a hypnotist uses flashing spinning lights on people. Like we get all these suggestions fed to us all night through television." He seemed to go into a kind of verbal reverie, talking to himself, reciting something, she thought, as much as talking to her. Like he was rehearsing for an exposé. "People even know, they make jokes about how TV brainwashes them to buy things. I read they use frequencies that make you go to sleep, and into a hypnotic state, and they put in subliminal messages." Then he seemed to catch himself and glanced at her. "You think I'm, like, paranoid."

"I think you're into conspiracy theories." Then she did that snaking move with her head like her friend Siseela, and did her best black-chick imitation. "It's all good, G."

He snorted, and it was his way of laughing.

But that tightening feeling was still nagging her. Adair forced it to the back of her mind. *Think about something else.*

She thought about wandering by Cleo's house, letting Cleo see her with Waylon. Cleo had gone from being her best friend to acting like Adair was a loser. Sometimes, anyway. They were barely talking, because Adair had been becoming friends with Cleo's boyfriend, Donny, a good-looking, way-too-serious black guy who was into African-American politics and could've played basketball, but didn't want to because he thought it was a stereotype.

But Donny had been dating Cleo a long time; Cleo with her sparkling blue eyes and blond hair and her confidence. Cleo had been getting more and more popular, and Adair was just one of the tolerated kids, not someone to be punked, but not really popular.

But then she decided that it would be just as shallow as Cleo to show Waylon off. And her other friend, Danelle, acted real bored when her friends talked about men, or hung out with men, as if it was so puny and stupid, but Adair knew it was because Danelle was overweight and defensive about not getting dates. Anyway, Danelle was on the other side of town.

Instead, she decided that it would be okay if they ripped off some drinks and got a little loose, just a little. He could even kiss her, and touch her breasts if he wasn't too heavy about it. So she said, "You want to see if we can steal some of that peach schnapps? My mom doesn't notice how much there is. My dad's not supposed to drink, but my mom has a drink sometimes."

"Sure, schnapps, whatever. I got sick once on peppermint schnapps, though—don't ever offer me that peppermint kind. Hey, what the fuck is that?"

He was staring past her into the sky over Rattlesnake Canyon. That's what the kids called it, because the animal control workers came out once a year to put rattlesnake traps up around there. It was really just some nameless little ravine at the end of a dead-end street, with a tiny creek you couldn't see for the bushes, a trickle that dried up much of the year. Steep slopes choked with undergrowth, shadowed by pines. It would be pitch-dark now, a hostile place defended by ticks and poison oak and rattlers. One time she'd seen a procession of migrating California brown tarantulas coming out of it; you could almost hear cartoony theme music accompanying them as they tiptoed along. Freaked out some of the ladies of the street.

But now there was a screaming in the sky over Rattlesnake Canyon.

A screaming light that seemed to hang there, coruscating, keening to itself as if an extra-big star was having a raving anxiety attack. And then as they watched it—

The burning light arced down, screaming more loudly as it came, as if it were terrified of the impact—

And struck somewhere beyond Rattlesnake Canyon, on the far side of the protected watershed.

About a second and a half after it came down, the shock wave reached them, the ground shivering, carrying with it the *ow–oomp!* of its impact. A flash of light outlined the piney skyline blue-white. Leaves quivered down from the maple tree looming over the sidewalk as the ground shook. Adair grabbed at Waylon to hold on, and he instinctively put his arm around her.

Then the dogs started up, every last one barking all at once, all over Quiebra Valley.

He realized he'd put his arm around her, and she realized she'd grabbed him. They stepped self-consciously away from one another. She looked at him.

But he was staring toward the place the screaming light had come down.

She looked toward the canyon.

"God! What was it? Shit, it musta been an airplane crash!" she burst out, to cover her embarrassment. "Maybe the terrorists blew a plane up—or crashed it into the refinery! There's a refinery over that way! God, if it was that, we got to get out of the area—it'll poison the whole town!"

"A plane? No fucking way!" He spoke without looking at her, not taking his eyes off the horizon. "It was a fucking UFO crash! That is so *tight*! We gotta get there before the Majestic 12 assholes cover it up!"

He was already hurrying toward the gulch.

"Waylon? Wait up!"

"A fucking crashed UFO, dude!"

Adair sighed. She didn't like it when guys called her *dude*, though the term had nearly lost its gender. "A UFO? Yeah, right. Way more likely a—a helicopter or something. Or a meteor."

She started after him. He was almost running now, toward Rattle-snake Canyon, faster and faster.

"Wha-at? The way it hovered there before it crashed?" he called to her, over his shoulder.

"It was probably coming right toward us so it only looked like it was hovering."

They were running toward the dark tangled brush at the dead end of the street. People were coming out on their porches, their balconies, shouting from house to house, looking for the source of the commotion.

Then Adair grabbed his arm and, puffing, pulled Waylon to a stop. "Wait wait *wait*! We can't go through the canyon, there's no path, it'd take all night and we'd get all poison-oaked up. It's overgrown like big-time."

"So what! This could be really cool—"

"I know, I know, but we got to get there some other way. It looked to me like it came down by Suisun Bay—where the Sacramento River comes out before it gets to be San Francisco Bay."

He snorted a laugh and shook his head. "You talk like I'm supposed to know where that is. Christ!"

"I know the bays around here because my dad's a commercial diver—oh, just come on!"

By the time they got her cousin Mason away from his bong and into his van, got gas in it, and got him to make the necessary turns, there were already state troopers, two trucks of firemen, several coastguardsmen, a couple of sheriff's deputies, and three or four dozen onlookers at the crash site. Probing lights were stabbing around, but most of them were focused into what Adair supposed was the site itself, under a disused dock beside a closed-down sea-food restaurant overlooking Suisun Bay.

Maybe half a mile to the west, the Carquinez Bridge made a black-iron silhouette against the sky, its girders picked out in lamplights, its roadbed streaked with headlights.

The crash site was yellow-taped, but most of the cops, along with the firemen and the coasties on the small white cruiser idling in the water near the smashed-in dock, were staring into the steaming gap where thick beams had been smashed into smoking flinders. The dock itself had crunched down into the water.

Adair and Waylon and Mason got out of the van, and all the men in uniform ignored them. Firemen in yellow slickers stood by with fire extinguishers and hoses, but there was no fire to put out.

"The fucking thing smashed right through the dock!" Waylon said.

"Whoa," Mason said. Which was more or less what he said to almost anything.

"See that shit down there," Waylon said, pushing through a crowd of ogling college students, right up against the yellow tape. "That thing down there's glowing, man."

Adair looked and shook her head. "I don't think so. It's just the lights on the dust and stuff. You can't make out much of anything."

"It's a fucking UFO," Waylon said. "I'm telling you. But they're gonna say it's a fucking weather balloon."

"Huh," Mason said skeptically, gazing at the broken-backed dock. He had his trenchcoat on, was scratching meditatively in his scraggly overgrown soul patch. He had floppy pants hanging off his ass and an *Enjoi Skateboards* T-shirt under the long, greasy coat. Mason was almost thirty-three but dressed fourteen years too young. "A UFO. I dunno, dood."

Adair said, "If we could just get closer . . ."

"Wouldn't, were I you—that stuff's probably radioactive," said an owlish college student with large round glasses, lank blond hair parted down the middle. Campus Republican at Diablo Valley CC, Adair supposed. He wore the kind of shirt that should have a pocket protector, and he did have the pompous air. "Best let the authorities handle this." His smug condescension was familiar to her, and then she recognized him: Larry Gunderston, a senior when she'd been a freshman, college student this year.

"*Riiiiiight,*" Waylon said, snorting. "Trust authority! Buy Enron!"

Then it was Waylon who was looking past Gunderston, at the sky, and Adair who was saying, "What are you looking at?"

"Shit. They're here."

"Who?"

"Majestic 12. It's all laid out in this book I got. I mean, it's like . . . even in a PC game, *Deus Ex*—"

"That's all, like, urban myth," Adair said.

Mason bobbed his head at that. "Yeah, huh. I saw this thing on the Discovery channel, at my aunt's house. Most of that shit isn't true, that black helicopters shit—"

That was the moment the black helicopter landed.

Beating the air with its blades, rattling the asphalt with blown leaves, the chopper came down on the weedy driveway of the abandoned, boarded-up restaurant. There was a designation on its tail, D-23, but otherwise it was dark and unmarked. The men who got out, however, wore uniforms.

"U.S. Air Force," Waylon muttered. "I'm telling you—probably the team they send out whenever there's a crashed saucer."

"Actually," a black deputy sheriff said, smiling broadly as he walked along the yellow tape toward them, "it's a crashed satellite, what I hear." He glanced toward the water. "Funny thing is, I had two reports it crashed out in the middle of the bay. So how'd it get clear over here?"

Waylon was staring at the three uniformed men who'd arrived in the chopper. They were talking to the cops, pointing up the road. One of them was definitely carrying a Geiger counter.

"What else I hear," the deputy said, "it's all melted half to slag, but you can see that's what it is, a satellite kinda deal. NASA on the side and everything. All they'll say about it is, 'It's one of the smaller ones.'" His broad smile shone toothily in the dimness; he was a big guy, straining his uniform, and he was sweating though the wind had risen, brisk now. Adair thought she recognized him from the D.A.R.E. program at school. She looked at his name tag. SPRAGUE.

"*I* remember you," Adair said. "What up, Deputy Dawg."

Mason shot her a *Be cool, I'm holding!* look.

But Deputy Sprague smiled at her. "Hey, I remember—you were the one calling me that. Where was it, over at Quiebra High, right? How those Cougars doing?"

"They suck."

"That's what I heard. Listen, you kids need to get on home. Nothing cool going to happen now, we all just waitin' around till they can get a salvage rig out here, and that's going to take hours—"

"*Nothing cool*, he says!" Waylon blurted. "Deputy, a *black helicopter* just landed and some spooky guys just got out. I mean, they're probably military intelligence—so like, what?"

Deputy Sprague chuckled and shook his head. "Son—"

"Waylon's sort of excitable about stuff like that," Adair said, and instantly regretted it when Waylon shot her a look.

"What I think is interesting," Gunderston said, "is that they must've been tracking this thing, but there was nothing about it on TV, the Internet—nothing. When that other satellite fell in the ocean near Australia, the whole world was watching."

"*Exactly*, dude!" Waylon said. "And those guys in the black chopper—they're like secret operatives and shit—"

"I got it on the radio, son," Deputy Sprague said, chuckling. "They're Air Force guys who've been tracking this thing, is all. That's not a black chopper, that's dark green. And it probably wasn't on TV because it caught them by surprise, too. It fell with no damn warning." He went into more of a cop mode, his body language changing to emanate authority as he raised his hands palms outward. "Now, ya'll move on out—they're not even letting the Channel Five people down here. Everybody got to go—that's all of you folks!"

Adair looked closer at the helicopter, its rotors still whirling. "Okay, it's dark green."

Waylon whispered to her, "We should try to get around the cops, get closer—"

But then it hit her. Salvage!

"Deputy Sprague, my dad does commercial diving and salvage—and he's only a mile from here!"

"If he gets his rig out here . . . I mean, hon, I can't guarantee—"

"Mason! We gotta go! Now! I gotta tell my dad!"

"Whatever," Mason said agreeably.

"Okay," Waylon said, as they trotted back to the van, "but I'm going to get out at the top of the road and circle back through the brush up there. I'm gonna watch this thing."

"Whoa," Mason said. "You are insane in the fucking membrane, cuz, ya kna'mean?"

Dad was in his pajamas, in his open bathrobe, in his slippers, and in a funk of depression—he'd probably gone off his meds again—leaving his personal imprint on the living room sofa. He was hunched, scowling, over an old, scratched-up acoustic guitar. "I can't remember the chords anymore," he muttered as Adair came in.

Dad's long face and long nose seemed longer when he was depressed, because his head was ducked. His dark eyes seemed more like a lost bloodhound's.

She wondered for a moment if he was going to have another breakdown. There'd been only that one time; he'd just sort of frozen up, like a computer running too many programs, and wouldn't speak for two days, shook his head. He'd hung around in his pajamas a lot before that, too.

But she remembered, then, going to work on the boat with him when she was little: how proud she'd been seeing him in his diving gear, grinning at her, giving her a thumbs-up as he went over the side.

More than once he'd saved lives. People stuck belowdecks in boats run aground, the hold slowly filling.

It was hard to remember that guy, looking at him now.

"Dad, there's a salvage job! Right this minute!"

He struck a sour chord and shook his head mournfully. "Now? They have to contract with me—"

"Nick?"

Mom came from the kitchen, a sponge in her hand, shaking her head with that practiced expression of disgusted amazement she had. "You need *work*? Hel-*lo*? Sometimes you have to *go where the work is*?" She looked at Adair. Her sharp features, those forever-down-turned lips, seemed skeptical, disbelieving anytime she looked at Adair. "Where's the job, Adair? And why are you jumping up and down, like there's ants in your drawers?"

"I'm trying to tell you that—that there was *a crash*!" She didn't want to say that it was a satellite. Explaining would just mean more delay.

"A car? Someone run off a pier?"

"No, it's a—an aircraft or something. A small craft kind of thing. Dad, there's government guys out there. It's at the end of Norton Slough Road—where that old dock was, on Suisun Bay?"

Mom looked interested. Government checks could be pretty big, for divers. She walked across to her husband on her quick, small feet and firmly took the guitar from his hands. He didn't react except with his usual slumped appearance of passive hurt, which was, Adair knew dimly, some indirect form of aggression.

"Nick, we need the money. No matter what you and I decide to do—the money's going to be necessary. Get up and get over there. Don't even go to the boat, your gear's ready in the truck."

"I don't think I could right now—"

"*Nick!*"

He twitched at the sharp, barking syllable, rather more than he needed to, and sighed deeply, got up, grunting with apparent effort, and went into the bedroom to change. Adair wondered if Dad had already decided to go, but he'd forced Mom to yell at him so he could make her look like a bitch again.

A guitar stand stood beside the sofa in the cluttered, untidy living room. Adair thought there was almost an affection, a wistfulness, when Mom walked over and put the guitar on the stand. The way you put an urn with the ashes of the dead on a mantel.

"Mom, what'd you mean?"

Silkie, their Siamese cat, jumped up onto the little lamp table beside Adair, exactly where she wasn't supposed to be. An old cat, with kinked tail and patchy fur. Instead of pushing her off the table, Adair gave her what she'd come up there for, a scratch behind the ears, a rub on the top of the head. "Silkie silk, you old silkie silk." Silkie looked up at her with cloudy eyes and gave out a gravelly noise of response. But Adair was still waiting for her mom to reply.

Mom ran her chewed-up nails through her wispy hair. "What'd I mean about what?"

"You said something to Dad just now about 'no matter what you and I decide to do.' "

"Nothing in particular." Mom turned to go back to the kitchen.

Cal was there suddenly, in the doorway to the hall that led to his bedroom. "She meant the divorce. They're talking about getting a divorce."

"Cal?" Mom didn't look at him as she spoke. She went into the kitchen, saying, "Don't talk when you don't know what you're talking about. I realize that's hard, when you're almost a grand total of nineteen years old, but just don't." The rest of it half-muted, coming from the next room. "—just try."

Cal was taller than Dad or Mom, with a head that seemed slightly too big for his body. He'd let his hair find its own destiny with thick brown dreadlocks. He wore horn-rim glasses, precisely because they were ugly, and cutoff oversize army pants, a camouflage jacket, a Rodney Mullen T-shirt stained with pizza sauce. His pale, heavy-jawed face wasn't particularly reminiscent of Mom or Dad, which elicited, from time to time, the usual "should've kept an eye on the cable guy" jokes. Jokes that made Mom laugh nervously, Adair had noticed.

Cal looked at Adair, then tilted his head toward the backyard and went down the hall to the back door. She knew what that meant.

She went out the front way—holding the front door open for Silkie to go out, too—and walked around the house through grass a month overdue for cutting. Silkie vanished into the shadows.

Adair met Cal beside the rain-warped glider in the backyard; the yard with its high grass and small lemon tree. Even in November, there were dewy lemons in it. She couldn't remember why they'd started meeting in the backyard that way. It started about the time they felt their parents were listening in on them.

"You're full of shit," she said as she walked up to him. "They're, all, scowly and mean twenty-four/seven, it's been like that for years. Nothing's any worse than before. They're not breaking up."

"That's funny you saying I'm full of shit—when you're steaming it from the ears. Beyond that, of course, you suck."

"You suck, moron," she answered, as expected.

"You suck, retard-o-girl." Then in his world-weary explaining-things-to-the-little-sister voice, he said, "But *no*, uh-uh, that's totally what they're talking about—divorce. Dad's all stressed out about money and they just . . . hate each other."

His voice broke, just barely, when he said those last three words.

"They *don't*. Oh, hey, you should see what happened over at Suisun Bay. I didn't want to say it, they wouldn't believe me. The cop there said it's a crashed satellite! What if Dad could be their salvage guy? That would be, all, national TV news and shit. He could get some big-ass work from that."

His eyes widened. He looked at her with his head tilted. "Now you're really full of shit. Satellite!"

"No, it is! And there's like military choppers and stuff. Just ask Mason, he was there!"

" 'Kay, I'm gonna go check this out. But you better be right about the job. There goes Dad in his truck."

She sat down on the glider swing, which was broken; she could sit on it, but it didn't glide anymore. She shook her head.

"They chased us out, though, Cal. They won't even let the TV news van in there now." Something occurred to her then, and she looked anxiously after Dad's truck. "I dunno, that thing down there could be radioactive. They'll give Dad a protective suit or some-thing, won't they?"

"I don't know. Most likely." His voice was husky with excite-ment as he gazed off toward the bay. "Suisun Bay . . ."

She chewed her lip, thinking about Dad down there. "It's the access road to that closed-down restaurant, where there used to be a dock—"

"Oh, *hell* yeah!" He snapped his fingers, on his left and right hands at once, the way DJ MixLord did when he was about to scratch some old vinyl. "I know that place! We used to go to that dock at night to smoke pot and listen to our boxes. Fuck it—I'm gonna check it out, too. So they chase me off, so what."

"I did see a guy with a Geiger counter."

"Radiation. Yeah, right. It's a chunk of metal that fell in a hole. I mean, come on, bee-atch? How dangerous could it be?"

3

Nick knew at a glance he'd have to bluff his way past the U.S. Marines standing on the other side of the yellow tape. But they looked as puzzled as everyone else about all the hubbub that surrounded the ruins of the dock. Sometimes, clueless people were a way in.

"Boys," Nick said, approaching, carrying his light diving gear. Taking in the soldiers, the Coast Guard, the chopper; feeling excitement rise in him. "I'm the salvage crew, at least for starters. I've got to have a look before I decide if I need to bring in the rest of my people." Sure, like he had employees anymore.

He glanced past them. A couple of guys in white lab coats, one with a Geiger counter, stood at the stoved-in dock.

Where were the local cops? Left, already? The Feds must've chased them off.

A few coastguardsmen stood by the dock wreckage, a few more watching, leaning on the rail of the white boat chugging in idle, just offshore. He might be too late; the coasties had their own divers.

The taller of the two young jarheads scratched his crew cut and put his helmet back on. His friend had a big, slightly crooked nose. Both of them had carbines slung over their shoulders on straps. "I'll have to get that cleared through channels. This is DIA territory now—NSA, the whole route."

The shorter marine, a stocky guy with a self-important expression, turned the other a stern look. "Yo, bud, can that *DIA* talk—that's need-to-know shit, man."

Nick thought, *DIA? The Defense Intelligence Agency. That's the military's CIA. And they're keeping it quiet.*

"Anyway," the taller marine said, irritated with his pal's reproach, "I'll have to run it by Sergeant Dirkowski. They put him in charge till—"

Nick snapped his fingers just as if he really recognized the name. "Dirkowski! That's who I'm supposed to talk to." Nick patted his pockets. "Shit! I've got a fax here somewhere. Maybe I left it on my desk."

A stocky man in a Green Beret uniform—ruddy-faced guy with pale blue eyes, pig-shaven under the beret—strode over to them, looking sharply at Nick as he came. A sergeant, Nick noticed. He took a chance, and said, "Ah, Sergeant Dirkowski!" The sergeant carried something that seemed a cross between a little walkie-talkie and a cell phone. Plunging ahead with his bluff, Nick went on briskly, "I'm your salvage diver." And handed him a card.

Dirkowski looked at the card. His thin lips flickered a smile. "You are, huh. Well, Mr. Leverton? I'm afraid this is a government operation."

Nick wasn't going to give up easily. This thing looked like a decent payday. He needed to show his family he could do something right again. Hell, he needed to show *himself.* "Sergeant, I do government contracting all the time. They don't have enough trained deepwater guys. Now this looks shallow to me, here, but I'm still your best man—"

"Sorry—" Dirkowski broke off as a voice crackled from the small walkie-talkie thing in his hand—a new model to Nick. He gestured "wait" and put the little instrument to his ear. "Dirkowski. Yeah, do tell. What do you mean, am I surprised? Never surprised by snafu, just surprised when there isn't one. Well, two hours is no good. Waitaminnut, I might have something else here." He lowered the walkie-talkie and looked appraisingly at Nick. "So you're a salvage diver? We don't have a diver on the boat we have here, and the boat coming with a diver doesn't have working grapples—not that'll work on something heavy as a satellite. How soon could you get down there?"

"I, uh . . ." Nick cleared his throat, playing for time till he could think this out. *A satellite?* "You sure there's anything left to pull up? I mean, if it came from space—and hit a dock . . ."

"Tell you something I don't want to hear repeated—it hit the water out there first, at an angle, almost like you'd skip a rock. It went under, came up again—one of the orbital control rockets must have refired—and smashed down here from about, maybe, a hundred yards up. So, could be it's partly intact."

Nick stared. Was that possible? For it to hit the water and then jump up and—

"Well?" Dirkowski snapped, looking at his watch. "Can you do the job or not?"

"Uh, yeah! Anytime you want. In a hot minute. Once I've got my boat here, I mean—" Except for the uniform, Dirkowski looked more like a hungry plainsman than a spit-and-polish Green Beret. "I—I have to do that, if you don't have a crane with salvage grapples. I've got a small crane, the hooks, everything you need but—"

Dirkowski shook his head. "No time. I'm going to have to—who the hell is that?"

The Green Beret was glaring toward a converted fishing trawler easing up to the remains of the dock. The coastguardsmen were shouting, waving for it to move off. But the boat, with only two running lights, came on anyway.

Nick knew the boat by its silhouette. "Actually, that's my boat, *Skirmisher.* My son's at the wheel, I expect. The kid's thinking ahead."

He smiled at Dirkowski, who nodded. "Okay, I'll call Washington, authorize your craft."

Nick ducked under the yellow tape, thinking, *All this security. What the hell is down there?*

"I should be pissed off, Cal," Nick was saying as he adjusted his mask, preparing to step backwards off the deck of the *Skirmisher*.

Shooting some lube into the winch, Cal grinned at him. "Hey, Dad, I got here when you needed me here. I got the instincts, man. I got skills."

They were on the deck of *Skirmisher* and Nick was feeling too good about getting this job to give the boy hell for running his boat behind his back. It had worked out, and it felt good to be on a deck with Cal again. Last two years, Cal hadn't shown much interest in anything except DJ culture and raves.

"Yeah, well, you're never again to run my boat without asking me. This time it worked out. But listen, you don't talk about this shit. You signed that paper, too, Cal. You're eighteen now, you swore, when you signed that paper, you'd keep your mouth shut about this. Nondisclosure. It's not that big a deal, it's not like the public doesn't know but—they take it seriously." He gestured toward the sergeant.

"Dad? I'll be frosty."

"All right, get that winch going. I want to take the hook down with me, in case it's an easy rig-up—which isn't likely, but—the hell with it. Here goes."

And with that, he stepped off backwards and dropped into the water, his head tilted so the water pressure didn't pop his mask off.

Cool darkness closed over Nick, shutting off the surface sounds. Now there was just the sound of his exhalations bubbling, the background rumble of two idling boat engines.

Then there was the light, shoreward, maybe twenty yards off, where the coasties' searchlight sliced the water under the smashed dock.

He'd been a little stunned when Dirkowski had confirmed the

thing was a satellite. It could've hit all that ocean, all that bay—even his own house.

But it had hit this little dock, right in the middle. Like it wanted something to break its fall at the end; something near the shore.

Funny how inanimate things seemed to take on a life and destiny of their own. When you were in salvage, hoisting safes and barrels and classic cars up out of the water, you thought about those things.

He looked up expectantly and there they were: Above, in black silhouette, hung the three big, blunt-point, jointed metal hooks on the line lowering toward him like some sea creature reaching down.

He took a small flashlight from his belt, switched it on, grabbed the nearest hook, and swam, towing it behind him, toward the crash site.

He angled himself downward, almost burrowing into the old familiar pressure, till he was a few yards over the bottom. A kind of foul gray glaze of processed sewage and boat-spew clung to things down there, making the sand striations on the bottom aluminum-washboard colored, sealing a sunken tumble of old truck tires into the muck. Even a living crab, sidling out from under some drunken boater's sunken beer cooler, was coated with the drab fuzz—like the bay's bottom was moldy.

That was Suisun Bay. It made him want to get out to the Channel Islands with Cal again, where the water, at least, was honest seawater.

He was a few yards from the leaning pylons that stood like damaged church pillars, with those lights shining down from above.

He shivered in his wetsuit. A ruined church? Odd, the thoughts he was having. Like some part of his mind, equally submerged, was trying to tell him something.

Closer . . . He reminded himself to try not to touch the pylons and beams leaning over the crashed thing; the wood had been cracked, smashed open, and he could see the yellow wood bright beside a tarry black coating. The beams had to be precarious. This was a lot more dangerous than he'd let on to Cal and Dirkowski. But risk was why he got paid pretty well—when he could get the work.

Kicking down into a deeper, heavier coldness. Bubbles streaming. There, a gleam of metal under the wooden wreckage—an irregular oval in the sand. A few angular projections thrust out of the grimy sediment on one side.

Closer. The exposed part of its curved hull was like a giant cracked metal eggshell, silvery and blackened, mostly buried in the sand, with the pylons and splintery beam ends and depth-muted lights all around it.

He squinted along the beam of his own flashlight. The satellite might be thirty feet long, all told. Nothing much to hook on in the exposed surfaces. Dirkowski had said it was shaped like a cylinder, with communication extrusions and rocket vents. The parts projecting out of the sand looked fragile, like they'd just break off. He was going to have to dig out around it, find something sound to grapple. Maybe have to loop some chain over those pylons first, pull them away from the thing for clearance. He hoped he didn't have to use a sand sucker. He'd have to borrow one from the Maritime School.

Nick swam closer, into another, heavier fold of water pressure, and into colder water, within reach of the bottom. A single, sickly, hand-size fish darted past his mask.

He thought he saw a bright metallic movement within the jagged crack along the top of the satellite's hull. His light flashing off its parts, he supposed.

All in all, though, it was surprisingly intact. But from what they'd told him, it'd come down at a shallow angle. Maybe this satellite *had* sort of chosen this place—because he'd heard Dirkowski say something about "firing orbital control rockets" as it came down. And how it hadn't received orders to do that.

Nick had heard that a lot of the more expensive satellites had small rockets on them, used for correcting orbital position. But from what he'd read, the correctional rockets weren't designed for atmospheric reentry. Weird that the satellite had "decided" to fire rockets to slow an entry it probably wasn't designed to make.

Questions rose in his mind like the streams of bubbles around him.

Had the DIA themselves fired those rockets remotely, brought it to this spot? Had they slowed its descent so it'd come down intact? Was it even an American satellite, or some kind of stolen Russian bird?

But then he saw the markings. Those weren't Cyrillic letters. He could make out some of the part that wasn't hidden by sand and cloudiness:

NATIONAL AERONAUTIC S

Below that:

DEPARTMENT OF DE

And the usual enigmatic array of numbers and letters that must mean something to some bureaucratic bean counter somewhere.

So this is one of those NASA-military collaborations.

As he thought all this he flipped close enough to brush sand away from the edges, looking for a fixture to hook. Just pulling it out of the sand might tear off any part he grappled to, though. Sand liked to hold on to things, once it had them. No, they'd have to dig it out.

He was floating almost upside down, angling his feet upward over the satellite, kicking now and then to keep from being nudged back up by water pressure. The lights from above danced around him, wavering in surface moil and splitting on the sand, on the metal edges of the satellite's shining fracture.

Dirkowski had said the radiation level was negligible, but best not to touch the thing with his bare hands.

Still, he could save time if he could get the grapple into that crack, grip some of the superstructure under the hull. He reached into the crack.

He felt around. Something . . .

It felt like something was reaching up, in response, from inside the satellite. A string of bubbles, maybe—but like it was feeling around. And its touch stung very slightly. Could be he was feeling some sort of residual electric charge.

The stinging passed. Then he felt something else, almost like a girl touching his palm teasingly with her soft fingers.

Testing, tentative, almost playful.

* * *

A second dark helicopter, marked only with D-23, had to wait for the first to take off before it could land. Major Stanner jumped down before the Blackhawk had quite set down, and—instinctively ducking under the whipping blades, one hand securing his hat against the rotor blast—he jogged over to the ruined docks.

Sergeant Dirkowski was there, talking into a cell phone. Stanner knew him from the DIA; he'd gone out on some black ops in Pakistan Stanner had helped plan.

The Green Beret broke the cell phone connection and saluted as Stanner approached. Stanner returned the salute. "Sergeant. That doesn't look like a Navy SEAL vessel."

"No, sir, the SEALs couldn't get a man here with the equipment in time. This man said someone had called him to replace the SEAL diver—"

"What man, where?"

Dirkowski nodded toward the water. "He's already down there, sir."

Stanner's mouth went dry. "Dirkowski . . . you tell this man that there was . . ." He couldn't remember if Dirkowski had been briefed on this bird. He thought not.

"I warned him there was some radiation danger—not to touch the thing directly."

Stanner grunted, shaking his head. So he hadn't been briefed. Great.

Stanner walked over to the gently lapping shingle by the wrecked dock. He watched the diver's bubbles on the water. As he watched, the bubbles stopped coming up.

Standing at the rail on the deck of the *Skirmisher*, Cal squinted down into the murky water. He couldn't make out much of anything, despite all the light from the surface. Sometimes he saw his Dad's spotlit shape, in wallowy outline, but then he lost it again as the light broke up on the dark waves.

Cal had let *Skirmisher* drift in the rising tide toward the crash site, so he was nearly over the top of it, as Dad had instructed him. Dad's cable had paid out for a while, and then stopped moving.

Minutes passing.

More minutes. Nothing from below.

He'd been waiting too long, hadn't he? He tugged on the cable, sharply, two times, to let Dad know he was asking if all was well.

He waited, his hand on the cable, so he could feel the slightest twitch of response.

Still nothing.

Dad had geared up with only a single tank of air. It was one of the small tanks—an inspection tank, he called it—for ease of movement. For a quick look around. Fifteen minutes. It had been that already, hadn't it? And he couldn't see Dad's air bubbles anymore.

That Air Force officer seemed concerned, too. The guy who'd come on the second chopper. "Hey, kid!" The officer shouted at him, from the shore. Looked like a captain or a major or something. "He supposed to be down there that long for a first inspection?"

"Uh, no! You got any divers here?"

"We got a rescue diver over here!" one of the coastguardsmen yelled from the boat. "You want him to suit up?"

Cal hesitated. It would tick Dad off big-time if Cal sent a rescue down when Dad didn't need it. He looked down into the water— just darkness and wavering light. He wished Dad had taken a mask with a headset in it, so they could stay in radio contact—but theirs was broken, and they couldn't afford to get it fixed. And Dad had wanted to get down there fast, to make the job his own.

He looked at his watch. Definitely—he was down there at least two minutes past his tank's capacity.

"Fuck," he muttered, looking around for a mask and tank. He was going to have to go down himself.

He figured he knew what'd happened. The satellite had smashed into the dock, which meant a lot of heavy broken timbers down there—shit too heavy and waterlogged and mired in the muck to float up. Some beam from the dock might've fallen in on Dad.

He could be screaming for air right now.

Feeling tears burning to escape, Cal pulled a mask on, shouting to the coasties, "I'm going down—be good if you send a man down—"

"Send a man down to what?" came a voice from the water.

Cal leaned over the railing. There was Dad's pale face against the dark water, looking up at him, his mask pulled onto the top of his head.

"What the hell, Dad! You know how long you were down?"

"So it was a few minutes extra, so what. I know how to conserve air after all these years."

Cal looked at his watch. More like five minutes extra, he thought. Damn, his old man had *mad skills*.

But five minutes without air? That wasn't really possible, was it?

Suddenly Dad was there, vaulting over the railing onto the deck like a young man despite the weight of his tank, the cold water, and the exertion.

Cal remembered that you looked for signs of strange behavior in a diver who had been down too long. He might have a mild form of oxygen deprivation—dementia or something. But Dad was already over at the winch, throwing levers so it'd slowly start taking up the slack.

The Air Force officer came alongside in a launch from the Coast Guard boat. "The boat there, Major Stanner coming aboard."

More laboriously than Cal's dad, Stanner climbed up the ladder and swung himself onto the deck. "You're starting your equipment already?"

Dad nodded. "It's ready to go. The support structures happen to've fallen in a configuration that shouldn't cause any problems. I haven't started the real lifting yet—if you don't think it's ready to come up. But I was able to clear the sand away. It should be solidly grappled."

Stanner raised his eyebrows. "You cleared all that sand away? From what we could make out, it's half buried down there."

Dad turned to look blankly at Stanner. "Maybe the sand was loosened by the impact. It's quite clear now along the upper half of the hull. But the S.N.G. module looks to be cracked. I expect its contents have been destroyed."

Cal looked back and forth between his dad and Stanner. The major's face seemed to go stony, all of a sudden.

"What'd you call it?" Stanner asked.

Just a flicker of hesitation from Dad. "I said satellite module. Why?"

"I thought you said something else." Stanner looked at him again. Cal's dad gazed unflinchingly back.

Shit, the old man could be chilled steel when he needed to.

Finally Stanner glanced at his watch, looked at the cable slicing down into the water, and said, "We've got a small navy vessel coming to take it aboard, be here any minute, so we'd better have it ready. I don't want it out in the—" He broke off, glancing at the shore. Then he turned to Cal's dad and said, "Okay. Let's hope you know what you're doing. Hoist away."

Waylon thought he might be crouching on an anthill. He pictured the ants looking for a good spot to start burrowing under his testicles. He scratched and shifted on the hummock.

The grassy hummock—*hey, I'm on a grassy knoll, dude!*—was on the hillside in the thicket of fur and oak trees overlooking the old restaurant and the smashed dock. He stood up, to let his blood circulate, shifting his weight from foot to foot, watching the navy vessel—what was it, a PT boat?—hauling ass toward San Francisco Bay, with that big metal thing they claimed was a satellite tied down under a tarp on its aft deck. It might've been a satellite. He hadn't been able to see it very well.

Probably was. Which was disappointing.

He shifted around on the hummock. Scratched one knee against the other. *Was* something crawling up his legs? Ants? Something else? Hadn't Adair said all kinds of nasty shit lived in this woods?

He left the hummock and climbed up on a nearby tree stump. Probably get termites up his pants, too.

He had to hunker down and peer between the trees to watch the boat. He made out three boats. The coastguardsmen were following the Navy boat, some kind of escort. The trawler that had winched up the Unknown Artifact, as Waylon thought of it, was tooling off in a different direction, piloted by that older kid, Adair's brother. Her dad—he thought it was her dad, though he was a ways off and Waylon had seen him only one other time—was walking toward his truck.

Waylon wished he had binoculars. He thought he'd seen ordinary English-language lettering on the side of the thing when it was hauled up, but he was too far away to be sure. Well, it was under a tarp now anyway.

He was getting cold and damp and wanted to check his pants to see if he had any unauthorized visitors of his own.

He sighed. Time to go home. He tended to put off going home because Mom's anxiety attacks were back big-time, and if it wasn't the anxiety attacks, she was plastered, and it made him feel like shit when she was drunk.

He heard a persistent rattling. It went lower in frequency, became more distinct, a thudding—and then he saw it coming.

It was a single light, approaching low over the trees. The tree-tops tossed about as it came.

"Oh, shit. The black chopper."

The same one. He could see the markings on it, D-23.

And as he said *the black chopper*, a searchlight switched on, making a thin column of harsh blue shine down into the trees. A doe, with ears like a mule's, ran from the questing blob of light.

The chopper changed direction, coming right toward him, its searchlight probing.

"Fuck this," Waylon muttered, and started off through waist-high ferns, the trees seeming to run toward him as he skidded along the slope.

He fell, sliding on his ass through blackberry vines, feeling them burn across his skin. The chopper boomed overhead, the trees surging in its wind, leaves caught up in its private dust devil, spinning into his eyes.

He stopped hard against a mossy-slick pine tree, goose-egging his shin on it. "Shit!" he hissed, and ducked behind the tree as the searchlight swept over the bole where he'd been a moment before, and passed on. The chopper carried its wind and restlessly probing searchlight with it, back into the farther reaches of the night sky.

Heart thudding, tasting metal but feeling a certain elation, Waylon started down the hillside, skidding toward the road. His leg ached, his face stung with blackberry thorns, and he had a long walk home. Maybe his mom'd be asleep when he got there.

Suddenly he stopped, aware of hunched, stealthy movement in the shadows of the slope below him.

That deer he'd seen, probably. But he kept still and watched.

After a moment, he made out two pale faces peering up toward him, catching moon and starlight where it dappled through foliage. No more of them was visible.

They were about seventy feet away from him, but he thought he knew who it was. Two of those marines who'd come to replace the cops. He had seen them earlier, from the brush close by the road.

Now they seemed to raise their heads and sniff the air, to listen like animals. It almost looked as if they were down on all fours, but they couldn't be; it must be that they were leaning their hands on a steep part of the hillside.

They were climbing up toward him.

They came on, seeming almost to glide effortlessly up the hill-side. They were so quiet, so stealthy, it was like they were on some kind of combat training exercise, creeping up on the enemy camp. And it was like they were moving in tandem—*he moves and I move, he moves and I move*—fast as lizards up the hill.

This thing has me freaked out. I'm imagining shit, Waylon decided. They were just climbing the regular way, looking for him because someone had seen him, and they were worried he'd spotted their crashed UFO—or whatever it was.

But suppose they caught him. Would they have to *liquidate* him, to keep the cover-up secure?

I'm just being paranoid. It was just a satellite, and they don't want the bad publicity. They just want to scare me off, like the guards at Area 51 with their threats.

But even as he thought all this, he climbed back up the hillside, through the trees, and then started down again, diagonally this time. Moving laterally away from the two men. He'd seen a path on the far side of the dock, along the edge of the water, probably used by fishermen—Chinese and Latino guys who fished in every bay he'd ever seen, no matter how polluted the water was.

He reached the road and sprinted for the rocky path, made it, and ran past little poplar trees and big juniper bushes, threading between boulders and chunks of concrete left here to provide a tide break.

He paused a couple of times to see if he was being followed.

Maybe. Something was rustling back there. The doe stepped into the moonlight, then bounded off. He waited and didn't see the soldiers. He moved on.

Fifteen minutes later, Waylon found himself rounding a small point that stuck out into a little inlet. On the other side, not even a quarter mile away, was a brightly lit marina thronged with sailboats. Beside the docks was a steak and fish restaurant.

He followed the curve of a gravelly beach to the marina. As he passed below the surf-and-turf place, he heard people on the restaurant's deck, which extended over the water under strings of twinkling lightbulbs, talking and drinking as they waited for a table. Someone was speculating about what was supposed to have crashed into the bay.

"I heard it was a small plane," a woman said.

He almost felt like telling them—telling *someone*—what he had seen, telling them about the chopper and the unnatural soldiers who'd harried him through the brush.

But he was too tired to be laughed at.

He trudged up a boat ramp to the road, stuck out his thumb, and got a ride back to Quiebra with some drunk college students who made fun of the bramble welts on his face.

Thinking to himself, *Of course they were after you, dude. Ever since the terrorists flew those planes into the World Trade Center and the Pentagon, the fucking military's been even more paranoid, ready to nail anybody who sniffs around. If that wasn't a crashed UFO, it was probably a spy satellite. Some sort of top secret shit. What did you expect? The Shadow Government will track your ass down if you get in its way.*

When Waylon got home to the condo, his mom was asleep on the couch, snoring loudly, with the TV on but the sound off. The Shopping Channel. She liked to look at the chintzy things they hawked, but she never bought anything. Her long curly bottle-blond hair was straggling over her open mouth. Wine coolers were lined up on the coffee table, and cigarette butts were spilling out of the ashtrays.

She was still wearing the dark blue dress suit she wore for her paralegal job; she was about forty pounds overweight, and spilling out of it. He pulled her shoes off and drew her long wool coat over her like a blanket.

Then he turned off the TV and went to take a shower.

November 24, midmorning

Lacey Cummings stood on her porch, looking at the eight-foot-high bird-of-paradise plant that nodded in the smoggy breeze like some otherworldly bird. She looked at the sky, blue overhead and gray-brown above the eastern horizon. Then she looked at her packed bags on the doormat and thought, *Am I ready to go or not? Have I got everything?*

She was on the front porch of her rented L.A. bungalow, waiting for the cab—thinking it was crazy to take a cab in L.A. If you weren't part of the limo set, you bought a car. But she had sold her car; she was going to the train station, for the Coast Starlight to Berkeley.

She wondered if she should call Roger. But since when were you obligated to tell your ex-husband where you were moving? She'd kept his surname because she liked the sound of it better, but she barely stayed in touch. Still, it bothered her not to tell him she was moving out of town. Not that he'd really give a damn. He was more interested in hearing from his agent about his new spec script.

She decided she just wanted to go. To Quiebra, of all places: to see sister Suze and niece Adair and nephew Cal and just forget her life here. So she took out her cell phone, put her finger on the button, about to switch it off—and of course that's when it rang.

She sighed. Hesitated—and answered. "Herrrre's Lacey," she said into the cell phone.

"Lacey, you still in town?" It was Chuck Fong, her editor at the *L.A. Times.*

"Can't talk, Chuck, gotta catch a train to Berkeley."

"Come on, you can give me a minute. We're talking about your career here, Lacey. You've been with us eight years, and I've always backed you up. One time, one time only, I couldn't do it and—"

"Chuck, my mind's made up. I just—"

Naturally the yellow cab chose that moment to show up. A bearded guy in a turban looked at her from the driver's seat, and she waved. He got out to help her with the bags.

"Lacey, claiming our publisher is in league with death squads? What did you expect? Come on, that was extreme and unreasonable."

"I didn't say he was in league with them, I said he was covering up the activities of death squads in Colombia, because he's backing the right-wing agenda down there. Get the Colombian oil, no matter who gets hurt. And why? Because he's also on the board of a major oil company, and the newspaper was bought by a multinational, and because he's got ties to the—"

"Do you know how paranoid you sound? In these times we have to be tough. You've got to be supportive of antiterrorism efforts."

"I support the war against terror. I don't support death squads. You wouldn't run my column about death squads, you were censoring me, so I'm taking my toys and going home. I'm sick of L.A. I need to get away."

"I can't guarantee you'll be able to come back."

"Is that another way of saying, 'You'll never work in this town again'? I'll tell you what, Chuck. If you tell me you'll run my column as written, I'll take my bags out of the cab that's waiting for me over here."

A crackle—she thought she'd lost the connection. But then he said, "I can't do that. He won't let me."

"Then I'll send you a card from the Bay Area."

"Lacey—"

Another call was coming in, and she broke the connection to Chuck and took the call waiting as she picked up the remaining bag and walked over to the cab. "Lacey here." She put the bag in the trunk.

"Lacey? It's Suze."

"Calling to tell me not to come? You Bay Area types don't want the sleazy Angelenos up there?"

"I'm calling to make *sure* you're coming. Thanksgiving plans, for one thing. The kids are stoked."

Lacey got into the backseat of the cab, turned the cell phone away long enough to tell the driver, "Union Station." She shut the door and said, "Suze, I'm coming unless you don't want me to."

"Of *course* I want you to!"

The cab started away. Lacey looked through the back window at her little house, the palm tree, the bird-of-paradise plant. Jerve, the little kid who lived next door, was skating up and down the sidewalk on his silvery scooter. "Then I'm coming. I'm in the cab on the way to the train station."

"I wish you were coming on the plane. It's faster."

"I don't take them unless I have to. What's the hurry? I mean, are you okay?"

"Yes, I just . . . I'm a little scared, I guess."

Lacey rocked back in her seat. It wasn't like her strong, athletic, independent older sister to admit being scared. "Go on."

"It sounds so stupid. It's Nick. I just—he's so distant and . . . I don't know."

"Since when has he been Mr. Warmth?"

"I know—especially when he gets depressed. But he's been

doing pretty good. I had to sort of push him to take a job recently. You know how he gets in that defeatist mind-set."

The cab drove up the on-ramp and slid onto the freeway. "Yeah, I remember Nick's 'why bother, it won't work.' But that's nothing new."

"It's . . . just that he goes off to work but he's really *secretive* about it. Doesn't even take his gear. I thought he was having an affair, but . . . Then this morning he said something weird. I mean, I came into the kitchen and he was standing at the sink and he didn't hear me, I guess, and it was like he was talking to the air. He said, um—what was it? He said something about a 'conversion.' But he didn't seem to be talking about religion."

"Um, he smoking pot again?"

"No. I don't think so. It's like—like he's really gone into some odd kind of . . . fugue state."

"You think he could have given up his meds, and not told you? People don't like to talk about it when they go off antidepressants— or on them either. He could be having a kind of withdrawal from medication."

"You know what, I thought maybe he hadn't been taking his meds. You're probably right. I'm going to see if I can get him to start again. See how you make me feel better? I need you around here to straighten me out when I get crazy."

Lacey smiled. "Whoa, you must be worried, admitting I might know something you don't. I'm coming, 'Sister Act.' "

Suze laughed at the allusion to the time they'd dressed up like twin nuns for a Halloween party.

"Okay, we'll be there. Call us if the train's delayed."

"I will. Bye."

Lacey switched the cell phone off, looked out at Los Angeles. A boulevard unreeled below the elevated freeway like film from a canister, and she wondered if she could really let L.A. go.

She thought she probably could. Her life was taking a sharp turn, and the cab was taking the exit for the train station.

November 24, 11:30 P.M.

Larry's dad had gone to a Civil War reenactment planning session after work, calling to tell Larry to heat up a frozen pizza and do his homework. But Larry Gunderston had been playing this particular computer game for three and a half hours, with pizza crusts still littering his desk. His back ached in the desk chair; his fingers had stiffened up. But whenever his Jedi character broke through to another level—killing a great many of the enemy to get there—the feeling that came seemed to suck him onward like a slipstream.

It would've been four hours, but he'd paused to go on-line, to the *Trek* chat room, where they'd talked more *Star Wars* than *Star Trek*, and now he was thinking about going back on. He'd try again to talk his on-line friend Allison into sending him a picture, if she was in the ROM-exchange chat room. She was reluctant, hinting she was no *Vogue* beauty. He didn't care, even if she was overweight like him. He needed to think that maybe there was a girl somewhere who—

"Larry? What the heck there, boy, you said you were doing your trigonometry!" His dad was suddenly there in the doorway, a man with narrow shoulders and wide hips, the same thick round glasses as Larry. "I'm gonna call your mom and have her come over and talk to you. I know how you love her lectures." Mom and Dad were separated; she lived in Oakland.

"I finished the trig," Larry lied. "It didn't take very long. I thought you were going to have a beer with those guys after the meeting."

"Only two guys showed up. Nobody seems to know where the other ones are. The whole thing is—never mind, dammit, do you know what time it is? You've got finals, kid. This really *does* go on your permanent record."

"It's just preliminary credits till I get into San Francisco State, Dad."

His dad had come to stand scowling over his chair, staring into the game. "Larry, if you make big swings with your lightsaber that way, the Sith'll get you. You have to make short, aggressive swings. Here, move, let me show you."

Larry sighed and got up, let his dad sit down. His dad could waste as much time on a computer game as he could. "I guess I'll . . ."

Dad was already hunched over the screen, his mind projected into the computer-animated world of the Jedi.

"Yes. Take the dog out, Larry, before you go to bed. Buddy needs to . . . uh . . . See, you have to—hell, I died, but you know what I mean. Did you save that game?"

Larry found the poodle sitting tensely by the front door. He attached the leash and let the poodle drag him outside and down the sidewalk. Most of the houses were dark, except for some TV glow in the occasional picture window. There was a shiny row of silent cars along the curb; boats in some of the driveways were covered with wet tarps. Nothing else. Yet the night seemed almost alive.

It was funny how vivid things seemed outside for a few moments when you first "came up for air" after hours of playing a computer game. There'd been a light rain, and he could smell the soil and the junipers in the damp freshness; and the stars looked sharply blue-white between the clouds. He let the little white dog tug him to the corner across the street from the cemetery, and immediately a movement that didn't belong caught his eye.

He peered into the slightly overgrown cemetery—a patch of rolling green below the protected watershed and the tract homes on the other three sides. Most of the tombstones were of the old standing granite variety, but there was a swath of the easy-maintenance stones flush with the ground, and it was through there that three figures were crawling along.

At first he thought they must be coyotes, hugging the earth as they crept up on some jackrabbit, but as his eyes adjusted he saw that they were people. He couldn't see how old or what type—though one of them appeared to be a mostly naked woman.

Must be teenagers playing some kind of war game or . . . vandals or . . .

He thought he ought to tell his dad—who'd probably call the police. There had been vandalism in the cemetery before. But he needed to get a closer look. And if the woman really was naked . . . He urged the dog across the street, past the low fence and into the cemetery. Buddy snuffled at a fresh grave, where silk flowers struck a bright note against the flat gray stone. Larry looked for the crawling people, couldn't find them at first.

There they were, about forty-five yards ahead of him, among the old tombstones now, emerging from behind a group of mossy, rain-streaked upright stones. It was like these people were crawling in triangular formation: the pasty old man—he looked vaguely familiar—taking point; the Chinese guy who ran the kung fu place at the mall, coming behind on the left side; and on the right, a young blond woman wearing only bra and panties, whose long hair was mucky with lawn clippings from dragging on the ground. They were creeping toward a big hole, which at first Larry took to be a waiting grave. But then he saw it was shaped more like a trapdoor, about three feet square, and a sudden spray of dirt came out of it, like a giant gopher was kicking soil out of the way. The three figures kept the same distance from one another, the same crawling formation, but still they moved in fits and starts, as if going from slow-motion to fast-action at random—and yet they did it all together. *Pulling* their way across the ground.

Larry's attempt to process what he was seeing went something like:

> *Insane drug users*
> > *or maybe*
> *Satan worship cult doing some ritual in the cemetery*
> > *or maybe they're*
> *People gone insane from some poison in the water*
> > *or*
> *Murderers hiding their deed with this strange behavior*
> > *or could be*
> *I had a computer-game overdose leading to epilepsy and I'm*

> *hallucinating this*
> *but*
> No, *this is real—let's go back to the Satan cult.*

He finally settled on a combination—*drug-addled insane Satan cultists vandalizing the cemetery.*

He knew he needed to tell someone what he was seeing. But for one thing he found it difficult to stop looking at that girl, her long white nude legs pumping against the grass, as the three figures crawled silently toward that dirt-spouting hole. Larry backed up in revulsion and fear, half stumbling, but not able to look away.

Then something made his stomach lurch—a woman's head extended from the hole in the ground on a metal stalk. The head rotated, and she saw him. A middle-aged woman, her hair in disarray, her eyes blank but seeing him. He could *feel* her gaze; the feeling made his testicles retreat up against him.

The other three, the crawlers, stopped dead—and turned all three heads at once, sharply, to look at him, as if they had seen him, too, when the head from the hole had seen him.

Then they started moving again, changing course, coming toward him. Moving faster now. And their bodies were changing. To facilitate speed, their arms and legs seemed to come apart and grow; their limbs *sectioned and extended* on ratcheting metal linkages. Their mouths opened—all three at once—and silvery tendrils extended from between their lips, wriggling toward him as if to sniff the air.

The dog was barking frantically.

And then Larry turned and ran, yelling, "Dad Dad Dad Dad *DAD!*" Half dragging the dog behind him till the leash suddenly went slack in his hand—but he didn't turn to look. Some distant part of his mind was amazed at his own speed, his legs outpacing the thumping of his heart as he ran through to the street, around the corner toward home.

The dog somewhere behind him barked wildly, yelping. Then . . . Silent.

He heard a siren whoop briefly behind him, as he ran up to the porch. Then his dad was on the porch, and a police car was pulling up in front of the house. Dad was opening the front door, frowning.

Larry collapsed against his dad, gasping for air. His skin flickered with points of heat as his lungs tried to catch up with the demands of his astonished muscles. Dad was staring at him.

"What the heck, Larry?"

"Dad." Panting. Trying to speak. "The . . . in the cemetery . . . people. Things. Crawling. Chased me."

"What?"

Then the cop was there, coming up the walk. A tall, blue-eyed white guy with a lazy, unconcerned manner as he took out his report book. A name tag on his uniform shirt said J. WHARTON, QPD. "Evening. Had a call about people running through the park? Vandalism, something like that?"

"You saw them?" Larry asked, peering past him at the street. He saw no one back there except Mrs. Solwiez, in her nightgown, gaping out her front door across the street. The police car's lights were flashing silently.

"I saw you, in the cemetery, is what I saw, son."

"Well, something—someone was chasing me."

He rattled out a version of what he'd seen—he found himself toning it down from what he remembered, afraid it would sound like he was lying—and the cop and his dad exchanged looks. Especially at the naked-girl part. The cop skeptical and amused; Dad puzzled, annoyed.

"That your story?" the cop asked.

"Yes. It's what happened. You could go see the hole in the ground yourself."

"I'll go take a look. But you know they were replacing some stones in the cemetery earlier this week. That might've made the hole."

Larry's dad turned to him with a suddenness that made him jump. "Son, where's the dog?"

Larry blinked. He looked at the broken leash still clutched in his hand. "The dog? He . . . got loose. Oh, no. Oh, God, Buddy."

The cop shook his head sadly. "Have you ever searched your son's room, sir? I have to say that we're having a real problem with teen drug use here in town."

Dad scowled. "Not Larry. Uh-uh. He's got his vices, but potato chips don't make you hallucinate. I mean, I'll look, but . . . I have to assume there was something out there, Officer Wharton. I'm going to go take a look."

Suddenly Larry felt a flush of love for his dad, a feeling he hadn't had for ten years or so. The old man was okay.

Wharton shook his head ruefully. "Well, I don't think you should walk around in the cemetery without permission after dark, sir, especially if they've been digging the place up. You might step in a hole. But I'll tell you what, I'll look for you. We'll swing by and see what we see and I'll come back later. But in the meantime, why don't you come with me to the station, to make a report, and the boy here—I think we should have him looked at. There's a doctor at the hospital, on call, for psychiatric issues."

Larry was outraged, but all he could do was gape and say, "Oh, Jesus, I mean—I'm not—I mean, jeez—"

It took Officer Wharton a few minutes, but he talked Larry's dad into it. They got in the patrol car—which made Larry feel kind of important, though he knew that it was stupid to feel that way, considering the cop was assuming he was stoned or crazy—and they drove around the cemetery. Saw no one. Not the dog either. They stopped at the front gate and called to Buddy a few times. No response.

"I'll find him later," Dad mumbled.

Then they drove to the hospital. Wharton went in with Larry, spoke to some nurses in hushed tones, signed some papers. Larry found himself alone in the emergency room, watching late-night TV on the set in the waiting area.

Eventually he told his story to a lady psychiatrist the cop seemed to have dated or something—she nodded when Larry told her the cop's name—and the doctor decided Larry needed some kind of anti-anxiety drug for now. Maybe he'd had an epileptic seizure of some kind, so they might have to change his meds later. Larry felt as if he was being treated like a complete lunatic. They acted as if his feelings about the whole thing were off the map and meaningless.

While Larry was at the hospital, his dad went off with the cop to make some kind of statement. Why that was necessary, Larry couldn't understand. His dad hadn't seen anything. Just him. Normally they'd just write a report in their little book.

But, hey, Larry decided. *You have to trust someone. You could trust the cops, after all. Couldn't you?*

They never found the dog.

4

November 25, night

"Why's she coming here on a train?" Cal asked, staring dully down the tracks into the thin fog. They could just make out the headlight of the oncoming train and the big blunt steely outline of the engine.

"Sometimes," Adair said, "you can seem so smart and sometimes you're just, like, retarded. Why does anybody come on a train?"

They were on the tarmac near the tracks at the Emeryville train station. Across the tracks, past a chain-link fence torn up at the bottom by tramps, was a shopping center with a movie theater, a bookstore, even a jazz nightclub. Beyond that lay the freeway and the bay.

"She doesn't like to fly," Adair's mom said. She had girl's soccer league that afternoon, and she was already dressed in her white short-sleeve Quiebra High shirt, white shorts, and white sneakers, and her silver coach whistle was hanging around her neck. Adair wore a dress she called her gypsy dress under a jacket from American Eagle.

Adair noticed that Cal wore the same clothes as yesterday.

The train whistled. Getting that quirky look in his eye he got when something was bothering him he didn't want to talk about, Cal said, "Whoo whoooooo! Hey, Mom, can we blow your coach whistle back at the train?"

"Don't be silly," she said vaguely, as she shaded her eyes against the sun breaking through the clouds and watched the train pulling up.

He grabbed her whistle, started blowing on it though it still hung around her neck. *Tweeeeeeee.*

Mom only stared at him, as if she was some kind of cryptographer trying to decode what he was doing.

Seeing that he wasn't going to get a rise from her, Cal dropped the whistle, shrugging.

The train clashed its wheels, squealed its brakes, and came to a grudging stop, reeking diesel. A chubby, blank-faced porter walked up to the first car with portable steps, put them down in front of the nearest door, and waited to help people off. An elderly white-haired woman got off, waving at Adair's mom—and then looking away in embarrassment as she focused her weak eyes and realized that she wasn't the daughter or niece she'd been expecting. Wearing a look of disappointed abandonment, the old woman walked past them toward the station.

Then Mom's sister Lacey climbed down from the train. To Adair, she looked the same as she had three years ago. An attractive woman with long chestnut hair, bangs cut across her forehead, a Long Beach tan, a softer, more humorous face than Mom's. But then, she wasn't married with kids, and she was younger than Mom.

Lacey wore oxblood dress pants that looked like they might've come from Macy's, a gold link belt, a white silk blouse, tennis shoes that didn't quite go with the rest of it. Just a little makeup. Mom almost never wore any either.

Lacey's nails were oxblood, too, but pretty short, because she typed a lot, Adair supposed. She was a journalist.

"Hi, you guys!" Lacey said, wheeling two hefty American Tourister bags up to them. "Thanks for picking me up." She beamed at her sister. "Suze! You look great!"

Lacey embraced her sister, and after a moment Mom returned the embrace. Lacey stepped back as if to appraise her, looking a little puzzled by something.

"Glad you could come," Mom said. She said it brightly, but with no real conviction.

"Well, I guess I'm committed, 'cause I put a lot of my stuff in storage. I've been sort of mulling moving out here. Into the city, probably, if I can get a job that'll pay for the rents you guys put up with around here."

"I can't advise it," Mom said. "The rents are . . . horrendous."

Lacey's eyebrows went up. "You were just saying what a good thing it was for me to come, just last night." She chuckled, hiding her hurt behind a mask of amused indifference, and grinned at Adair. "Your mom has turned mercurial. Wait a minute, that can't be Adair, not after just three years. Not this gorgeous babe. No way." She turned a facetious scowl on her sister. "What've you done with my niece, and who is this imposter?"

Adair smiled at the joke, but Mom had a peculiar blandness in her face as she looked back at Lacey. "What do you mean?"

"Hello, Mom?" Adair said. "It's a joke?"

Mom smiled. "Hello? I was joking, too."

"And look at Cal!" Lacey went on. "All-star something or other. Damn, they grow kids big now. You helping your dad with the business still?"

Cal looked away. "Not lately."

Mom turned to Cal. "Cal? Isn't there something you're supposed to do?"

"Uhhh . . . no?"

Adair turned him a look of slack disgust. "Get her bag, dumbass!"

"Oh, okay, I was going to, whatever," Cal mumbled. He took the larger of the two bags, and they started toward the parking lot.

"There *are* wheels on those bags, Cal," Lacey said, smiling, seeing Cal was carrying it by his side. "High technology. It's the latest thing."

"Oh, yeah, huh."

"What a dumbass," Adair said.

"That's twice you called me that. Next time you want me to fix your computer you can just shit-can it."

"Then you suck," Adair said matter-of-factly.

"You suck."

"You suck." She dropped back to walk beside Lacey. "Hey, you're gonna be here for Thanksgiving?"

"I will."

"It'd be so cool if you moved out here, Lacey!" Knowing she was bubbling a bit but meaning it. There was something reassuring about Lacey, right now.

"You could help me pick out an apartment, if I decide to do it," Lacey said. "I sold my car just to have enough cash to pay down on a nice place. You have to have big security deposits, I've heard. Key fees and all that."

"It's not so bad now, with the dot-com collapse," Adair said. "Rents have gone down some."

"I've got some applications in with the local papers, but I'm not even sure I want to work for them. To tell you the truth, I think I'm going to take a couple of college classes or something, till I figure out what else to do. I've already found a little local school to give me that ever-elusive sense of purpose."

"I recommend the colleges in San Francisco," Mom said, unlocking the car. "They're much better."

"Oh, no, Diablo is good. It's one of the best ones!" Adair burst out. Wondering why Mom so obviously didn't want her sister to go to school around here. *Is she trying to push Aunt Lacey away?*

"Diablo is exactly the one I picked," Lacey said, smiling at Adair. "Give me the school named after the devil, every time."

Cal and Adair laughed. Mom just smiled faintly.

November 26, morning

Lacey opened her luggage on the single bed. They'd given her the room that doubled as Nick's office.

She was puzzled by her sister—and she wasn't sure what was puzzling her. It was partly what *wasn't* happening. It'd be more like Suzanna to help her unpack, chattering the whole time about where she could put her things, asking if she needed anything, telling her about towels—but Suzanna had simply shown her in and silently left her here.

Normally when they saw one another, Suzanna would take her aside for a recital of complaints about her husband and the kids, and then, after getting it off her chest, following up with how great her husband and kids were, after all. That's how she always was, and it was fine with Lacey. But nothing like that this time. Suze seemed distant the way people are when they're angry but don't want to talk about it.

But Suzanna appeared at the door with clean towels. "You can use that bathroom off the office, while you're here. Before you go. Have it to yourself."

Lacey looked at Suzanna, trying to find the right tone. "So, Suze. How're things with the kids?"

"Fine."

"Just fine? How's Nick?" She lowered her voice. "You were worried about him?"

"Why would I be worried about him? He's better than he's ever been." She seemed to mean that. She laid the towels on the bed and turned to go.

"On the phone you said—"

"Oh. I was wrong. You were right. It was just the meds. He's back on them. We're fine."

She turned away again.

"Suze, wait. Seriously, are you mad at me for anything? I put my foot in it somehow?"

Suzanna paused at the door and looked mildly back at her. "Not at all. Why should I be angry?" She seemed truly in the dark.

"Okay, whatever. Never mind." Lacey went back to unpacking, and Suze wandered off toward the garage.

Lacey was pretty much through when she heard the triple scream. The scream of tires, the scream of an animal, the scream of a girl.

She rushed out front and saw her niece, Adair, kneeling in the street; a dull-faced pale young man in a rather shabby military uniform stood by what appeared to be a brand-new Ford Expedition sport utility vehicle. It hadn't any plates yet. And Lacey's sister, Suzanna, was walking calmly over to the SUV.

"Adair, honey, come away from there," Suzanna was saying.

"Suze? What happened?" Lacey asked, coming out into the cloud-filtered daylight.

Then she saw the red puddle spreading out from the small, crushed remains. The young marine—that was a marine uniform, wasn't it?—was staring at the dead cat.

"*Silkie!*" Adair sobbed.

The marine became aware of Lacey, glanced up at her as she approached, and it seemed to her that he adopted the appropriate expression of remorse at that moment.

"Oh, my God, Adair, that was your cat?" Lacey asked, squatting to put her hand on her niece's shoulder. Adair turned away from the wreckage of Silkie and buried her face in Lacey's shoulder. Her only reply was a nod and sobbing. "Oh, jeez, I'm sorry, hon. The poor thing."

Lacey glanced up at Suzanna and the young marine. They looked at each other, Suzanna and the soldier, and then at the cat.

His uniform was dirty, torn here and there. Buttons were missing. The knees were green. Very unusual for a marine. Near unthinkable. He must've been out drunk somewhere in a park, Lacey supposed.

"Corporal," she said, noticing his stripes. "Were you driving drunk around here?"

"No, ma'am," the marine said. "But I'm sure sorry about the cat. She just run out in front of me."

"She does that," Suzanna said. "It's no fault of yours. You can go on now. I'll clean this up."

The marine nodded. "Thank you, ma'am. But I'm sure sorry about the cat. She just run out in front of me."

"You said that," Lacey muttered. *Exactly that*, she thought.

But the marine was already getting into his Ford Expedition. He backed it up and drove around them. And drove away.

"Suze," Lacey asked, "do you want me to pick the kitty up and you can take Adair into the house?"

"No, I'll do it. I'll just get a shovel."

Lacey drew Adair to her feet and put an arm around her to guide her into the house. "I hate those SUVs," Adair said. "Big killing machines. People love to get in big killing machines. I *hate* them!"

An auspicious start for my visit, Lacey thought.

Aloud she said, "I know how you feel. I'd have called a cop to check if that jarhead was drunk, but—" She broke off, not wanting to say anything about her sister's odd indifference. "Anyway, sit down, honey."

They sat on the sofa. Lacey saw her sister carrying a big shovel from the backyard toward the street, passing on the other side of the window, just two yards away, so that Lacey could just faintly make out the song that Suzanna was singing to herself as she went to pick up the dead cat. *"Time of the sea-ee-sonnnnn . . ."*

Adair had her face in her hands. "Silkie was my friend since she was a kitten. We grew up together."

"I know. It looked like she died instantly—but I don't know if that's much consolation."

Adair looked up at the shadow passing over them, her mom striding by the window, carrying the cat on the shovel to the backyard. "Mom's going to bury her back there where the gerbil's buried, by the rosebushes. She used to say that if we bury pets under rosebushes, we see them again in the roses."

"That's kind of nice, really."

Adair nodded, wiping her eyes, and got up. "I'm gonna find something to bury Silkie in." She went dazedly into her bedroom.

Lacey went out back and saw Suzanna digging a hole, not under the rosebushes but on the side of the house near a can full of yard clippings. The cat was lying on the dirt beside her, its back broken, eyes open and staring, tongue sticking out.

"Suze? Don't you want to put the kitty under the rosebushes?"

Suzanna continued digging, making a perfect little rectangular grave, as if she were born to miniature grave digging. "Why?"

"Because you told Adair it was nice to do that when she was little, I guess."

Suzanna looked up at her. "I did? I guess I'd forgotten. Okay."

She pushed the dirt back in the hole with the side of her tennis shoes and went briskly over to the roses and began to dig as Adair came out carrying an old, torn pink silk pillowcase.

Adair stopped, looking at the cat. "I can't."

Lacey took the pillowcase and knelt beside the dead cat. Trying not to look at it too closely, she eased its still warm body into the pillowcase. She got only a little blood on her thumb, but more blood began to soak through the pink pillowcase immediately. She carried the cat over to the new hole Suzanna was finishing—finishing with remarkable dispatch.

Once finished, Suzanna went to the garage with the shovel and didn't come back. Lacey and Adair lowered the pillowcase gently into the hole, and Lacey filled it up, pushing the dirt in with her hands, as Adair tearfully said, "Good-bye, Silkie, you were a hella good cat." She hugged Lacey quickly, once. "I'm sorry this had to happen as soon as you got here."

"I'm sorry you had to lose your kitty at all. I had a little dog, and when it died from old age it was like my own child died. Some people say it's silly, but . . ." She shrugged.

They stood there awhile, looking at the little grave together. After a while, Adair let out a long, slow breath and went back into the house.

Lacey found Suzanna in the garage, gazing placidly into the cryptic electronics inside the back of an old boom box.

"Trying to decide if the batteries are dead?" Lacey asked.

Suzanna didn't even look up from her inspection of the old CD player. "No."

Lacey waited. Suzanna said nothing else.

Finally, Lacey said tentatively, "You know what, I'm a little puzzled. I mean, you had that cat a long time, too. Aren't you . . . I don't know. I mean, you always loved animals."

Suzanna stood. Seemed to think for a moment, staring into the middle distance. Then she said, "I'm very sad about it. I guess I'm just, you know, at this point in my life, a little blasé about pets. And it looked like she died instantly. Would you like some instant coffee?"

"Um, sure." Suzanna went to the door from the garage to the kitchen, and Lacey turned to follow her.

And then stopped, turned to listen, as once again she heard three screams.

It was from a street or two away, this time. But it was remarkably similar:

The scream of tires, the scream of a small animal, the scream of a child.

5

Adair walked home from the bus stop, carrying her backpack of books over one shoulder. It was making her shoulder ache. *Should have left them in my locker.* She didn't think she'd get herself to crack a book tonight.

It was already getting dark. She saw that the few remaining jack-o'-lanterns were even more sunken in, their grins loonily lop-sided now. She thought about her friend Danelle, who seemed sort of happy that her parents had said they were moving. At least she could've acted sad to be leaving her friends. But then Adair was her only friend, just about, and most everyone had treated her like shit at school, it was true.

A turkey vulture wheeled overhead and swept away; blackbirds trilled repetitively from a red-blossomed bottlebrush tree beside the sidewalk. It hadn't rained for a while, and she'd heard newspeople worrying there wouldn't be enough water in the snowpacks to replenish the reservoirs. Leaves that should have been pasted to the street rattled dryly ahead of her in the breeze, toward Waylon.

He was standing behind the bole of a liquidambar tree, a little ways down the street, waiting for her. Like he was hiding, but watching for her. Which was kind of weird.

"Yo, Mister Waylon," she said, walking up. He was dressed just like he had been a couple weeks before, when the satellite had come down, she noticed. "Hardly seen you around school."

"I haven't been coming much. My mom's been a basket case and . . . I just felt like keeping my head down, sorta." He looked past her down the street, jamming his hands in his pockets.

"There some reason you're acting like you're hiding?"

He hesitated, looked at her, then back at the street. "You see those marine guys driving around?"

She felt a taut anger constrict her throat. "Those pricks. One of them killed my cat. Ran Silkie over."

"Lot of people lost cats around here."

"And he just mumbled and drove away. Fucking asshole."

"I thought that—that they were following me, those guys. More than once. I think it was because I was spying on the satellite thing."

She put just a shade of teasing mockery in her voice. "So now you're all 'it's a satellite' and not 'it's a UFO'?"

He shrugged a reluctant concession. "I think it was a satellite. It looked like it. But they're up to some shit. It could totally have, like, reverse-engineered technology from Area 51 in it or something. They reverse-engineer shit from UFOs."

" 'Kay."

"No, they do!"

" 'Kay."

He snorted. "Okay, fine. I've got a book I'll show you about it."

" 'Kay. I'm getting cold."

He looked at the street, then at her, then at the sky. "I could walk you home."

She sighed. She'd hoped saying *I'm getting cold* might induce him to put an arm around her. "You could walk me home, yeah. But then I'd be home."

"You don't feel like going home, either?"

"No. My parents are just 'whatever,' no matter what happens lately. They don't fucking care anymore. God, it was so lame on Thanksgiving last week. They just went through the motions. Lacey was so embarrassed for them. She moved out to a hotel. Mom kept hinting. She has so changed. It's all fucked up."

He looked at her curiously. "You didn't used to cuss this much."

"I didn't used to feel like it so much."

"Well. My mom makes a big deal about Thanksgiving. She kept it together pretty well. Cooked the turkey and we watched football. Which she likes. She gets off watching those linebackers. Like I care about football."

"But that's nice you watched it with her."

He shrugged and fell silent. So they just walked for a while, passing the turn onto her block. At the corner they saw Mr. Garraty pushing his wife in her wheelchair up the walk to the ramp that led to the porch of their ramshackle ranch-style house. Mr. Garraty was limping. Mrs. Garraty was on the stout side, a round-faced old woman with bottle red hair, swelling ankles showing under her long woolen coat. Her husband was a stooped man in a heavy knit sweater, once tall and now getting humpbacked, his sagging cheeks pale, his eyes watery gray, his hair a wisp on his head. Both of them were in their eighties. Adair remembered her mom saying the Garratys should be in a retirement home or with children, someplace they could be taken care of.

They started up the ramp, and Mr. Garraty started to lose traction and the wheelchair slid back a little, his wife giving a little squeak of anxiety at this. Then Waylon surprised Adair by stepping up behind them.

"Lemme help you with that," Waylon mumbled. Mr. Garraty was startled and looked at first like he was going to yell for the cops, but then realized this punky-looking kid was actually trying to be helpful. Adair followed them, pleased, as Waylon helped push the old woman onto the porch.

"Thank you," Mr. Garraty said. "I've been meaning to fix that ramp. The tar paper on it came loose last year. It's a mite too slick."

Mrs. Garraty stared at Waylon and Adair for a moment through her coke-bottle glasses, frowning; then she smiled, making a great many lines in her face suddenly stand out. "Oh, that's Adair, Suzanna's girl, Benny," she said.

"Well, for heaven's sake, as if I don't know that," Mr. Garraty said. "I remember her when I was doing the electrics over at her grade school, she was always asking questions." He smiled at the memory. "And this is her young man, who helped us up here, I expect."

"Benny, good gosh, you have no reason to blather out your presumptions like that," Mrs. Garraty said.

"Uh, well, anyway," Waylon said, genuinely embarrassed. "I was just—we were just—so anyway, we've got to—"

"Why don't you kids come in for some hot chocolate?" Mrs. Garraty asked. "It's the least we can do."

Mr. Garraty chuckled seeing the expressions on their faces. "Look at that, now, you've scared them, Judith. The thought of sitting around in our old kitchen with us. I'd be looking for an out myself if I was this boy here. What's your name, son?"

"Um, Waylon?"

"You're not sure?"

"Sure, I'm—yeah, it's—"

Adair poked Waylon. "He's teasing you, dumbass. We should go, Mr. Garraty, it's nice to see you guys. We've got to go home."

Mr. Garraty was already turning away, unlocking the front door, mumbling as he fumbled with the key. "Well, thank you, Waylon, Adair. You startled me, there, but I'm glad you came up, I might've—darn this key."

Adair tugged at Waylon's arm, and the two of them went on their way, Adair waving good-bye to Mrs. Garraty as her husband backed her wheelchair through the door. She vanished through the door, sitting down and backwards, waving.

Adair looked at Waylon. "That was really—"

"Shut *up*," he said, wincing.

So she didn't say it. But she thought, *He helped them without thinking about it. That's what he's really like.*

She kept hold of his arm.

December 2

Major Henri Stanner stood outside the Cruller on a cool morning, sipping from a Styrofoam cup and looking down what passed for the main drag in Quiebra. The Cruller's house coffee tasted like some artificial-flavor designer's idea of essence of almonds, and maybe vanilla.

He turned and glanced back into the coffee shop. The red-haired lady behind the counter smiled at him and turned a patient look of gentle inquiry to a little old lady whose greatest joy, probably, was deciding whether to have the almond-paste bearclaw or the apricot-jam filled. Maybe the coffee was second-rate, but the place was better than a Starbucks; it belonged here, had been here for years. It felt singular, and singular felt friendly.

It was an awkward little town, in some ways, he thought, with its attempt at drumming up business for the merchants by calling the little main drag Quiebra's "Historic Old Town"; with its increasingly uneasy mix of ghetto-refugee black kids into Jay-Z and 50 Cent and low-slung sedans, and white kids into Kid Rock and four-by-fours.

He'd been looking the town over for a week, off and on, while supervising the site. He was beginning to like the place, warts and all. And he was worried about Quiebra.

He dropped the coffee half-finished into a trash can and started for the police department. He was wearing his Air Force officer's uniform and getting curious stares from some of the passersby. A tall, gangly teenage boy looked at him speculatively.

"Yo, officer," the boy said. He wore a Raiders jersey, a lot of pimple cream discoloring his face. He shifted a backpack from one shoulder to the other. "Can you get me into the paratroopers?"

"I'm not a recruiter, son. Sorry." Stanner slowed enough to be polite, talking as he sidled by.

"Whatcha doing here then?"

Stanner snorted to himself. The generation of bluntness.

But he smiled and said, "I'm visiting a friend, is all."

Going to have to ditch the uniform for sure. Get into some civvies after today.

He waved and continued on his way. The police station was tucked into something called the Quiebra Department of Public Safety. You had to look close to see the word *Police*. The building was shiny-new, all red tile and stainless steel, part of an L-shaped complex that included city hall and the fire department.

A white-haired lady in a flowery, white-collared dress was on the other side of the counter's check-in window. She glanced up when he came in, looked curiously at his uniform. She wanted to ask . . .

But instead she called the duty commander for him: a small Filipino guy, crisply uniformed, with brisk movements and bright black eyes; QPD COMMANDER K. CRUZON on the little plastic name tag under his badge.

"Yes, Major, can I help you?" Second generation, no accent.

They shook hands. "You're the first guy got my rank right this week."

"I was Air Force for ten years. An MP."

"You're doing all right here. Say—" Stanner flashed his NSA liaison ID below the level of the counter so that Cruzon could see it but the secretary couldn't. "—could we talk in private?"

Cruzon frowned at the ID in its little case. Stanner could tell he was reading the whole title to himself: *National Security Agency: Department of Defense Special Intelligence Liaison.* His eyebrows went up, and he nodded.

"We could talk," Cruzon said, "but that ID doesn't get you any special privileges around here."

"Talk's all I'm after."

"Then right through here, Major Stanner. We'll go to the conference room. Bettina? Buzz us through, please."

On the way to the conference room they ran into Leonard Sprague, the deputy from the crash site. "What's this?" Stanner said. "The sheriff's department crammed in here with the municipal cops, too?"

"We were just tradin' some notes on narcotics," Sprague said, shaking Stanner's hand. The black deputy towered over Commander Cruzon. "You here about the crash still? I thought you guys were outta here and gone."

"Could we go into the conference room? It'd be good if you could come along, too."

"Sure, I've got a few minutes, Major. I've been wondering about some things myself."

They sat around a rickety metal and plastic table, drinking even worse coffee than he'd gotten at the Cruller. The walls were painted concrete; there were some high windows, and an urban planning chart on a wooden tripod.

"You haven't asked why I wanted to speak to you, Commander."

"Call me Ken. I figured what it was about. It's not every day we have a satellite crash around here. We were expecting a lot of press. I was surprised there wasn't anything on the TV news." He looked at Stanner with a combination of amusement and a kind of sharp attentiveness.

Something's worrying him, Stanner thought.

"Yeah, well," Stanner said, as if it weren't a big deal, "we were caught off guard. We didn't know the thing was coming down till it was already on its way. I just happened to be in the area, so I was dispatched over here. It's a project that I did have some—"

Shut up, he told himself angrily.

"—some experience with. Anyway, there just wasn't any time to warn people. There were some people at NASA who were a little embarrassed, so they didn't want any publicity, either."

Cruzon nodded but didn't seem convinced by the explanation. He kept his eyes on Stanner's face.

The little guy's a human polygraph, Stanner thought. *He knows I'm lying. Good for him. But he won't call me on it unless he has to.*

"So, Major," Sprague said. "You're still here in town?"

"You guys do me a favor, call me Henri, or Henny if you prefer—some of my friends call me that."

"Henri—like ornery?" Sprague asked, grinning.

"I hear that one now and then," Stanner said, chuckling politely. More like almost every day.

"Henri, that's French, huh?" Cruzon asked.

"My mother was French, name of DuMarche. I'm named after her dad. He died the day I was born. I should just get it over with and change Henri to Henry."

The two men both nodded slowly, watching him, waiting. He'd stretched out the small talk as much as he could, and it wasn't going to make them trust him any further.

Stanner said, "Okay, you noticed I'm still here in town. It's just that we want to make sure there aren't any *issues*, any side effects or problems with the satellite, ah, in any of the towns near the crash site. This town is the nearest."

" 'Issues,' " Sprague said. "What issues exactly?"

"Plutonium?" Cruzon asked, leaning forward. "That it?"

Hearing that, Sprague sat up straighter in his chair.

Cruzon was just saying out loud, Stanner supposed, what had been worrying the little cop, ever since the crash. Certain high-performance military satellites were powered by plutonium; solar power wasn't enough for some orbital spying operations.

"No plutonium," he said. "Maybe another kind of toxin. What it is—okay, wait a second here. Fellas, you must realize that there may be national security issues involved, or I wouldn't be here. I'm supposed to make you sign something where you guarantee that if you repeat any of this you give us your firstborn or your left testicle or something—but I'm going to skip all that if you'll just tell me you won't talk about this to anyone but me."

Cruzon compressed his lips. "I won't gossip about it. I won't talk to the press. I won't consult with anyone else in the department—but that last one is a *probably*. It's about, I won't say anything unless I have to. It's, what you call it, provisional. If I think lives are going to be at risk, here . . ." He shrugged.

"All that goes for me, too," Sprague said.

They looked at Stanner; they waited.

Stanner tried to keep his face relaxed as he came to the lie he had to tell. "All right. There was a *possibility* of a toxic chemical release at the crash site."

He shifted in his seat, unable to get comfortable. But it wasn't the chair, it was the way these two were watching his face that made him feel like squirming.

He gestured vaguely. "This toxin—once in the water it might come up in bubbles. Might've drifted over the surface, maybe a small cloud that couldn't see in the dark. Chances are, even if that *did* happen—and I don't have any evidence that it did—nothing but a squirrel or a snake or two's going to die before it dissipates. We detected nothing at the site when we were there. But see, we might've lost a canister of this stuff. It might've broken open down there in the water and leaked out later on—after everyone who was working out there already took off."

Jesus Christ, he thought. *What a crock! Am I sweating? I'm having to make up one fucking lie after another. I shouldn't be in fucking intelligence if I can't be cooler than this, goddamn it.*

Usually he analyzed statistics, satellite imagery, sometimes directed small-scale insertions. Until he'd started working with the Facility, he'd always worked on foreign projects.

Having to lie to American citizens bothered him. A couple of perfectly good cops, too. Maintaining a cover story hadn't bothered him, working overseas. But here . . .

Still, he kept his face relaxed, his voice dismissively casual, as he went on. "We doubt there was a leak. This is all just, you know, a routine health check because there were civilians around."

"Yeah, well, forgive me if I'm a little doubtful about this concern for civilians, there, 'Ornery,' " Sprague said, tapping the side of his little Styrofoam cup. "I used to work over in south San Francisco. Military dump out there's been poisoning some of those neighborhoods for decades. They won't clean it up. What the hell, they figure, that's ghetto, let 'em get cancer."

Stanner nodded noncommittally. "That's not my bailiwick."

"What's the effect of this chemical?" Cruzon asked. "You said maybe some dead squirrels. So it kills you dead?"

"It would kill a man, undiluted. But by the time it reached anybody in town the gas would probably be pretty diluted, and all you'd get would be behavioral anomalies."

Cruzon and Sprague exchanged looks. Then Sprague scowled at Stanner. " 'Behavioral anomalies'? What the hell's that mean? I mean, that could be my wife's whole family."

"Well, I'll tell you," Stanner began. "No, let me just ask you. Have there been any, like, out-of-the-ordinary incidents?"

"Such as?" Cruzon asked.

"Violent behavior that seems to—to have no explanation. Or, are there any highly unusual break-ins?"

Sprague stared at him. "You sure I shouldn't be worried about my own exposure, too, Major? I feel fine but—should I have a blood test?"

"No, it would've hit you by now, Deputy." Stanner grinned. "You seem okay to me."

"What's this toxic stuff called?" Cruzon asked.

"I've told you everything I'm cleared to tell," Stanner said, feeling as if he was coming out with his first honest remark all day. "Can you help me out, here?"

Cruzon shrugged. "Unusual violence—no. Nothing unusual."

"Might be best not to eat fish from that area, too," Stanner said. "I'll see about getting an advisory issued on fishing. Let out that it's a sewage leak or something. Don't eat the fish from around there for a while."

Sprague shook his head in wonder. "A sewage leak. That what you're going to say? You people find it pretty easy to lie to folks."

Stanner managed not to show how much the remark startled him. At least, he hoped it didn't show. He toyed with his coffee cup and didn't reply.

Cruzon had made a tent of his fingers. "Unusual break-ins, you said, before? Why exactly would there be—"

"Uh, this toxin," Stanner improvised, "affects the brain, has a sort of pack-rat effect on some people. Kind of an OCD symptom. They start obsessing about stuff. Objects. Often it's shiny stuff. Like, say, electronic parts."

Cruzon looked at him. "Electronic parts. A chemical that makes you obsess about electronic parts?"

The raised eyebrows said, *Sounds like bullshit to me.*

Stanner thought, *Why couldn't I have drawn a stupider cop? Lord knows there are enough around. But not this time.*

Cruzon leaned back in his chair and gazed at the ceiling as if he had crib notes up there. "Well, actually. There was a little vandalism at the high school. A vocational class, the electronics shop. Last night."

"Huh," Stanner said. "Electronics shop. When I was a kid it was woodshop or metal shop and that was it. Anything stolen?"

"I'm not sure."

Stanner nodded, shrugging unconcernedly. "Well. Maybe I'll look into it. But there's probably no connection at all. I wouldn't worry about it."

He smiled again, hoping they couldn't see him shudder.

6

Adair went to get some clean clothes for school from the dryer, and found her mother wandering around in the garage. Her mom was walking back and forth, in repeating patterns—like a mouse stuck in the patterns of a maze long after the maze has been removed.

"Hi, Mom," Adair said, bending to open the dryer door. She'd put the clothes in the night before; they were still barely warm. Her bare feet, under her nightgown, were cold on the concrete.

Mom didn't answer. Adair straightened up and glanced at her, yawning—but the yawn was a fake, to cover the disoriented feeling she got, watching her mom walk around, and around. Mom walked over to Dad's tool bench. She touched the tool bench twice, shook her head, then turned around and walked across the garage, skirting a stack of boxes containing half-broken diving equipment. She stopped at the wall; reached out and touched the dusty plasterboard. She said, "Perimeter. Someone please. Perimeter. Volume. Someone."

"Mom?"

Mom ignored her. She went back to the tool bench. She touched it twice, shook her head, then turned around and walked to the farther wall. She touched the wall.

"Mom!"

Still no response. Mom walked to the bench. Touched it twice. "Perimeter. Please."

Adair got a squeezing feeling, like she'd felt when Dad had his breakdown. Was Mom having a nervous breakdown of her own? Was the whole family fundamentally defective? Maybe someday they were going to find her, too, wandering around in the garage, touching walls and babbling.

Then the door opened suddenly behind her, and she jumped. "Go to school, Adair," Dad said, hurrying past her. He walked over to Mom, put his arms around her, and whispered something in her ear. Mom struggled—her arms thrashed—and then she went limp. Dad caught her, and she straightened up. She saw Adair watching, and she put her arms around Dad.

They hugged.

Then Mom said, "You shouldn't catch us playing these little games."

Dad and Mom looked at her. Then both of them *leered* at her.

Adair backed away and turned to rush through the kitchen door. She heard her parents laughing.

She stopped in the kitchen, trembling, to listen.

"Reinstall?" Dad's voice came dimly from the garage.

"Reinstall," Mom said, her voice calm and cheerful.

Adair went to her bedroom and started getting dressed. She started crying partway through putting on her socks, with one sock still halfway onto her left foot. She sat there leaning over, with her hands on the sock, and just sagged like that, her head against her knees, crying.

Cal was walking by. He stopped at her door and stared in at her. "What the fuck are you crying about?"

It sounded harsh, but she knew it was as close as he could get to letting her know he was worried about her.

She made herself stop crying. "I don't know. I don't know how to describe it. There's something wrong with Mom and Dad."

"What? They're fine. They started spending a lot of time together again. They go off together for hours. Shit, they hardly hung together at all before this—this—"

She turned to look at him. "Before what?"

"I don't know. Before they started—hanging together. I guess."

"You haven't seen them do anything weird? Or felt like they were—I don't know—it's like they've been brainwashed, or joined a cult or something."

"They're not in a cult. Those people make their kids join, too."

She picked up her shoes and stared at them. "Yeah. What if they do?"

"Do what?"

"Make us join, too."

He growled in his throat with exasperation. "Join *what*?"

"Mom was doing this weird thing in the garage, then Dad made her stop, then they acted like it was some kind of sexy role-playing game or something."

"Oh, so they were getting sexy with each other? Fuck, mind your own business. How the hell you think you were born, Adair? If they're getting, like, all intimate and stuff, it's a *good* thing."

"You don't understand. But I don't know how to describe it. I mean, you wouldn't believe me."

"You know what's going to happen?"

She could tell he was getting really angry. His voice got all flat, and he was hugging himself in that bottling-up way he had.

He went on, "You're going to fuck things up. You're going to make them all self-conscious or something. You're just freaked out because they're giving each other more attention than little baby Adair for once. And it bothers you and you're going to fuck up their getting back together. Just cut it out! Leave them alone! Or they're going to fucking break up!"

He turned and stormed away down the hall.

She thought, *It's me. It's not them. Maybe. I'll ask Lacey. I'll talk to the counselor at school. But except for that I'd better shut up because it's probably something wrong with me.*

And she pulled on her other sock.

December 3, late morning

"How come we have to move, Dad?" Larry asked.

They were just getting into the station wagon. Gunderston put the key in the ignition as Larry got in beside him, buckling his seat belt.

Larry asked him again, "Seriously, Dad, I mean, an hour ago we were fine at home."

Larry paused, thinking, *Maybe not fine. But at home.*

He went on, "Then the big rush, some emergency. I never did get what it was. I mean it's dumb—are they going to pay for our hotel?"

"Yes. They are."

"But what's it all about? Why do we have to leave?"

Gunderston shrugged. "Because . . . there's some kind of toxic leak or something—from a pipe under the cemetery."

Larry thought, *The cemetery.*

He hadn't mentioned what had happened that night. Where Buddy was. None of it—not since they started taking him to the doctor. That creepy doctor had hinted that if he didn't stop talking about it, they might put him away somewhere.

Larry expected his dad to start the car. Instead he just sat there, looking gravely at Larry—a long look, unusual for him. Dad rarely looked right at people.

Then he looked quickly away.

Larry wanted to tell his dad something, and couldn't figure out how to say it. The medication made it hard for him to think. Finally, he said, "Well, shouldn't we call Mom first, before we just go?"

"It's only temporary. I'll tell her we're staying at the hotel for a few days. Everyone on the street is going somewhere. It's just . . . temporary."

Larry looked at his dad again and tried to decide what had changed in him. True, Dad wasn't interested in talking *Trek* or *Star Wars* or Harry Potter or the Civil War or role-playing games anymore. He didn't watch the sci-fi channel with Larry—or he hadn't until

Larry had asked why he wasn't watching it. Then Dad had said, "Of course I'll watch it with you."

But it wasn't all that so much. It was more like standing in the bright sun but feeling like you were in the shade. Things didn't feel the way they should *where* they should.

He decided he was going to stop taking the meds. He wasn't sure why he'd made the decision. But he knew he had to get his head clear so he could think about this.

But maybe I should be taking them. Maybe there really is something wrong with me, he thought.

Up and down the street, people were packing things into cars, getting ready to leave. But no one was leaving Quiebra. The firemen standing at the corner, watching silently from their QFD cars, had insisted that everyone evacuated stay somewhere in town. An evacuation—but not far. They had to be there for some kind of health checkup. They'd all be told about it later, "when everything is ready."

Dad started the station wagon and they drove away, on their way to a room-and-board place over the Chinese restaurant in Old Town Quiebra.

Larry wanted his mom.

He wanted his dog.

He wanted his dad.

7

Bert Clayborn was sitting in the uncertain sunshine on the small deck of his duplex. His condo's back door faced the ocean, and he was eating a late lunch of tomato-cheese salad and watching the gulls wheel and dive over the beach.

A crash from next door; the wall vibrated. Another crash. Things breaking, the girl yelling something he couldn't make out. That Derry girl, half Pakistani, all goth, who'd dropped out of Contra Costa College—an unpredictable, possibly bipolar girl with visible mood swings. Knowing that, he wasn't inclined to call the police; it was more likely she was assaulting her own apartment than being assaulted.

He drank off the rest of his chardonnay. He allowed himself one glass before going to teach a class. He had taken over a class at Diablo Valley College near the end of term for Darryl Winsecker, who had taught a literature class and who'd suddenly dropped out of the job for "the indefinite future." There were rumors of long-term alcoholism rehab. Darryl hadn't settled for one glass of chardonnay.

The phone rang, and Bert grimaced. He was pretty sure he knew who that was. It was that time of year. He just didn't want to answer.

He knew it would be his younger brother, Errol, and he knew that Errol was going to invite him to spend vacation break with him and his wife, Dory. Dory with her ever-patient, faintly puzzled look whenever Bert spoke. And their videogame-obsessed kids. Errol would want him to come see the family for Christmas, and Bert knew he should go. It would be healthier to spend the holiday with someone; it'd be good for his relationship with his brother—but he just didn't want to go. And he didn't want to tell Errol why.

Because I don't want any more well-meaning "help" from my family, or any more pitying looks because you think I'm either gay or a loser just because I don't get married.

Another crash from next door, and weeping. Should he go over there? But every encounter with her had been like gazing into Edgar Allan Poe's maelstrom. And the phone was still ringing.

He sighed and stood up. But he didn't go next door or to the phone. Instead he stood there and watched the gulls some more. White birds, starkly aerodynamic wings with black tips, Nature's genius in their design—they could do maneuvers beyond the most cunningly wrought aircraft. Graceful and raucous, determinedly survivalist but brattily pushy, garbage-eating scavengers, too. Nature increasingly imitating people, having to accommodate itself to people. But then there had always been scavengers and parasites.

The phone stopped ringing. The crashes from next door ceased, too—though he could hear her talking loudly and cursing.

He could see a big swatch of plastic trash washing up on the beach. *Thoreau would have been apoplectic, seeing what we've done to this planet,* he thought. *And in fact—*

The phone started ringing again. He sighed and went to answer it. "Yes?"

"Bertie!"

His heart sank. "Hi, Errol."

"Listen to that enthusiasm when he says my name! Bad time to call?"

So he's not without some *perception, anyway,* Bert thought. "No, I just have a class to teach this evening. Getting set to go."

"Right-o. But what about getting set to come and visit us? A Connecticut Christmas, Bertie!" Errol began doing his Bing Crosby imitation. " 'I'm dreaming . . . of a white . . . Christmas . . . bah bah booh dah booh dee oh . . . with every Christmas card I write!' "

Although Errol was a, God help us, science fiction writer, he was heavy into old movies. "Are you trying to torture me into agreeing to come?" Bert asked, sighing.

"You can make fun of me all through Christmas vacation. I'm paying the airfare, the whole shebang."

"That's not necessary."

Bert was distracted by a sudden shout from next door. *"Fuck you, you're not going to do it to—"* There was more, but it was garbled.

He brought his attention back to the phone call. "If I want to come, Errol, I can go on-line, get a good fare." He was touched, despite himself, that Errol wanted him to come out there badly enough that he would offer to pay his way. Errol could be a little cheap sometimes. Maybe he was genuinely lonely. Sure, he had the wife and those kids—but she had that weird little martyred thing going, those sad smiles, and the kids were completely indifferent to their father except when he didn't show up to see them play soccer. Then they trotted out their own sulky mockeries of their mother's crucified smiles.

"I'll try to come." He heard a police siren from the complex's parking lot, and the disappointed whine running down as it was switched off. Maybe the cops were coming for the slightly mad girl next door, after all. He hoped she was all right.

Errol chattered on, asking, "So how's the old love life? And I don't mean old in the 'needing Viagra' kind of way. You dating anybody?"

"There must've been a mix-up, Errol, when they were making Jewish mothers. You got accidentally put into a male Gentile's body instead."

" 'So, vy don't you get married, already?' But Jewish mothers are usually right, man. And listen, there's someone I want you to meet. I mean I know, she lives in Hartford, and you're on the West Coast, but, you know what, I was talking to Professor Shremminger, over at Connecticut State U, and he thinks that it's been enough time since that wrangle over tenure. You could come back—"

"I don't want to go back there. I've bought a place out here."

"You can sell that little hovel."

"Errol, you're my younger brother. I'm supposed to tell you what to do. You're role-reversing on me here."

"Sell that place, come back here, go back to work at the university. I mean, you and I know they passed you over, but a lot of those guys are gone now. I think there's a chance you could get the Thoreau chair."

Bert hesitated. That was tempting. But it wasn't really likely.

"No, Errol. I burned my bridges. I called them Nazis. And unfortunately they aren't Nazis. I mean, it's unfortunate because I'd be vindicated if they were. They're cronies of Bill Buckley, but they're just conservatives, and I sounded like a crank."

A doorbell chimed next door, and he heard the young woman screaming, *"No no no, you can't come in, I know what you are, I won't I won't!"*

"My neighbors are having a run-in with the cops here," Bert muttered.

Errol slid that right into his thesis. "You see? Living out there in California, with the lunatics? And sometimes you *are* a crank. Like with the women. I swear sometimes, Bert, it's like you stick to bachelorhood because it's some kind of political ideal. Hey, married people live longer, man."

I just don't want to settle for comfortable misery like you've got, Bert thought. But he said, "I just don't feel I can relate to the women I meet. If they're not shallow, then they're insanely career driven. And I can't believe you've got me talking about this crap again. I'm proud of being an aging bachelor, and let's leave it at that. Maybe I'll come out for Christmas. I got to go, man. Work. Thanks for calling. I'll call you back tomorrow."

Bert hung up and looked at the gulls once more. They were diving for garbage floating in the ocean.

Then Derry—with her bone-white hair and dark skin and four separate piercings at her nose and mouth—burst through her back gate and ran onto the beach. She was wearing nothing but a long T-shirt that didn't quite cover her ass, her short brown legs pumping as she ran away from the cops. She stumbled in the sand and fell—and two Quiebra PD officers stalked up to her. One of them glanced over at Bert; smiled and shook his head ruefully.

"Drugs!" the cop said. Bert recognized the guy—Officer Wharton.

Bert nodded, watching as they caught the writhing, sobbing girl, one of them expertly pinning her, the other locking the handcuffs in place. "I'm not on any fucking drugs!" she yelled, turning her dark eyes to Bert. "I'm not! They put their conversion thing in me—" Her eyes dilated, terrified, her mouth quivering between the words. He could see some other piercing, flashing at the back of her tongue. Kind of far back in the throat for a piercing. She was yammering on and on as they manhandled her—not too roughly—toward her condo. "—they tried to change me and I was fighting it. If you get mad and you try, you can stop it from taking you over—sometimes you can—and they can't let you fight it and—please call somebody outside. They have to be outside the—"

They dragged her back into the condo, and presumably out the front. After a while he heard the cop siren Dopplering away.

Bert sagged into his deck chair, surprised at the emotion he felt after seeing the girl dragged away. He'd barely known her. He'd suspected she was crazy. But he'd have felt this upset, he supposed, even if he hadn't known her at all. She was in distress, and with mental illness, real paranoia like that, there was so little they could do. The poor kid. There were so many insane people around—especially living on the streets in Berkeley and San Francisco—sometimes you wondered if some pollutant was behind it, or some sort of epidemic virus.

He sighed, and thought, *Move on, Bert. Work up ahead.*

He got up to toss the remains of his salad over the low wall to the beach—hoping his neighbors didn't see it, they hated it when he did that—and watched first one gull, then a scrapping flock of seagulls converge on it.

Then he went to find his coat and car keys. He hoped the car would run.

Adair was at school, trailing along after Waylon, after-hours. He was going to Mr. Morgenthal's electronics shop. Waylon was working on some kind of radio that could, he thought, pick up "secret government frequencies" he'd read about at disinfo.com, only he told Mr. Morgenthal it was an ordinary CB and that he wanted to use some school equipment.

Adair was feeling shitty. First of all, she still felt uncomfortable around her parents. That weird ritual in the garage. Some kind of sex thing? Hard to believe. But what else could it be?

She felt like she was a mute, or a ghost; she was around people, but she couldn't talk to them, not about what was on her mind. There was Waylon, but she felt reluctant to talk to him about what was happening with her parents. His theories about things were always so extreme. She had opened up a little at lunchtime, though, saying, "You know what, I just feel like there's something wrong with my parents, like the whole town is off, but—maybe I'm just imagining it. But my mom and dad, I don't get it."

He just chuckled dryly and shook his head. "Tell me about it. My mom is *so-oo* fucked up. And my dad—he got mad and just said, 'the hell with 'em both.' Well, maybe he didn't say the hell with 'em both, but he acts like that. We haven't heard from him in . . ." There was a little catch in his voice when he said that. He seemed to brood about it for a while, and she didn't feel like she could say any more. Even though she felt that whatever was going on was a whole lot worse. She didn't want to diminish what he was feeling, but she didn't know how to explain. It sounded insane when she tried.

So even though she was walking down the hall with Waylon, she felt a stab of loneliness. Cleo hadn't even called to tell her she'd dyed her blond hair with Day-Glo blue streaks.

Danelle had moved away, and Siseela was someone she saw mostly only at school.

And here came Cleo and Donny around the corner, walking together but not as close as they used to, Cleo with her blue streaks, Donny's hair in short dreads. Cleo on her cell phone; Donny checking his beeper. Handsome with high cheekbones, a strong chin, Donny could be an actor, but he wanted to run for office someday.

Siseela came up then, too, from behind—a gangly girl with cornrowed hair, bland blouse, and always a long skirt, because her parents were Jehovah's Witnesses. She got a lot of sympathy for being stuck with Jehovah's Witness parents, and her having to pretend she believed in that bullshit just to get along.

All of them carrying books or backpacks, the kids clustered near the door of the shop. Waylon, who was "about as social as the Unabomber," as Cal put it, sighed and leaned against the wall with an impatient look toward Morgenthal's classroom; not wanting to talk to the group, wanting to go in, but knowing that Adair wanted him to wait for her.

She thought, *Maybe he's into me, if he acts like that. Waiting for me when he wants to do something else. But then why doesn't he make a move or something?*

"Lookit Cleo's hair," Siseela said. "She all like that singer Pink, only she's Blue."

"I think it look good," Donny was saying, talking to Siseela.

Adair knew him: he'd say "it look good" to Siseela. Adair had heard him say, "I'm fittin' to go to UC Berkeley, I get accepted," to Siseela. Black English. But the day before, he'd said to Adair, "I've applied to Berkeley, and I think I can get in. I'm not totally sure." With perfect diction.

But then, half the white students were deliberately talking in Black English. White kids affectionately calling each other "nigger," even. The black kids called them "white niggers"—or "wiggers."

Donny, anyway, had a jump on being a politician. He had the instincts.

With Waylon squirming restlessly, the group talked about movies, complained about the jenky dances at the Youth Center, how the school was getting all shabby and "hella ghetto," Cleo said, oblivious to Donny's glare; he thought that expression was racist. And about how Siseela was getting her navel pierced without her parents knowing, and how she was going to hide it from them. Then she related with horror that they were going to make her do that door-to-door Jehovah's Witness thing soon.

"I'm not gonna be no JW pod people, yo," she said. They talked about how a bunch of people had had their home PCs or Macs stolen. Donny said he'd heard that sometimes the computers had just been torn apart, parts stolen, and that brought up how there had been some kind of big rip-off from the electronics class, and some people's cars had been stripped—and how freaked out they were. One of the kids was suicidal without his computer: ate two bottles of Tylenol and half his mom's Valium, had to have his stomach pumped.

Adair was covertly watching Waylon all this time. He had perked up at the talk about the thefts, then went back to ticking away at his Palm Pilot screen with the little stylus.

Finally he stared into the tiny screen, nodded to himself, blew his lips out noisily, and walked off, going into Morgenthal's electronics shop.

The vice principal stalked down the hall with that why-are-you-guys-hanging-around-here-after-hours look, so the kids broke up. Waving good-bye to Siseela, Adair started to go after Waylon.

Cleo stopped her. "Hey, is he your big thing now?"

"Waylon? He's my friend. And guess what, a friend is a big thing for some people."

Cleo didn't take that bait. She just gave her hair a toss. Donny was backing toward the door, gesturing to Cleo *come on, if you're coming*, but not necessarily urgent about it, and it looked to Adair as if Siseela was waiting for Donny at the exit door, maybe hoping that Cleo wouldn't come.

Adair thought, *Good for you, Sissy.*

"So you going to get a piercing now, too, Cleo?" Adair asked, just to keep Cleo there.

But Cleo shot Adair a cold look and went off to try to retrieve him.

Adair shrugged and for Siseela's benefit—behind Cleo's back—made a fuck-you finger at Cleo.

Siseela, looking Adair's way, laughed and made an I-got-your-back sign with her hand.

"I still can't believe it," Mr. Morgenthal was saying to Waylon, as Adair walked into the electronics shop. "Why would the kids do this? I mean, it's all for them—for their lives! For their *future.*"

He was almost in tears, looking around the ravaged electronics shop. There was something shocking in seeing a teacher about to cry. Especially a big, round, red-faced man like Mr. Morgenthal. He was always jolly and patient—except some days, when you could tell he was hungover. He wore his shop overalls and had his thinning brown hair slicked back. His thick-fingered hands were trembling on his desk as he sat behind it looking at the smashed-open oscilloscopes, the torn-open ham radios, the gutted hard drives.

"Whoa," Waylon said, staring at the wreckage.

"Now you sound like Mason," Adair muttered.

"And there's no room in the budget to buy everything again." Morgenthal's voice quavered.

"You can probably get a lot of new stuff donated by some of those Silicon Valley places," Waylon said. "Get better stuff now, maybe."

Mr. Morgenthal brightened a little. "You have a point." But then he scowled again. "Still, I don't understand this. Now, maybe I shouldn't assume it was the kids who did this. Only, I thought it was some of our kids because, you know, it looks more like vandalism than burglary."

He went on and on like that for a long time, speculating, trying to understand.

He was such an emotional man for a vocational electronics teacher, Adair thought. You'd think they'd be all cool and analytical, like a

Vulcan. "You could get extra credit, helping me clean up, Waylon," he said finally.

"Actually," the man in the doorway said, "I'd appreciate it if you didn't touch anything just yet."

The three of them went silent and stared at the stranger. But was he a stranger? He looked sort of familiar, though his clothes didn't belong to the vague memory Adair had of him. He was wearing chino slacks, an Arrow shirt, an open zip-up windbreaker. Tall, lean, good-looking guy. Then she knew what it was: he should've been in uniform. She'd seen him out at the satellite crash site, hadn't she?

"My name's Stanner," the man said, in an unhurried, vaguely friendly sort of way. "Major Stanner. Could I talk to you in private, Mr. Morgenthal?"

Stanner ambled over to the desk, casually showed Morgenthal some kind of ID—blocking it from the kids with his body.

Morgenthal's eyes widened, seeing the ID. Adair wished she could see it.

"The police gave me a call," Stanner went on, glancing at his watch. "Wow, it's getting toward dinnertime. Anyway, we think—" He glanced at the kids. "You guys still here?" Stanner turned to Morgenthal, raised his eyebrows.

Morgenthal stood up and said, "Sure, I—yeah." He turned to Waylon and Adair. "You kids, out! Thanks for coming by, Waylon. I'll let you know about the class; we'll do some book work next time maybe."

Stanner smiled reassuringly at Adair and Waylon. She thought there was a kind of wistfulness. Like he really did wish they didn't have to leave.

But Waylon had red spots on his cheeks, and he was chewing his lower lip. He seemed mad about something. You could tell he recognized the guy, too.

Waylon crossed his arms. "I'm staying. Hey, look, you people ought to come clean about this shit. Serious."

"Waylon!" Mr. Morgenthal said sharply. "I won't have that kind of language in here. Now go outside, please!"

"It's no big thing, Waylon," Stanner responded, using Waylon's name as if he were one of the school administrators, with that kind of informal authority.

"You were at the crash site, man. I recognize you," Waylon said. "And there should have been stuff on the news about it, and there wasn't, so that means a cover-up, like when the CIA covered up how they smuggled crack into south central L.A.!"

"I don't actually have anything to do with crack dealing in Los Angeles, Waylon," Stanner said, seeming mildly amused.

"You deny you were at that crash site?"

"I helped out when I was in the area, yes. Just coincidence. I'm looking into something else. Equipment stolen from some schools, that might be used in domestic terrorism. It's not really a likelihood, but we follow up all the little things nowadays. So there you are, you dragged it out of me."

"You mean I dragged your cover story out of you, dude!"

Morgenthal groaned. "Waylon, for God's sake . . ."

"And I'm not CIA," Stanner said, chuckling. "I just do a little investigating for the government."

"Bullshit, man, the fucking CIA has a hand in everything, and chances are that satellite was theirs! Surveillance shit! The CIA fucking shot Kennedy and Malcolm X and Martin Luther King, dude. Don't tell me they're not—"

"Waylon!" Mr. Morgenthal barked, his face bright red. "I warned you, and I'm writing you up for this! Now get out or I'll have your mother in here!"

Waylon winced at that. "Yeah, like she'd show up," he muttered, going to the door, Adair with him. Then he stopped and turned to glare at Stanner, who smiled and waved at him. Waylon looked as if he might charge Stanner to try to shake the truth out of him.

"Come on, Waylon," Adair said hurriedly. "He's not going to tell you anything. What are you going to do, chain yourself to him? Let's go."

After a few tense seconds—Waylon glaring, Stanner smiling patronizingly—Waylon let her steer him out into the hall. But he pulled away from her and stood to one side of the doorway, trying to eavesdrop.

Stanner emphatically closed the door, nodding at Waylon and Adair in a friendly way as he shut it firmly in their faces. They heard him talking to Morgenthal, but they couldn't make out a word through the closed door—even with Waylon pressing an ear to it.

"Fine," Waylon said, straightening up. "But I remember that motherfucker. I'm going back out to the crash site. There's some heavy shit going down."

"You heard him. He was here about, you know, some other thing completely."

"Oh, sure, and he's here 'coincidentally' for two different things? How do we know there's not a UFO connection in this whole thing? That thing came from space—okay, it was American made, but how do we know the aliens didn't shoot it down, or didn't, like, climb into it or something?"

Trying to sound like she was half joking, she said, "Do you know how nuts you sound?" They walked out into the crisp late afternoon. He was right that Stanner was probably lying. But UFOs didn't feel right. It was something else.

Waylon, she saw, totally loved the theater of it all. It kept his mind off other stuff, probably.

She looked at him as they walked along the avenue. She was almost running to keep up with his long angry strides.

"You going to the bus stop?" she asked.

"Till I get a car."

She'd been hoping maybe that evening he'd make his move. Not that she'd let him get very far. But she wished he'd make a move anyway. A little making out couldn't hurt anything. She might even give him a hand job. That much was okay. They ended kind of gross, but she didn't mind too much. It was just reproductive fluids and DNA.

But he was staring straight ahead, and she could almost feel what he was thinking. It was practically right there in the air. *How to get over to the site?*

"It'll be dark in an hour or so," she said. "Let's go tomorrow morning."

"What? No! Tonight! Hey, you think that fucking stoner cousin of yours would give us a ride?"

She sighed. "I thought you said something about how I should, like, come over to meet your mom?"

He looked at her in surprise. "I did?"

"No, you didn't. I was being sort of sarcastic. But . . . you could ask me to meet her."

He stared at her. "Why?"

She ground her teeth together. "Never mind. Forget it."

Mom, this is Adair. She's sort of special to me.

Yeah, right. Like that was going to happen. He was weird about people going to his house.

"So you want to go check out the crash site again or what?" he asked, staring off toward the Suisun Bay.

She blew out her cheeks. She didn't want to go to the crash site—but she didn't want to go home, either. She felt more and more uncomfortable at home, since Lacey had moved to the motel. "I'm starving. If we can go to Burger King, or something first, I'll call Mason, and we'll see what he says. If he's not too stoned out."

"Tight," Waylon said. "We go to Burger King and then the crash site. Um, you got any money?"

8

Vinnie "Vinegar" Munson was just noticing the feeling in his hands that meant it was getting cold. His fingers felt distant and clumsy. He said, aloud, "Look out, brother, the wind'll lock handcuffs on your extremities like Officer Rhino." The lady standing next to him waiting for the light glanced at him, knowing he wasn't talking to her. That he was just talking. He knew she thought he was "one of those guys." To all of them, he was "one of those guys," but to Vinnie Vinegar he was doing exactly what was necessary and right. "It gets routed to New York like lost luggage," he explained. He wasn't looking at her, but this time he was talking to her. She didn't know that, because he was turned away from her and talking in the same voice he'd used before.

Then the light changed to WALK, which made him feel good. It was all's-right-with-the-world when he crossed the main street— the only big street—of Quiebra's Old Town, at exactly the moment when the lit-up hieroglyph of a man began happily striding along in that golden-white electric glow that meant *Yes!* It always bothered him when it changed to the red glowing hand that said, *No! Don't cross!* and he was only three-fourths of the way across.

He knew perfectly well that the red hand was there to warn

people not to start off crossing the street, because they'd be caught in traffic when the light changed. What, was he retarded that he didn't know that? He was forty-six years old, and he had read the entire *Encyclopedia Americana* and understood everything but some of the physics parts, and he certainly wasn't retarded. But the red hand bothered him. Couldn't they put up some kind of machine that jumped up and stopped people *behind* him, so that he didn't have to look at the red hand saying *No!*

"The red hand," he said aloud, "is not meant for you." He had to tell himself that a few times, till he was past it. He was afraid it would come down and burn his face with a red hand imprint, the way Mom used to slap him, but of course, it never did. His therapist would have said, "You don't really believe it's going to do that, you're just letting some tension go, worrying about it. That's one of the ways you release tension."

But he still worried about it.

He got past the red hand, then walked past the boarded-over place that used to be some kind of big butcher shop and still had a sign on it, QUIEBRA'S OWN LAZY AGED MEAT. People made jokes about that sign, jokes his mother called "unsuitable." There was a silly drawing of a lazy cow on the sign. Mother had explained there'd been some idea that aged meat was tastier, but it made him think of roadkill. Once you started thinking about roadkill, it was hard to stop. He hated thinking about roadkill.

He looked at his watch. It was 5:32. That sequence of numbers irritated him. It implied *5432* but it left out the *4.*

At 6:00 he would watch *Starbots*. He knew it looked childish, watching a cartoon every day, but this was a Japanese cartoon, and it was so beautiful he didn't understand how anyone could resist watching it. He didn't like other cartoons. He didn't like *Sponge-Bob*, he didn't like *Scooby-Doo*. That stuff was childish. He watched *Crossfire*—without looking directly at the people in the show, but watching it anyway—and he understood every word. It was always about something that was in the papers. You couldn't say he was stupid. It was just that in *Starbots*, everyone was a Hyperdroid, even the bad guys, and if they got killed, they vanished in a shower of sparks. They didn't lie there rotting, picked at by turkey vultures, like the roadkill on Quiebra Valley Road. The streets in the show were of some shiny synthetic stuff. Nothing was dirty or unsymmetrical on *Starbots*. Even the bad guys were beautiful; they didn't have warts or wrinkles or snot.

When Zaron and Lania transformed into Starbots, they unfolded with perfect symmetry, like flowers. They made little jokes at each other's expense, but they didn't call each other rude names. They were always loyal. They never touched each other, except once in a while one would help the other stand up after a magnetic blast had knocked him down. Vinnie didn't much like touching people, but he could do it if he had to.

The Starbots Interworld Station was a beautiful place, even with its villains. "How could anyone not want to be there, instead?" he said aloud, as he started across the footbridge over Quiebra Creek. Down below the little wooden bridge, rushes were bending and ducks were coursing in the stream. "Show me a duck and I'll show you a whole way of loving muddy little bugs," he said, glancing down. Which was, of course, exactly the case and nothing less.

Vinnie was thinking about *Starbots*, and how he needed some vinegar to purify his tongue, and hoping there were still some pickles at home, as he hadn't had any vinegar for more than an hour, and he was toiling up the path that wound between houses and copses of trees to his and Mom's house, on the crest of the ridge overlooking Quiebra, when he saw the squirrel's jaws unlock, and something came spinning from its throat.

It had seemed like an ordinary squirrel, furry red-gold—not really the color of the red *No!* hand, not actually. Ordinary red squirrel color. It ran in that darting, stopping, darting hesitating way the squirrels used, up the trunk of a eucalyptus. Then it stopped at the place where the tree bole opened into branches, and it tilted its head to stare into a mess of leaves that might've been a bird's nest.

That's when its jaws opened way wider than they should be able to, and the silver darting thing came out of the middle of its throat, and it struck just like a snake at something. He saw that the squirrel wasn't striking at an egg. It had snapped up a piece of something shiny, maybe the clockworks case of an old wristwatch, without its band. So it must be a crow's nest, because he knew that crows stole shiny things and put them in their nests. And there was a squirrel with a piece of a watch in its mouth. Then the watch spun around in its mouth so fast it blurred, for a full ten seconds it spun there—and then vanished inside the squirrel. The squirrel's mouth snapped shut with a spurt of blue sparks.

Then the squirrel seemed to notice Vinnie; to turn a minatory black eye toward him. The eye extended out from its head an inch or two on a little silvery stalk and tilted this way and that. Then the squirrel thing rolled up into a ball, just like a pill bug, and *rolled* down the trunk, without falling, just like it could stick to the wood, and it rolled off across the sloping ground between the boles of some trees, rustling the dry leaves as it went.

He stared after it. His mouth was open, and he snapped his own mouth shut, afraid that sparks would come out from between his own lips. But they didn't.

He heard a fluttering sound and looked up to see a blue jay glaring down at him. It was completely silent. It just stared and stared. Without a sound. Which wasn't normal for blue jays. They were never silent for long. They used up a great deal of energy screeching. He had tried to explain the inefficiency of this to them. This silent blue jay cocked its head—and then he noticed that it hadn't any legs. It had little metal hooks instead of legs. Its head slowly rotated on its neck all the way around, unscrewing, till a little silvery worm was able to come out from the opening in its neck. The worm in the blue jay pointed its metal tip at him—and the tip quivered really fast like one of those New Year's Eve paper toys that uncurl and shake themselves at you and make a rude noise.

Then the blue jay rolled itself up like a pill bug, tucking its head between its fish-hook legs, rolled down the tree—and rolled away. It didn't fly. It rolled.

Home for Vinnie was uphill from here—but he ran home.

When he got home he put on the Beach Boys song "In My Room" like he always did, and he got out his journal. He wrote about the squirrel and the blue jay in his backwards book, still breathing hard as he wrote, but he didn't tell anybody about it, not even Mom.

He didn't want them to think he was the kind of person who saw things like that. It was hard enough to get people to be fair.

December 3, night

Cal was sitting with his mom and dad watching TV and wondering why it felt so fucked up. It was what Adair used to call Family TV Night. It was pretty much the last thing they did willingly and happily together. And it usually felt okay. Adair wasn't here, so tonight it wasn't the whole family, but that wasn't the problem.

He thought about Adair insisting something was wrong with Mom and Dad. He'd yelled at her for saying it; maybe he'd yelled at her because it was bothering him, too.

There *was* something with Mom. Was she pissed off at Dad? She wasn't laughing at the show, and she kept looking at Dad. She would glance at him, then at the TV, then she'd look at him again. He watched the TV and laughed, right along with the laugh track. He turned and smiled at them warmly from time to time. At least, the smile seemed warm.

So what was bothering her?

Cal wasn't sure. Yet he almost knew.

For once, it occurred to him to just right out ask her. But you couldn't ask your parents stuff like that—*Why are you acting so weirdly, Mom?* At least, not in his family.

A commercial came on; during the commercials he whipped out his Palm Pilot—the expensive one he'd gotten so cheap on eBay— and checked his E-mail. Tapped out a reply to his friend Kabir in Palm Pilot graffiti: *Can't go to mall tonight . . . family shit . . .*

The show came back on, with dull inevitability, and he folded up the Palm Pilot. He wished Lacey was here, but she'd moved to a motel.

It was hard to think of her as Aunt Lacey. She seemed more like an older sister. She was pretty cool. She seemed to be ready to deal with whatever came along no matter how screwed up it was. She never got annoyed. Sometimes Lacey seemed puzzled by Mom but never pissed off.

The sitcom wended its predictable way. "What a loser show," Cal muttered.

"Would you like to change the channel, son?" Dad asked, and he didn't seem sarcastic about it. He changed to another channel. A talk show with a bunch of women talking about breast implants. "How's this one, son?" he asked.

Son? "Uh . . ." His dad knew better than to think he'd watch something like that.

So he changed to a WWE show. Wrestlers heaved themselves around the ring. "How about this one?"

"Oh, I don't—"

He kept flicking through them, too fast to judge, until finally Cal stood up, almost convulsively, and said, "Actually, I'm gonna take a walk."

He started for the front hall, hesitated in the archway. Felt like he should say something more, but he wasn't sure what.

Then his dad said, "Sure thing, son," and turned the TV off. "Certainly," he added. He got up and went out into the garage. Began rustling around out there. Mom just sat in the chair, gazing toward the TV.

Then she looked toward the garage. Then back at the blank TV. Then at the garage. Then back at the TV. It was freaking Cal out.

He turned to go, and she said suddenly, "Cal?"

Her voice sounded almost strangled. As he turned back to her, he wondered if she had something caught in her throat.

"What?"

"Cal." She was looking at him, then at the garage. Then at him. Then at the garage again. Then she lifted up her left hand, and she stared at it. And the hand twitched.

He got a twisty feeling and asked, "You okay, Mom? Should I get Dad?"

"Dad? No! No." She stood up awkwardly, took a step toward him, twisted her head about on her neck as if trying to clear a crick, opened her mouth, and said . . .

Nothing.

She simply stood there, breathing loudly, with her mouth hanging open. Making—he could barely hear it—that faint strangled sound.

Something was seriously wrong with his mom. "Okay, that's it, Mom! I'm getting Dad!"

"No!"

Cal hurried over to her, reached for her.

She took a step back from him. As if afraid. She made that strangled sound again.

He hesitated. "Something—caught in your throat?"

"Yes. No. Sort of. Maybe. Cal, it took me all this time. It can be fought. It can be—"

Then Dad was there, in the kitchen doorway. He was staring at Mom. His lips were moving.

And Mom suddenly seemed fine. She smiled and said, "Jeez, something caught in my throat, there."

It seemed to Cal—he wasn't sure, because he saw it from the corner of his eye—that Dad had mouthed those words silently as Mom had said them. *Something caught in my throat.*

No. Not possible.

Mom was smiling at him. "Go on, go on your walk, Cal. Certainly. Go right on ahead. We'll see you later, son."

Cal looked from one parent to the other, then shook his head in wonder. It was rare for either one of them to call him "son." Not that they acted like he wasn't their son. They just didn't call him that. Calling him that sounded like something from one of those old shows on TV Land.

A feeling rose inarguably up in him that he had to get somewhere far away, as fast as he could—and he didn't know why.

"Actually, Mom? Can I borrow the truck for a couple of hours?"

"Certainly." She turned very suddenly and went toward Dad. The two of them went into the garage.

Certainly? Normally she'd have given up the keys only after an argument, especially with Dad watching.

Whatever. This was his chance to get the truck.

He got the keys from the hook on the wall, went out to the curb, and got in the car. He started it—and just sat there.

He tried to think of somewhere to go.

Mason hesitated in the doorway of the kitchen, watching Uncle Ike cleaning his rifle in the living room. He didn't like to be around Uncle Ike when he was cleaning his gun. Ike was a big guy in a hot-pink bowling shirt and shorts and flip-flops; he had receding red-blond hair and freckles and enormous hands. He'd sit there at the coffee table drinking Bud and cleaning that 30.06, and it just made Mason paranoid because he knew that Uncle Ike had flipped out on Aunt Bonnie, at least once, which is why Aunt Bonnie had gone to her cousin Teresa's place to live. At least, she said, till Ike went back on antidepressants—or amphetamines.

When he wasn't on amphetamines he would alternate between glum disinterest, vague friendliness, and manic rages. And here he was cleaning that gun. In movies the hit man cleaned the gun right before he shot someone.

"When you gonna clean this house, you little prick?" Uncle Ike said, ramming a long skinny brush through the bore of the rifle.

Mason looked around. Dirty clothes lay about the floor, which was otherwise papered over with cast-aside old issues of the *National Enquirer*. The beer cans and pizza boxes had been shoved off the coffee table onto the floor to make room for Uncle Ike's cleaning kit and the rifle.

The kitchen was worse. The place smelled rank, too, but you mostly smelled that only when you came in. Once you were inside a while you didn't notice it anymore, unless you got near that big pile of garbage teetering over the trash can.

"We need to get some chicks in here," Mason said. "Clean this shit up, Uncle Ike."

"You're the chick around here," Uncle Ike said. "You get to earn your way by cleaning the house. You don't work, you don't bring any money in. You sell pot to eat on, but you don't give me any of the money."

"You said you didn't want any narco-money."

"That's not what I'm fucking talking about. I'm talking about I get my ass to the bowling alley five nights a week to hand out those stinking bowling shoes and hear people whine about the lanes not working, and you're here watching fucking *Friends* and *Seinfeld* reruns on TV."

"Hey, whoa. I got laid off, okay. I'm gonna get on over at the Square Deal garage."

"Even those fucking crooks wouldn't hire you. Now fucking clean the house, you little prick."

Mason said, "Fuck you, man. I'll sleep in my van."

He went out the door, fast but not neglecting to slam it. His plan was to smoke a few bowls, then go to a pay phone—his cell phone had been shut off—call up his young cousin Cal and see if he could get something to eat at his house. Cal and Adair were barely related to him, only by some kind of twice-removed in-law thing he couldn't remember, but they treated him like a fucking human being, unlike Uncle Ike. That asshole.

He went to the van, hearing Uncle Ike shouting behind him, through the door, something about *don't bother to come back*—and stopped by the driver's side door. A brown and white Ford Expedition was weaving along the street.

"Whoa," Mason said, fascinated. "He's got to be all fucked up on something."

But then he saw that the driver was weaving with a purpose. He was chasing something down the street. A cat, a fat fluffy-white cat too panicked to get out of the road. But there—the cat spotted a wooden gate, darted right up and over to safety. The Expedition slowed down; the driver was a young guy with a scruffy haircut, a dirty uniform of some kind. He glared after the cat. Then he seemed to sense Mason, turned to look at him—and smiled, his whole face transforming.

He rolled down his window and leaned out of the SUV. "Howdy, pardner," the guy said.

Mason recognized him, then. He was one of those two young marine guards they'd run into down at that site where some kind of military shit had fallen from a plane or something into the water.

"That cat do something to you, dude? Don't be, like, running cats over. That's our neighbor's cat."

"Oh, I wasn't really going to hit it. I was just chasing it a little ways."

"Oh." Mason was losing interest, but he couldn't quite look away from the guy's unblinking regard. "So, uh, hey, where's your friend?" Mason added, for something to say. "The guy who was with you down there at the bay. The other jar—marine guy."

"Ah, yes, you were there. I retrieve you now," the marine said, his smile broadening. "My friend? I'd like to know myself. He didn't adjust well. He just fell apart. Some do well and some don't. You know, I think you'd do rather well. You'd just fall right into place."

"Say what?" *This motherfucker*, Mason thought, *is crazy. He must be, like, AWOL and shit, too. Bad news.*

Mason dug around his pocket for his van's keys, then he saw he'd left them in the van. And the van door was locked. "Shit! I fucking locked my keys in the van!"

He heard a car door open, looked over to see the marine walking toward him. His uniform was missing some buttons, and there were oil stains on the shirt. The guy had left his car running and left it in gear, and it was slowly, very slowly, starting to roll by itself down the street, angling randomly toward the curve.

"Cuz, marine guy, you left your car in gear."

The marine nodded, smiling, completely unconcerned, and stepped between Mason and the van. He put his hand flat over the lock on the door of Mason's van, and there was a clicking, a sound of tumblers, and the little black plastic cylinder of the door's lock switch popped up, all by itself. "There you go," the marine said.

"Whoa," Mason said. "How'd you do that?"

"So yo," the marine said, "you wanta smoke a bowl or something?"

Mason only had a pinch or two left. "You got any? I'm about flat."

"Sure, I got some. Gung ho, man. Let's get in the back of your van."

Mason was on automatic, in a way, after that, not questioning anything, and they were in the back of the van in about twenty seconds, the SUV forgotten. Mason dug his little brass pipe out from under the driver's seat, turning to see the marine crouched, not offering pot, not reaching for the pipe, just crouched—and opening his mouth really, really wide.

It was impossible to open it that wide.

Mason made a squeaking whimper that sounded funny in his own ears, and recoiled, turned to climb over the driver's seat, to escape out the front.

He got partway, then something grabbed his ankles and pulled him irresistibly into the back of the van.

9

Carrying coffee in a Styrofoam cup from the Cruller, Bert surveyed Winsecker's night students as he entered his classroom, and found it about as he'd expected. Three or four elderly ladies looking for the "personal growth" they'd heard about on *Oprah*; four or five aspiring writers of both genders and varying age; a couple of gay middle-aged poetry enthusiasts who could probably quote Whitman—at least they wouldn't be completely clueless; and a smattering of high school kids probably looking for extra credit to make up for something they'd failed.

He did notice one bright-eyed lady, about his own age, with chestnut hair, a notebook open on her desk. Roll call established that her first name was Lacey, and she was new to the class.

Bert wrote his name on the blackboard. *Mr. B. Clayborn*. Some teachers went with the just-call-me-Sam thing, but Bert, though only forty-one, was to some extent old-fashioned.

"Welcome back to Adventures in American Literature. As you no doubt have heard, I'm taking over for Mr. Winsecker for the rest of the year. I do things my own way and will be assigning exactly what I please. The class title has the word *adventure* in it, but we won't be reading the abominable Mr. James Fenimore Cooper or the overdiscussed Mark Twain—delightful as Mr. Clemens may be. Instead we'll be focusing on the transcendentalists in the first half—"

A middle-aged man raised his hand. A rumpled, heavyset man with a smug expression and a book on the Civil War sitting beside his notebook. "Will we be discussing Civil War literature?"

"Well, Mr. . . ."

"Gunderston. Ralph. You had my son in your—"

"I remember! A senior last year, I think, in my high school class. I see the resemblance!"

This brought a titter of laughter to the class, and a puzzled, irritated look to Ralph Gunderston.

"Mr. Gunderston—Ralph, if I may—the short answer is: *barely*. That's how much we'll be discussing Civil War literature. We're going to try to understand what American writers thought about life. Today let's consider Thoreau, Whitman, and Emerson as radical thinkers—as radical as Karl Marx."

Lacey's eyes were calmly attentive the whole time, and she asked a couple of intelligent questions. He kept finding excuses to look at her.

After class, as the students filed out and Bert packed up his briefcase, Lacey approached him—a little shy, yet unafraid—asking if he could recommend a biography of Thoreau. Something about being a journalist, some piece she was writing.

On impulse, he offered to loan out a book. She accepted the biography he carried with him. He felt a sort of astonishment as he handed it to her. He never ever loaned books.

She was saying something about being new to the area. Living over in Quiebra.

"I live in Quiebra, too," he said. "And thank God it's unfashionable, because that makes it the only place in the Bay Area a teacher can afford to buy a house. Anyway, the only place that's not an urban combat zone."

The last person he'd loaned a book to was the last woman he'd been serious about. Juanita Collins. She hadn't returned any of his books, and eventually she'd stopped returning his phone calls. Then he'd heard she'd married some high-powered attorney. And that had hurt. He could imagine her comparing life with a community college teacher with life as a wealthy lawyer's wife.

Lacey nodded, watching him curiously. "Well, I've got to catch a bus. I haven't gotten around to buying a car yet up here. I sold my little old L.A. freeway-flea."

"A journalist, you said? What sort of topics?"

"Reporter, columnist. Irresponsible high-handed political opinionating, that kind of thing."

"Really. I'd love to read some irresponsible opinionating." He astonished himself again with what was an almost out-of-control boldness on his part: "Did you say you're catching a bus? It's kind of cold out. I can give you a ride back to Quiebra. I mean, normally I couldn't—if you were a young—I mean, it would look wrong my offering a ride to one of the—the freshmen girls, but I mean, not that you're old—" He could feel his face burning. He shook his head. "Oh, Christ."

But she was laughing softly. "I'd appreciate a ride. It's cold up here in the Bay Area. I'm used to Los Angeles."

Listening to Armand Van Helden on the CD player—world hip-hop rave-rap by a DJ with a German name—Donny stopped his '91 Thunderbird at the stoplight between the shopping center and the strip mall and glanced at his watch. Sort of late.

But he didn't feel like going home yet. What was the use of Pops giving him his own car if he couldn't drive around in it after school? He'd caught up on his homework using the computer in the school library; there'd been plenty of time because two of his teachers hadn't shown up, and he'd heard the PE teachers weren't around either, like there was a major teacher-hungry virus going around. He had the beeper they'd given him and they hadn't beeped him, so it must be cool. All the same, he thought he ought to call Moms, at least. There were upsides and downsides to being an only child.

When he'd dropped Cleo off, pretending he was going right home, she made fun of him for being Mr. Responsible all the time, and all he'd said was, "Ask Chris Rock." She hadn't known what he'd meant. And he was beginning to suspect he might have to deal with being in two minority groups.

Maybe Cleo was suspecting it, too, the way she looked at him when he had said he wasn't ready for sex.

It wasn't like she was really all sexed up and hot for him. She just didn't want to be a virgin anymore. Donny thought he ought to play along, but he found the thought vaguely repulsive.

He sighed. Really, he'd always known. Ever since seeing that movie where Wesley Snipes was mostly naked. Siseela was going to be disappointed, too.

He looked at himself in the rearview mirror. *Are you or aren't you?* He shook his short dreads, just to watch them bounce a little. Then looked around, hoping no one had seen that. The only possible witness was that big greasy-haired guy in the *Starbots* jacket—Vinnie something—wandering down the sidewalk, turning his head sharply away when cars drove past. Talking to himself a mile a minute, as usual. That made Donny decide to do some digital-camera shots for his Web site before going home.

He got the camera out of his backpack, and when the light changed he turned left and pulled up in the driveway of the shopping center, blocking Vinnie's way long enough to catch his worried, oblique look in the digital camera—his anxious, sagging face turned away under the streetlight.

Two shots. Then Donny waved at Vinnie, because he felt a little bad about scaring him, and drove into the parking lot. He always captioned the pictures on his Web site; that was part of the art. He decided he'd title the picture *Vinnie Hides Right out in the Open*.

There: Four white dudes, nineteen or early twenties, were gathered around the front of a Trans Am with its hood up, under the bright parking lot light. Probably on their way somewhere and the car had started fucking up. They all four had sagging pants and baseball caps turned backwards, and they were all leaning to look into the engine: a great shot. He pulled up next to them, opened the window, took the picture. Click: the four of them in almost identical clothes peering fixedly into the engine. He'd caption it *Destiny Omen.*

Then one of them looked up, glaring, and snarled, "What the fuck you think you doing, nigger?" and gave him the finger, and Donny snapped the finger and the angry white boy, too. He'd caption that *What the Fuck You Think You Doing, Nigger?* even though the guy followed up by grinning at him and making a dismissive gesture that meant he was just kidding. Then Donny recognized him: Lance something-or-other, he'd graduated last year. Held back a year, so he was almost twenty when he graduated. He was a gangly dude with an overbite and a shaved head under his backwards Oakland A's cap.

Donny drove around behind the Trans Am and then up parallel to it, and did a gruff-cop imitation. "What seems to be the trouble here, you boys? Give me a urine test, right now, goddamn it."

Lance laughed and came over to the car. "I'll give you a urine test on your whitewalls, dude." He thumped fists gently with Donny. "Hey, Donny, what's up. You got that T-bird shinied up. Doing some snapshots and shit? You gonna put me on that Web site?"

"Might. That 'What you think you doing, nigger' shit deserves to go up so everyone can see what a high-class fucker you are, Lance."

Lance laughed. "I know. I'm . . ." Then a kind of enigmatic sadness came over his face. He looked past Donny at a family coming out of the Albertsons; then he took a spindle of papers from his back pocket and handed Donny one. A leaflet.

HAVE YOU SEEN ROY?

> Roy Beltraut has at this time been missing for more than 24 hours. If you have any information about his whereabouts it will be treated confidenchially. Please call.

And there was a phone number.

Under the text was a blurry black-and-white picture of Roy in a basketball uniform. Donny had played some pickup basketball with him a couple of times. A pretty decent guy, red-haired and shy, and really tall. He decided not to point out that *confidentially* wasn't spelled with a *ch*.

"Man, I played ball with this guy," Donny said. "He run away?"

Lance looked glumly at the picture of Roy in Donny's hand. "I don't think he ran away. Call me later, that's my number there, I'll tell you the whole story. I don't want to say it around these fucking guys." His voice dropped low. "Some of them talk on-line a lot. They might mention my name."

"What's on-line got to do with it?"

"Tell you later. I think the phone's okay." He turned away, then stopped, seemed to think a moment, then turned back to Donny. "I'll tell you one thing though—Roy's parents don't give a shit he's gone. I'm doing this myself. Dude was my best friend." He added wistfully, "He asked me to come with him to the cops, and I didn't go."

His voice had dropped to less than audible. Donny shook his head. "The cops? What about? What's up with that?"

"Just—call me. There's some shit going down. I figure maybe you'd help me organize a meeting or something. You're a guy who does shit like that. Like you got them to build that skate park for the woodpushers, and that protest about there being no black history day at the school. So . . ."

"So what is it?"

Lance shook his head decisively. "I don't wanta talk about it here. Actually, give me a call and we'll arrange to meet. I'm not even sure about the fucking telephone."

Donny looked at Lance, weighing him up. The guy tweaking on amphetamines?

"Okay, whatever. I'll call you. Later on."

Donny drove around behind the shopping center, where the loading docks were, hoping to catch a bum foraging out in the Dumpster, get another picture. From back here, the shopping center was fortresslike. A copse of small leafless sugar maple trees stood just beyond the edge of the tarmac, and up the hill.

A movement caught his attention. Something shaped all wrong was swinging through the trees.

He swung the car around so the headlights pointed in that general direction. Put it in park and got out to stand beside it. He wanted to get whatever it was on camera. He figured it was some kind of sloth, maybe, swinging through the trees like a monkey. He raised his camera—and froze.

It was a dog—up in the trees. A midsize terrier was *swinging through the trees* like a monkey.

It had some kind of metal tentacles instead of its front paws, metal spines waving around on its back, and faceted glass eyes.

"Fuck!" Donny blurted, and convulsively snapped the picture. The thing reacted, and was gone in a flash of fur and slinking chrome into the bushes up the hill.

He went a few steps up a thin trail, but water was trickling down the slope and he only slid back down in the slick mud and couldn't see the thing any longer.

He went back to the idling car, shaking, and sat down behind the wheel. *Okay,* he thought, *that was like somebody's escaped pet monkey, with maybe a chain leash on it, and I saw it all wrong.*

He looked at the snap on the screen in the back of the digital camera.

It was all murky, half-hidden by branches. Could be a stuffed toy thrown into a tree. Wouldn't convince anyone of anything.

He shook his head. It hadn't been what it had seemed.

He decided he wanted to go home. See Moms and Pops. Thinking about them made him feel funny. They'd been really distant lately; gone from home a lot. Way more than ordinary.

He drove around the shopping center to the parking lot. Maybe he could get Lance to come back and they'd find the thing and . . .

Lance and his friends were gone. There was only a pop-eyed fat lady, wheezing as she carried a bag to her car.

He drove into the street, thinking that he wasn't going to tell his folks about what he had seen in the tree after all. Maybe he'd tell

Adair or Siseela. But even they wouldn't believe him. His parents would think he was on drugs. And he never took drugs. Mostly never.

He found himself driving home fast, breaking the speed limit by enough that one of the neighbors, that old woman who always came outside in her bathrobe on Valleyview, shouted, "Slow down!" as he passed. He didn't even slow for the speed bumps on Wright Street; the car bounced and clanked, maybe dented the muffler.

He was relieved to find both parents' cars parked in front of the big ivory-colored house, Moms's gold Saturn and Pops's silver Jaguar. His mom was half white, half Asian; his pops, a surgeon, was "blacker than some, black enough," as he put it; a tall ex-college football star who'd made a lot of money specializing in sports medicine. He'd put the San Jose Sharks right, more than once.

He parked, hurried into the house. "Yo, you guys!" he called. He just wanted to see them. He wasn't even sure why. "Hey, yo, your beloved tax write-off is home!"

There was no answer. Just the overloud pendulum tocking of that antique grandfather clock Moms had bought. The whole house was furnished in expensive antiques Donny was afraid to touch.

He looked at his watch. Sometimes they went to bed by this time.

He went up the stairs and listened in front of their bedroom door. He didn't hear the bed squeaking, so it wasn't that. He tapped on the door to their bedroom. "You asleep?"

Still no answer. He felt as if he should assume they were asleep, and just go down and get on-line or watch TV or something.

But he couldn't assume that. He didn't know why, but he had to *see* them in there, asleep, together. He had to know they were all right.

Like my parents are my kids, he thought, chuckling nervously at himself.

He opened the door softly, not wanting to wake them. There they were, lying side by side.

They were lying on the bed, on their backs, fully dressed. They just lay there, silently.

They had their eyes wide open.

For a moment he had a frantic thought that they were dead, because they were so still and it was as if they weren't even breathing.

Then they both turned their heads, at exactly the same moment with exactly the same motion, and looked directly at him.

"Hello, son," Pops said.

"Um." His mouth was so dry it was hard to speak. He licked his lips. "You guys—okay?"

"Certainly," Moms said.

"Certainly," Pops said. "We're just resting. Having a talk."

"Son," Moms said, "there's a blood test coming up at the school soon—"

Then she broke off, and turned her head as if listening to some willfully intrusive thought. "No," she murmured. "Not yet."

"Okay, whatever," Donny said.

He closed the door and went to his own room, thinking, *It wasn't like it seemed. What's wrong with me?*

Endless delays, trying to leave the school. Bert and Lacey cornered by the chatterbox who organized class schedules, the security guard confused about his parking pass . . . But Lacey had already taken to calling him Bert.

A light rain started up, as Bert finally drove Lacey out of the parking lot in his old Tercel. He hoped to God the little car didn't break down on the road again. The ramshackle little vehicle embarrassed him even when it ran.

Bert shook his head, wondering at himself again. He hadn't really cared what anyone thought of his car until today. Had it been so long that a little attraction made him irrational? But it had been only six months since he'd last gone to bed with a woman, though that thing with Emily hadn't lasted long. Nothing had lasted long since Juanita. He had convinced himself he was going to ease into a comfortable bachelorhood and accept a lonely death with existential fortitude.

The rain was just enough to require wipers. When he switched them on they almost scratched the glass. He was way overdue to have them replaced.

"Must be tiring, teaching a class so late in the evening," she said.

"I'm sort of used to it. Keeps me out of trouble."

"Me, too," she said gravely. "I'd be gambling away my life savings if I weren't in the class." He looked at her curiously, and she laughed. She was kidding. "Everything's a gamble—that's what I got from that passage you read, from Whitman."

They spoke of Whitman and Auden—she had a liking for Auden, it seemed—until they got to Quiebra Valley Road. Here every sort of tree, each type in its clump, hunched thick green mysteries in close beside the narrow highway. Now and then on the shoulders of this dark, curving stretch of wet asphalt were white wooden crosses with artificial flowers and deflated mylar balloons.

She turned her head to look as they passed another cross. "Those are all from people who died here? Jeez, that's three or four now on this one stretch of road."

"We had a big speeding problem on this road. It's really twisty and narrow. They killed kids with their cars, and the families put up those crosses. We got a good commander over at the Quiebra PD, guy named Cruzon, he put up a whole series of checkpoints to catch the drunks. Got the DA to do some prosecution, too, improved the situation some. But those kids are still dead."

He glanced at her, wondering how she'd take that hint of his basic pessimism. He could see the good in things, but the dark side was always there, too. And he wouldn't turn his back on it. Foolish to turn your back on it.

But she was nodding. "Yeah. People lose their kids, there really isn't any closure, any resolution to how they feel."

The wipers screeched and swished across the windshield; the rain beaded and blew in trails, up the hood of the car.

They were quiet. He thought about how he had just met her. It wasn't wise to ask a student for a date, even an adult like Lacey. But then—

Something fell from an overhanging tree limb, clattered and sparked onto the hood, and scuttled up onto the windshield.

It was a handful of somethings. Little pieces of irregularly shaped metal—or metal-threaded glass? Driven by the wind and the slap of the wipers, he supposed, they seemed to twist about to reorient themselves, fitting together, almost in the shape of a little animal, a lizard or—

"Look out!" Lacey burst out.

Then he saw it, too.

Headlights were blazing toward them, a truck's horn was blaring.

Working hard to keep from jerking the steering wheel in a panicky way, he steered sharply onto the shoulder. The little car fishtailed, bouncing, heading toward the gorge. Then it stopped on the edge of a steep drop-off to Quiebra Creek, so abruptly that both of them whiplashed.

The car shuddered, and the engine died.

10

Vinnie Munson sat with Mother Munson; Vinnie on the small sofa; Mother, a scrawny, wispy-haired woman, twisted half-sideways in her heavily padded recliner, under a comforter. Just the two of them in the cluttered, close little living room of the bungalow. He was watching MTV with the sound turned off; she was giving him her usual running commentary.

Sometimes Vinnie looked at the screen directly, but when he felt the pictures pushing on his eyes, he had to look away and follow it out of the corners of his eyes, with quick glances. Taking in the mostly naked girls dancing around behind the black rap stars with big gold chains swinging over their taut chest muscles; girls spilling out of limousines behind the man as he came out posing and rapping, tilting his head rhythmically this way and that so his dark glasses caught the light. Mother explained why it was bad, as he listened and watched.

"You see that's whore behavior right there, please," Mother was saying. "That's unsuitable. Showing your boomies because you want to be in that man's video. For money. On the *Dean Martin Show* he had some dancers in short skirts, but it wasn't whore dancing like this. That's just unsuitable."

Mother's eyes sparkled. They were having a great time. She'd have been disappointed if he'd turned off this disgraceful programming.

The video ended, and they had one of those crazy MTV animations where the word *MTV* blew itself up and reassembled like a monster or something. Vinnie had to look away. He didn't like that. It was too much like the brain cartoons that tormented him at night.

"I won't be in that rectangle when they're washing my hair that way," Vinnie said.

"Well, I should think not," Mother said. She always had something agreeable to say to him, though she understood him only about half the time. But half the time was ten times more than anyone else. She liked to criticize the things they saw together, but she meant it kindly. When on Sundays they went to the International House of Pancakes they all knew her there and they made sure to heat up her maple syrup and there was one girl who brought Vinnie extra pancakes, extra bacon. He couldn't look directly at her, when she was there, but he saw her in window reflections, or out of the corner of his eye, and she was a thin little woman like his mother, only young. Mother talked about how Vinnie had charmed that girl, and he sometimes actually laughed his barking laugh at that. It took a lot to make him laugh.

Next they were going to have *The Real World* on. Mother let him turn on the sound for that. She liked to comment on how badly behaved those kids were and feel sorry for the ones who sounded lost. There was one on lately named Lorena who would start crying about how the others put her down, and Mother would say, "Oh, the poor honey. You see what she's gotten into? She's a good girl and they act like that. Oh, that's a shame, Vinnie. Do you want some cocoa?"

She made him cocoa and popcorn, and they ate it together, watching young people whine on *The Real World*. He loved cocoa. He loved popcorn. He loved his mother. He wished he could let her give him a hug more often, like she wanted to, but it took a lot of inner preparation for that. Anyway, she knew he loved her. He always made her a valentine with his own hands, for February 14.

So they just sat in the living room together and watched *The Real World*. As much as he could watch it directly. He didn't have to think about the machine blue jays or the pill-bug squirrels. He didn't have to think about the voices from his seizures. He could be with Mother, and they were happy just being together like this.

It was bliss.

"Oh, hell," Bert muttered as the engine died. "I'm sorry, Lacey. Son of a bitch. I can't believe it. Are you all right?"

"Yes." She rubbed at her neck. "It's okay. Not even any real whiplash, I don't think. You?"

"I'm just mortified, is all. Something fell on the hood and I was staring at it and I must've crept over the center lane—just after my self-righteous speech about the drivers around here!"

She chuckled, nodding. "The world likes to remind us."

"When we're being pompous? Definitely. Holy cow, my heart's pounding."

She looked at the hood of the car and along the edges of the windshield. "I don't see anything now."

"Oh, but it was there. It must've been something like tinsel blown off one of those mylar balloons—from the crosses. I thought it was going to block my vision, and by God it did, just by being distracting."

"I know, I saw it, too! I mean, it's not there now. Whatever it was. It didn't look like tinsel. Little shiny things, like tiny puzzle pieces. My guess is it's something from a power pole. An electrical conductor thingie that broke off or . . . something."

He tried to start the car, but it wouldn't, and from the whining, clicking sound of it he'd jarred something loose in the already balky starter. "It's probably nothing major but . . . Last time I tried to fix the car myself I broke it worse. Do you have a cell phone?"

"I do. Right here in my purse."

But the phone didn't work; it crackled and muttered and wouldn't connect.

"Wouldn't you know it. The one time you really need one. Well.

Shall we walk till we find one of those yellow call boxes?" He peered up the road. "Those emergency phone things."

"Sounds like a plan." They got out into the rain—slackened, now, to a fine mist. Once more, Bert squinted down the road, looking for a call box. There wasn't one.

She whistled softly, and he went to stand beside her on the verge of the drop-off to the creek. "Look at that, Bert!"

They stared off into the darkness, below the road—the darkness he'd almost plunged the car into. They'd hit the shoulder right where the screen of trees parted for an opening into the narrow gorge of Quiebra Creek, maybe a hundred feet below. "Jesus! It must be the deepest part of the canyon here! The damn car would've turned over two or three times on the way down!"

Then he looked at her, wondering if he'd scared her, saying that.

But she was grinning. "I know! That'll sure as hell wake you up, won't it?"

A lot of other women would have been angry, or at least anxious, at a close call like that. But she reveled in having survived, at the closeness of it.

"It's funny there isn't a guard rail here," she said, leaning to look into the gorge. "Oh! I see! There was—only it's down there now!"

Bert followed her gaze and could just pick out the twisted white metal ribbon of the guard rail, tangled with the hulk of an old SUV, crumpled into a cluster of boulders, forty or so feet below. "Oh, yeah. I remember that one. That SUV's been down there for months. Leaking gas into the creek, no doubt. They really should've hauled it out by now. And fixed the guard rail. But for the grace of God, we could be down there with it."

Lacey turned back to the road, set her face toward Quiebra.

"Shall we?" she said matter-of-factly.

They buttoned up and started off toward town. The rain stopped altogether, and clouds broke open around the moon. The trees dripped. The moonlight was strong when the clouds allowed it;

sometimes it was muted as the clouds slid past and the darkness would mass around Bert and Lacey.

He glanced back at his car and sighed. "I'm sorry. That truck. I shouldn't have let anything distract me."

She looked at him; her smile caught the moonlight through the trees. "Not at all. It's not so cold now. Not an unpleasant night for a walk. I was startled by that stuff on the windshield, too. I'd have done the same thing."

Bert growled to himself. "That . . . blankety-blank trucker."

"You can say it! Tell it like it is! Witness!"

"That *fucking* trucker should have stopped to make sure we were all right." After a moment he grunted to himself, conceding, "Could be, the dumb son of a gun didn't even see us go off the road. It happened around the curve from where he went."

The night released the sound of their footsteps and not much more. He started to relax a little, look around, enjoy the walk a little; the trees dripping, the mulch exhaling a delicious, deep odor of leafy decay—odd how some kinds of decay could be pleasant. Maybe because it hinted about life closing the circle, about energy being released from what had been inert.

"It's funny," he said, "we're not far from town. There are ranches around, and freeways on the other side of those hills. But this area here is sheer wilderness. Nature keeps asserting herself. We destroy one aspect of the wildness and it finds a way to come back."

"But sometimes it's like some alternative nature keeps trying to grow out of our society—machines, electronics, media. Nature co-opting technology—it's like technology has become a—a wilderness."

He nodded. "I know what you mean. People are in such a strange state now. They're so much at a remove from real life, at least in America. It's like we live in 'media world,' like . . . in a dream. And we just kid ourselves into forgetting about the wilderness—about the *wildness*. But—" He gestured at the woods lining the road. "—it's savage and it won't go away. Maybe it just finds new shapes."

She looked into the darkness where the breeze made the tree-tops toss and hiss. When the wind eased, he could just hear the creek, like a crowd of whisperers. He was surprised they hadn't heard any owls yet. But the moon shone on him and Lacey between the shadows of the trees.

Maybe this little adventure could turn out to be a good thing. Maybe they would look back and laugh someday at how they'd gotten closer sooner because of his shaky driving. She'd say, "And you should have seen him, slapping his forehead, 'I'm so mortified!'"

Fantasies, he thought. *I'm turning into a damned teenage boy around this woman. Errol would say, "Aha, see, what'd I tell you!"*

He glanced at her and she returned his glance. He looked self-consciously into the darkness of the gorge to their right.

That's when he heard the soft, rattling, scraping sound, of something following them, down there.

Mason refused to get out of the van and refused to say why.

"He's paranoid 'cause he was smoking that dope," Waylon muttered. "Forget him, let him stay in the van."

Adair looked at Mason and thought, *There's something he's not telling us.* He'd hardly said anything since he'd picked them up.

She shrugged and followed Waylon through the rain down toward the shattered dock. There wasn't much evidence left of all the activity, now; the rain had erased most of it. Just the interlaced tire tracks of big vehicles, some torn yellow police tape lying on the ground like old Halloween streamers.

She paused for a moment to look at this arm of the bay, as Waylon pushed obliviously on ahead.

Occasionally a gibbous moon broke through the clouds and splashed a silver path on the slowly heaving water; this inlet of the bay dappled with sprays of rain that chased each other across the surface. Out toward the middle she could just make out the dark line of waves created by the current from the Sacramento River flowing into the delta and the bay. Adair could see, almost on the farther shore, the lights of a small boat chugging along, toward the bridge. She couldn't quite make out the boat itself; it looked like a cluster of lights laboring along, dipping with the rhythm of the waves. It was about the same size as *Skirmisher*.

She wanted to go out with Dad on the boat again. She got sea-sick in winter weather and it was cold out there, so she usually avoided it—but now she wished they could be out on the bay together. Only, Dad hadn't taken *Skirmisher* out since the satellite.

In fact, he hadn't done any work that she knew about for weeks. What were they living on? Maybe he'd gotten the check from the government for hauling that satellite up. But he hadn't mentioned it.

She sighed, and her gaze lifted to the hills on the other side of the bay, where someone had their Christmas lights up already—well, it was already December—and the strings of lights sparkled in candy-tone colors between the ghostly orbs of streetlights.

"Hey! Adair!" Waylon called.

She joined him on the wrecked edge of what remained of the dock. She pushed with her foot at a mostly broken-off end of timber, and a nail-studded chunk came loose, fell spinning into the water. It sank, then bobbed up again, drifting to clunk against a tarry, barna-cled pylon. She said, "You know, it's weird to think a fucking satel-lite crashed right here at our feet."

Waylon nodded. "I heard that. Shit. Look at that—the edge of the wood all charred. What's weird is that anything of the dock made it. Man, I'd think there'd be just, like, splinters left."

She turned to him in a sudden burst of conspiratorial excitement. "When Cal was working on it with Dad, he heard someone say some-thing about the satellite slowing itself down. It was like the way they said it. That it didn't exactly crash. It was more like it landed."

He stared at her. "Holy fuck. It *landed*?"

"Well, crash-landed. I mean, if you think about it. It's amazing that it, you know—"

"—that the satellite wasn't smashed to pieces! Damn! You're right!"

She felt a sort of glow inside. She'd shown Waylon she could help; she could be part of his quest. Maybe she could get him to make some kind of move, anyway; because maybe he appreciated her now a little more.

Mason honked the horn on the van, behind them. She glanced back, could just see the outline of his head. "He's getting nervous alone back there. Or bored."

Waylon muttered, "Just cool your fucking jets, Mason. Shit. We've only been here, like, a minute."

She shivered and hugged herself. "It's cold out here."

She looked at him sidelong, hoping the hint would get him to put his arm around her, but he just kept staring into the water.

Clueless shithead, she thought, suddenly angry. *You don't know what you're missing.*

She caught a flickering from the corners of her eyes, turned and saw that Mason was flashing the headlights. He was getting seriously antsy. Or scared.

Waylon pointedly ignored him. "There should've been reporters all over this thing. But nothing. Just gossip. The Feds have got to be suppressing this shit." He nodded to himself. "You know what? I'm thinking of calling some media. See, if reporters get onto this, they could shake things up, force NASA and whoever to answer some questions. We might find out what it was all about. They could use, like, the Freedom of Information Act. That's a law that—"

"I know what it is," she interrupted snappishly. "I got an A minus in civics, 'kay? But that Ashcroft guy and his pals closed down that Freedom of Information Act thing. They used the terrorist stuff for their excuse."

He looked at her with a renewed interest. "Huh. That's right. I forgot that. You keep up on this stuff, huh?"

She was irritated at his surprise, especially after thinking, before, that she'd impressed him. "No, I'm a stupid high school bimbo who doesn't think about anything but rock stars and getting on the pep squad. Why would I have anything else in my head?"

He blinked. "You mad at me for something?"

She snorted. "No. Forget it. Just forget it. Anyway—anyway, you won't be able to convince anyone there was a satellite here. Unless you can get Deputy Sprague or somebody to back you up, they won't believe you."

"What about your dad? He could testify or whatever."

"Nope, he's sworn to secrecy. Me and Cal had to promise, too. I could get him in trouble if I talked to the papers about it. So don't tell them about him, or he'll kill me."

He looked at her. "Kill you?"

"Not really, dumbass. You know what I mean. You're the one who's all paranoid."

He looked back into the water. "Deputy Sprague. Maybe he'd talk to the press if I like outed him on this shit."

She shrugged. "I'm cold. I'm going back to the van."

"Shit, this isn't cold. You whiny California people, man, you little beach bunnies don't know what cold is."

"It's cold to me." It seemed even colder when the clouds closed over the moon and it got darker. "I'm going."

The rain went from mist to hiss onto the back of her neck as she hunched toward the van. She glanced at the dock, but Waylon was still just standing there, a silhouette, gazing down into the water.

He wants to play Mulder, she thought. *Fine. But I don't feel like being his Scully.*

She stopped halfway to the van, feeling a stab of reluctance to go to it, and not sure why.

The van just sat there, with its headlights off now—hadn't he had them on before?—like a rectangular block of metal and darkness. Just a box, with some glass on it and a seething kind of quiet.

She was getting one of her feelings again. That's what it was. She didn't want to go near the van. Her feelings weren't visions, and they weren't all that specific. But they were also usually right.

Then the van's driver's side door opened and Mason got out, but it looked all wrong. He was getting out backwards, like he had turned around in his car seat, then had gotten out of the van without turning back around.

Why? Unless there was someone behind the van. Someone he didn't want to take his eyes off of.

She moved a little to the right, trying to see better, a little closer to the van, and realized his body was facing her after all. Only *his head* was facing backwards. Completely backwards. As she watched, it rotated on his neck like it was on a turntable. It kept going, all the way around, the other way. Then it stopped moving, back where it had started: facing backwards.

Her stomach lurched as he turned toward her again.

No, the whole thing had to have been a trick of the moonlight. That thought made her pulse slow a little.

"Mason?"

He didn't answer.

She thought she saw something moving, around his feet. Like, a small animal of some kind. A bunch of small animals. She couldn't see, in the darkness, what they were. They started coming toward her.

For the second time, Bert offered his coat to Lacey to supplement her own; a second time she refused. He was starting to shiver, even with it on. The occasional car had passed, but neither of them felt comfortable hitchhiking. Not yet anyway.

The moon came and went with rolling clouds. The breeze rose and shook a little rain off, then died away.

He glanced behind him. The sense of being followed came and went like the moon. Now it was gone again.

He shrugged the feeling off and trudged around yet another curve beside Lacey—Bert on the outside, reflexively sheltering her from the road, but wondering if really he should be sheltering her from the sucking darkness of the canyon, the steep slope between the clusters of trees to their right. Fir trees now becoming eucalyptus; peeling, menthol pungent eucalyptus soon replaced by liquidambar and miniature chestnut overawed by tall poplars; some of the trees evergreen, some of them stripped of their leaves. Now and then a gray-bearded palm tree. It was central California's arboreal polyglut, as he thought of it, and the ecologists hated the way native trees were being crowded out by the interlopers.

He was getting hungry and footsore and cold and the only yellow call box they'd come to had been vandalized. "A really useful piece of technology," he muttered now, "that call box, and those barbarians had to yank the phone off it. Why do they do things like that?"

She shook her head, chuckling. "I'm sure I can't imagine."

"I heard that someone broke into Morgenthal's electronics shop over at the high school, stole a bunch of stuff. Maybe it was the same people. You can sell electronic parts of certain kinds, and some metals, if you know where to go. I think I'd rather believe that than blind vandalism."

"You prefer barbarians with a plan?"

"Something like . . ."

Was it that sound again? Rattling the gravel in the darkened slope beside the road's shoulder?

". . . like that."

There was something up ahead now, something small, oozing along close to the ground. A low, slinking four-legged shadow. Two green-gold eyes shining in the moonlight, regarding them coldly.

"Ooh, a kitty cat!" Lacey said, suddenly sounding like a little girl.

It was. A thin black cat, probably feral, padding toward them with its head ducked down. It paused to sniff the air, to look into the gorge; then came on again.

"Maybe that's what I thought was—" He broke off, rethinking how he wanted to say it. "—what I heard making noise down below us there, sort of pacing us. He must've outflanked us. Hiya, cat."

Lacey squatted down to greet the animal. He was tempted to warn her that it was probably feral, but it rubbed its skinny flanks against her, purring like a toy engine. She scratched it behind the ears. "Oh, look, Bert, it's got a mark around its neck where it had a collar. Some creepy jerkwad must've abandoned it out here. Or her. I think this is a girl cat."

But then she straightened and stepped back as the cat suddenly arched its spine, hissing, ears laid back. Not at Lacey, as Bert had thought at first, but at something behind them.

* * *

Adair hadn't quite run away, when the little round black things began to roll toward her along the ground, like dark independent yo-yos.

She'd backed away from the van, then turned and trotted up to the dock. But Waylon was gone.

"Waylon!"

She looked back toward the van. Something small—several somethings—were rolling toward her.

She saw a larger movement in the trees, near the path along the shore that led to the marina. Was it Waylon? She hoped so. She ran that way, her heart pounding louder than her running feet.

"Waylon?"

The figure moved off into the trees. She followed, stumbling over a rotting log, falling, her hand sinking into a yeastily redolent cold mush she knew to be a kind of shapeless orange fungus she'd always found repulsive. She made a hissing sound of disgust and wiped her hand on leaves—which turned out to be stinging nettles.

Swearing under her breath, she got up and stumbled onward, her hands burning. Where was Waylon?

"Waylon!" She said it as loud as she dared, her voice hushed but carrying.

Someone whispered back. She couldn't quite make out what they'd said. *Come here*, maybe?

But she stopped where she was. The voice, whisper or not, hadn't been Waylon. She was sure of that.

"Hey, cat!" Bert called after it.

But the cat darted past them and shot off into the darkness. There was a feline screech, and a furiously tangled follow-up screech, then silence. Bert looked at Lacey and shrugged. Then the cat trotted triumphantly out of the shadows of the gorge, back into the moonlight, carrying something shiny in its mouth.

Bert stooped for a closer look. It looked like more of that stuff that had hit his windshield. Why would a cat show interest in that?

But then he saw the shiny stuff squirm, and the way it moved made him think of a lizard. It writhed, squirmed again—

And burst apart in the cat's mouth, in a shower of silver parts.

The cat opened its jaws to hiss, and the last of the stuff fell away. It seemed to coalesce, then catch a wind, to roll away into the darkness. But the wind had long since died.

Lacey went to the cat, who permitted herself to be picked up.

Shaking her head, Lacey looked into the shadows. "What was that thing? It looked alive. Sort of."

"Yeah. It did look like that. Like it was alive. But I don't see how it could've been. It was metal, I think. Or maybe it wasn't. Actually, I don't know what the hell it was."

More movement, then, in the darkness below. He looked over the edge, toward the creek, as a wash of moonlight fell. Was that someone? A man, a young man in a tattered military uniform, climbing up the hillside toward him? Moving like a lizard, too, in fits and starts, up the side of the slope.

Then the clouds moved over the moon again and darkness drew over the scene.

Maybe someone down there needed help. Or maybe there hadn't been anyone there at all. He'd been feeling spooked for a while, now.

Once, while hiking in Northern California, after hearing the local people telling Sasquatch stories, he'd seen a bigfoot among the trees, just beyond a clearing; saw it as evening darkness came onto the woods. But as he had moved closer to the thing, the bigfoot had resolved into a shadowy, wind-swayed bush.

He shrugged. Maybe he hadn't seen the guy down in the gorge. "Lacey? Did you see anyone down there?"

She came to stand beside him and look into the shadows. The moon broke through the clouds again, and the slope was empty. "Nope. You saw somebody?"

"I guess not." He turned to look at her. "You going to adopt that cat?"

"Have to. Can't leave her out here, can I? Only, only, I'm staying at a hotel till I get a place. I can't impose a stray cat on my sister.

She's already making me feel like—well, I'm looking for living quarters big-time. But meanwhile . . ."

He said resignedly, "You're not the take-the-cat-to-the-shelter type, are you."

"No." She looked at him steadily. "No, Bert, I'm not."

"So it's me, isn't it?"

"You could always tell me your condo doesn't allow cats."

"I just hope the gulls don't eat her."

She pointed. "Is that a car coming?"

Headlights were racing toward them. Lacey was looking at the oncoming lights as if she were considering hitchhiking, after all. "Yeah," he said.

Bert turned for a last look down the hillside; could see nothing in the darkness. But . . .

Something *was* there. He could feel it, watching. He could almost feel it thinking about them.

The cat in Lacey's arms looked down there, too. Its tail swished sharply.

The headlights drew close—and slowed. It was a sheriff's cruiser, and as it pulled up, Bert bent over to get a better look at the driver.

He knew this guy, a black deputy who interfaced with the local PD a lot. He thought the deputy's name was maybe Sprague.

"Deputy, we're awfully glad to see you," Lacey said.

Sprague rolled down the passenger's side window. "Truck driver called, said he thought you mighta gone off the road. He wasn't sure, and he felt bad he didn't stop to look, so he called us . . . and here you are, by gosh. Well, climb in." Glancing at Lacey, he added, "You going to bring that flea-bitten old cat with you in my cruiser?"

She smiled at him and stroked the cat.

The deputy sighed. "The things I allow women to do. Come on, I've already called for a tow truck. We'll get your car to town."

Adair couldn't stay where she was any longer. But she didn't know where to go.

The van just sat there, about sixty yards off, on the gravel area across from the dock.

Something was rustling in the darkness. She couldn't tell where it was exactly. Or what. Maybe just a deer or a skunk.

Great, her hands burned from nettles, she stank from fungus, and now she was going to get skunked.

Was there someone crawling, in the shadows, under that old, broken-down redwood?

I've been imagining things all night, she thought. First Mason with his head like it was on a turntable. Then those little balls of shadow.

She took a step toward it; and there was renewed rustling; a glint of metal. An angry trilling.

She stepped back, and the motion stopped; it fell silent. She stepped toward it once more, tentatively—and again the angry bristling, the sense of an unseen hornet's nest, about to swarm at her.

She drew back again. *It's like it's guarding some border,* Adair thought. *It's warning me to stay on the other side.*

Or maybe to stay inside.

She tried calling Waylon again, shouting this time. "Waylon!"

"Yeah! Adair!"

She heard him coming noisily through the underbrush.

"Where'd the hell you go!" she shouted.

"Where were *you?* I went to look see if there was any surveillance stuff up there."

He was still a few yards away.

She said, "Did you feel like . . . something doesn't want us to—" Then she broke off, staring.

Light swung in dual beams across the trees, strobing through their trunks, passing on. Headlights. Someone was driving into the gravel lot.

It was a black SUV. It pulled up on a sloped area, stopped at right angles to the van, almost nose to nose. Adair heard the *crick-crick* sound of an emergency brake, and then someone got out, leaving the headlights on. In the beams, stretching across the open ground, Adair saw the little dark shapes that had been moving toward her.

One was a ball of fur with little steel claws. Another wasn't a ball at all; it was living line: a snake. But it wasn't weaving curvily the way snakes usually do. It was moving like a centipede in a straight line. Straight as an arrow. Moving yard after yard with no rippling movement at all. Like it was dead and being pulled on a string.

"Do you see that shit?" Waylon asked, half stumbling up to her, looking where she was looking. He saw it, too.

Then the figure beside the SUV—seemed as if he'd been talking to Mason—got back in the driver's seat, drove the SUV slowly across the rough ground, swaying and bouncing a little as it came, right toward them.

And as the vehicle approached, the little things that had also been coming toward them darted off into the woods, as if spooked.

The SUV pulled up. Waylon and Adair walked out into its head-lights, shading their eyes.

Major Stanner got out and walked toward them. Mason moved slowly up behind the major.

"Are you kids all right?" Stanner asked. He stepped into the headlights so they could see him more clearly.

Mason was still coming up behind Stanner. It seemed to Adair as if he was moving stealthily. And she thought she saw something shiny in his hands.

Well, so what? Why did it bother her? It wasn't like he was the type to get violent. He probably had a cell phone or something.

Stanner was saying, "Listen, I have to tell you, the satellite—I guess you know about that—it might've leaked some fuel. The fumes could make you sick. You could hallucinate, and—you just definitely don't want to get exposed to this stuff."

Waylon just stared at him.

But Adair was relieved. At least this was something like an explanation. "Jesus," she said. Was that what it had been? "Actually I *was* sort of seeing some stuff."

Mason was raising a hand behind Stanner. Adair thought about warning him. But it couldn't be what it looked like.

Stanner was asking, "But you don't feel—nauseated or anything?"

"No," Adair said.

"Then it's not serious. You'll be all right."

Waylon seemed to break out of his reverie then. "So that's the latest bullshit cover story? What, a fucking gas leak?"

Unruffled, Stanner looked at Waylon. "That's it. That's the 'latest bullshit cover story.'" A kind of steeliness rang in his voice, then. "Take it or leave it."

Waylon hesitated, sensing the warning.

Mason seemed to twitch behind Stanner.

Adair stared. "Um, listen."

Then Mason stepped up beside Stanner. There was nothing in his hand—though she could've sworn there had been.

Must've been the fuel stuff, affecting her mind, she decided.

Mason grinned at them. "Yo, you dudes! I try talking to you and you're all scamperin' into the bushes like little humpity-bumpity rabbits and shit."

Waylon only glanced at him. Then he spoke pointedly to Stanner. "Last time I was up here, I saw some weird shit in those hills."

Stanner nodded. "Like what?"

Waylon opened his mouth to tell him, then just shook his head. "You already know."

"Not necessarily, Waylon. Tell me."

"People who weren't acting entirely like people, man."

Stanner nodded, slowly. "That's kind of vague, kid. You have some kind of proof?"

"You don't need proof, dude. You already fucking know."

Adair glanced at Waylon, impressed by the bluff he was playing out.

Stanner looked at Waylon for a long moment. He didn't deny anything. He looked like he wanted to tell them something. But then his mouth pursed. He shrugged, and turned to Adair and Mason. "Anyway, it's just not smart to stay out here any longer. Another one of those fume clouds catches you—"

Waylon snorted. "Fume clouds. What bullshit. The only fume clouds up here are the ones Mason generates, man."

"Dudes, can we go home?" Mason said. "I'm burger starved. I am, like, burger bereft. I am experiencing a serious burger deficiency."

Waylon took a step toward Stanner. Adair could see he had made up his mind to confront the government guy. But Stanner turned on his heel, walked briskly to the SUV, and got in.

"Wait, tell me one thing," Waylon began.

But Stanner just waved and backed up, drove his SUV up to the road. He stopped there and waited, engine running, his brake lights burning—to make sure they left.

Adair managed not to run to the van. The others came along behind. She started to get in, then decided to look through the van first.

She bent over and looked under the dash, behind seats.

There weren't any weird little ball things in it. Maybe it had been fumes.

Mason drove them home. And he seemed just like Mason. Mostly.

11

Vinnie was out of pickles, but he'd brought along the little pickle jar because it had vinegar juice in it. Watching the bank, he drank vinegar juice and nodded to himself sagely.

He said aloud but discreetly, "Yes. Yes, it does appear to be the case. Reality is what is the case."

After all, what else was there to be said? They *were*, yes, weren't they? Certainly they were.

He was standing just under the small porch roof that sheltered the front entrance to the Presbyterian church, behind the bank in Old Town Quiebra, at about one in the morning. He hadn't been able to sleep, and he often went for walks at night when he was restless. He had come the long way, down the road, around a corner, down another road, around another corner—all in order to avoid the woods. He didn't wish to take part in the woods; he had seen the wrongness of the squirrel and the wrongness of the blue jay, and he sometimes heard them muttering and conspiring outside his bedroom window. He had once seen, at the edge of town, the crawling man who hadn't quite grown into himself right—judging from what some of the animals were saying—and he didn't want to take part in that, either.

And as he wrote in his backwards journal, he did not wish it to take part in him.

He thought about that, as he watched a team of casual, unhurried people empty out the bank. "The world always seems to find another way to be intrusive."

There they were, emptying the bank, taking all the money from it at one in the morning. There was the nice lady who worked at the front desk of the police department, and there was Mrs. Bindsheim from the Cruller, and there was that old hippie garbage-head Sport, and there was Mr. Andersen the insurance agent, and there was Mr. Andersen's ten-year-old daughter, and there was a child of about five, a Hispanic child he didn't know, and there were Mr. and Mrs. Swinchow, and there was that red-haired Malley girl, and there was Mr. Funston, and there was that fat lady who sang so loudly in the Catholic choir you could hear her on the street when they had those special masses, and there was Reverend Grindy, and there was Mrs. Chang, and there was that man from the Sikh temple with the turban who owned the liquor store, Mr. Roi. There was Bubbles Gurston, and there they all were, emptying all the money out of the Bank of Quiebra. They were bringing out money and—he could glimpse this through an open door—they were rifling safe-deposit boxes.

The thing was, Mr. Funston and Mrs. Chang both worked at the bank. So they were in on it. And Mr. Andersen, as Vinnie well knew, hadn't spoken to Mr. Funston for ten years, but here Mr. Anderson was, cheerfully handing Mr. Funston a bag. Now a policeman came out of the bank, handing a big bag of money to that small child, who didn't act like any child at all as he took the bag of money and carried it up a ramp to tuck it neatly in the back of the big U-Haul truck along with the other bags and boxes. No one spoke as they went about this work. They seemed friendly and efficient—they even smiled, some of them—but no one spoke.

In eleven minutes and twelve seconds, by Vinnie's watch, they were quite finished, and they closed the bank—which Mrs. Chang locked back up with her key—and they all got in the back of the U-Haul with the money, except for Mr. Funston who was driving the truck.

Even the kids and the policeman, whose name Vinnie didn't know, got in the back of the truck.

Then Mr. Funston drove the truck away. All without saying a word.

Eleven hours and twenty-two minutes later, Vinnie heard people on the street talking to a *Contra Costa Times* reporter about how the bank had been looted in the night by unknown persons.

Vinnie told people all about it, of course, saying right out loud, "I saw the whole procession like a pageant with everybody marching together, the people who work at the bank and the cops is what stole it, the red hand was helping, too, but I saw it happen not on TV but in a parade, someone could ask me who did it."

But they just made those snorting sounds and turned away, or else plain ignored him, like he was babbling. He didn't get worked up about them ignoring him. He was used to it: people around here made a point of not listening to him, though he was nearly always right.

December 5, late afternoon

Having labored through a thicket of willful student disinterest in his morning class at Diablo, Bert was driving his repaired Tercel through Quiebra's suburban streets under a diffused-blue sky, the clouds charcoal smudges. Slowing for speed bumps gave him time to examine the reason for the speed bumps: local kids. Baggy-clothed junior-high-schoolers on the sidewalk practicing skateboard jumps, "ollies, grinding"—terms he knew from working at the high schools. He passed them and found himself peering into open garages.

It seemed to Bert that the occasional open garages displayed cross sections of personalities: this garage immaculately ordered; that one ordered but they never throw anything away; here was one more like his own, a repository for whatever he didn't want in the house, disarrayed.

He passed the high school, kids with backpacks, others peeling their cars out of the driveway, crossing the street to cadge cigarettes.

Mixed couples, but rarely black and white in friendly groups; Hispanics in both groups; Asians mixed, probably only if they had good English. All the kids trying out their posturing, or boldly darting across the street in traffic.

That squat Hispanic kid with the shaved head and the droopy pants—Bert remembered seeing him and his friend there in a "sideshow" he'd stumbled on, when he'd worked late in the Diablo library. The sideshow had taken over a corner of the stadium parking lot, car stereos providing a hip-hop soundtrack for the drunken, laughing crowd.

They were watching six or seven cars spinning donuts, the cars taking turns—sometimes two at once—squealing in tight circles, roaring in and out at one another. Some of the kids darting into the path of the cars like toreadors with bulls and jumping out of the way just in time, laughing, bottles in their hands, all in a cloud of blue smoke from exhaust and burnt rubber.

Bert worried about these kids. He wondered if the ones he was going to meet, Lacey's niece and nephew, went to sideshows.

He veered with his usual sloppy turn onto the freeway, into the stream of hurtling dusty metal; he went two exits up the freeway, left the freeway for Pinecrest, followed it around past the dark, thicketed ravine the kids called Rattlesnake Canyon.

Two blocks more and Lacey and the kids were there, waiting outside a sun-faded ranch-style house more or less like the others except it was the only one on the block that'd let its grass grow wild and weedy. Lacey and a teenage girl and a boy who looked like he was just about college age. The boy wore a black hooded sweatshirt and multipocketed black pants; the girl wore a jeans jacket, an untucked white blouse, white jeans that had been elaborately drawn on with a blue ballpoint.

Lacey wore a navy-blue sweater-jacket that zipped up, jeans just tight enough to show some curves.

They crowded into the little car, Lacey introducing Adair and Cal. "You got your car fixed. Was it serious?"

"Serious, no. Embarrassing, yes. I'm still mortified."

"I had a good time. Eerie but good. Hey, I read the Thoreau biography."

Lacey and Bert talked about the Thoreau biography he'd loaned her. She had brought it along, to his astonishment. In the back, the kids maintained their distinct silences, Adair tensely listening to the adults; Cal sullen, making it obvious that he'd been dragged along.

They ate at one of those places that decorated with weathered junk nailed to the walls, sleds and baseball bats and antique toys and outdated signs, in an attempt to fabricate a carefree atmosphere. The waitress recited her canned greetings, then the specials—"like a hostage with a gun to her head, reading the kidnappers' demands," Lacey said—and that made the kids grin and loosen up a bit. The food seemed to have been prepared, frozen, and then microwaved. But the kids seemed to enjoy their Thai chicken quesadillas—a "contradiction in cuisine," said Bert—and Lacey seemed amused by the argument two drunken balding men were having at the restaurant bar over the Oakland Raiders versus the 49ers.

"Niners are saggin' with Rice gone," Cal said solemnly.

"I wish I knew more about sports," Bert said, a bit apologetically. "Maybe we could go to a game. You guys could give me a lesson."

"The Niners' starting quarterback and the backup quarterback are both learning fast," Lacey said, and went on exchanging arcane football wisdom with Cal for twenty minutes.

Cal talked about how he was getting back into playing guitar—Lacey had prompted that, showing him some chords she knew—but when Bert asked them about their dad's diving business, both kids got quiet and glum, and he sensed he'd made some kind of faux pas.

"So how's school?" Bert asked, somewhat desperately. "Is there a class in school you don't hate? I mean, I shouldn't assume you hate school."

"You can assume that," Cal said, sticking a finger in the dregs of his virgin strawberry margarita, sucking the syrup off.

"I've finally got a computer science teacher who knows more than I do," Adair said. "For years, every time any of us took one of those classes we always knew more than the teachers, and they made us do stupid stuff we'd already done when we were, like, babies."

"I use a computer for work, and when I try my hand at a little academic criticism," Bert said, "but I understand them about as well as a cargo cultist understands an airplane." The kids looked at him blankly; he decided not to explain what cargo cultists were. "What is it you like about the class?"

"Computer science?" Adair smiled, staring off to the side at a fakily rustic NO SWIMMIN' AT THIS HERE SWIMMIN' HOLE sign, hung cockeyed on the wall above her. "I like how you can write code, and it's all, logical, or it's like communicating with something. I don't know, it's like we have this artificial-life program where you make these fractal patterns react with each other in certain ways, and you set up actions and reactions and it just gets a life of its own and it comes from math, from numbers—from just the way things *are.*"

Cal grimaced at Adair; Bert and Lacey smiled at each other. "That's a great way to think of it. Computer science giving life to math—or finding the life in math."

Adair shrugged and Cal snorted, as if to say, *The adults are patting us on the head, oh, how nice.* But Bert could tell Adair was pleased, and even Cal seemed surprised by what went on in his sister's head.

Bert thought, *They're so caught up in technology. Computers, MP3s, CD burners, downloading whole movies, laptops, augmenting their own videogame platforms with chips ordered on-line, doing most of their homework research on-line, spending hours in chat rooms and instant-messaging—* he'd heard kids talk about all that and more. Not to mention television, cars, portable CD players.

He wanted to quote Thoreau. *We are conscious of an animal in us, which awakens in proportion as our higher nature slumbers. It is reptile and sensual, and perhaps cannot be wholly expelled.* He wanted to talk about the idea of a higher nature and a lower nature. He wanted to ask them when they'd last looked beyond the digital landscape; when they'd really opened up to the sky and the sea and the forests, and to one another—and ask if it were possible that their obsession with the technology of distraction was deafening them to the message of God's creation.

But Bert kept quiet. He kept his mouth shut because he knew he'd just come off pompous, and because teenagers justly despised self-righteous lecturers. Too, teenagers knew that if they were addicted to all these things, it was because they'd been conditioned to them by adults who were just as bad, or worse; who reduced them to a consumer demographic.

So Bert just smiled and nodded and said they did well to hone their skills.

After dinner, it was just getting dark when they drove to the Quiebra waterfront park for a view of the predicted meteor showers. As the sun moved toward the ocean, they walked along the sandy path between clumps of muck-reeds and stiff spare beach grass, watching for the legendary green flash in the otherwise neon-tangerine sunset.

When the teens had walked on ahead a little ways, Lacey asked, "Bert, you know that metallic stuff we saw the other night, that seemed . . . like it was moving by itself?"

"Well, yeah. I remember. It did sort of seem—I'm not sure."

"Have you seen any more of it? Or anything else strange?"

"Lots of strange things. Well, that night when my car died on us, there were some things. I thought we were being followed a couple of times. Just a feeling of being watched. But my imagination was working overtime out there."

She chuckled. Then she became thoughtful, her voice hushed as she went on. "You know, the Bank of Quiebra was looted. I heard a weird story about it. Something someone saw out their window. And Adair . . ."

She told him about Adair coming to her with stories of her parents' strange behavior. Mom's behavior in the garage. *Reinstall? Reinstall.*

"I told her that it was probably something perfectly normal going on—and she was just, you know, misinterpreting. That she should talk to her parents about it. She said she was . . . scared to. Not uncomfortable talking to them—*scared.*"

"Scared to talk to them? Why?"

"She said it was hard to explain. She seemed so sincere. And it's not like I didn't notice a lot of strange things lately about Suzanna and Nick myself. I did. I feel like I let Adair down. Like I turned my back on her when she needed me, Bert, by not taking it seriously enough. Now I wonder if it could be to do with all this other stuff."

"All what other stuff, exactly? What do you think it is?" Privately wondering if the other shoe was dropping here—if he was finding out Lacey was actually a bit crazy. That would be his luck with women, all right.

"What is it? I don't know. There's so much secretiveness around here. I don't think it was like that last time I was here. And weird things stolen all over town, and a woman at the café this morning said that someone was torturing animals around here. I asked her what made her think so, and she said she saw a bird with machine parts in it, like someone had shoved these things into its body and let it go."

"Jesus! What a grotesque—" He broke off, thinking. "Unless, maybe it was some kind of tracking device. Zoologists use them."

"The way she described it, I don't think so. I guess I just think . . . there's a story in this town. There's something going on. I keep getting the feeling that people are *hiding* something. I'm going to look into it. Either it's my journalist's intuition, or I need to see a doctor."

Bert considered. "I *have* felt as if some people seem—weirdly distant. Like they're doing something together, and they're not including me—and I'm glad to be out of it. I mean, beyond my usual alienation. But . . ." He shrugged. "It's just a feeling. Nothing, really."

"Maybe it's more than nothing. But if you see anything—"

Cal dropped back to them. "Hey, I saw that green flash thing! That flash that's in the sunset sometimes."

He pointed and they peered at the setting sun, but the flash had passed; no one else saw it. They watched the seabirds, small black coots bobbing on the water; the coots were contrasted by elegant white seabirds vanishing into the surf, to come up half a minute later with small crabs in their beaks. The ever-present gulls rose and dipped.

When the sky darkened enough so they could see the evanescent blue-white streaks of the meteor shower, Bert found himself reciting, " 'Who falls for love of God shall rise a star.' "

Cal looked around. "Yeah, it's all pretty and stuff." Deliberately teenagering it up. "It's sav CGI." He grinned at his sister. "It's *good graphics.*"

Bert thought, *The kid knows how a guy like me thinks even when I don't say it out loud. It's a mistake to underestimate these kids.*

Still, tell them the story. "When I lived back east," Bert said, "I went to an art museum in Concord where they had a touring exhibition of the greatest impressionists. Some people came down to see it and they videotaped it. And they looked at the van Gogh through the camera lens—never once looked at it with their naked eye. Though they were there in the room with the original."

Lacey laughed and shook her head. "Yeah. I hear you."

Cal shrugged and looked annoyed. Sensing he was being lumped in with those clueless tourists.

They walked on, and suddenly Lacey said, "Ben Jonson?"

"What?" Bert said. "Oh, that line I quoted. Yes. *You* get a gold star," and he patted her head.

"Ha, ha, a gold star," Cal muttered. "Fonn-ee."

Lacey took Bert's arm, then, and for a while, after that, he felt that all was right with the world. So what if she might be a little crazy.

She watched the falling stars. "They say meteors brought life to the earth—amino acids, proteins, or something that life is built up from probably came from some other world, and dropped into the ocean." She looked out at the sea. "But was it by accident or design?"

"I've always wondered. Maybe when you look close enough there's no difference. There's that whole 'intelligent design' controversy. But who knows."

Bert watched another blue-white scratch appear on what seemed the dark surface of the sky, another meteor. It seemed to him, for a moment, that the heavens were dramatizing the oneness of things, the above taking part in the below, the sky unifying with the earth. Below among the wet rocks a gull tugged at the decaying remains of a small manta ray, death cycling back into life again; the usual duality, separation of the individual from the whole, seemed removed for a moment.

Was Lacey his last chance, and would she treat him, finally, as Juanita had done? Was he stuck, mired in his work? Had he made one too many fatal missteps in his life?

Those doubts were always with him and had become part of him. Yet for a moment, feeling connected to some immeasurable wholeness glimpsed in the sky and horizon, stars and stone, he was set free.

Lacey looked at him, as if sensing it. Her eyes were shadowed, but he could *feel* her regard.

Then Adair broke the spell. So quietly Bert could barely make it out, she said, "Falling stars can be something else, too. Planes crashing or—satellites."

"There's a great mystery about a fallen satellite," Lacey explained, seeing Bert's puzzled look.

"Oh?"

"They're not supposed to talk about it. Something to do with their dad's salvage work."

"Everything's been fucked up since then," Cal said suddenly, stopping to stare angrily up at the knitting clouds.

Lacey looked at him but said nothing, and after a long, pensive moment they walked back to the car. Bert wondered what wasn't being talked about; what hung in the air like a meteorite, refusing to fall where it should.

They drove back to the Pinecrest area without talking much, slowing now and then to look at the Christmas lights shining in strings of blinking charismatic colors against the houses. Car culture was big in Quiebra, and at one house a classic 1940s Plymouth was outlined in Christmas lights; just the car, not the house. And here was the O'Haras' house, Adair said. It was like a starburst of lights—and as they stared, Bert realized it wasn't just overdone, it was *strangely* done. The Christmas lights seemed randomly strung, or like the scruffy webs of black widows, lacking beautiful spiral symmetry but with their own arcane design. And the same strings of lights looped from the O'Haras' to the house next door, which was completely dark, the blinking light-chains crisscrossing like scribbles. Yet almost in a recognizable pattern, a cryptic message of some kind, like the mutterings of a lunatic.

Bert felt increasingly uneasy, looking at the patterns in the strings of lights. It was just as if a message was written there, in some language he couldn't quite read.

"Better get you kids home," Bert said.

He drove them right there, without any more delays.

December 6

Half an hour after school, Waylon found Mr. Morgenthal at his workbench in the electronics shop tinkering with some kind of radio receiver, it looked like.

Waylon stepped in close to look at what Mr. Morgenthal was working on—curious about what he'd managed to salvage after the vandalism and theft. And then stepped back again. It was the smell. Mr. Morgenthal had a harsh smell about him, which wasn't usual. It was like he hadn't bathed. There was also a burning smell, like a toy train transformer that'd been left on too long. But maybe that was from the project—looked like he'd done some soldering.

Waylon realized that Mr. Morgenthal was staring at him. But smiling. What was that look, like, all ironic? Had he forgotten some assignment?

"So," Waylon began, "you got a new project going after all, there?"

"After all? It's a satellite dish. It's modified."

Waylon saw that it was one of the smaller satellite dishes that people put up, but Mr. Morgenthal had changed it, had soldered a lot of little parts to it in a mesh of wires. *Hella sketchy*, he thought.

Mr. Morgenthal went on. "Modifying a satellite dish for greater power. There was a diagram in *Popular Science.*"

He said it with that smile and that stare, as if testing to see what Waylon would think of the explanation.

Waylon just nodded.

"Was there something you needed, Waylon?"

It really was like the guy was mad at him or something but had made up his mind not to say so. "No, I didn't need anything special. Um, I guess you got some of your stuff back?"

"My stuff?"

"That was stolen?"

"Stolen?"

"Uh, yeah? You know, the vandals and the stuff that was stolen?"

"Nothing was stolen." Mr. Morgenthal turned back to his tools. "That was just . . . a misunderstanding. I had given permission for the materials to be used and forgot about it. I have everything I need. However, class is going to be suspended for a while."

"Suspended? This one? Where do I go when I used to go to shop?"

"Wherever you like."

"Yeah, well—" Waylon laughed. "—the principal might have some different ideas."

"Oh, you'll find that Mr. Hernandez is completely in agreement. Now if you will excuse me."

"Sure."

No one would care where he went? That was cool. But then again, it sucked.

Every kid he knew had picked up some sense of what you needed, to grow up healthy. How could you not get that, when they talked about it all the time in sitcoms and shows like *Boston Public* and TV movies and HBO specials and all that shit? *"Yo, man, I got no role models, my uncle is all I got and he's always fucking up and at home we're all stayin up till three in the morning and shit, knamean? What? I'm sorry, I mean he's always screwing up."*

But, whatever. No electronics class, that was one more hour a day he could use for his investigation. Maybe it was all, destiny and shit.

But still, it was fucked up.

Waylon turned and walked slowly to the door of the classroom. Looking around as he went. Almost nothing was left in the room except the workbenches. All the students' tools were gone along with the electronics.

He looked at Mr. Morgenthal—and he got a feeling. Just a sad feeling.

He went into the hall. Yes, definitely feeling sad and not knowing why. Like somebody had died but he didn't know who.

But then again, he did know: Mr. Morgenthal had died.

12

Adair was almost home from school on that same clammy, overcast afternoon, with the sun seeming crabby and ungenerous behind chimney smoke and mist, when she saw old Mr. Garraty pull himself up onto the roof of his house.

She stopped and stared, watching him dangle from the metal gutter along the edge of the roof, and thought his ladder must've fallen, somewhere, though she couldn't see one. A cat poised on the roof, a tabby cat, as startled as Adair was. Maybe he was trying to get to the cat, and then the ladder went down.

But there was no ladder.

And the old man was doing a brisk pull-up, grabbing the corner of an eave to draw himself up onto the roof in a second, as easily as a cartoon superhero.

"Mr. Garraty?" she blurted.

He stood up and turned to look at her, his head turning remarkably far around on his shoulders. "Adair, isn't it?" His body turned toward her, to match his head—or that's how it seemed to her. It reminded her of Mason—that same illusion. His tool belt clacked as he turned, screwdrivers bumping into wrenches.

He seemed to be leaning toward the ground a bit and should have pitched headlong to the grass, but he didn't. He just stood there a little crookedly, smiling at her. A peculiar look in his eyes— though there wasn't anything definitely wrong with that look.

She cleared her throat. "You okay, Mr. Garraty?" She was dimly aware that there wasn't much sense in asking if he was okay. In fact, he seemed unusually okay. He had just done something more suited for an Olympic gymnast than an old pensioner in Quiebra. "I mean, is your cat okay? Are you up there after your cat? Do you need . . . a ladder? Or anything?"

He turned to look at the cat, and the instant he looked at it, the cat backed away hissing and vanished over the crown of the roof.

"No, that particular parasite—that cat—is not my property. That's a stray or a neighbor's cat who's been acting like he owns my roof. No. Not my cat. No." He turned to look at her, and his expression was exactly the same as it had been. The same smile. The same appraising eyes that seemed to be weighing her up. "You've grown," he said. "In the last few weeks."

She blinked. "I have?"

"Yes. About an eighth inch." Then he turned to look at his wife, Mrs. Garraty, who was clambering up the roof from the back of the house, something in her hand. She came to stand with the confidence of a circus performer on the peak of the roof. Just stood there, with a sort of satellite dish thing in her hands, a contrivance about the size of a garbage can lid. The comparison to a lid seemed natural because it looked to Adair like it *had* maybe been made partly from a metal garbage can lid, but with a lot of wires spread over its surface, radiating from the center.

Then it registered: Mrs. Garraty hadn't been out of her wheelchair for a couple of years at least. And now she was standing up on the roof of a house.

Mrs. Garraty looked at Adair balefully, and then it was as if she remembered to smile, but the look stayed in her eyes.

What a look it was—she had to be forty or so feet away and way above her on the roof, Adair decided, yet somehow that look came down at Adair like someone throwing a lawn dart at her head. Adair felt like sidestepping.

"We're putting up a satellite dish," Mrs. Garraty said. "My husband found it in *Popular Mechanics*. Do-it-yourself. Homemade. They're quite popular. You'll be seeing quite a few of these. Save a lot of money. Free satellite TV, young lady. And you can't beat free, can you?"

The whole conversation was taking place between the people on the roof and Adair on the ground, and Adair was getting a crick in her neck, but she couldn't turn away, couldn't help staring up at them. She felt someone else nearby, and turned to see Mr. Than, that nice old Vietnamese guy who lived next to the Garratys, standing in his yard with his rake in his hand, staring up at Mrs. Garraty, too. His mouth was open. He was as surprised as Adair.

Mr. Than and Adair exchanged a look of mutual confusion: neither understood it, but neither one felt quite right about asking.

"Chinese medicine," Mr. Garraty said. "You should appreciate that, Than. We went to a Chinese doctor. He's given us a marvelous . . ."

He looked at his wife. She stared back at him.

Then he nodded and turned back to Mr. Than.

". . . *ginseng*," Mr. Garraty said. "He gave us a marvelous ginseng."

"Oh!" Mr. Than said. "This ginseng I must try! I take some, too, but nothing that—my goodness, do you think she is safe up there?"

"Oh, I'm fine, Mr. Than." Mrs. Garraty laughed. "As you can see, I'm more than fine. Glad to be out of that chair. Feeling much better now. Ever so much better. Here you go, dear."

She handed her husband the homemade satellite dish, as if she were handing him a box of tissue.

Then she turned and walked confidently down the far side of the roof. She was out of Adair's line of sight.

And Adair heard a thump. It sounded exactly like Mrs. Garraty had fallen! "Oh, Mr. Garraty, was that—"

Mr. Than had heard it, too. "Your wife—she is all right? I hear maybe something fall? Hey, Garraty, she okay?"

Garraty was ignoring Mr. Than. He was stationing the satellite dish on the peak of the roof, turning it just exactly so. It didn't point at the sky, but across the rooftops.

Then Mrs. Garraty, safely down on the ground, stepped around the side of the house into the front yard and looked first at Adair and then at Mr. Than. "Why, I'm just fine, thank you."

Adair looked at Mrs. Garraty's feet. Grass was stuck to the tops of her little white tennis shoes. Adair had the irrational suspicion that Mrs. Garraty had jumped down from the roof and landed on her feet in the backyard, sinking in the dirt to the tops of her shoes. That wasn't possible, of course.

Mr. Garraty was focused on screwing the plate at the base of the support for the homemade satellite dish onto the rooftop with vigorous motions of his wrist.

"Now, if you'll excuse us," Mrs. Garraty said, "I don't want my husband distracted up there. He might—"

"—might fall," her husband said at the same time she did. Exactly the same time.

As he spoke, barely audible, he was looking at the screws he was turning to fasten the satellite plate into the roof.

"My goodness, awfully heck of good ginseng," Mr. Than said, shaking his head in admiration as he went into his garage.

Adair nodded and said, " 'Kay, you guys have fun. Bye," and turned away, began walking home. Walking quickly.

She glanced back to see Mr. Garraty—having finished screwing the plate down in a remarkably short time—taking the wire from the homemade satellite dish in his hand and directing it through his fingers along the down-sloping rear side of the roof as he walked out of sight toward the backyard. Then there was another *thump* sound. A few moments later, the yowl of a cat. A furious yowl.

Adair stared at the Garratys' house for a long moment. But in her mind's eye she was seeing her mom and her dad. There was some kind of continuity between her parents and the Garratys, as if an icy stream had overflowed first through her own house and then through theirs. There was a wrongness, badly disguised but not something she could challenge without seeming like she was all bipolar or something.

Mom and Dad. The Garratys.

Adair turned shivering away from the Garratys' house and went home as quick as she could.

But getting there, seeing her mom go into the garage—and lock the garage door from the inside . . .

She didn't feel much better at home. She turned up the heat. It just seemed so cold all of a sudden.

December 6, night

Henri Stanner felt a strange kind of relief, being here, away from Quiebra, and a strange kind of vulnerability, too. He always felt watched, anytime he came to the Biointerface division. Even after they'd run his cornea print and let him in. He wasn't sure they watched everyone, or not closely. But he was sure they watched *him*. Because of his ties to the Facility. A camera partway down the corridor tracked him whirringly as he strode by.

This wing of the Stanford Research Institute's B.I. division was quite ordinary looking. An ordinary institutional corridor—white walls, strips of white lights, locked white-painted metal doors that masked startling experimentation. The click of his heels echoed as he reached the intersection of two corridors. Here were more cameras. He paused to watch as a young, pale, narrow-shouldered technician in a white coat walked by, muttering to himself, glancing at an electronic clipboard, looking up ahead, back at the clipboard, muttering some more. The technician walked by the camera; it didn't turn to follow him.

Stanner waited a few moments, then walked by the camera.

It swiveled to keep him in view.

He nodded to himself, and just kept going till he found room 2323. He pressed the button in the intercom fixture, spoke his name. The door buzzed.

Inside was a plain blond-wood desk, behind which stood a

pearly-white metal column about six feet high and two in diameter. Its camera lens swiveled and took him in.

"State your name again, please," the computer-generated voice said from the column.

"Major Henri Stanner."

"That name checks with appointments and voice-print records."

Interesting that I never gave a voice print knowingly, Stanner thought. *But it seems one was taken anyway.*

The door to one side of the desk clicked and swung inward, and Stanner walked through to find Bentwaters and Jim Gaitland sitting at a conference table.

Captain Gaitland was a stocky man with an easy, sleepy-eyed look to his face, ears that stuck out like a cartoon making fun of listening too hard; he wore his Marine Corps uniform.

"Look there, Gaitland's in uniform," Stanner said. "Is that supposed to be a message? Add some kind of official glamor to this meeting? I've seen you in uniform maybe one other time in fifteen years."

"No reason to go undercover today, Major," Gaitland said, with his easy Tennessee drawl. "Have a seat." He tapped a digital tape recorder built into the tabletop. "You want to give a report, I'll have it transcribed later."

"I don't know as I should give a report to a guy I outrank," Stanner said, sitting. "What, no refreshments?"

Bentwaters, wearing lab white, nodded abstractedly. "We'll have three coffees with cream and sugar on the side," he said—to the air, which meant someone or something was listening from outside the room.

"Rank isn't really of the essence here, it's more about seniority," Gaitland said, adding, "Sir."

Bentwaters looked at Stanner speculatively. "I do sense some hostility here, Stanner."

A young black woman came in carrying a tray; she wore a tight green dress, nothing lablike about it. As she bent over to put the tray of coffee mugs, creamer, and sugar on the table, Stanner couldn't help admiring the taut expression of her figure through the fabric.

I've been way too long without getting laid, he thought. She smiled at him and left without a word.

He took a deep breath, took a cup of coffee, and turned to Gaitland. "I'll tell you what, Captain. I keep getting this funny feeling in Quiebra—that probably the Facility knows as well as I do how far it's gone. And it bothers me. That town should be subjected to a quarantine, to evacuation pending individual evaluation of each person there. I don't care what cover story the Pentagon uses. Hell, any number of terrorist scenarios will do. But—" He took a sip of the coffee, which tasted burnt, and put the cup down. "—but don't wait. Tell them to do it now. *Now*."

Bentwaters hunched back in his chair and then looked fixedly into his coffee; he wasn't as good as Gaitland in hiding his feelings. And clearly Bentwaters was scared.

Gaitland's body language was the opposite of Bentwaters's. He leaned back, as if relaxing on his porch, and his eyes went hooded. "Well," he said musingly, "I don't think they're going to go for that without some kind of physical evidence of real contamination. Serious contamination."

Stanner stared at him. "You weren't there at Lab 23, Gaitland. But you had to see the videotape before we burned the place out. Any contamination that leads to *that*—"

Gaitland used a pen from his inside coat pocket to stir sugar into his coffee. "You don't know there's any contamination, not for sure."

"I saw breakouts on a fucking grotesque level of biointerface, there in the woods around that town."

"Where's your proof? Where are your samples?"

"I'm not going near them without some sort of contamination-proofing. But I know what I saw, Gaitland."

"In broad daylight?"

"It was at night. And there are two missing marines out there. What the hell you think happened to those boys, Gaitland?"

"I heard something about that. When a couple of enlisted men don't show up for roll call, it's something called AWOL."

Stanner grunted. "Both of them? From that site? Then there's equipment stolen all over town. Some of it I don't know what they'd use it for. But some of the parts are perfect for biointerface backup. Micromodify the silicon and—"

"Now hold on there, Major," Bentwaters said, "you're jumping the gun. We don't know they can modify components to that extent."

"Their whole imperative is to experiment and find new ways to proliferate," Stanner replied sharply, struggling to keep his temper. "You got any sources tell you about a bank robbery?"

Bentwaters seemed shaken at that. "Bank robbery?"

"The Bank of Quiebra was looted top to bottom and there's been no FBI in there. Which says to me that someone stopped them from investigating. I mean, a robbery that big and it's only local cops? So I figure that the Facility has a handle on this thing already."

"You're presuming a hell of a lot, there, Major," Gaitland said coolly.

Stanner pushed on relentlessly. "I heard a story that a whole crew of *local people* were involved in the robbery."

"They're capable of Internet savvy," Bentwaters said, "so why wouldn't they steal funds that way, if they could? Electronically, digital robbery."

"Because there are firewalls, and that might get five or six other agencies involved, if they're detected. It could bring the whole damn country down on them. They must know the Feds are holding off on them—a little matter of bureaucratic paralysis." He looked at Gaitland when he said that. "They're playing their cards close to their vest. If they show up stealing money in the system, digitally, they force our hand. And we'd be watching for it, too. Instead, they steal actual, physical cash, and use it to buy the equipment they need. And that's *high camouflage*—exactly how they're supposed to be."

"You're hypothesizing," Gaitland said. "Guessing. You don't know. It could be just an ordinary gang of thieves stole that money."

"All the parts you'd expect they'd want have been bought up for twenty miles around Quiebra," Stanner said. "I spent most of the day yesterday checking."

"Oh, Jesus," Bentwaters muttered.

Gaitland shot him a look of warning. To Stanner he said, "And you think they're using this stuff for proliferation? They can't have everything they need to accomplish that."

"You know damn well they can manufacture whatever else they need themselves," Stanner retorted, leaning forward. "What they're buying is transmission equipment, communication infrastructure, prosthetics, and components for 'the cradle,' the makings of imprints for further proliferation—for one thing, all the etching chemicals—"

"Etching chemicals," Bentwaters muttered. "Doesn't sound good, Gaitland."

Stanner sat back and took a pull at his coffee. "Not quite as bad as Quiebra PD coffee but almost."

"I wasn't aware that you spoke to Quiebra PD," Gaitland said, watching him.

"I asked them questions. I stuck to a moderately believable cover story. They gave me some leads. Now, look, the breakouts can't convert just anyone, anytime. They haven't adapted the conversion principles yet for everyone. They're doing it selectively, at first, I figure. So it's not completely out of hand. Not yet. But they're going to get faster and better at it—and soon. We've got to act, Gaitland, right now."

"Come on," Bentwaters said, frowning, "conversion has to take a while in itself even when they've got what they need."

Stanner shook his head. "They were getting better and better at it, even before Lab 23. They're doing it a molecule at a time—but that can be faster, rather than slower. I believe it can be done in maybe a minute, in some cases."

Gaitland leaned back, looked at the ceiling, and spun his chair slightly. He made an *uh-hmmm* sound deep in his chest, just loud enough to be heard. At last he said, "I'll make that recommendation. But they may want to send in their own teams for confirmation."

Stanner had been in intelligence a long time. Gaitland was a fair-to-middling liar. Not bad, really. But just another liar and Stanner knew, by now, when someone was improvising to keep him on a string.

"Gaitland, you guys are watching this already. There are people who want to learn just how fast it'll spread."

Bentwaters squirmed in his seat. "You're saying we're using the people in this town as lab rats? That's pretty insulting." He cast a doubtful glance at Gaitland.

"I doubt it was the original intent," Stanner amended. "But maybe they figure since it's gone this far, it's too late—and they'll just see how far it'll go. Maybe they've decided that the town is fucked either way, so they might as well gather some useful data."

Gaitland's eyes flicked at him and away—making Stanner think he'd guessed rightly. He went on, "But people go in and out of that town. And so do *they*, Gaitland."

"Actually," Gaitland said, "I don't think they go very far—if they're there at all, I mean. They have to protect their cluster. They still have a main organizing cluster, wherever they are. The brain. Have you found it?"

"You dropping *your* cover story, Gaitland?"

"I'm not confirming anything. This is all hypothetical. Have you found a central organizing cluster?"

"You mean—" Stanner allowed himself a thin smile. "—the 'hypothetical' cluster?"

"That's what I mean. Yes."

Stanner shrugged. "No. I'm not so sure there is one. They might've innovated beyond that. They're constantly experimenting. The animal-redesign models I've seen in the woods around there prove that. They're trying out new modes all the time."

Bentwaters frowned. "Gaitland's right—if there's a cluster, and there probably is, they won't go far from it, at least not till they've established other clusters elsewhere."

Stanner felt a chill go through him then.

Other clusters elsewhere.

He stood abruptly. "I'm going to get proof that this thing is out of control, Gaitland. If that's what I have to do. But I'll tell you something—I think it was out of control days ago."

Gaitland shook his head. "I don't think you should make another move out there without orders."

"You're telling me to stand down?"

"I don't outrank you—I know that. But I am conveying an order from upstairs."

"I want it in writing."

"You'll have to wait for that."

"Then," Stanner said, "it doesn't apply. I'm going back into the field."

"I don't think the brass is going to be thrilled about loose cannons booming away in that town, Stanner," Gaitland said coldly.

"That's *Major* Stanner to you, asshole," Stanner said.

He saluted Gaitland and walked out. The cameras turned whirringly to watch him, until he left the building.

13

Adair was lying on her back in bed, limp, still, her knees drawn up; her head was tilted, so she could look at her computer. Now and then one of her knees would sway back and forth a few times, metronomically, but mostly she just lay there unmoving. Inside herself, though, she was all jumpy, kinetic.

She wanted to get out of the house. No homework—two of her teachers were out sick or something—and she didn't want to stay home tonight. She didn't have any money; Dad and Mom said there was no money for allowances, all of a sudden, and lately they wouldn't even pay Adair and Cal for extra chores. So no money, she couldn't go anywhere.

Siseela had had her computer stolen, and she was, like, the only one Adair talked to on-line lately, except for Waylon, now that Cleo was playing Princess Bitch. A lot of people had just sort of disappeared from on-line. Most of the regulars, gone. There was a school chat room, and some people would be there.

But now, after everything else, Adair was unable to get her computer to work. The monitor was just a blank blue-white glow.

At last she sat up, then got to her feet, feeling a little dizzy. She kicked through her junk to the hall and looked in the door of Cal's room. He was stuck here, too, because the car wasn't working. Someone had trashed the engine, torn all sorts of shit out of it, and Dad had taken the truck. Dad was gone a lot without explaining where, and the bus that used to come through their neighborhood had stopped running, and where would you go with no money? Mason wasn't answering his phone, either, and Cal's friends had gone off to college.

"Hey, Lump," she said, which is what she called him when he sagged in his room playing his Game Boy Advance. She looked vaguely around the small room. The rectangle of the single bed against the wall, the desk and the laptop that sat on it were the only oases of order in the layered chaos of Cal's domain. Paperback books and random diving gear and a pizza box and a couple of old McDonald's bags and some *Electronic Gaming Monthly* magazines half-torn, lying like dead birds in the mix, and peeling Tony Hawk and Limp Bizkit and Moby posters on the wall. Cal's cheap red Gibson-knockoff guitar was leaning on a boom box, and some sound equipment and clothes were spilling from the closet. Mom and Dad had made them clean up a lot more, before.

Then she thought, *Before what?*

Aloud she asked, "Can I use your computer, Lump?"

"Lumps don't have computers." He didn't look up from the game.

"My darling cool handsome smart big brother, can I use your computer, please? Or can you fix mine?"

"What's wrong with it?" Still not looking up, his thumbs clickety-clacking on the Game Boy like insect mandibles.

"It's not booting, nothing. Power's going in. It was fine yesterday. I want to go on-line."

"I don't want you to go on-line on my computer. You download hella MP3s and you leave them on instead of erasing them and you're gonna get me a virus—"

"Cal, I won't. I just want to talk to someone. I'm going crazy here."

"It's totally fucked up here. That's for fucking sure. But, no, you can't use my computer. Go away."

"You suck. Where's Dad?"

"You suck. I don't know."

"You suck. What's Mom doing?"

"You suck. She's in the garage. Again."

"You suck. We could watch a video or a DVD."

"You suck. DVD player's broken. VCR's broken, too."

"Shit." She felt so bound up, like a spring about to snap.

She thought of getting into Dad's booze again. But she remembered all that puking, after the last time, and having to pretend she'd had stomach flu. So instead she said, "At least look at my computer. I'll stand here and whine if you don't. Whine. Whine. Whine. *Whi-i-ine.*"

"Fuck!" He threw the Game Boy down so it bounced on the bed. He continued to sprawl there a moment, glaring at nothing. Then he lurched up and went growling to her room, half tripping over a bowling ball.

She followed him to her room. He kicked her backpack out of the way and went over to her IKEA desk, looked at her computer, scowled, and hit reset. It didn't.

"Huh," he said.

He leaned over the desk and looked at the back of the computer.

"Well, fuck," he said. "No wonder."

He pulled the monitor toward him and to one side, which in turn pushed the keyboard so it fell off the desk to dangle there by its cord. He turned the computer's hard drive box around.

"Watch out! You're wrecking my keyboard."

"Shut up if you want me to fix your—oh fuck, it's—well, look— did you try to install some hardware and leave it half-done or something?"

"What? No."

"Look at this."

She looked into the back of the computer. Wires were sticking out, torn ends; there was no motherboard. There was no RAM.

He snorted and shook his head. "Somebody reamed out your computer, Adair. For real."

She started to cry.

Cal nodded. He understood: Her computer was totaled.

Oh, no. *Her computer.*

When Waylon got home, his mom was asleep on the couch again. She was dressed for work, except for being shoeless.

He tossed his heavy backpack on the floor near her head, hoping the shake of it would wake her.

It did. "Hi, baby," she said, opening her eyes halfway and stretching.

She sat up and shook her long dyed platinum hair out of her eyes.

"Had trouble sleeping last night," she said. "I almost fell asleep at my desk at work this morning."

She didn't smell like liquor, and he didn't see any bottles around. She was supposed to be staying sober.

But she could have pills. She was just as likely to take those as she was to suck up the wine coolers. And the way she kept smacking her lips like her mouth was so dry, that was a pill thing.

She caught him looking at her as if he was wondering, and she frowned. She didn't like it when he acted like the parent.

Then you shouldn't make me do it, he thought.

He went into his bedroom and turned on his computer and the classified frequency scanner he'd worked up. He got that certain frequency with no problem and listened to it for a few minutes. Was it all code? Not exactly.

He switched it off.

He felt too jangled right now, with his mom being the way she was today, to really think about it. He just wanted to eat something and see Adair and maybe . . .

He went into the living room. Mom was still lying on the couch, staring moodily at the ceiling. He asked, "There anything to eat?"

"Um, not really. I'll send out for pizza, I guess. We should really conserve money though. I got laid off today."

His heart sank. It wasn't just the money worries that would come.

It was also that he knew that without a job she'd fall apart and slip into that swampy place she lived in sometimes. When she was un-employed she tended to smoke a whole lot of cigarettes and watch a lot of daytime TV, instead of looking for work. Then she'd get depressed because she didn't have any work. Which made her smoke cigarettes and watch daytime TV and then she'd start the heavy drinking again. It'd been like this before.

He thought about calling his dad. But he couldn't quite imagine doing that. What would he say? Send more money?

What am I, he thought, *a family court judge? Fuck that.*

But the idea lingered, as he went to the phone. It wasn't about money.

He knew his mom had moved out here against his dad's wishes. Dad could even do some shit in court to get them back to New York State. But he'd heard Dad tell a lawyer on the phone that he didn't want to take Mom to court because "the boy would be caught in between." Sometimes he wondered what his mom told his dad in private, and if there was a reason for his dad not being in touch.

He stood over the portable phone—transparent purple plastic—and gazed down at it. But he didn't call his dad. He hit *3* on the speed dial for a different phone number.

"Quiebra Quick Pizza," said a bored teenage voice.

"Yeah, a double cheese pizza." He gave the name and address and added, "That you, dude? It's Waylon."

"Waylon, oh, yeah, what's up, dude." It was Russell, whom Waylon had met a few days before. Introduced by Mason.

Waylon said, a little softly, "So, dude, you know about that extra spicy you mentioned? The other day?"

"Yeah."

"Some of that, too. Like, one packet."

"I gotcha."

They hung up. His mom called from the bathroom, "You ordered extra spice on it? You know I don't like spicy stuff."

"That's on the side, Mom."

Since it was some pretty strong marijuana, he thought, it should really be on the side. He had twenty bucks stashed away, he'd slip Russell for the dope along with the money his mom gave him for the pizza.

He'd been trying not to start smoking pot again. He couldn't get any homework done when he smoked, and it made him kind of paranoid. If Mason was any evidence, it made you forgetful and stuck in a rut. But on the other hand, he just felt like getting stoned.

He went to the window, looked out in the gathering darkness toward Rattlesnake Canyon. Had he been paranoid that night? He hadn't been smoking. And Adair had seen some shit, too. Worse than him. Toxic gas?

Bullshit. Major Tightass was lying about that—maybe about a lot of stuff. But who knew what exactly?

If he could find out, maybe he could get some kind of deal for an exclusive story or something with the *National Enquirer* or Fox TV. Help him and Mom get out of the hole they were going to slide into now that Mom was laid off. Maybe he'd go on-line and ask again if anybody else had seen anything weird in Quiebra.

But he didn't want to say too much to anyone, not yet. He wanted to get a line on what had happened so he could be the one who got paid for it.

He imagined himself talking gravely on television about his experiences. *I knew something was up because of the helicopters and the lack of reporters there and stuff like that. You could just feel it in the air. I knew I had to find out the truth.*

He smiled. That would be so cool, to nail those liars on national TV.

Hadn't Adair said her aunt Lacey was some kind of reporter? Maybe he could set up something through her. Some kind of deal so she didn't steal the story.

Mom was washing her face in the bathroom, putting on that moisturizer shit that women use. She was saying something about how she was so sick of being a paralegal, she was really kind of glad they'd laid her off. She wanted to do something else. She even went by the bank in Quiebra to apply there, but it had got robbed big-time and it was all confusion in there. There was some kind of internal investigation and the bank was closed till they finished the investigation into some kind of inside job thing, but then banks don't pay very well anyway.

"I'll probably end up being a paralegal again. But then again . . ."

She was just nattering on the way she did when she felt guilty about something.

Maybe she was . . . was *seeing* someone. There was the manager of the apartment building—seemed like the dude was interested in her. But it was just too gross to think of that big fat bald doofus handling his mom.

Suddenly he felt a leaden heaviness in his chest and arms. Like he wanted to just lie down on the couch and go to sleep himself.

But he wouldn't be able to sleep. So he chose his other refuge. The computer.

They'd take half an hour getting the pizza here. So he went to his room, went on-line to see who was on from his buddy list. Maybe Adair was on.

Yeah, there she was, probably instant-messaging with people from school. She shot him an IM, telling him something about her computer getting wrecked.

WAILIN2003: *Your computer? Fuck! What are you using?*

ADAIRFORCE3: *My brother's old laptop . . . it's really slow and hard to type on . . . it sux bigtime . . . not having a computer is the ass totally the ass. I have to hide this one my parents are being weird pretending they didn't wreck my other I feel like I'm going crazy without my computer I had all this art on it and I can't work on it cant even do half my homework its just the suckass shit . . .*

And then she was telling him about that old Garraty dude he'd helped with the wheelchair, climbing the roof.

> ADAIRFORCE3 : *They were all of a sudden like Chinese acrobats or something, these geezers—*

He couldn't credit that. She must be making a wack weirdass joke, he supposed, playing with his head. He typed a response.

> WAILIN2003: *Whatever, but checkitout Morgenthal says nobody broke into his shop or stole nothing now. He's all, "Stolen?, hello nothing was stolen." It was a misunderstanding and I'm all, whatever dude.*

> ADAIRFORCE3: *You didn't believe what I said about the Garratys, did you. You suck. G2G. Dinner now.*

Then she was gone.

Had he pissed her off again somehow? It seemed like he had before, too—that night they'd gone out to the crash site, too. Pissed her off, some way.

He figured he'd go see Adair after he scored. It felt good, being around her, even when she got irritable for no reason he could make out.

He wondered if Adair smoked pot. If she didn't, he wouldn't offer her any. He didn't want to get her started.

He'd been to enough AA meetings with his mother—and AA had almost as many dopeheads as alcoholics now—to feel weird about smoking dope. You couldn't feel like it was normal after you went to those meetings, even if you still felt like doing it. Even just pot. Too many people had problems with "just pot."

But sometimes you had to find a way to change how you felt.

It was dawning on him, more and more, that he felt like shit. Just like total fucking shit.

December 8, late afternoon

Bert was a little disappointed when it turned out Lacey had come over with an agenda besides seeing him.

"Come on, Bert, I want to show you something," she said, standing in his front door. "You'll have to drive."

It was a clear but mildly cold and windy day. Small clouds scudded with almost desperate haste; dead leaves spun across the windshield.

He followed her directions, drove to a street he had passed many times, off Quiebra Valley Road: 1970s tract homes overgrown with trees, altered with renovation, most with a boat on a trailer or an RV.

"There, pull up over there," Lacey said. He pulled up and she pointed. "See that? Anything strange about him?"

"It's kind of late in the day for a postman—but some routes are like that," Bert answered. "He has a beard and he's wearing shorts even though it's December—but really he's an ordinary postman, for the Bay Area. What about him?"

"He has two bags. One is his regular post office bag, and one is a canvas bag on his other shoulder. He's taking mail from one bag and something else from the other bag and putting them in the mailboxes. The something else is a four-by-seven padded brown envelope, each with a lump in it. One for each house, all the envelopes identical. There—a man is coming out, ignoring his own mail, and taking the little padded envelope."

Bert tapped his fingers on the steering wheel. "Well, so? It's some promotional thing, and he had so many to deliver he organized them into a separate bag. And people are curious about what it is, a free sample or something."

"I've seen several people ignore their mail and go for the little bag. And I waited. And they never came back out to look at the other stuff."

"Huh. All I got at my place was a circular for a pizza parlor in El Sobrante."

She watched the postman, as he went from one house to the next. "I've been driving around, checking this out for two days. It's certain neighborhoods more than others. Especially in the north end of town. But it's spreading from one neighborhood to another."

Bert felt uncomfortably warm; it was blustery outside, but the car windows were shut and the sun was low to the horizon, glaring through the windshield. He rolled a window down and said, "Now you make me want to see one of these packets."

She cleared her throat. "Well, it's funny you should say that. I stole six of them from houses where the people weren't home."

He looked at her and had to laugh. "You stole the U.S. mail? Can you say 'federal offense,' Lacey?"

She was digging in a big handbag. "Yes, well, I don't think it *is* the U.S. mail, Bert. Here."

She handed him three identical padded brown envelopes. Each envelope had a metered postmark. There was no return address, though the law required one now, and the packages were addressed to 333, 444, 555, and so on, all on Candle Street.

"There is no Candle Street," Lacey said. "I've checked. And those envelopes came from adjacent houses—and the numbers didn't match the houses. And look at the addressee names. 'Gable, Cable, Able, Sable' and so on. And those street numbers—"

"It's just . . . nonsense. Like a prop."

"Exactly. Like camouflage. And not very good camouflage. But then it didn't have to be."

He tore open one of the envelopes. Inside was a little mechanism about as big as a walnut: a computer chip affixed to a hemispherical, silver device he didn't recognize. He tore open another envelope. The same device. No note, no letter.

"And what do you think this thing is?" he asked.

"I have no damn clue, Bert. But look close at it. No manufacturer's hallmark, no numbers on it, and it looks sort of handmade, doesn't it?"

"Sort of. Jesus! You don't think it could be a small bomb?"

He was a heartbeat from throwing it out of the car window, when she said, "I took one out to the beach and tried to get it to explode. I tossed rocks on them, and I tossed a couple in a fire. Nothing."

"What? Lacey! Holy shit, you might've blown your head off!"

"Well, I was pretty sure it wasn't a bomb. And I stayed back as much as possible."

"Look, let's do the simple thing: Let's go ask the postal inspector."

She sighed. "You know, I started to do that. I went to the post office. I asked to see the postal inspector. They gave me a strange look. They sent me to the inspector's office. The inspector was a perfectly ordinary man, behaving in a perfectly ordinary way." She looked at Bert very seriously. "And looking at him, I felt a terror . . . like I've never felt before. It was like something inside me was warning me, *Don't say anything to him about this.* So, I didn't. I said I'd made a mistake and I left."

She looked at a leaf blowing across the hood. "You think I'm . . . ."

He looked at the envelope. He looked at the postman. He looked at the little mechanism in his palm. "No. I don't think you are . . . imagining things. I may ask the inspector myself, though."

"You know what," she said suddenly. "There's a whole syndrome of unusual numbers of people in this town asking for psychiatric help—thinking they're imagining things. Just over the last week or two. I met a doctor at the library. I asked him about some of the things that Adair told me she saw."

"Wait, a doctor in the library? How'd you know he was a doctor?"

She was a little embarrassed. "Well, he was sort of hitting on me, and it came out in the conversation."

"I thought so. And you had a nice long conversation with him?" He was teasing her—mostly.

She looked at him with feigned innocence. "You don't want me to have long conversations with guys who are hitting on me? Why not, Bert?"

"Oh, go on with your story."

"Okay. He said doctors all over town are hearing from people who think they're suffering from some kind of paranoia. I said I'd go to the hospital and ask—and he suggested I not do that. He wouldn't say why. He said he himself was beginning to mistrust people at the hospital. And then he got real embarrassed, and he said, 'Listen to me—I sound paranoid myself.' "

Bert watched the postman, coming up the street. Coming nearer. Another house. Then nearer yet. "I should just . . . go over and ask him. He must know. I should just . . ."

"So, why don't you?"

He looked at the envelope. "The fake addresses. Other things—tell you the truth, I . . . would rather the guy not know I'm curious."

She nodded. "I'm scared to ask him, too."

He started the car. "Come on, let's see if we can find out what these devices are. Probably some banal explanation."

"Who are you going to ask?"

He turned onto Quiebra Valley Road. "Morgenthal, over at the high school."

"Hey, there's Adair! And her friend!" She pointed and he saw they were passing her niece and a lean, stooped, spiky-haired boy he didn't recognize. Both wore oversize hooded sweatshirts and sloppy fatigue pants. "Pull over, Bert!"

He pulled over and she rolled her window down.

"Aunt Lacey!" Adair seemed genuinely glad to see Lacey.

"You guys need a ride?"

"Sure! Oh, this is Waylon. That's Bert and my aunt Lacey."

The teenagers piled into the car, Adair effervescing a bit about how she'd been wanting to talk to Lacey, Waylon making a grunting noise that might've been "Hi."

"Before we set off," Lacey said, "Waylon, Adair said you know a lot about electronics?"

"Some," he allowed grudgingly. "My dad works in it and I picked some stuff up, sort of."

Lacey handed him one of the little devices they'd found in the envelopes. "Know what that is? It's a little local mystery—to me anyway. Hundreds of them are being delivered to houses around here."

He balanced the little hemisphere in his hand, turned it over. "Weird. No . . . not exactly. I mean, this little round part here—you can see the wire going in this hole here—it looks like a transmitter.

The whole thing looks like it's supposed to be on something bigger, maybe."

"They came in these envelopes." Lacey showed him one of the envelopes. "They look sort of fake."

He looked at them and said seriously, "Could be a mind-control device."

Adair rolled her eyes. "God, Waylon, come on. Not everything is a conspiracy."

"How come they're being passed around in this bogus envelope by the hundreds, then?"

Adair took the thing in her hand, and her expression changed as she looked at it. "Acually, I've seen one of these before. I think . . . my dad had one. In the garage. He was connecting it to something else."

Lacey raised her eyebrows. "Well, then, let's just go ask him."

"*No!*"

They all jumped a little in their seats, surprised by Adair's vehemence.

She went on, looking out the window, "I can't talk to them. I'm scared to."

Lacey nodded as if she understood.

Waylon spoke up suddenly. "Something weird is getting broadcast around here. You want to hear it? My mom's not home, she's . . . out today. The house is, like, sort of fu—sort of a mess. But if you don't mind . . ."

Bert and Lacey and Adair were standing behind Waylon, in his moderately malodorous room—he'd hastily cleared a path through the dirty clothes on the floor—and looking over his shoulder as he worked what he called the classified frequencies scanner. It looked to Bert like a sort of ham radio that Waylon had wired into his computer's hard drive. Waylon tapped the computer's keyboard to search for "anomalous frequency transmissions." They passed through what was clearly some kind of jargon-heavy military band, through a lot of crackle and dimly heard nattering, and then to a bandwidth that seemed to leap out as if it came from right next door.

"This is totally not a legal band, here," Waylon said. "And this is the one I've been trying to figure out. Near as I can make out, it's from here in town."

The voices coming from the speakers overlapped in a cacophony of cryptic relayings of numbers and apparently encoded phrases. "One-oh-one-oh-one-one-oh-oh-one. Protocol 7655, an outer representative. Emergency conversion at 76 Meriwether Street. Hilltop Mall, basically ours. A new shipment prepared, seek Cluster approval, All of Us 6777777 priority . . . reset H. Robins . . ."

"What the hell," Bert breathed.

"You see?" Waylon said.

"Who do we talk to about this?" Bert said, turning to Lacey.

"It's all so . . . ambiguous," she said. "I'm going to hold off a few days and just gather information. Carefully."

Adair nodded. "I don't know how to explain how I know—but it has to be careful."

"You and Waylon, can you help me with this?"

Adair grinned. "Totally!"

Waylon scowled. "I've got my own plans to expose this stuff."

Lacey smiled at him. "Think I'm going to scoop you? Tell you what, we'll share a byline. But if there's anything going on that's as secret as this seems to be, then it means, maybe, that someone's being hurt, or endangered—otherwise why hide it? So we have a moral imperative, Waylon, if you know what I mean. Only, let's wait till we have something concrete."

Waylon turned to listen to the radio. "Listen to that shit, dude. Listen to that. And tell me I'm just paranoid."

December 8, evening

Stanner waited for his daughter on Pier 39, in San Francisco, "at the seals." Just about dinnertime. So far, it was dinnertime for the seals and not for him.

A chill wind off the bay made him zip up his windbreaker. He leaned against the rail, trying to find a spot without gull droppings. Behind him were the shops, the noise of the tourists on Fisherman's Wharf. In front of him, the hissing sea, sporting some white-caps now.

Shannon had wanted to see the seals. She was into nature. She had Sierra Club calendars at her desk at work, he'd noticed, when he'd gone to visit her there, in Chicago. Were these seals or sea lions he was looking at? He thought, looking at them squirm and bark and loll, that these were sea lions. He'd heard the animals had made these rocks home over the last few years, taking over a little corner of an inlet off San Francisco Bay, right near the pier.

The beeper on his hip vibrated, and he looked at the number. Bentwaters's SRI office. Stanner had scrupulously avoided getting back to them. But maybe he'd better talk to Bentwaters.

He looked around for Shannon, didn't see her. So he took out his cell phone and called.

"Yeah," Stanner said, when Bentwaters answered. "What's up?"

"Stanner? You haven't been returning our calls."

Stanner hesitated. Should he speak freely? It might be used against him. He decided to take the plunge. "Last message I got said I should blow off the investigation. I'm not going to do that yet— and I don't want to be in the position of having to refuse to take orders. You don't outrank me—so I can talk to you."

"If you're smart, you won't go back to that town. The Facility doesn't know what to do about it, Stanner. There's a kind of paralysis of disagreement."

"So they're convinced it's spreading?"

"Yeah. They've sent a few people through. They've found a frequency being used for a certain level of communication between the cluster and the breakouts."

"How far's it gone? I can't tell, short of holding some guy down and cutting him open."

"You were right, they can't do everyone just overnight. They have to create the microinterfaces, and that takes time. So they're doing some neighborhoods faster than others. Apparently they're experimenting with animals, and combinations, and they're using them to control the perimeter. Pretty soon they'll seal it off completely. So what can you hope to accomplish? You may as well come in from the goddamned cold."

"I'll tell you what, I think that town can be saved. Listen, you remember the blanking system we were working on?"

"That takes access to a huge in-place transmission system, or a hydrogen bomb or something, to generate a pulse big enough—"

"No, listen, dammit. There might be an infrastructure, an in-place system we can access, if you can get me a design for an EMP booster that could be hooked into a microwave transmitter. It has to be based on the design the Facility has—the one we modeled."

"I don't know."

"I could test it. We might just be able to save the rest of the town before they go to the next phase. They seem to be able to convert some people easier than others, and if they just make people disappear, it causes too much of a stir. So they're doing it bit by bit. It gives us a little time, Bentwaters."

"Why some people and not others?"

"I don't know. But I found a house where I was sure of the parents; they're building a transmitter only the All of Us would use. But I'm pretty sure the kids aren't converted yet. Parents are often converted but the kids left alone—at least at first. It depends on the kid, seems like. For one thing, young people seem to be generally resistant—maybe neurological, maybe psychological, maybe, maybe growth hormones, who knows? I mean, there are some neurological systems that don't work. We knew that about cats, for example, but we're not sure why. This resistance principle could be extended, too. We could work up some kind of injection to give people. But in the meantime we have to stop this before it gets—"

"Hi, Dad."

Stanner almost dropped the cell phone into the bay when Shannon walked up and leaned on the rail beside him. "Bentwaters, I have to go. I'll . . . think about being in touch." He hung up and turned the cell phone off.

His daughter wore a pinstriped suit dress and coat. She was petite, like her mom. Half Japanese.

"Stop what before it gets where, Dad? That sounded like one of your more sinister phone calls."

"Oh, stop what? Stop women from becoming high-ranking officers."

"Dad!"

"Kidding, I'm kidding. No, stop my having to do any more paper-work. So, hi. You know what, I think those are probably sea lions and not seals."

"Hi," she said, still looking at the sea lions. "Yeah, sea lions."

She barely looked at him as she spoke. He could tell it was going to be one of those meetings. She was brooding about her mom's sui-cide again, maybe.

"So what brought you through town?" he asked.

"What brought *you* through?" she countered. "Or are you not allowed to say, double-oh-ten-thousand?"

When she'd been a teenager, she'd found out he was Air Force intelligence. He was a spook, and she related that jokingly to James Bond, who was some kind of naval commander as well as a spy, and he'd said, "Well, I'm not double-oh-seven, I'm more like double-oh-ten-thousand, way down the pecking order and I sure don't have a license to kill. I don't think I even have a license to punch in the nose."

Of course, he'd killed quite a number of men. But he liked to pre-tend that was someone else. And it had never been like James Bond. The men who were killed in James Bond rarely begged for their lives.

He'd tried to stay away from field work, after one too many "on-site liquidations." Tried to stay in the technical side of things. But sometimes the technical side of things took a little walk out into the field and started hunting around.

"What am I doing? Oh, some orbital mapping stuff over at the NSA. Technical gobbledygook. I pretend I understand it and they let me stay on the job a few more years."

"You sound like you're already thinking of retirement." She looked at him with renewed interest, her short glossy black hair bobbing with the quick motion.

"Oh, I think about retirement every day. I'm not old enough to get full benefits though. So I keep putting it off. But it's what I'd like to do."

He gazed at her. Just taking her in. She was petite and intense like Kyoko had been. The same deep black eyes. You didn't often see truly black eyes; usually "black" eyes were really dark brown, but Kyoko's had been black and fathomless.

If I'd fathomed her, he thought, *if I'd asked more often how she was feeling, she might've finally told me the truth.*

He felt his eyes burning and looked away from Shannon. "Look at those big lugs out there," he said, nodding toward the sea lions. "People throwing them fish. Big lugs just lying back sunning and eating. Man, that's the life. Smelly but easy."

"They do smell, don't they? But I don't mind. Once when I went snorkeling in Mexico—"

"You went to Mexico? You never told me that."

"I sent you a card, Dad."

"It didn't get to me."

"Because you move around too much." She glanced at him, and there was some satisfaction in that glance. Like she'd found a way to underline the instability his rootlessness had brought to her life. Or his being rooted, anyway, in the Air Force. And how could you have roots in the air? "Anyway, the sea lions swam right to my snorkel mask, and one of them bumped on it with his nose, just to be playful."

She smiled at the memory, and Stanner smiled, too, thinking of his daughter enjoying that little encounter with a sea creature.

He nodded appreciatively. "So, how's work, Shannon?"

She shrugged. "I'm not getting a promotion. I swear they have a glass ceiling. I'm the best PR person they have."

"*Those* people have a glass ceiling? I thought their whole trip was being liberal, some kind of 'green' investment firm, right? You'd think they'd be pro-women to a fault."

Then he realized she was glaring at him. Just like Kyoko, she hated it when she wanted to bitch about something and he was "oh, such a Mr. Reasonable Male" as Kyoko had put it.

How could he explain? He couldn't tell them that he'd seen things that'd break your mind if you didn't convince yourself, at every last chance you had, that the world was a reasonable place after all. That enough of it was, anyway. That it wasn't all shadows within shadows and unquestionable directives to do the unspeakable.

He couldn't tell her about the dreams he'd been having, seeing that Burgess kid smashed into jelly, and in the dream Burgess yelling at him to push the table harder, get it over with, *for god's sake, kill me!*, and him trying to say, *no, no, it isn't me, I'm not doing it, fella, I'm not, I swear, it isn't me.*

All he could do now was get a sheepish look and add lamely, "But then I wouldn't know about glass ceilings."

"Being a white establishment middle-class male, you haven't experienced glass ceilings? Who'd of thunkit. You got that right, Dad. Come on, let's get something to eat."

At least she was calling him Dad. They walked along the pier, up to the street. "You didn't say what brought you out here, Shannon. I'd like to think it was to see your old pop."

"I'm pushing a line of cruelty-free cosmetics, perfume, that sort of thing. The company's here; the investors want me to meet them. Give 'em a boost."

Shannon picked a restaurant redolent of seafood, sharp with the smoke that rose from blackened fish. New Orleans–type cooking, Stanner supposed, which he disliked. It didn't matter. He just wanted to look at his daughter and remember when she was little, building sand castles with him in Florida, back when he'd had the NASA posting, Kyoko smiling as she watched them from her beach towel, from behind her dark glasses.

They got a table too near the jazz band. He didn't like jazz either, and they were remarkably loud for three guys with a stand-up bass, a hollow-body electric guitar, and a trap set. He ordered some bouillabaisse and she got the salmon. She seemed glad the music made it hard for them to talk much.

Afterwards, his daughter let him kiss her cheek good-bye, and was noncommittal when he invited her to spend some vacation time with him in the spring. He watched her get into a cab to go to her hotel.

Then he went to find his rented SUV, that big pain-in-the-ass glossy black thing, thinking about Kyoko and Shannon, so that he almost didn't notice the guy who was tailing him.

But over the years he'd developed a lively feel for being followed. There was no doubt about it: Someone was following him, a stocky blond guy in a cheap blue suit, no tie, walking down the street about half a block behind, acting real casual, remembering to yawn with boredom and to stare witlessly into store windows.

Had the agency stopped trusting him so much they had him followed? Could it be the other side of the tracks at the DIA? Or someone else?

Stanner ducked into a doorway and waited to take the bull by the horns. Must've waited maybe ten minutes, but the guy had realized he'd been made. He dropped back, stayed clear.

Even so, the tail probably wasn't far away. Stanner waited; waited till it got cold in the doorway, and he decided the hell with it for now.

He went to the SUV and drove back to Quiebra, thinking he'd have to change where he was staying and his car, too.

Because he realized, as he hit the Bay Bridge, that he had been picked up again. He was being followed by a whole team in three cars; one ahead, the other two strung back through the traffic. Not real good at it, but fairly professional.

He figured it was Gaitland's people. And he figured that Bentwaters had told them he was an official loose cannon now. He had crossed over.

December 9, night

It was a fog-sticky dawn in eastern Quiebra Valley, and Evan Metzger didn't want to be up and about, trudging across the overgrown old ranch from the truck to the barn, having to step around horseshit and dogshit. He was paying that fucking greaser to clean up out here, and still there was crap everywhere. Probably hadn't cleaned out the kennels while the dogs were gone like he was told, neither. Someone was going to get his ass kicked and his pay docked.

He lit a cigarette and blew a weary stream of blue smoke as he walked up to the barn. Look at that, fucking Jeff or Carlos had left the barn door open; it was supposed to be locked up. *Sheriff come through here, he could look right in there and see the dogfight setup, get the animal-control people all over our asses.*

Tired, tired as a son of a bitch. He'd been fighting his dogs against some pretty well trained bulls, fighting 'em half the night over in Alameda County, and despite winning most of the fights, one of his best dogs had died and his bait dog—a small scared-looking redbone mutt that'd refused to fight, making it good only for baiting—had been torn to pieces the first night out, which was bad luck since it was better if they lived a few fights. That way you didn't have to keep replacing bait dogs.

Then some of those nigger cocksuckers had given him a lot of shit about paying off on bets, which had meant having to wave his .45 around and shout the signal word to Donkey, who'd come in on his flank with the shotgun right on time. And what with the two guns and Metzger being a weight lifter with his head shaved and a Special Forces T-shirt—not that he was ever in the Special Forces, having been kicked out of the army for going AWOL from boot camp—the fucking jigs had backed down and paid up on their bets, but Donkey'd had to watch his back while he loaded his dogs into the truck. The whole thing, along with the bourbon and the crystal meth, had made him edgy, so when one of the dogs had been slow about getting into the truck he'd stoved in its ribs with a kick—one of his best pit bulls—and he'd end up selling it to a nigger for twenty bucks so it could be used as a bait dog before it died—if it lived that long.

Metzger was bone tired and he could smell his own stink. He was glad that grinning bastard Donkey'd gone home. He just wanted to take a bath and swallow a handful of Valium and hit the sack. But best make sure the barn was wired like it was supposed to be for his first big home dogfight, tonight.

Distantly aware of the dogs barking in the back of the truck. Maybe he'd just leave 'em in their cages for the day, that'd make 'em nice and mean an' lean for the fight. Treat 'em hard puts an edge on 'em, his old man had always said. The last letter from prison had been a lot of babble about being born again, but he knew his dogs all right.

His half brother Jeff had supposedly spent all day wiring the barn with the miniature stadium lights, but Jeff was pretty spun on the crystal and he'd forget what he was doing and end up carving his name in a post five hundred times or something.

Metzger went into the barn and thought it looked okay. The barn's stalls had been pulled out—he'd done that himself—and the homemade bleachers were set up around the fighting pit. Looked like Jeff had the lights up all right. Metzger found the switch and threw it just to make sure the spots were properly setup.

Two things at once, then:

The dogs setting up a big barking, yelping at the truck—

And the spots shining on Jeff's bloody, naked, gutted body in the center of the dogfighting pit.

It was like the dogs were reacting for him; he couldn't believe it enough to react himself. Jeff was cut open from sternum to groin, an empty shell. His organs were there, on a tarp to one side, stacked like a produce pyramid with someone else's—because there were at least three human hearts, there, lots of other body parts.

"Oh, fuck . . . oh, *mother*fuck . . . Ohhhh, fuck fuck *fuck!*" was all that came out of Metzger.

He backed away from the body, fumbling for his .45, then realizing he'd left it in his jacket, in the truck. He turned and bolted through the door—and stopped, seeing Carlos, the skinny, big-nosed greaser who worked for him, standing there in his boxer shorts and guinea-T, crying like a baby. Just standing there crying with the morning mist swirling around him over the dirty ground between the barn and the truck, and those little hopping things around his legs.

Carlos babbled something in Spanish and pointed at the hopping things.

They were made of feathers and fur and pieces of metal all tricked together and spastic with activity. That one was about as big as a small cat, and its twitchy head was a rooster's, its quivering legs metal jointed pins; its shivering body was like the middle part of a rattlesnake; at its butt end was another head—a drooling skunk's head, looked like. Both heads snapped at Carlos, beak and snout snipping, drawing blood as the thing jumped in.

But *that* one, now, was more like a ball, rolling along, its head that of a rat tucked up between its stunted legs, its body sort of rolled up, all kinds of little living wires extending from it all spiny, as it rolled up to connect, in some way that was hard to see, with that other thing that had a blue jay's head, a squirrel's tail, its middle parts all sort of wired together with lengths of exposed muscle tissue and pumping organs under plastic coatings, and wires that seemed to twist within themselves like they were made up of thousands of tiny restless little things. It seemed to connect with a round critter that was all feathers and beaks and nothing else, and with another thing that seemed made of fishhooks and eyes and fur.

They all mingled one with the next, the way the wall shifted when you were stoned, creatures amalgamated of things that should never be connected at all. They danced together to make a sort of sketchy man-shape in the air that was circling around Carlos, not letting him go more than a step before it flowed to block his escape, wherever he tried to run. The things chattered to themselves in voices that were almost animal and almost human and almost like talking heard from a distant radio station lost in static, as they darted in and out to rip small pieces from Carlos, cutting him up little by little in an even way, strips and ribbons torn away from him all the way around, flaying him in snip-snaps at the same neatly calculated levels, spiraling ruinously and bloodily up him as he spun around flailing. Blood spotted the dirt more and more thickly.

There was a man, too, or something close to a man, at the back of the truck—opening the cages of the pit bulls.

Metzger automatically shouted at the raggedy figure—

"Oh, fuck, don't open those cages!"

—and in reaction the guy's head revolved on his shoulders, swiveling like a periscope to look backwards. He had only one remaining eye. In place of the other eye was just a red hole in his head, and his clothes were the tatters of a uniform. Maybe a marine uniform. Then the tattered marine seemed to speak to the dogs as he climbed up on the truck—crawled up the side of it, really, almost defying gravity by gripping the side of the truck with stretched-out arms and legs—as all six pit-fighting dogs came stalking out of the back of the truck toward Metzger.

"It seems a waste," the man clinging to the truck said to Metzger. "Your Mexican friend will be used, some for fuel and some for parts. But you—I just want to see them eat you. I used to like dogs, and maybe there's some of that left in me. But the All of Us is also modeling justice scenarios. They figure there'll be some resistance to complete absorption, and they may need social controls. So we get to punish people for being assholes now and then. It's all an experiment. The All of Us loves experiments—maybe because it was one."

While Carlos fell wailing under the hopping shapes, the things of fur and feathers and hooks that carved him apart worked with surprising efficiency from the outside to the inside.

Metzger saw the dogs' intention in their eyes, in the rigidness of their bounding bodies.

He turned to run into the barn, but never got through the door. The dogs leapt as one and knocked him down and then there was a tearing agony at one with their growls and delighted yips as they wrenched him this way and that and tore him to pieces and ate him. They were eating him alive.

The last things he saw in life were their foaming jaws and the man above who crawled up the side of the barn, pausing to look down at him with his one eye. And then a sheet of blood drew itself over all the world.

14

Joe Sindesky had given up trying to get comfortable. He had a comfortable bed, he had taken all his pills, and it was even warm enough in here since his grandson had brought him that space heater. He didn't have to yell at the cheap bastards who ran this retirement home to turn up the heat. His arthritis was bothering him only like a house on fire, not like a forest fire, and he sure as double hell was tired enough to sleep.

He was hoping to die in his sleep, the way Margie had. And he hoped it was going to be soon.

But lately he'd been tormented by the old memories. He might have to start taking that Zoloft stuff again. He was remembering Anzio, and Omaha Beach. Especially the beach, how he'd had to abandon his own cousin, Little Benjy, just leave him to die—Benjy who he'd pledged to his aunt to look after, and he'd even pulled strings to get him put in his outfit. Joe'd had to leave Benjy writhing on the sand bleeding to death from a 9mm round in the breadbasket, because Joe was a sergeant and he was expected to move the platoon up onto the beach. They had to protect those engineers who were going to bust open the bunker, and he'd had "the mission first, the mission no matter what" drilled into his head over and over, and it was ten times as strong because this was fucking D day for god's sake, but Little Benjy, all of eighteen, was screaming, *Please, don't leave me, Joey.*

"Shut the fuck up, Benjy," Joey muttered, "it's sixty goddamn years later and I'm tired of hearing it."

But I bled to death all alone. You weren't even there to hold my hand. Maybe you could've carried me on your back.

They'd have nailed me, I moved that slow, carrying somebody.

You see? It was your own ass you were worried about, not the mission, Joey.

"Shut the fuck up," Joe said again, getting carefully out of bed and crossing the little studio room to the closet. He moved slowly because it hurt to move fast, but mostly because if he tripped in the semidarkness, with only the nightlight on so he could go to the head if he needed to, why, he'd have cracked a hip, at least, and be stuck in bed, in misery, till he died. A man just didn't heal good at his age.

As he pulled the photo album down, he wondered yet again why God kept them alive so long past their use—yet let so many nice kids die young. He felt despair tighten over him, familiar as an old, ill-fitting coat.

He had lived with despair a good long while now. It was like the way they lived with humidity in New York, like the way people lived with the dryness in Arizona. Despair was part of the atmosphere of his life, something he accepted. Only, tonight, maybe it was just too much to accept. Maybe the time had come.

He'd have done himself a while back—he had enough nerve for that anyway—except Father Enzena said it was a mortal sin. Or was it a venal sin? He couldn't remember. Maybe he hadn't heard clearly. It was hard to tell what that goddamn Filipino priest was saying in his mushy Tagalog accent.

Oh, you got used to the Flips, they were okay; he just wished they'd speak clearly, because you felt like a fool, fiddling with your hearing aid all the time.

He could go over to Berkeley; they had an Irish priest over

there, but they were all liberal sons of bitches, giving their blessings to gay marriages. Always in hot water with the diocese. How could you trust a priest like that?

He hobbled over to the chair beside his bed with the photo album and opened it toward the back where there were more pictures of him and Margaret together.

There was Margie in her elegant sun hat. She loved those fancy sun hats.

He suddenly felt himself weeping: it just came over him all of a sudden. He missed her, had missed her for thirteen years, though she was crazy senile at the end—but it was more than that. It was feeling that he had no purpose without her, and without work. That was what made him want to cry.

He couldn't manage a garage anymore; the figures confused him; he got the billing mixed up. He had done some volunteer work, but it was so hard to get around now. And a lot of people just treated him like he was a grumpy old busybody.

So what did that leave you? You were in a waiting room, is all it was, and what was in the next room? Death. You were waiting to be erased from the world. Until then, all you had was playing cards with Mrs. Buttner and that old bald-headed yahoo with the big age spots on his head, could never remember the guy's name. That was about it. What the hell kind of life was that? And TV nowadays embarrassed him. My god, those Victoria's Secret commercials made you ashamed to watch TV with your grandchildren. You could tell the kids and grandkids were all just putting in time, when they came to visit.

Oh, shit, he was crying again.

Well. Fuck that Filipino priest. The real reason he'd held off was because he had been afraid the saints wouldn't let him see Margaret in the next world. But he had to admit it—

Had to admit he'd stopped believing in a next world. What did priests know? Literally dozens of them arrested on child molestation out in Boston. Even more in Ireland. If they hadn't been molesting, they'd been tolerating it. How could you trust a bastard like that? Child-molesting priests, homosexual priests, they had to be liars, and that would include about heaven.

He'd been raised Catholic, but being a practical man, a nuts-and-bolts man, he'd really never been able to believe in anything he couldn't see.

Sure. It was all a scam. He'd always suspected that. Not that he'd want his grandkids to stop going to church. But then again, if you couldn't trust the fucking priests to keep their hands to themselves . . . Oh, the hell with the whole fucking thing.

He had the .32 in his drawer, under some papers. They didn't know about it, of course. Residents weren't supposed to have firearms. People got crazy senile and paranoid in their old age, and they really shouldn't have firearms, no. So he'd had to smuggle it in.

Feeling a real sense of purpose now, and silently laughing at the irony of it, Joe got up with a grunt and hobbled over to the little rolltop desk. Dumped out the pencil box, found the little key he'd hidden at the bottom, and fumbled at unlocking the drawer. The lock took a minute, what with the shaking of his crooked fingers, but finally he got it unlocked and got the pistol out.

He held the gun in his hand and admired it. He'd had it for fifty years. He'd kept it in good repair. He made sure the safety was off. He cocked it and raised it to his mouth.

"Hello, Joe, whatya know?" said a voice from the doorway. "Is this good timing or what?"

Joe was so startled he almost pulled the trigger. But he managed to ease off. He didn't want anyone to have to *see* him blow his brains out.

He lowered the gun and squinted at the dark figure in the doorway. He hadn't heard the door open, but then that figured, with his ears being as bad as they were.

"Who's there?"

The figure reached to turn on the lamp atop the dresser. Joe recognized him. It was Garraty.

"Why, Garraty." Joe glanced at the clock. It was one in the morning. "How'd the hell you get in? They don't allow no visitors at this hour. Place is all locked up. Security guard and the whole business."

"Well, I'll tell you."

"Speak up, dammit."

Garraty spoke a little louder, closing the door behind him. "I was just saying, Joe, I did in fact have to kill that security guard. Ran into him when I jimmied the back door. He was a foul-mouthed little punk anyway. I can't imagine you feel sorry about him."

Joe blinked. "You say you killed him? Oh!" He chuckled because it was expected when someone was pulling your leg. But he didn't feel like laughing. "Damn, you had me there. I don't remember that kind of sense of humor from you, Garraty. Well, hell, I'd make small talk and ask how your missus is but—"

"She's better than she's been for twenty years."

"—but I figure you must've noticed this gun."

"I did," Garraty said. "Seems I got here at the perfect time. Just a moment later and *boom!*—a terrible waste."

Joe felt a warm pulse of hope. Maybe there was another way. Maybe somebody gave a damn. Maybe . . .

"Now, look," Garraty went on, "we go way back. Elks together for twenty-five years at least since I moved out here. I know what time of day it is, Joe. I understand how you feel. I'm here to tell you I've got something better than putting a bullet in your head."

Joe groaned in disappointment. "Oh, no. You're born again, ain't you. Is that all it is? I hate that stuff. Goddamn it there, Garraty, I'm Catholic. I was just now thinking it's probably a lot of bullshit, but it's *my* family's bullshit, and what do I want *your* bullshit for?"

"I'm not born again—not the way you mean. I'm not a Christian, Joe. It's not religion I'm talking about. Nope. It's better than that. It's real, you see. Let me show you something."

Then he did a handstand, right there in the middle of the room. Without any visible effort, no tremble in his arms. Joe just stared.

"I'm dreaming, is what it is," Joe muttered.

"No, you're not," Garraty said, flipping down to his feet again.

"I'm young again inside, Joe. Eventually, if I cared to, I could make the outside look young, too. So I'm told. I could do it, anyway, if it helps the All of Us. But I don't think whether I look old or young is important anymore. I don't care about that. I don't need sex, and if you don't need sex, why do you need to look good? Vanity? I've got something better than vanity. I've got life and power. You can have 'em, too."

Joe looked at Garraty and considered. Finally said, "You were in bad shape, last I knew. Something happened to you, sure. But why'd you come to me?"

"I've been assigned to you, Joe. We're recruiting the older folks first. They're much easier than the younger ones. We still have to attune for the brain chemistry of the younger ones, and we haven't got the thinking power to work that out yet. That's a big thinking. We tried a couple of the young ones, and they sort of worked and sort of didn't. One of them was in hand, for a while, but he got troublesome, and the other one is just wandering around in the woods, converting animals and keeping an eye on things in his own half-assed way. We're working on a test to sort out which kid's susceptible."

He paused. Smiled oddly. "Then, too, Joe, there's a temporary shortage of the communion wafer."

"The *what*?"

"That's what I call it, anyway. It's the special material that integrates the All of Us through the nervous system of the people we convert. It has to be manufactured. We still haven't got enough, and we had to build the mechanism to manufacture it. So we can't convert everyone, all at once. But pretty soon we'll have a new system. The stuff will be able to make *itself* more easily. After the launch, Joe, very soon. And then everything will speed up.

"So what you want to do, Joe, is get in on the ground floor here."

"Sounds like this new world of yours has got a lotta bugs in it," Joe said, stalling. "You can't do everyone, you got problems with the kids."

"Sure, but we're getting the bugs worked out. Then we'll start again on the younger ones, don't you know. Hell, even some of the middle-aged ones, they can resist a bit—and there are complications. They have to be reset."

"What's that, 'reset'?"

"Why, sometimes it means they've got to be killed, Joe." Garraty's smile never faltered. "The rest of the time we just need to restore them to status—if the person was already with us."

"Killed! You really did kill that security guard!" Joe felt a long slow chill slither through him.

"Certainly. He just wasn't suitable for conversion, for various reasons. Some people are like cats; we have trouble with cats, too. Cats—we don't care for 'em. Wrong brain chemistry. Hard for us to utilize, and the little buggers seem to sense us. Anyhow, when it comes to people, we prefer voluntary recruitment because the process is quicker, more foolproof. Of all the various systems modeled, voluntary recruitment is the most cost efficient.

"We've had to do a lot of experimenting, Joe. Some of the early formats were . . . a mess. But as you see, we've almost got it down to an art form now. The changeover can happen in a minute or two now."

Joe was trying not to look at the door. "And you're saying I don't have to take that last trip to the cemetery?"

"Funny you should say that. You have to go there in one sense. But not to die. We're using the cemetery, see. Central's there. It turns out to be the place where there's the best insulation against electromagnetic fields from the outside. We have a risk problem with—" He broke off, seemed to be listening. "No need to go into that with you. Well, you ready to be rejuvenated, Joe? What do you say?"

Joe shook his head. "Garraty—or whatever you are—you can kiss my ass. I figured what you are, more or less. And I'll tell you something. I ain't much—but I ain't ever going to be *that*."

"Joe, what else have you got? A choice between the misery of old age, isolation, endless loneliness—and oblivion? Old age is a bitch,

Joe. I remember when I realized I was getting old. I was in my early fifties. It's like being told you have a terminal disease, and seeing the first symptoms of that disease come on you. That's how it felt. But not now, not the way I am now. This way, Joe, you live pretty much forever."

Joe swallowed. His mouth was suddenly so dry, it was hard to do. "Forever?"

"Well, there's a little something called entropy that will eventually take its toll—in maybe ten thousand years."

"Ten thousand!" It made him tired just to think of it. "Ten thousand years? You've gotta be kidding."

"Maybe longer. If you join us, all pain ends for you, Joe. All sickness. All weariness. All sadness. All uncertainty, gone. It's all over with. You get to be part of something beautiful, growing like the patterns in a snowflake. You'd be useful again! If only you could see it the way I do, you'd say yes in a hot second."

"But, I wouldn't be me anymore."

"That's only partly true. They leave you a vestige. It's enough. How much were you ever really yourself anyway? People kid themselves about that, Joe. Why, one moment they're in a good mood, then they're angry and hurt. People are as changeable as fog in a wind, Joe. Wisping this way and that. That ain't real anyhow."

"Speak for yourself. Tell me something. You folks are from, what—outer space?"

Garraty shook his head, smiling. "Not at all. Right here on earth. We're not alien creatures, not at all. What we are—all you need to know is, we're part of something grand now. My missus and I are happy as hell in it. Lots of your friends, too, Joe. Why Harry Delveccio just joined us, and he's going great guns."

"Harry! He's one of you?"

"He is. Happy as a goddamned clam. Was him who suggested you."

"Whatever he is now suggested me. Harry would never do that. So you, whatever you are, you're all one thing, really, eh?"

"Yes and no—but more yes than no."

"It's like—" Joe felt his heart squeeze in his chest. "It's like something's eating the town. One person at a time."

"We don't literally eat human flesh—though we would if we ran out of other fuels—oh, I see. A figure of speech. Yes, people are . . . consumed into the overall organism, digested, in a way, made part of the All of Us. But it's not as if they're eaten."

"Bullshit. You've been eaten. You're eating my town."

"Call it what you like. After you, I'm going to be going from room to room here, converting. We need the framework, dontcha know. So what do you say, Joe? The easy way? The way that wastes the least energy, works fastest? All you have to do is open your mouth and close your eyes and blank your mind and—think *yes*."

Joe snorted and shook his head. He leaned a little forward as he said it. "No."

"You mean that? The other way is slower and it starts with a reset. Hurts like hell, and it's so inconvenient to the All of Us."

"Inconvenient to the All of Us." Joe was pointing the gun at Garraty now. "Fuck the All of Us. I don't think you're going to be recruiting anywhere here tonight, goddamn you, you misbegotten coldhearted son of a bitch."

Garraty smiled—and then he had Joe's gun in his hand.

Joe felt the gun go. It was a bullwhip crack, the way Garraty's hand moved. Joe's hand still stung from it.

"This can't be, this ain't what I—" Joe began.

It was almost inexpressible. He had allowed himself to visualize a bunch of ways it would end for him, but this sure as hell wasn't one of them.

Then again, maybe it wasn't so strange. Really, it was just another way for the world to go on rolling right over him.

But there was no reason for him to take it sitting down. He'd taken it sitting down all his life, watching television, dying a little more each night in prime time. The hell with that.

Garraty smiled blandly. And Joe knew Garraty was about to kill him.

Joe stood up and lurched at him, hands balled into fists—and Garraty stopped him dead, grabbing him by the throat. Joe felt like a small boy in a big man's hand.

Garraty put the gun aside, on the bureau, then he brought his free hand over to Joe's head.

Joe got off a yell or two, but that was something the night nurses had learned to ignore; old folks yelled in the night all the time, what with one thing and another. And of course the security guard wasn't around to hear it.

December 10, morning

Helen Faraday prided herself on not suffering fools. She'd been serving the Lord as a lay minister at the Quiebra Church of Jesus the Annointed for eighteen years, devoting all her spare time to it. It was she who'd seen to it that the previous minister, Reverend Dalbreth, was hounded out after he was found sleeping with a married lady, and it was she who told Mrs. Lambert that her son Eli had been feeling up that Pakistani girl in the baptismal room after hours—leading to a confrontation, which led to Eli running away to become a heroin addict in the city now, which just showed that character will out. Certainly she wasn't going to accept Reverend Nyeth's young wife building some kind of sick Internet-porn device in the church basement. She'd heard Mary Nyeth making a sexy joke to another of the church's ladies, and she'd seen her holding those little Bible-study boys a bit too close if you know what I mean, and it was very likely she was some kind of child-porn person. Of course, Helen couldn't come out and say that without proof. But she would get her proof today.

So here she was early in the morning, before anyone else, going down the stairs into the old Witnessing Room. They didn't use it anymore, since that incident a couple of years ago where that confused widow Mrs. Runciter had become convinced the Angelic Tongues were telling her the church was overrun by demons, and she tried to attack the minister and had to go to the hospital, and the laying on of hands had put her in that screaming fit that never did end.

Remembering the incident made Helen a bit nervous about descending the rickety stairway, flashlight in hand, into the dark church basement, where the skinny hysterical Judy Runciter had writhed and made blood foam from her mouth as she pointed at each of the church leaders in turn and screamed "Satan sucks through you, Satan sucks through you! Aghibia-habya-meleth-takorda-sha-bababba!" over and over again.

Mrs. Runciter had smashed the lightbulb and begun clawing at them in the dark, and no one had ever replaced the light down here, after they'd all run screaming upstairs. The Baptists coming out of the church next door that Sunday had thought it all quite smirkily funny as the Church of Jesus the Annointed members milled frantically in the parking lot.

Helen paused, hearing the stairs creak under her. She was a trifle overweight, enough that she was a tad worried about these stairs collapsing, and she could hear herself breathing, so strangely loud, through her mouth. The air seemed musty and cold and heavy.

She swung the flashlight beam around as she reached the bottom stair, and there was the old braided rug, and the upright piano, both of them coated in dust, and a trail of footprints leading through that dust. The footprints went from the stairs to the low stage at her left, where a cobwebby purple curtain stood, slightly parted. Beyond it was the machine that mumbled to itself, said things that were like what she supposed the Internet had to be. Babbling that made no sense. And she'd seen Mrs. Nyeth down here, standing over the machine.

She crossed to the low stage and stepped up on it, pushing through the curtains. There was the workbench set up against the wall behind the curtains, the plastered wall painted with a cartoonish mural of Jesus leading two smiling children into a rainbow-arched heaven.

Her flashlight found an entirely different sort of contraption on the workbench now, something like a satellite dish but not exactly. It didn't give out a sound like the other machine had, as she played the flashlight over its parts. The only sound was the creaking . . .

. . . of the basement stairs.

She turned and saw both the Nyeths coming down here: Mrs. Nyeth, a slight red-haired figure in a brown shift and little flat shoes, leading the way; Reverend Nyeth, a man in a turtleneck sweater, with a high forehead and a perpetually purse-mouthed, skeptical look, following with his flashlight.

Helen switched off her own flashlight and retreated into the dim back corner of the stage area, near the curtain.

"Well, whatever it is you have to show me, Mary," the reverend was saying, "I don't see why it couldn't wait till I put a lightbulb in down here." He paused to look around. "It's absurd, you know, not using this space just because someone lost touch with her common sense."

"I agree, Charles," Mary Nyeth said. "I have been using it, in fact. As for a lightbulb, the new models won't need them, and you'll be one of the new models."

"I'll be what?"

"Never mind. I'll show you, right in here."

Helen held her breath and tried to make herself small as Mary Nyeth stepped through the curtain and showed the contraption on the workbench to her husband.

"What the dickens is that thing? Where did it come from?"

"It's a transmitter, Charles. It boosts a certain carrier wave. I made that transmitter myself."

"You made it? Come now."

"Lots of people have been making them. Haven't you seen them around town?"

"Now that you mention it—Mary, what's going on? Will you tell me, in heaven's name?"

"Just relax. It won't hurt, not so much, if you relax."

Then Helen watched as little Mary Nyeth took her larger, more powerful husband by the throat and bore him down backwards, the reverend struggling and calling, "Mary, what? Mary! What—*don't!*"

And she watched as Mary knelt on her husband's chest and

extruded a bristly, living metal stalk from her mouth and forced it down his throat from her own.

Helen didn't scream—she only *just managed* not to scream—but she knew Mary must have noticed her pushing through the curtain and fumbling through the darkness to the stairs, clawing her way up them on her hands, and barking her knees and shins.

She got out the side door and to the little parking lot—some corner of her mind was amazed she could move as quickly as that—and she got to the minivan she used to take the kids to Vacation Bible School and was driving away before Mary came out, staring after her.

And Helen thought, *Mrs. Runciter was right after all.*

But she daren't say that to the police. She'd have to get them to come out here with some other story.

When she got home, breathing hard, slick with sweat under her dress, she dashed right to the phone on the kitchen counter and called 911.

"Yes, hello?" Her own voice sounded shrill in her ears. "I want to report . . . an attack. A woman attacked her husband at the church. She forced some kind of metal thing down his throat."

"And your name?"

"Helen Faraday." Oh, Lordy, her mouth was dry. She felt faint, dizzy.

"Stay where you are and we'll send someone over."

"No, please, send someone to the church."

"Certainly. Just stay where you are."

The line went dead, and Helen hung up. Then it occurred to her that they hadn't asked what church or which people.

She found that she was afraid to call back, though she wasn't sure why. Well, the police would be here in a few minutes. She would tell them which church. And who.

Mrs. Nyeth killed the Reverend Nyeth, at the Church of Jesus the Annointed, she would say.

But was that woman Mary Nyeth? It was hard to think of her as Mary Nyeth now.

Helen allowed herself some of the rosé wine she kept for special occasions, and she was almost calmed down when it came to her that she had seen a lot of those transmitter things around town—things like the device this demonic woman was building in the basement.

Why should it be a surprise that the devil was using technology? Porn had exploded across the Internet, television had become hideously sexy, and people babbled on cell phones when they should be praying.

Then something more occurred to her. The transmitters were everywhere in Quiebra, so this must be some kind of citywide conspiracy. How far did it go? How could they get away with it, without the help of—

A sharp knock came on the door. A new wave of panic swept her from her stool at the counter, sending her dashing to the back door. She would go through the back gate into that little dirt alley between the houses and get away from there.

But the police were outside the back door, too, and they didn't bother with an explanation. There was a white officer named Wharton, from his name tag, and a Chinese-looking one named Chen. They just grabbed her by her forearms and dragged her screaming into the back of the police van in the alley. It was one of those big black-and-white vans, and there was a short, dark-skinned, sorrowful-eyed Hispanic man in there, cuffed to a metal post.

She struggled and yelled, *"Someone help me!"* and almost pulled loose. Then one of the officers—she wasn't sure which—hit her, once, just above the right ear, with some kind of truncheon, and she fell sick and dizzy to her knees, close by the Hispanic man. They grabbed her wrists roughly and cuffed her, then climbed out, without saying a word. She felt hot wet blood running down her ear, onto her shoulder.

They slammed the back doors of the van with a steely clang and got in the front, started the engine. And drove the van away.

"I'm sorry they've hurt you," the Hispanic man said.

She looked up at him—wincing at the pain the movement caused—and she burst into tears. He nodded sympathetically as she wept and the van drove on and on.

After a couple of minutes, she swallowed her sobs and asked, "Where are they taking us?"

"I think, to the cemetery . . . or to a building near it." He had no Latino accent. Central Californian. "From what I could find out, there's a tunnel in an old barn there that goes under the cemetery."

She saw then that he wore a police blouse, but it was torn open, buttons missing, and his T-shirt was stained with blood. "You're—you're a policeman, too?"

"They're not police—not anymore. But I'm still a police officer. Yes. That's why I said I'm sorry." He spoke softly, so she could just make him out over the rumble of the van. He seemed to speak only as a kind of afterthought. She had the feeling he'd already given himself up for dead. "It was my job to stop them," he went on. "Me and some others who found out. They haven't taken over all the department, you understand. They don't seem able to change every-one over at once. They have to make something—something they use in that changeover first, and that takes time. A few of the fel-lows at the station are left, and some of them only kind of half know. I was suspicious, called over to the Justice Department, Oakland PD. I called all over the Bay Area. I even tried to call Washington." He chuckled sadly. "I thought I *was* talking to the Justice Depart-ment and the Oakland PD. Only, I wasn't. They've taken over all the phone lines. They monitor cell phone output, too. Calls out to any kind of law enforcement office are routed back to . . . I don't know what you call it, some kind of switchboard they control. And you're not talking to who you think you're talking to. If there's any-thing in the call that's dangerous to them, they arrange for you to be picked up. If it's like a liquor store robbery, they switch it over to the real cops, I guess, and you wonder why you have to report it twice. I could have gone to Oakland in person, but they watch you too close for that." He shrugged and swallowed hard. "Lots of peo-ple have been taken, the way you and I have, when they tried—tried to call for help . . ."

His voice trailed off. The van rumbled on, and she felt close to throwing up on the floor. She made *urp*ing sounds, but she kept it down.

After a time he added, "Yeah, they—they have the town pretty well sealed off, and they watch places that could be dangerous to them, outside town." His voice broke, then. He turned his face away from her.

"What will they do to us?"

He didn't answer her for a while. Then, as the van was pulling up somewhere, he said, "If they can convert you, they will. Or they'll kill you and use you for parts."

Helen started praying, then, and went into a kind of trance, even speaking in tongues, as the back of the van opened and they came and collected her and the Hispanic cop.

She kept waiting for God to intervene, as they dragged the two of them onto the red-stained wooden floor of the old barn, but—as they methodically cut off the little dark policeman's head—she began to suspect that God wasn't going to answer, this time.

December 10, afternoon

Ms. Santavo was a petite little woman, shorter than Adair, who wore ladies' business suits that she had to have specially made for her. They didn't make them in children's sizes. She was actually half Vietnamese, half Filipino, if Adair remembered rightly, married to a Mexican guy named Santavo.

She had a psychology Ph.D., and maybe she was using it on Adair, here in her office at the high school, but it didn't feel that way. Adair'd had several meetings with Ms. Santavo, back when she thought her parents were going to get a divorce and she hadn't been able to concentrate on school stuff. Ms. Santavo had always been really nice and she'd done some kind of therapeutic talking-through that wasn't really part of her job, just to try to help. Ms. Santavo was good at making Adair feel like an adult working things out with another adult.

On her desk, Ms. Santavo had a lot of those little toys for grown-ups you got at Earth Gifts and places like that—the miniature Zen sand garden, the baseball-size version of the globe with purple lightning jumping toward your hand when you touched it, the panel with colored sand that made artful-looking shapes when you turned it upside down and shook it, the frame with tiny magnetized diamond shapes of chrome that you could rearrange into any shape you wanted. Adair was playing with that one, absently, as they spoke after school.

"I know what you mean," Ms. Santavo was saying, sipping a can of Diet 7UP. "I am not real likely to walk up to my own mother and say, 'Mom, I think you're acting very strangely'—not unless it's really necessary. If she seemed to be developing Alzheimer's, I might have to say something like that. It would be really hard."

Adair was thinking about what Ms. Santavo said, but her hands were shaping the magnetized metal pieces into an almost familiar outline. A woman with long hair, in rough silvery silhouette. "It's not just . . . being afraid of how she'll feel about it. Hurting her feelings. It's . . . hard to explain. I don't have any good reason. That's what's, like, freaking me out. Being afraid of them for no really good reason. That's why I thought, maybe I should see a doctor. Maybe, there's something wrong with my mind. Maybe. I mean, feeling like your parents aren't human anymore. Both of them, not just my mom—that's just sick, isn't it?"

"Oh, you know what, before I'd jump to the conclusion that you're sick, I'd check out the less drastic possibilities. Like that there might just be a misunderstanding about what's going on. Look, let's have your mom come in—talk to her, the two of us. What the heck, if that doesn't work, we'll see about doctors."

Adair felt pinned to a board, like a butterfly. She felt like she had to say yes. But she didn't want to. "Yeah, sure."

Ms. Santavo picked up the phone, called Adair's house. "Hello, this is Ms. Santavo, calling about Adair. No, she's fine, I just wanted to know if we could arrange a time to meet, talk over some issues that seem to be bothering her? No, it's not an emergency but I think the sooner the better.

"Well, sure, if you like. Okay. That'll be all right. See you then."

She hung up, frowning—and then remembered to smile for Adair. "So, a preliminary step—your dad wants to meet with me alone."

"But you talked to my mom."

Ms. Santavo shrugged and smiled. "Well, she seemed to have been anticipating the meeting. She said your dad planned to come, instead."

Adair nodded. She felt like warning Ms. Santavo about something. But she didn't. Because she wasn't sure what the warning should be—or even why she wanted to make it.

It was 9:53 P.M., and Vinnie had come out to listen to the noise from the bar—the way he sometimes did at night, never going in, just listening—and he was disappointed. Usually he heard laughing, arguing, people whooping, television noise from the ESPN that was always on because it was a sports bar, and music. And, of course, the sounds of glasses clinking. But it was so quiet in there now.

Vinnie screwed up his courage and looked through the window. The bartender, Ross, a stout balding guy with fading blue tattoos on his forearms, was standing behind the bar with his hands in his pockets, looking up at a football game on the TV over the rows of bottles.

Except for Ross, the bar was empty. Where was everyone? Vinnie'd always felt a sense of communication and sharing with the people in the bar, even though they usually weren't aware he was out here listening on the sidewalk.

He didn't look at his watch. He knew without looking that it was exactly 9:59.

Instead he looked up at the streetlight. Moths fluttered around it. You didn't usually see them much this time of year, but there they were. But they weren't batting at the lamp the way they usually did, leaving strobe trails of randomness behind them. Now the strobe trails were all in precise patterns, like pictures of electrons circling an atomic nucleus.

As if sensing his puzzlement, two of the dusty white fliers detached from their mothy orbit and flew down at him like dive-bombing hawks—not like fluttery moths at all. They streaked down in straight trajectories. When he stepped back from them they stopped in front of his face, one moth in front of each of Vinnie's eyes, hovering there in a way he'd never seen a moth do.

Looking into their little moth faces, he saw tiny little jointed metal sensors emerging from their eyes.

He thought he heard a voice, then. *"This one for the All of Us?"*

And another voice replying, *"No. His programming is problematically atypical. Seven Meridian green, polarized. He is suitable only for parts."*

Somehow he was aware that they weren't talking to each other. He was hearing something in his mind that the moths were hearing, too.

The moths were like remote eyes for the things that were talking.

One of the voices said, *"Who shall we send?"*

"They are busy with conversions. There is no urgency with this one. He is socially externalized."

Socially externalized?

Angrily, Vinnie clapped his two hands together in front of his face, crushing the moths.

But he knew it wouldn't help. Two more moths detached from their lamp orbit, dived impossibly hawklike down, on their altered, metal-threaded wings, and followed him home.

15

Adair and Cal were outside on the broken glider, both of them with hands in their pockets against the foggy bite of a December morning. It was a Sunday.

Adair watched ghosts of fog lift off the roof as the sun brightened. The wisps lifted up—as if trying to get to heaven, she thought—and then they vanished as if judged and found wanting.

Cal kicked at an old cat toy that had belonged to Silkie. Then looked over at the spot where Silkie was buried, under the dormant rosebush.

"Sometime I wish it would get really cold here," Cal said. "It never snows. It's all bland and shit. I wish everything would be covered under snow. Just blanketed over, like all dead white."

Adair said abstractedly, "It's like that song, 'I'm Only Happy When It Rains.' Only you want snow to be happy. So you're *never* happy because it *never* snows."

But she was thinking about Mom. Sometimes it was like Mom'd been trying to tell them something and never could say it. Impulsively, she said, "My counselor told me to look for other explanations for what seems wrong with Mom and Dad besides . . . whatever it is. Like how they were about my computer and . . . stuff. So I guess, they're acting weird because they're thinking about a divorce? I mean, like they're back to thinking about it?"

"I don't think that's it." He kicked angrily at the grass. Then he took a piece of stick gum from his pocket, started to unwrap it, but it was old and stale and the wrapping was stuck to it. "I think they're lying to us about shit. About where they go. About . . ." He shrugged.

"Well," Adair said, "come on, shit, Cal, you were acting all, 'Don't say there's anything wrong with them, they're happy now.' And now you're all, 'They're lying to us.'"

"Okay, so, maybe, I'm not so sure now." He looked at her. He looked back at his shoes. Then suddenly he stood up. "Come on," he said decisively. "I want to show you something in the attic."

"The attic? What were you doing up there?"

"Looking for some old scuba gear of mine. I was gonna go out and find a job without Dad, because he hasn't been taking me with him. If he's been going out to the boat at all. Which I don't think he has, because I rode out and looked at it and it just hadn't been moved. I mean, you can tell. So I went to the attic—oh, just fucking *come on*."

Adair growled in irritation. He was always ordering her around. But she followed him.

The entrance to the attic was a ladder built into the wall in the pantry. He climbed up, pushed open the little door near the ceiling, and climbed through to the little catwalk. She followed him only after she saw that he had switched on the naked lightbulb.

The attic ceiling was low, so they had to walk stooped over; they shuffled like a couple of knuckle-dragging apes to the center of the space, past a lot of old scuba gear and cobwebby boxes and layers of insulation.

Cal knelt by a suitcase in a corner, opened it, and pointed. In the suitcase were stacks of hundred-dollar bills, all in bill wrappers, and an empty bag that said BANK OF QUIEBRA. Some of the stacks had been torn open and reduced to smaller piles. Adair squatted down and picked up a bill. It looked real. She dropped it and rocked back on her heels.

"Oh, shit, Cal. What's it from?"

"I've been . . . scared to ask. But I'm going to fucking ask them now."

"Cal, I don't think we should. I'm scared to."

"Why?" He didn't seem to be asking as if he didn't know the answer. It was more like he wanted it to be confirmed.

But she only shook her head and swallowed. And then coughed—the dust up here always did that to her.

"Come on," he said. "This is bullshit. We have to know. I'm going to ask Mom. Sometimes she seems like . . . she wants to tell me something."

They went back to the little attic door, climbed down the ladder, and found Mom and Dad in the garage. They were side by side at Dad's workbench, tinkering together with what looked like a home-made satellite dish, a lot like the one Mr. Garraty had built.

Cal stared at it for a moment. "Whatcha building there, Dad?" he asked.

Dad was screwing a motherboard to the back of what looked like the old wok Mom had used for cooking maybe twice—the "dish" for the satellite channel pickup, Adair guessed. He'd punched holes through the wok with some tools from the boat that he usually used for repairing scuba tanks.

Without looking up, Dad answered, "I'm making a satellite-station antenna. The specs were in *Scientific American*."

"I heard it was *Popular Science*," Adair muttered.

"Yes, it was in *Popular Mechanics*, too," Dad said. He finished tightening a nut and put his hand out—and Mom handed him a sol-dering iron.

Adair looked at her mom, who began unspooling some solder. Dad used the soldering iron, so that a little curl of smoke rose. Then he put it aside with a grunt and crossed the garage to rummage through a box of loose electronic parts.

Adair prodded Cal—and he nodded. Whispered to their mom. "Mom, can I talk to you?"

She didn't respond. Cal persisted, putting his hands on his mom's shoulders, in a way he never had before.

"Mom." He looked into her eyes. He squeezed her shoulders. "Mom, I saw them bring that suitcase. That man from the bank? I saw the suitcase full of money in the attic." Cal licked his lips, and went on. "Hundred-dollar bills. And I saw the Garratys get a visit at night from those people, too—and get another suitcase. And somebody reamed out the bank. There's something going on, Mom. Some people are up to some shit, and you guys have gotten into it. I thought maybe, payoffs from the government, maybe there's a radiation leak or something from that crash, some shit like that, and, I don't know, they just took over the local bank to pay people off. Mom, come on, goddamn it."

Her lips were moving but nothing came out.

Then she froze—and turned her head fast, queasily fast, to look at Dad rushing at them.

Dad made himself look angry; that's how it seemed to Adair. He was *doing* angry. "Cal! Leave your mother alone!"

Cal took a step back from his mom, and her face cleared and she smiled sunnily and she walked out of the garage.

"We were holding some money for some people," Dad said, the anger dropping away as if it had never been there, replaced with weary reasonableness. "It's to do with a special real estate transaction. You wouldn't understand. The IRS would make it impossible if we didn't do it this way. We've turned the money over. I don't want any more whining from you kids about computers. You've both been spoiled for years. That's going to end. I promise you it's going to end, when—" He broke off. He seemed to consider, then made a dismissive gesture, with a wry expression on his face. "Look, forget it. You kids go on out and have some fun, okay?"

He went back into the garage, closing the door quietly behind him.

Cal turned to Adair, and it scared her to see tears starting in his eyes. She couldn't remember the last time she'd seen him cry. "You see?" he said, his voice breaking. "That bag . . ."

"What bag?"

"That fucking Bank of Quiebra bag shows everything he said was a lie. A fucking lie."

Then he went into the house, and after a moment she heard his bedroom door slam. Then System of a Down came blasting from his CD player. She could tell when Cal was in a good mood if he was listening to his rave-mix CDs. But he listened to bands like System of a Down and Linkin Park when he was in a bad mood. He turned it up so loud it began to distort, which was, she muttered, "Hella loud," and she waited for her mom and dad to complain.

But the door to the garage never opened. They never said a word.

December 11

"So how's your investigation going?" Bert asked, as he and Lacey got out of the car. They were in the parking lot of an apartment complex along the beach, looking to find her a place not far from his.

"Actually—" She lowered her voice. "—I'd rather not talk about it till we're somewhere more private."

Bert shivered. The sky seemed a noncolor, horizon to horizon, maybe technically gray, with a thin cloud cover. He led Lacey up the imitation-redwood steps over a rain-darkened wood-chip-and-bark-dust embankment, toward the manager's office.

He felt a small thrill, going with Lacey to help her find a place to live. It wasn't going with her to find a place for them to live together—but it wasn't all that far from it. There was something intimate in it.

A week's worth of mail was piled on the gray synthetic carpet in front of the door of the manager's office. Bert peered through the glass pane to one side; the office was empty, looked deserted. The phone on the desk looked as if it had been taken apart.

They heard a thump from the roof. "Sounds like someone's on the roof," Lacey muttered.

They moved back till they could see up over the roof's edge. The manager—a Latino guy in coveralls, with big dark eyes and gray hair and a mustache—was familiar to Bert; he had once been the handyman for Bert's own condo complex.

"Hey, Jaime!" Bert shouted, waving from the little square of grass that passed for a lawn.

Jaime looked down at him incuriously. He was setting something up on the roof, some kind of antenna. "What you want?" he asked flatly.

"Your sign says you have some rentals available. Lady here would like to see them."

"She can have one. The doors of the empty ones are . . ."

His voice was lost in a gust of wind. The murmur of the sea. "What?"

"They're unlocked. Electricity is on. She can move in anytime she want."

"What? The application? The price?"

"No application. Townhouse seven or eight. Twelve hundred a month. Leave checks in box. That's all. I cannot talk now."

Bert and Lacey looked at each other, then at Jaime on the roof. Bert shrugged. "It would seem you have a place to live, if you like the way it looks—and they're all pretty much alike."

"You must have a lot of pull with him. Not even a credit check." She shook her head in wonder.

Bert shrugged and they walked up to the building to look through the empty condos. But he thought, *I hardly knew that guy at all.*

They walked around the complex. From here you could see more of the roof—and other roofs.

"Will you look at that," Lacey muttered, pointing.

He nodded. "I'll be goddamned."

As far as they could see, weird little homemade antennas of varying size and shape and sophistication sprouted from rooftops. Some were satellite dishes—but modified, strangely wired-up satellite dishes. Others were made out of odds and ends—pots and lids and even hubcaps. Transmitters or receivers of some kind, all pointing in one direction, and none of them aimed at the sky.

One on every roof.

"You remember that little electronic transmitter, Bert?" Lacey said, after they'd stared awhile. "I think I saw one on that thing the manager was putting up on the roof back there. But it was too far away. I can't be sure."

He glanced back at the apartment building. "He's getting down now."

"He is? Good! Come on!"

"Lacey . . ."

But she'd already started trotting, half running back toward the building, well ahead of him. In a few minutes she was up the aluminum ladder, still leaning against the building.

By the time he started up the ladder after her, she was already climbing down.

"Let's get out of here," she hissed. "I need a drink."

They headed back to the car, got in, and drove back to his place. "It was there?" he asked. "The transmitter thing?"

She nodded. "It was there."

December 11, evening

Adair was going out to the sidewalk, to walk over to Siseela's, when she heard the music from the basement. It was sixties music. Like Dad and Mom had listened to, sometimes, after they'd drunk a little Chablis. Feeling a faint lift of hope, she went around the side of the house and into the backyard.

She stood just outside the squares of light from the windows, gazing down into the basement.

The basement rumpus room, as Mom called it—though no one in the house was quite sure what a rumpus was—had a much-torn leather couch; a coffee table with some framed photos of Dad and Cal posing on the deck of *Skirmisher*, both in scuba gear; and a worn Persian rug Mom's sister Lacey had given her, over which Mom and Dad were doing a stately four-step to "Time of the Season."

Adair lingered, watching her mom and dad dancing.

They would pass by below her, inside, right under the basement window. Dancing by the liquor cabinet, where that schnapps was—and then out of sight. Then after twenty seconds or so, they danced back into sight, slowly spiraling by, Mom's head on Dad's shoulder, and it looked, sometimes, like she was crying. His face was . . .

She couldn't read his face.

Then Mom raised her own face, tear-streaked and happy, to his, and he kissed her, an open-mouthed kiss.

Adair felt a mingled rush of both happiness and embarrassment, seeing her parents kissing that way, and she had to look away.

Thinking, *I was wrong, they're okay. It was me.*

She turned to go—and out of the corner of her eye caught a flurry of quick movement, down in the basement. She thought she heard a sharp *crackle* sound. She turned back in time to see Dad drawing his hand back from Mom's neck. And she was slumped in his arms. Her head tilted unnaturally to one side.

But he seemed to still be dancing, dragging Mom's limp body out of the window's line of sight. Adair's throat constricted.

"Mom?" It came out as a squeak.

Then she was running across the grass to the back door, banging through and down the steps, two at a time, opening her mouth to shout for Cal to call an ambulance.

There were Mom and Dad, embracing, kissing, both very much alive. Mom breaking the clinch to turn to her, her cheeks flushed, her eyes glassy with rapture.

"What's the matter, baby? You never saw us kiss before?"

"No, it's not—I thought—I thought—I heard someone fall or something. But, I guess not."

They were both smiling at her. Without speaking.

Mom looked like she had braces or something. Had she gotten braces? Adults did sometimes.

But, no. When Adair looked again, the flash of bright metal was gone.

They just kept beaming at her. Just to make them *say* something—and maybe going with a kind of instinct—she said, "Did they—did you find out anything more about that satellite?"

Dad waved dismissively. "Oh, just an old weather satellite. But we're not supposed to talk about it. It belonged to the military. They study the weather, too, you know. And they're embarrassed about it almost falling on San Francisco. Big secret. Kind of silly. Won't have to work much now, though. They paid me so well I could almost retire."

Adair almost said, *What, from one job? I thought you gave up smoking pot in the eighties, Dad.*

But instead she said, "Um, you kids, have a good time."

Okay, Adair thought, *I know why they're talking in this wack kind of way. They're hinting I should go. They're all . . .*

Don't even think it. It wasn't what it looked like. But it's so cool. They're together again. And I had to be weird about it.

She turned and climbed the stairs, stumbling once and painfully barking a shin in her hurry.

December 12, night

Cal stepped back from the sideshow, when the exhaust rolled toward him, making him cough.

The cars were roaring in donuts and figure eights, mad close to each other, through a thick blue cloud that rose to draw a thin film over the stars. Three cars were showing moves: a rebuilt Mustang, an older Accord, a Trans Am. Maybe eight other cars were parked around the edge of the crowd, some facing in toward the sideshow with their headlights on, so that they were lighting the impromptu event. The crowd of kids around made collective *ooh!* and *aah!* noises and scurried back, screeching when the Accord, spinning in place, nearly ran them down. Someone threw a wine bottle that smashed on the concrete between the cars.

The sideshow was in the big concrete lot where a group of warehouses had once stood. The crumbling rims of old building foundations stood around the edges of the big open concrete space. Grass poked spottily through cracks. To the north was the Sacramento River. To the south and west, a little under a quarter mile off, lay Quiebra. To the east was a woods, the long narrow strip of woods around the area where the satellite had crashed.

Cal had heard two guys earlier, at the Burger King, arguing about that.

"*No fucking way a satellite crashed.*"

"*Way, dumbass. Get a clue. I fucking watched them pull it up.*"

"*A satellite would've made a big huge crashing hole, man, like a catastrophe, and it would've been all over the fucking news.*"

"*This one slowed down in the atmosphere.*"

"*You're full of shit, dude. That's like impossible. No wonder you fucking flunked physics.*"

Cal had worked hard at not thinking about the satellite—not thinking about when his dad came up out of the water. So he'd left the Burger King and come out here, to get his mind on something else. But there was that woods.

The cars roared and spun, and the kids laughed and threw quarters and empty beer cans. He heard two boys bitching about how their computers had been jacked, and how fucked up that was, and their parents just didn't care and *fuck* them, they didn't understand.

But some people still had their gear. It was like that story in the Bible where they put ashes on some doors in Egypt, and God's plague passed those houses over. Some of the kids had CD cases and were selling pirated computer games and MP3s and video ROMs to each other; others were talking to people elsewhere on wireless handhelds.

A girl stepped up beside Cal; a pretty blond, compact little thing in white jeans and a tight off-white sweater. She had a little red plastic purse on a strap on her shoulder. Cal recognized her; she was some friend of his sister's, or had been.

"Cleo, right?" he said.

"Uh-huh," she said, opening the purse. "And you're Adair's big brother Cal."

She had pretty good tits, he decided. Nice round ass. He could get into that, though theoretically she was young for him.

It'd been a while since he'd dated. He hadn't been trying. The girls he knew lately seemed to irritate him in some way, and he just couldn't hang with them. He guessed it had something to do with the way things were with his mom and dad, but he didn't really want to think that through.

She took out a little brass-and-wood pot-pipe and a lighter. She had a small pink stationery envelope in her purse, and she pinched some pot from that onto the blackened screen. She lit it, inhaled, and passed it to him. Cal took a hit and passed it back.

The spinning, roaring cars seemed to slow down as the dope soaked through him. The cloud of exhaust seemed to turn iridescent and just slightly shimmery. He could feel the concrete vibrating under his shoes as the cars laid rubber.

"I didn't know you smoked pot," he said. He thought he saw someone moving at the edge of the woods. A ragged figure hanging back.

"Lot of shit people don't know about me," Cleo said.

Some kid in one of the cars had turned on his stereo really loud— the heavy-duty bass speakers thudded against the night—and it took Cal a moment to figure out who the band was. "That's Qurashi, that song, isn't it?"

"Either them or the Beastie Boys."

"Are the Beastie Boys still around? No, that kind of white, hard-rock hip-hop, it's definitely Qurashi." He waved the pipe away. "That's enough for me. After two or three hits the stuff makes me nervous. I'm fucking nervous enough already."

She had moved close to him, and he could feel the warmth from her hips. Some of the kids were dancing at the edges of the crowd. She glanced up at him, asking, "You wanta dance?"

"Won't, like, what's his name, Donny, get all jealous if I'm dancing with his Kool-Aid?"

"Not his Kool-Aid anymore. You know what? I think he's a fag."

Cal was genuinely surprised to hear this. She'd been devoted to Donny. "No shit?"

"I offered to give him head, and he said no."

It occurred to him to say that he wouldn't have said no, but that seemed lame.

She looked at him impishly. "So, do you want to dance or what?"

"Uhhh . . . Here?"

He was relieved when another car drove up and parked behind Cal. It was Donny. Cleo glanced at the car, but otherwise didn't react.

Donny got out and walked over to Cal. He had his digital camera in hand; now and then he got a shot with it. Cleo looked at him and walked away.

Cal realized he was relieved she was going, which didn't make sense. But it was how he felt.

The sideshow had become a small drag race around the edges of the concrete, and Donny and Cal watched it silently. Finally Cal said, "I keep expecting the five-O."

"I don't think the cops will be out here, tonight," Donny said. "They like us to keep busy with this shit. They got some other things going on."

Cal looked at him. "Like what?"

"You haven't seen anything? Noticed anything in this town? The cops are right in it, man. I'm not sure what it is, but there's going to be a meeting. I'll let you know when."

"I'm supposed to know what you're talking about?" But the cold feeling in Cal's gut said, *You know. You just fucking know, Cal.*

"Adair told me about some of the shit you guys've seen. For now, the best thing is just to keep a record of all this. And the other stuff. Because people who say too much too loud . . . disappear."

Cal looked at Cleo; she was drinking right from a bottle. "She used to do that, act that way?"

Donny shook his head. "It's part of keeping us distracted."

The sideshow went on and on, roaring ever louder at the night, gushing blue clouds; bottles smashed and someone fired a pistol into the air. And not even that brought the cops.

"What's wrong with this picture?" Donny asked, snorting, capturing the scene with the digital camera. Then he went back to his car.

December 13, late morning

Adair sat half-slumped at her desk, in second-period English class, yawning because she hadn't slept much. She'd kept waking up, seeing her dad whirling her mom in his arms like a dancer doing a routine with a lifeless dummy. She was tired, but she felt a burning tension in her, too. It was worse than just being tired.

She looked at the clock and wondered—where was the teacher?

Her mind returned with itching insistence to her mom and dad.

"What's the matter, baby? You never saw us kiss before?"

Adair shook her head.

I am one fucked-up chick.

Maybe she should talk to the guidance counselor again. About Mom and Dad. The stuff she thought she'd seen at the crash site. If that military guy was right, her mind might have been affected. Maybe she needed to get a blood test or something. Maybe a lot of them did. Maybe Ms. Santavo could arrange it.

She glanced at the clock. No teacher yet.

But then that thing with the money in the attic. My computer. It's not like they're not lying to us.

About a third of the kids simply hadn't shown up. That's how it looked to Adair, as she glanced around. And it was twelve minutes after the class was supposed to start.

"I don't think she's going to show up," Donny said. "A lot of teachers haven't been showing up. Your own mom hasn't been coming in, right?"

"She hasn't?" She didn't have her mom for PE, but it was true she hadn't even seen her around school.

"When you ask about it . . ." Donny shrugged. "Mr. Conracki says, 'Don't worry about it, just use that period for library time.' "

Other kids began drifting away from their desks, congregating in the back of the room, laughing, whispering, giggling, gossiping; others spilling out into the hall. Donny, Adair, and Siseela were the only ones still at their desks.

Donny glanced at the door. "I think I should tell you—you can tell Waylon and Cal—we're planning a meeting, to talk about some stuff."

Adair didn't ask him what the meeting was about. She knew.

"We could talk in a chat room."

"I don't want to talk about it on the Internet." He looked at the door again, his jaw working. "You know Roy Beltraut?"

She shook her head.

Donny said, "He was that tall redheaded kid, was a pretty good forward, scored eight points in two games."

"Oh, yeah. I remember him. He doesn't say much. But he's nice." Then it occurred to her Donny was talking about Roy in the past tense.

Siseela leaned forward and whispered, a little melodramatically, "Girl, Roy's gone. Just gone. Disappeared."

Adair said, "Well, so? He, like, ran away or something. People do. I mean, it could be lots of stuff."

Donny got up and moved to the desk in front of her, then leaned toward her and whispered, "Roy said *on-line*—in a chat room—that he was going to report something about the bank and about some other stuff he saw. He was going to report it to the police, and he said he didn't trust the cops around here, he was going to the state police. He was going 'right now' in his car, he said, and he signed off and no one has heard from him since."

"That doesn't mean—" But she broke off, thinking that it did make sense somehow. "Okay. Where's the meeting?"

"You know that big water tower up on Pinecrest? Tomorrow night at nine. And listen, don't bring any parents. Or tell them."

She swallowed. " 'Kay." Her own voice sounded small in her ears.

"Right now, it's hella obvious Mrs. Donner isn't coming," Siseela said, getting up. "I'm going to McDonald's."

Donny stood up, looking resignedly worried. "Good as any place. Everything is all, like, the default place to go."

*　*　*

Backpack slung over one shoulder, Adair made her way down the hall. Students were everywhere, talking, throwing paper wads, at a time when the hall should be empty. Some of them looked around, kind of scared. Then went back to pretending they were glad the adults were missing.

She went into the office and looked around. No secretaries. The principal's office looked empty. But she could see Ms. Santavo in her office, pulling a bunch of files—a big armful of them—from the file cabinet. She seemed to be dumping them into a suitcase.

Adair pushed open the little swinging gate that led into the office area, feeling strangely intrusive, and went through, half expecting some alarm to go off because she was entering this sanctum without an invitation.

She went to Ms. Santavo's office and knocked on the frame of the open door.

Ms. Santavo spun so quickly to look at her, Adair was a little startled.

"Hi," Adair said. She found herself looking at the suitcase, full of student files, and saw two more suitcases leaning against the wall. "Are you moving to another office?"

How come, Adair wondered, *Ms. Santavo didn't just take the whole file cabinet, if she was taking everything that was in it?*

Ms. Santavo looked at her in a way that made Adair think of a bird, cocking its head. Then she smiled. "I'm going to scan them all into a zip file, at home. Can I help you?"

"I was just—"

"Who am I addressing?" The smile never wavered.

"I'm . . . Adair?" Adair was a little hurt not to be remembered. "You helped me before, and some weird stuff has been happening."

"Oh, yes."

"And I was wondering—about Mrs. Donner? I mean, was the class cancelled?"

"Just go to the school library and—we'll let you know."

" 'Kay. Um, the other thing . . ."

Adair looked around. No one was there but she stepped inside and closed the door anyway. Ms. Santavo looked at her expectantly.

Adair hesitated, not sure where to start.

Mostly it was—what if her dad had really hurt her mom, and she hadn't imagined it? She just couldn't bear that to be true. She'd always assumed, on some level, somehow, that the troubles between her mom and dad were at least partly her fault.

They were always finding a way to let you know. *"We're sacrificing for you kids,"* Mom would say. *"Show some appreciation."* So if things were bad, somehow she felt it was her fault, and Cal's, because "it was all for the kids." And if Dad had flipped out, that was probably her fault, too, wasn't it? And that was one step beyond bearing.

So she plunged in. "Remember what we talked about? It's been—worse. I mean, it's stuff like, I thought I saw my dad break my mom's neck! I mean, it *looked* like he killed her, but then she was fine. So I know I'm seeing shit. I'm seeing stuff, and—other people are seeing stuff and . . ."

"And you're thinking of—therapy? Maybe going to a doctor, somewhere outside of town?"

The question took Adair by surprise. "Outside of town? Well, no. Just—someone. I mean, are there therapists for kids here in Quiebra?"

"Actually, there is someone." She went to the door and opened it. "Come with me. I'll introduce you. I'm going right by there on the way home. I believe that in fact today all your classes have been cancelled, anyway."

Confused, Adair followed Ms. Santavo to her car. Outside, a wind soughed at her face, stung her nose with chill. Pieces of the school newspaper blew up across the parking lot to wrap around her ankles, and she had to shake them loose as Ms. Santavo opened the car door for her. She got in the little car gratefully.

"Brrr. It's getting cold again."

Ms. Santavo started the car. "Yes. It certainly is. It's getting cold again. I've noticed that myself. It's cold."

Adair glanced at her. There was something . . .

But then Ms. Santavo started to hum a tune to herself.

Adair shrugged. She looked around the inside of the little car as Ms. Santavo backed out of the parking space and drove a bit too fast through the parking lot and into the street.

It was unsettling, leaving school like this in the middle of the day. Didn't they have to get permission from her parents or something? She decided that she was being a baby to worry about it, though.

The silence in the car wore on, and began to be oppressive. So Adair said, "This is a Prius, isn't it, one of those Toyota hybrid cars?"

"Yes, it certainly is a Prius. It's a hybrid." Then Ms. Santavo's face seemed to crawl within itself. Where had Adair seen that before?

And Ms. Santavo turned to Adair and said, almost imploringly, "Please, Adair, help me."

"What?"

Then Ms. Santavo's face became settled. "Help me understand what's happening with you. Won't you tell me what's going on with you and the kids? Are there a lot of kids, concerned, going to see therapists?"

"Um, well, they were freaked out about Roy. That kid who disappeared. Do you have any idea where he is?"

Ms. Santavo glanced sharply at her; held her gaze so it seemed to cling to Adair. They were driving along Quiebra Valley Road toward the countryside. "Why would I know where Roy is?"

Suddenly Adair felt a nasty tingling in her hands and the back of her neck. She hadn't expected the cold undertone of hostility in that response.

"I just meant, um, that since you're the school guidance counselor, maybe you knew if they found him, like he had just, you know, run away." She found herself afraid to look at Ms. Santavo. Who seemed to be driving the car without looking at the road, the full force of her attention turned to Adair. "Or something."

Adair noticed, too, that they were heading out into the country-side. There was nothing out here for miles but woods and cattle pastures, the occasional horse ranch.

"I see." Ms. Santavo was still looking at her—but she drove the curving, narrow road flawlessly, and fast, too, about fifteen miles per hour over the speed limit, with little fine corrections of her hands on the wheel.

She seemed to become aware it was odd for her to drive without looking at the road—and turned away, stared into the windy distance ahead.

They were about four miles from town already, Adair guessed. The wind was swishing the tops of the trees warningly; a turkey vulture, poised in a leafless oak, ruffled its shiny black feathers as they passed, its wattled-red head cocking at them.

As the car swept on, flawlessly taking curves, Adair realized, then, that she was scared, and wanted to get away from the car, as quick as possible, as far as possible.

She turned to look at Ms. Santavo, who seemed suddenly to realize she'd been behaving oddly.

"My protocol . . ."

"What?" Adair said, her voice shaking.

"Who else is worried about the things you were worried about, Adair? I want to know so I can help them."

" 'Kay. Could you tell me where we're going? There's no, like, therapists out here, are there?"

"Certainly. He has a house out here. He works out of his house. His ranch. It's a ranch out here. It's really nice. He has Arabian horses. He has cattle. You'll love this place."

They're all crappy liars, Adair thought. *It's like they're just now learning to do it.*

Then she thought, for the first time, *Who are "they"?*

Adair said, "Look, I don't want to do this today, not without talking to my parents. I don't really think I should do anything without their permission. I think they have to sign something. I mean, I just don't want to go. Let's—let's go talk to my mom first."

Ms. Santavo seemed to mull that before answering shortly, "I already have permission from your parents."

Even if that was true, it wasn't reassuring. "I don't want to go, Ms. Santavo. I'm serious."

Ms. Santavo didn't answer. She kept going. Then, after a stretched-out minute, she said, "We're almost there."

Adair thought, *Okay, that's it, that's all. How the fuck am I going to get out of this car?*

As if in answer, a sheriff's cruiser came swinging toward them, around the curve ahead.

Adair tensed, opened her mouth to yell, started to raise her left hand to signal for help—

But Ms. Santavo's hand clamped over Adair's left wrist. The pain was immediate and electric. She felt the bones start to crack.

"Silence!" Ms. Santavo said.

Silence equals death, Adair thought.

The cruiser was about to pass them on the left.

Adair shot her right hand out and jerked the steering wheel hard into the oncoming traffic lane.

Ms. Santavo let go of Adair's wrist and grabbed at the wheel.

Adair caught a glimpse of Deputy Sprague's outraged face; she could tell he was swearing, his hands taut on the wheel as he jerked it to try to avoid a—

Collision. His bumper cracked into the Prius's left front fender. Sparks and crumpling metal, the cars spinning, the air bags inflating as the Prius whipped around twice, Ms. Santavo going, "Ah, correctionnnnnnn . . ." as she spun.

Like a soft explosion, the air bags slammed them back in their seats, filling Adair's vision. And a smell of chalky chemicals went with them.

A tornado interval, seconds prolonged for what seemed like a long, long spin, as the car squealed in protest.

Adair clawing at the air bag, pressing hard on the floor with her feet, yelling, "Ohhhh . . ." The sound getting louder as they jerked to a stop. "Ohhhh, *whoahhhh—shit!*"

She felt a stabbing pain in her neck, then they stopped in a cloud of rubber smoke.

The air bags deflated automatically. Adair coughed up the white lubricant powder that drifted off the bags.

Ms. Santavo's hands pushed the remnants of the air bags away. But her face was crawling within itself. And, her voice hoarse, she said, "Yes, it's a hybrid," to no one in particular.

Adair didn't wait to see what Ms. Santavo would do. She thumbed the red button on her seat belt—the swelling wrist of her left hand screaming with pain as she did it—and jerked the car door open with her right hand, lurched out of the car, turned to see the guidance counselor leaning toward her, fingers dug deeply into the seat cushion up to the knuckles. Where Adair had been a moment before.

Adair backed away, then heard Deputy Sprague yell.

"Hey, there, girl, stay right where you are now!"

She turned to see him coming at her, looming and lumbering at her, hands clutching, his dark face a rigid mask of tension, angry and focused, and it was that chilling focus that made her turn and run from him, thinking, *He's one of them, too.*

Adair sprinted around the front of the Prius, then back around the steaming cop car, almost running in a circle around Sprague.

Picturing the Road Runner and the Coyote, she leapt feet first down into the gorge of Quiebra Creek, crunching down onto a steep slope coated with dead leaves and storm-broken branches, then slipping, tumbling, the whirling of the car all over again but in another direction, in the grip of a momentum that had its own plans for her.

She came to a sudden painful stop, smacking the back of her neck against a log. And found that she was conscious—but unable to move.

Deputy Sprague stood swaying, a little dizzy, between the smoking, crimped front end of his cruiser and the Prius.

What the fuck? Where had that kid gone?

He took a deep breath and steadied himself. *Get it together, Sprague.*

"Hey, young lady!" he shouted, toward the gully. "Come on back!"

Must've panicked. Well, this was a hell of a thing.

He turned to the woman in the Prius, bent to look in at her— and he grimaced with the pain in his back. He was going to turn up with all kinds of back problems later.

The driver looked vaguely familiar. Hadn't he seen her at the high school? Someone from the office.

"You okay there, ma'am?" he asked.

She gave him a strange look, her face sort of twitching. She started to get out of the car.

Sprague shook his head. "No, lady. Unless the car's on fire you stay right there till we check you out. You could have a concussion. You just sit and try to relax. I'll get on the radio and call for some help. We're going to get you thoroughly checked out—and I'll find that young lady who was with you."

Sucking air through his teeth at the pain, he straightened up.

The radio. Call for help.

A big extended-cab pickup truck drove up and slowed as it passed by the wreck, a couple of pale cowboy-hatted ranch boys gawking down at them. "Hey, uh, you folks need help there, uh, deputy?"

Great. *Ol' Deputy Sprague got in a fender bender out there right where he give us a ticket.*

"No, thanks, I'm calling it in," Sprague told the ranch boys. "We're okay, best keep moving, don't want to block up the road, thanks for asking," rolling it all together in one sentence as he waved them on.

They nodded and waved and drove on, accelerating to roar around the curve at a speed that probably deserved a ticket. Sprague walked stiffly to his cruiser to call for help.

Should have called even before he got out of the car, he realized, but he had been shaken up himself. The whole thing had been so damn unexpected.

He reached through the open car door for the microphone on the squawker—and someone pulled his gun from his holster, from behind.

"Don't touch that radio," the woman said. "I don't wish to be thoroughly checked out."

He turned, wincing at the motion, and saw the little dark woman from the Prius with his revolver in her hand, cocking it and aiming it at his head.

She went on calmly. "You might get a physician from outside of town. That would be a serious problem."

Her calm voice didn't go with her appearance. Her hair was mussed, her face streaked with white powder, her eyes big and dilated.

It took him a moment to fully understand that he'd let someone take his gun; now he really was going to look like a jackass. His own motherfucking gun.

And then he saw her hand tremble. She had it aimed at his head—and he knew she was going to fire.

He blurted, "Shit!" And he slapped down just as she squeezed the trigger, his hand knocking the muzzle down but not at the ground like he'd hoped. The gun kicked back hard in her hands, flashing and roaring, and he felt something punch him in the upper chest, an expanding circular wave of numbness that made him rock back against the car.

Sprague had been shot once before, and it wasn't as big a shock as it might've been for someone else. He managed to close his fingers around the revolver's cylinder, jerked the gun away from her, straight-armed her in the sternum with his other hand so she staggered back away from him.

Then his knees went all jelly and he started sliding down the car.

Sliding to a sitting position with his knees drawn up. The pain from the gunshot was really rolling now, an expanding rippling of white-hot burn that sucked all the strength from wherever it went. And it went all through him, again and again, one burning ripple after another.

Going into shock, he thought. *Call in. Get help.*

But his belt squawker wouldn't work here, he knew, in this end of the valley, with the high hills around, and he couldn't yet get to his feet to climb into the car.

The woman was moving again, slipping around the back of the car now. What was wrong with her? Why had she done this?

Something else was going on. That kid had been running for a reason—running from this woman.

Sprague coughed; felt a choking pressure building in his left lung. He figured it was filling with blood. He tried to remember what that meant for his chances.

It couldn't be good.

A wetness on his belly and lap made him more aware of blood pumping from the wound in his chest; it came out in pulses, feeling first hot as it hit the air, and then cold as it ran down his chest. His heart was betraying him: each time it pumped, it pulsed more blood out of him.

Slow down, he told it. *Get a compress over it*, he told himself.

But he couldn't think of how to do that. His mind was molasses.

He heard the little dark crazy woman speaking to someone he couldn't see. As if in response, there was a scraping sound, like a weight being dragged, and then a soft *whoosh*, then *clunk* as something was heaved—or jumped—to hit the top of his car. He could feel the impact as it shivered through the cruiser's frame; he felt it in his shoulder blades, up against the fender.

Then something was slithering along, moving nearer, over the top of the vehicle. He could just glimpse the big sliding movement out of the corner of his eye when he half turned his head.

Whatever it was, it was coming—crawling toward him, literally crawling over the car.

Then it leapt over his head.

And dropped to the ground in front of him, scuttling around crabwise to face him. The way the thing looked penetrated his growing fogginess.

Not exactly a thing—a *he*, maybe, a man, of sorts, on all fours, knees and elbows tucked in close to the body, clothes all torn up, face muddy and gouged, ribbons of flesh hanging on one side, the side missing an eye.

Even so, Sprague could just make out the guy's face. He put it together with the tatters of the uniform: Yeah, it was one of those young marine guards from the crash site.

The jarhead's hair was all overgrown, his face bearded and the beard all matted. His left eye was the one missing, its socket glinting a restless silver. A metal tongue licked from his mouth as he came toward Sprague in little twitchy fits and starts, literally crawling over the asphalt.

Sprague said, "Oh, no."

He raised his gun—but it felt so heavy in his hand now, it was hard to aim. He didn't think he had the strength to pull the trigger. He tried. It was like pulling a metal staple from a wall with one finger. The thing was poised to jump at him.

Fire the gun, goddamn it.

The gun fired, and a piece of the crawling thing's upper left shoulder exploded. The thing twitched and recoiled—slightly. Sprague knew that wasn't going to be enough.

Fire again, you bastard, shoot him! But the gun was too heavy. It sagged into his lap.

The crawling marine's head seemed to give a twist, and there was a sound like a tooth coming out of its socket, and the head extruded from his shoulders on a kind of jointed silvery-wet stalk, the mouth opening, opening wider, wider, jaws distending, visibly unhinging like an anaconda's.

The head whipped out to snap shut over Sprague's hand, ripping the gun away, and three, no, four fingers, too, tearing them away as easily as soft candy in its yellow teeth.

Sprague hadn't quite the strength to scream. He only moaned and looked at the dripping bony slivers where the upper right part of his hand had been.

Then the crawling thing's body crept up, still on all fours, moving just like a lizard to poise over Sprague. Its hand—something wrong with his wrist, something gray and wet there—grabbed

Sprague's left ankle and jerked him toward it so he slammed onto his back. He knew he'd cracked his head on the asphalt, but it was a distant sensation, a doughy kind of pain.

Then Sprague felt himself gripped—by what, he wasn't sure, something bristly on the underside of the crawling guy's body. Gripped and then dragged, leaving a red trail behind him. The marine was dragging him around the car, and it hurt to move that much, real pain breaking through the blanket of numbness. The pain and the shock was making it hard to care where he was going.

He was vaguely aware, as a darkness closed gradually but inexorably in on him, that he was dragged on his back, off the road, into mud, into the wet, overhanging brush.

The darkness was almost complete, but he could see the black cross of a turkey vulture soaring over, through the tree leaves. He was almost grateful when the crawling thing began its methodical tearing and rending.

The darkness filling more and more of his vision, like some kid with a black crayon scribbling his idea of *night* over the scene.

There was a final decisive rending and a sensation of arctic cold searing deep in his vitals. Then the darkness was complete.

16

Adair was starting to feel like she could move again. The rubbery feeling in her limbs was receding; the dizziness was a bit less. She could draw her legs up and turn a little.

Then she saw the silhouette of Ms. Santavo on the edge of the road above her. The quick movement of Ms. Santavo's head, peering down at her.

Adair bit the scream down into a whimpering sound, as gravel and clods of dirt and pieces of stick clattered down around her, dislodged by Ms. Santavo's feet as she skidded down the slope.

No. She wasn't going to be buried out here with Roy. She knew they'd killed Roy. She could feel it. Roy was dead.

She got a sudden, jarring mental image of Cal, talking to people on-line, not thinking about what he was saying.

And Waylon—the way he went on about conspiracies. They monitored the town's kids on-line somehow. Were they going after Cal now? And Waylon?

Ms. Santavo paused. Something was in her hand, maybe a heavy stick, like a club. She came on again, sliding carefully down to poise herself over Adair.

Adair got her feet under her, waited till Ms. Santavo was almost on top of her—and launched herself upward, propelling her head into Ms. Santavo's midriff. Which was a lot harder than she expected.

But Ms. Santavo tilted, fell full length backwards against the steeply angled slope, grunting, dropping a long black shape of some kind; losing her footing, sliding down so her feet became lodged under a curve of the stump.

Riding the energy of a sudden surge of triumph, Adair vaulted over the log and skidded further down the slope to the gully's bottom—and saw what it was that Ms. Santavo had dropped.

Not a club. It was a shotgun. A police shotgun.

She had a vague sense of having heard gunshots. What if she'd been wrong about Deputy Sprague? He must've been shooting at them.

Oh, god. Poor ol' Deputy Dawg.

She sobbed—but she bent, grabbed the shotgun, and almost fell over: It was heavier than she expected.

She heard Ms. Santavo getting up behind her, hissing—then she stopped, as if seeming to remember. "Adair! Wait, you're confused, you were hurt, we have to go to the hospital, Adair, come back with me!"

Adair ran parallel with the embankment, then angled toward the creek, jumped onto a low, lichen-painted boulder. Panting, she looked around.

Gray crags and round lumps of granite lined the creek here; most were little boulders, waist high and smaller, but there were bigger ones down toward Quiebra, and deeper brush, maybe places to hide.

Quiebra was a few miles that way—the way the creek ran. That much she was sure of. Looked like rain clouds gathering, too.

She jumped from one little boulder to the next, carrying the shotgun in her right hand, her left throbbing with pain at each impact, every time she landed on her feet. She almost lost her balance, carrying the shotgun. It took practice to get used to moving with it.

She ran on, darting between big boulders, jumping along the tops of small ones, through slanting beams of sunlight flashingly alternating with wells of shadow. She ran through clouds of gnats, and she slapped away bluebottle flies.

When she got to the cluster of big boulders, some of them ten feet high, it occurred to her that she'd gone the wrong way. The things like Ms. Santavo were mostly in Quiebra, weren't they?

So what. She had to get to Waylon and Cal. She had to warn people.

Stupid girl, she thought.

But she kept going, weaving in between big boulders, leaping along the smaller ones. The creek, smelling of frogs and minerals, seemed alive, seemed to rush along with her, as if it was encouraging her.

Her breath was coming in short gasps; her feet and knees were aching. She had to rest, get her wind back.

She paused on a low oval boulder, sticking partway out into the rushing water, and knelt, splashed water in her face, thinking, *Maybe this is a nightmare, and if I feel the cold water, I'll wake up.*

This was real. Ms. Santavo was homicidally crazy. And didn't seem like she was Ms. Santavo anymore. So maybe the same thing had happened to Mom. Maybe what she'd seemed to see through the basement window . . .

Adair shook her head. She couldn't think about that. Not now. She turned her mind away, like stopping a downhill run, fighting the momentum of that thought.

She had to focus on surviving, right now.

The water felt good and she was thirsty, but she knew not to drink it. Like most California creeks, it was contaminated with some kind of parasite. Some amoeba that gave you cramps and dysentery for months. She glanced back along the gully.

Parasites, she thought. That's what it felt like. There were parasites in Ms. Santavo.

And there she was, about sixty feet back, clinging to the side of one of the big boulders, her feet higher than her head, angled downward. Her feet were bare, and her hands were splayed: she was exactly like a gecko on a stone wall. Defying gravity—gripping, maybe, with those metal bristles Adair could just make out on one side of her torso, on her hands. Her blouse was torn open, her skirt was hiked up around her hips; the lines of muscles in the backs of her legs looked wrong somehow.

Adair felt sick, looking at her.

Then Ms. Santavo looked up, with a sudden exact motion of her head, staring right at Adair.

"Fuck you, whatever you are!" Adair shouted. It didn't help the situation—but it made her feel a little better.

She turned and started up again, jumping from boulder to boulder, going as fast as she could, headlong. The creek was wider here, and she had to splash through some shallows. Running crazily to get away.

At least she hoped it seemed that way. Around a bend in the creek, she picked a rock and jumped behind it: a big gray house-shaped rock. She waited, panting, her feet in an eddying pool of cold water that felt sort of good.

She told herself to get calm. To quiet down. To wait.

She pressed her back against the boulder and hefted the gun in both her hands, looking it over. She had fired rifles before, with her dad. Not shotguns. Probably it had a shell in the chamber. Ms. Santavo would have had it ready to fire. That red dot meant the safety was off, didn't it? She couldn't remember how to check.

Something rattled along the embankment to her left.

Her left wrist and the lower part of her hand hurt; it was swollen, blue in spots. The Santavo thing had cracked the bone. But her left hand only had to steady the shotgun; her right would pull the trigger.

She got as good a grip as she could with her left and put the index finger of her other hand gingerly into the trigger guard, just a little pressure on the trigger.

The creek hushed and chuckled—and then seemed to seethe more loudly, in warning.

And there was another sound. From directly overhead.

Heart percussing, Adair looked up—and saw the Santavo thing's face upside down. Her mouth opened, exposing a glimmering wriggle in there—as she tensed to jump.

Adair let out an involuntary squeak—but flipped the gun in her hands so it pointed upward, the barrel right along her own nose, and the motion pulled the trigger for her. The shotgun roared, and the barrel recoiled, to crack against Adair's forehead at the hairline, just hard enough to cut her scalp, and the *boom* made her ears ring.

Then blood dripped down, and it wasn't Adair's.

She looked up to see that the upper half of Ms. Santavo's head was missing—but she was still clinging to the rock, seeming frozen. She was dripping silver fluid and blood, all mixed together, and in the gaping concave place, like a broken-open melon, where the upper part of her head had been, was a nest of silvery things that writhed like maggots.

"Reset," Ms. Santavo muttered, her mouth dripping red and silver. After a moment, almost inaudibly, it added, "not applic—not applic—able—not—" Lips dripping fluid as they moved. Then the mouth quivered once more—and stopped moving for good.

Adair tried to scream, but her throat seemed closed up—and instead she ran, hugging the gun to her, toward Quiebra, her own blood pumping from the scalp wound, streaming into her eyes.

The world seemed to rush all wobbly, jerkily around her, past her: it wasn't like she was doing the running at all. The sunlight drained away into the sky, seeming to flow upward into the closing clouds and rain loosed itself, slithered down to paste her hair to her head. Sometimes she ran partway up the hillside toward the road, then she'd lose her footing and slide down and change direction, run along the creek boulders, but blindly, hardly watching where she went.

Adair fell again and again, slipping on wet moss, bashing both knees, cutting her elbows on rocky surfaces.

At last, she lay with her left leg in water, the rest of her sprawled on a wet gravelly bank. The shotgun—she hadn't dropped it till now, she realized with genuine surprise—lay near her. She was heaving there in a soft rain, letting the panic ebb a little.

She couldn't get up. Her heart and limbs were aching. Her breath seemed to cut its way out of her, it hurt so much. She lay listening to the creek. She heard the sound of cars and trucks. Now and then, she could just make them out, only a hundred yards away, up the embankment on the highway that paralleled the creek. Maybe someone up there would glance down and see her, if they looked between the trees.

But if they did, maybe they'd be the wrong people. Maybe it'd be better if they didn't see her. It wouldn't be wise to go up to that road. She had to find people she could trust.

And she felt a twisting in her heart as she admitted to herself that who she could trust probably didn't include her own mom and dad.

Finally, her breath coming more normally, strength returning, Adair got to her knees.

She grabbed the stock of the shotgun and pulled it toward her. She cleaned the mud off it, as best she could with the hem of her blouse, and then she hugged the shotgun again, almost lovingly.

She heard something moving in the brush, some distance behind her. She looked—but saw no one. Then a quick movement caught her attention, and way back there she saw a hairy face with an empty eye socket.

It wasn't looking toward her, but it was hunting her, slithering along in the leaf-crackling dirt at the base of the embankment. It was after her, for sure.

She watched it with a sickened fascination. The way it moved made her stomach twist. It was like it was pulling itself along the ground the way a climber would pull himself up a cliff. It mixed up horizontal and vertical. It moved on all fours, zigzagging up the steep embankment on the other side of the creek, maybe thirty-five yards back.

And she saw that its hands were stretched out from its wrists on metal extensions that pulled it along with pistonlike movements; its feet were on pistons, too.

She was afraid to move; afraid that if she did, it would see her. It would be wary of her now. It would have found the Santavo thing. It would be careful.

The thing zagged down the slope, and she vaguely remembered having run up that same part of the embankment, blindly, partway back. It was following her trail somehow.

Soon it would trace her to this side of the creek.

It went behind a boulder—so that she was out of its line of sight for a moment. She got up, slowly, each movement bringing a new ache.

She made up her mind. That fucking thing was going to have to work at it, if it wanted her.

Then she moved at an angle, into a patch of died-back black-berry brambles, and up the hillside, into thickening shadow.

December 13, late afternoon

The guard was a black-bereted, dress-uniformed man getting soft around the jowls in middle age. Hispanic guy, name tag said RODRIGUEZ. He knew Stanner by sight, from scores of visits here, to the big black cube that was the West Coast NSA headquarters.

"What the hell do you mean I don't have any clearance?"

The guard looked back at Stanner with an expert combination of blankness and crystal-clear rebuff. "That's right, sir."

They were standing on either side of a metal desk; cameras were mounted near the ceiling; a steel door was closed behind the guard; several screens were built into the desktop, which also held a computer monitor.

The guard glanced at it, in a way that said to Stanner that he was waiting for someone.

When he looked up again, he had an even more neutral expression. "If you'd like to wait, we'll see if we can get this cleared up, sir."

"Tell you what, Corporal Rodriguez, how about if you get me Captain Gaitland on the line."

"I'm afraid that won't be possible, sir, he's . . . in the field."

Stanner had a watery feeling in his gut—and the last time he'd had that, in Yemen, he'd been arrested by the Yemeni secret police. Someone was coming, all right. There would be clarification; all the wrong kinds of clarity.

"Okay," Stanner said evenly, "I'll go get my DIA pass from my car. That should clear it up."

"I don't think that'll be necessary, sir. If you'd just wait here . . ."

Stanner very conspicuously dropped his leather satchel onto the desk, so it looked as if he was coming back.

"I don't want any more goddamned misunderstandings," Stanner said in a flat tone of official displeasure. "I'll go get my full credentials."

He turned and strode through the door before the guard could hit the emergency lock-shut. He'd decided not to say, "Be right back," because that would only make the guy wonder if it were true, satchel or not.

And he wasn't coming back. They were going to take him into custody, if he let them do it. He could end up in Leavenworth, or worse, on some trumped-up beef, if they wanted to keep him out of the way.

Why, though? Why the loss of his clearance? He'd been acting under orders, with clear permission to investigate the "repercussions" in Quiebra. He'd handled the satellite recovery according to orders.

But he knew what it was: Gaitland had tried to warn him. And Bentwaters. And since he'd outranked Gaitland he hadn't waited for his orders in writing.

And he'd deliberately not checked his E-mail or answered his cell phone or his hotel phone for two days. He had suspected he was about to be pulled off this thing. But he couldn't let himself be cut loose from it till he was sure Quiebra was going to be all right, in the end. He couldn't retire not knowing for sure.

Maybe he could just back off, and the heat would ease up.

No. These people in Quiebra were American citizens, at risk. He was supposed to protect them, not play God with their lives.

234 | JOHN SHIRLEY

Fuck Facility Central anyway. He needed to *know*.

He kept moving at a brisk walk, which became a trot, till he was jogging toward the SUV, hitting the unlock button on his key-ring tab as he went. The car chirped in response, and he took the last three steps with long, fast strides, opened the door, started the car, and drove away, slamming the door en route.

It was a misty late afternoon. He hoped it'd rain; that would make a tail's work harder. More likely one would be waiting outside the gates.

Stanner saw that the guard at the parking lot checkpoint was in his glass booth, answering the phone. Probably getting the word to put down the barrier, to keep Stanner in the lot till they could take him into custody.

But before the barrier could come down, Stanner had hit the street. He was driving away at twice the speed limit.

I swear, sometimes it seems like American intelligence can't do anything right, he thought disgustedly. *The Black Beret hadn't even been told I was to be held, till I was already on to it. They should've had it all set up. It's a wonder that sorry son of a bitch Ames didn't walk away with the entire Company files. What's it been since then—years?—and they haven't learned dick.*

He realized he was already thinking of the military-intelligence complex as *they*—not as *we*. He snorted and checked in his rearview.

If they had a tail on him already, he couldn't spot it. Could be they were getting better. He'd lost the guys following him three times in the last two days, and it hadn't always been easy. When the sky was clear they could spot him with satellites.

He regretted losing his satchel. He'd had it for fifteen, maybe eighteen years. There was nothing much in it he needed; there'd been some statistics about break-ins down in Silicon Valley. Big computer-chip thefts weren't uncommon—the Russian mafia routinely sold stolen computer chips in bulk—but there'd been quadruple the usual number in the last few weeks. Chips and other cybernetic hardware taken; enhancement gear, most likely.

Then there was the bank. That big Quiebra bank job. The one no one knew about.

There'd been almost nothing about that in the media. Usually a bank job that thorough would've had reporters crawling all over the place. Not this time.

Theoretically, some of the liberal Democratic senators, and even a few Republican men of conscience, had put the stops on Project Truth—the CIA/Reagan administration term for a structured program of disinformation, using reporters, in the early 1980s.

After 9/11, the Justice Department was given carte blanche for reinstating control on the media. Ashcroft had gutted the FOIA, and the Pentagon proposed the Office of Strategic Influence under Brigadier General Worden—big taxpayer money for true and untrue propaganda. Money for lies, sometimes, to be spread internationally, to every medium, in aid of the war on terrorism. Publicly, the government had decided the OSI wasn't necessary—but it existed nonetheless. The first lie put out by the "nonexistent" OSI was that the office didn't exist. Irony as usual dogging intelligence.

Driving down the 101 to the Bay Bridge, slowing to not attract attention, Stanner reflected that he didn't really blame the government much. After 9/11, the siege mentality was to some extent really justified. There was a sense that a major part of the world ranged against America—and that sense wasn't entirely wrongheaded.

Still, who was to say the Pentagon wasn't pulling strings on the media the same way Project Truth did, in the case of that bank in Quiebra? Certainly they went to great lengths to protect the Facility. Stupid to think they wouldn't, really. They'd kept the satellite crash pretty quiet; he'd helped them do that himself.

He thought about Shannon. Where was she? Was she safe? Would they use her to bring him in, if he didn't come in on his own? Maybe he should warn her. God, would she be pissed off.

Dad, how dare you drag me into your paranoid little world?

He looked into his rearview mirror. Was that dark blue Ford Taurus following him? Maybe. A man and woman, looking ever so disinterested—but changing lanes, not long after he did, only a few cars back.

He looked back at the road, had to swerve to stay in the lane. Shit. They might realize he'd been watching them.

Fuck 'em. Let them follow till he got to the East Bay. He'd lose them in Berkeley. There were all those blocked-off streets he could use to throw them off, then he'd go over the hills, through Tilden Park, down into the back roads to Quiebra. He had a stop to make in Quiebra, before he went to the next level.

Somewhere in his Palm Pilot he had the home address of that Filipino commander in the Quiebra PD. Commander Cruzon.

The guy had been "out sick" the last week, when Stanner had gone to see him at the PD. This time he was going to Cruzon's house. They were going to compare notes. Whether the little son of a bitch wanted notes compared or not.

Bentwaters. The bastard had better come through: He needed to get that EMP transmitter design.

But he'd take something along, next time he went to see Bentwaters. Like a silenced machine pistol.

He wondered, as he drove onto the Bay Bridge, when he'd unknowingly crossed the line from the Same Old Bullshit to being in SDS: Serious Deep Shit.

December 13, afternoon

Lacey looked at the little green screen on her cell phone. The phone seemed to be in touch with its server. The battery showed a full charge—and she hadn't used it much since she'd charged it. But she'd tried four times, and the call just wasn't going through.

She was at a small window table in the Cruller, in what passed for downtown Quiebra. Her latte sat in front of her, untouched. She stretched, then rested an elbow on the table, and it rocked on its uneven legs, so that the latte slopped over. She muttered a curse and dabbed at the milky brown puddle with her napkin. Too big a puddle. She dropped the napkin into it and watched it soak the coffee up. Absorbing the hot coffee into its papery blandness, making it part of itself.

She shivered and tried the cell phone again. It seemed to be calling through now. She put the phone to her ear and heard a rush of static and the odd, jangling words again, something like the confusion that had come out of Waylon's frequency searcher. Then it was as if some atmospheric hand had lifted, and the line cleared; she heard it ringing.

"Hello?" It was Rueben's voice.

She had almost married Rueben, before meeting the guy who was now her ex. A few weeks ago, she'd found herself wishing she'd stuck with Rueben. But now that things were getting serious with Bert, Rueben was back into the "handy ex-boyfriend" category—only, it was hard to think about relationships at all just now.

"Hi, Rueben! Can you hear me okay? Cell phone problems around here."

"Lacey? Sure I hear you! Good to hear you, too. Hey, there was a rumor, uh, that you and—"

"Yeah, we broke up. I'm staying with . . . well, near my sister in Quiebra now. But, hey, did you get my package? My note with that, um, item, right?"

"What package? And what note?"

"I overnighted it to you. It's a sort of odd little computer chip on a—well, it's soldered to another device. It was in bubble wrap, inside the envelope with my note. And you've got that computer science doctorate, ought to be good for something."

"No, I didn't get anything from you. Why are you sending me odd little chips?"

"That's a long story. But I was hoping you could help me figure out what the thing is. I mean, it seems to be some kind of—of I don't know what."

"Nothing came. Have you tried to track it?"

"Um, I'm a little nervous about doing that at this point. To tell the truth, I didn't use my own name on the envelope. I used a nickname I thought you'd remember, and a fake address. I was nervous about this call, too, but I figure they can't monitor everything."

There was a long crackling pause. "Listen, are you okay? I mean, how about if I come and see you? Have you—I mean, uh, are you . . ."

"Am I getting paranoid, Rueben? Yes, I probably am. Maybe not paranoid enough, Rueben. That's what I'm beginning to think. Especially now. They must have intercepted that package."

Another staticky interval and she found herself staring at people going by on the sidewalk outside the coffee shop window. An elderly man, bent nearly hunchbacked, walked along with a younger woman, probably his daughter; they passed a middle-aged man with clubbed hair, a purple shirt and a silvery tie—a local real estate agent, going the opposite way.

"Lacey?"

Coming behind the real estate agent was a woman in blue jeans and Levi jacket, with long black hair and high cheekbones and black eyes—one of the local Indians. All of them seemed to glance at her, as they walked by. As if . . .

She shook her head. As if what?

"Lacey, yo."

"Oh, sorry, Rueben."

"I really think you should, uh—"

"Rueben? I'm going to be okay. Don't come to Quiebra, whatever you do. I'll call you back in a few days."

Before he could argue, Lacey broke the connection.

Two rather overweight teenage girls carrying Taco Bell bags were passing now. They looked at her. As if . . .

Snap out of it, she told herself. *Do something normal. Get some distance from it. Christmas shopping.*

She got up and went out, waving to the chubby lady behind the counter. She walked into a wind that was misty but not cold; she strolled past a beautician's shop, and then stopped in front of a small jewelry store. Maybe some earrings for Adair?

She went in and thought she must've mistaken the sign in the window. The jewelry counters were all empty, except for fragments, here and there; a single pearl earring lying askew next to what looked like a broken bracelet. Mostly just blank black velvet under the glass tops. Well, maybe they were changing all their stock over.

"Hello? Anyone home? Are you open?"

After a few moments she gave up and turned to go—but turned back when a woman came out of the back room. Late middle-aged, short and busty, elaborately coifed silver hair, blue eye shadow, jewel-rimmed glasses with an onyx-beaded croky. Her lipstick seemed smeared, and her makeup a bit blurred, as if she'd been crying.

"Yes?" the woman asked.

"Um, are you open? All your stock seems to be gone."

The woman looked hazily at the display cases. "Yes. It's all gone. We haven't got any to put out. It's gone."

"Right before Christmas? You must've had one heck of a sale."

"Oh, no. People just came and took it. They came and took it, you see, as 'resources' they said. They just took it. Stole it really."

"Stole it! What did the police say?"

"The police?" She seemed to sway on her feet. She clutched at the glass top of a display case as if she was afraid she might fall. "A lot happened in one day. Wasn't it amazing? You can't call the police now. You're not one of them, are you?"

Lacey swallowed. "One of who?"

The woman blinked hard, as if a harsh light struck her eyes, and stared down at the empty cases. "My husband tried to leave town— was going to talk to the state police. Said he'd be back yesterday, by noon. He hasn't come back."

And then she seemed to sink down, below the level of the display case. Lacey lost sight of her for a moment.

Lacey went and looked over the edge of the case. The woman was sitting on the floor, rocking back and forth, her legs cocked to one side, crying.

Lacey tried to think of what to do. "Oh, gosh, let me get you a doctor! Or—some family—someone—"

"No!" The woman looked up at her in sudden panic. Lacey could see the color draining out of her face. "*No*, please, for God's sake, *don't call anyone!*"

The woman scrambled to her feet and ran, stumbling in her hurry, into the back room, slamming the door behind her.

Lacey backed away from the display cases, and then turned, hurried out and down the street. She hurried against the wind, down a block, left a block, to the police station.

"This," she muttered, as she stalked up to the station, "is bullshit. I'm going to find out what the fuck is going on."

Inside, she found a man seated on the other side of the reception window. Not the woman who'd been there a couple of days ago, when Lacey had glanced through the window. A tanned fiftyish man with deep smile lines, maybe the faintest suggestion of a hair weave. But she knew him. Bert had introduced her when they'd run into him at the new bistro. It was the mayor—Mayor Rowse.

"Hello, Mr. Mayor. Are you, um, doing a police job, here? Or, just waiting for someone?"

"I'm filling in here," Rowse said, smiling, cocking his head to one side. "Certainly."

"Yes, well, that's unusual, isn't it?"

"Oh, no, not when the police are so very busy. Big project going on. Certainly. I was able to pitch in here. But how can I help you? Is there a problem somewhere? You wanted to report something?"

"Hm? Well . . ." She opened her mouth to tell him about the lady in the jewelry store. The woman's husband, the theft.

But she couldn't quite bring herself to say anything.

No, it wasn't *couldn't*; it was *wouldn't*. She didn't feel it was wise. She wasn't sure why. The mayor just looked at her. As if . . .

She shook her head. "No, no, I just . . . wanted to say hello to the lady that was working here. We had a nice chat but, uh, I've got to get some—some shopping done. I'll . . . talk to you later."

She turned and hurried out. And went to her rental car, and got in, and drove home.

Think this through, she told herself as she drove. *Decide what to do.*

But that wasn't exactly possible, somehow, to think it through. There weren't enough facts.

Except—she knew she needed to get out of town.

She had to find Adair and Bert and Cal—and ask them to go with her.

December 13, late afternoon

Captain Gaitland was driving the van; Lieutenant Magee, a big military cop who had black features but light skin, like Colin Powell, sat beside him; and a thickset Green Beret sat in the backseat: Sergeant Dirkowski.

Dirkowski was in uniform, but the others were in plain clothes. Each one had a 9mm Smith & Wesson automatic under his jacket. Behind Dirkowski was a big open cargo space, and in it lay an empty military-issue coffin.

On the floor of the van, next to Magee's leg, was a metal brief-case. On the side of the briefcase was what looked like a small stereo speaker grid.

They had just turned onto Quiebra Valley Road. "It seem to you like those Quiebra PD rollers back there were watching for us?" Magee said. "The ones we passed at the Shell station."

"No, sir, I didn't believe so," Dirkowski said. An Alabama accent.

It was funny, Gaitland thought, *how Dirkowski could be outranked by Magee but still be condescending toward him somehow.*

"Well, I think so," Magee said. "You sure we got enough person-nel here, Captain?"

"We need only one sample," Gaitland said, scanning the streets. Wondering how to pick one out. It'd be pretty awkward, walking up to people and running the scan over them. "We ought to be able to take one of them down, between us."

"We had three guys out here for observation," Magee pointed out, "and only one of them came back alive. Half-dead himself. Says the fucking breakouts keep experimenting with—what you'd call it—their form. Trying combinations of bodies, changing up the body."

"That's right," Gaitland said. "They modify bodies at the cellular level. And they seem to be trying for several models, little ones and big ones, for different jobs. So that means maybe they can do things we can't, uh, anticipate. Exactly. But a nine-millimeter round will stop anything, you put it in the brain."

But, he thought, *they could literally have more than one brain, in more than one part of the body.*

He didn't voice that thought to Magee.

"What I was thinking," Magee went on, "was we maybe should get Stanner here. He's been on-site. If those chowderheads in the observation team had consulted him, maybe they'd still be around."

Gaitland noticed Magee turning to look over his shoulder at the road behind. "You see something back there I should know about?"

"It's that police car. I mean, what if they took over the local cops?"

"It can't have gone that far." But Gaitland wondered. Aloud he said, "Stanner is AWOL. He's been out of touch. Seems like he doesn't trust us."

Dirkowski snorted.

Gaitland looked at him in the rearview mirror. "You got something to say about that, Dirkowski?"

"No, sir."

"Anyway, Lieutenant," Gaitland went on, turning to Magee, "we're trying to get Stanner back in hand—but he doesn't even take orders from us, not now. We've had to follow him to get some sense of what he's doing."

"He shook those boys," Dirkowski muttered. Adding, "Sir."

Gaitland ignored him. "He doesn't like the pace we're working at, and you know what, he can't make up his rules as he goes along and he's going to find that out."

"That fucking roller's got his lights on, sir," Magee said.

Gaitland sighed. "I'm gonna pull over. Everyone got their pistol permits, the special ID, all that squared away?"

Magee nodded. Dirkowski said, "Yes, sir."

Two cops were in the cruiser. Looked like a white guy and an Asian. Gaitland pulled over to the shoulder, but the Asian cop shook his head, pointing to a side road that led to a park, screened by trees, just up ahead.

"They don't want us on the shoulder," Dirkowski muttered.

Gaitland pulled onto the side road. But he reached under his coat and loosened his pistol in its holster.

The two cops pulled up behind them and got out of their cruiser.

Magee said, "Maybe we ought to have the detector on."

"How do we explain what it is, sir?"

"Go ahead, turn it on—and have your finger on the deprogram button," Gaitland said.

Hands shaking, Magee pulled the converted Halliburton briefcase up onto his lap and opened it. The mechanism inside was solid-state, filling the interior, the equipment covered in a gray plastic panel that showed two LCD readout windows, and two toggle switches under a metal cover. The switches were labeled ONE and TWO. Wires ran up from the device to the inside of the lid of the metal briefcase, connecting to the transmitter grid that looked like a stereo speaker. It had to be simple because none of them were Facility technical staff; they understood the device only in theoretical terms.

Magee flipped the switch cover back as the cops stalked up to either side of the car. The cops—Quiebra PD—had their .44s drawn, but held down against their thighs.

"Can I see your driver's license?" the white cop said to Gaitland. His name tag said WHARTON. The Asian was bending to look in at the other side. Was staring at that open briefcase and the arcane gear inside.

"Sure," Gaitland said. He took out his wallet, took out the license, and laid it on the wallet next to the badge, which today was Secret Service. The Facility could get them any sort of federal badge they needed, each one authentic.

"Secret Service?" Wharton said, sounding amused.

"That's right, and one military attaché. As federal agents, we're packing sidearms, of course, but we have the paperwork." Gaitland grinned at Wharton.

Wharton grinned back—an automatic, grimacing sort of grin.

Something about it made Gaitland feel like gunning the van out of here.

"What've you got in back there, behind the Green Beret?" Wharton asked. "Looks like a coffin."

"A box. Empty," Gaitland said.

The other cop—CHEN, his name tag said—straightened up and looked at his partner.

Wharton nodded to Chen. Then to Gaitland he said, "Yeah, we're gonna have to examine that briefcase, fella."

"Excuse me, officer, but—" Gaitland said, turning to Magee. He mouthed, *Hit switch one.* Turned back to the cop, to finish, "—but you've just seen our badges. You ought to be cooperating, not hassling us."

Magee flipped the first toggle. He went all stiff, staring at the readout. It said, *positive.* Meaning, these cops contained breakout components.

Meaning they weren't human.

"Get out of the car!" the cops barked, both at once. Raising their guns.

Magee didn't have to be told to flip switch two. The device in the briefcase hummed.

Gaitland looked at Wharton. The cop shivered, squinching up his face as if he was hearing an irritating sound that no one else could hear. He took a shaky step back.

Gaitland drew his own pistol and waited. Any moment Wharton would fall dead, at least in theory, as soon as he was deprogrammed.

Wharton looked at Chen—and both of them laughed.

"That," Wharton said.

"Is not effective because—" Chen said.

"—Because you have failed," Wharton said, "to—"

"—To take into account the anticipatory capability of the All of Us," Chen said. "All gateways have been closed; all frequencies shuffled. And now . . ."

Gaitland was already taking a bead on Wharton's head, but the cop moved with impossible speed and fired at the same time.

Gaitland felt a hot wet shattering in his chest and thought, *Why didn't I wear the Kevlar?* and that was nearly his last thought, as he heard them shooting Magee again and again. He felt another round hit him in the throat, this one feeling cold, and all the strength drained out of him as he slumped against the bloody Magee.

The last thing he heard was Chen saying to Dirkowski, "You can live, if you drop your pistol. We think we can use you. I mean, you can live—our way."

And Dirkowski saying, "You got it."

17

"Cal, dude, have you seen Adair?"

It seemed to Cal that Waylon was probably stoned. A certain red-eyed, glazed quality. A slight fuzziness in his voice.

It was just getting dark. They were outside the Burger King, where Cal was sitting at a metal picnic table trying to fill out his employment application form in the light from the restaurant window. He'd made up his mind he was going to move out of his parents' house, which meant he needed money, which meant he needed a job. He'd rather work on boats, but those jobs were hard to find in a steady-work way, short of joining the Coast Guard. The CG or the navy were tempting, but he didn't feel right about leaving Adair alone in town yet. He wasn't even sure why.

"No," Cal said at last, writing in his social security number, "I haven't seen her since she went to school. Lacey called looking for her, just before I came over here. And Donny called for her."

"Oh, man," Waylon said, "this is fucked up, it's jenky, man, it's like *voop*, she's gone. I just fucking hope she's not with Roy."

Cal stood up, shaking with what he told himself was fury, but maybe it was more like fear. "What the fuck you say? Don't say shit like that, not a word, Waylon, unless you *know*, man, that something happened to her—"

"Hey, whoa, chill—"

Cal stepped around the picnic table; Waylon took a step back. Cal snarled at him, "You come at me all mumbling to yourself, like a stoned pothead moron, about my sister. You been putting your hands on her, you fucking New York stoner?"

"No, dude, shit, you can ask her if I was doggin' on her. Ask her yourself if we—when we find her."

Cal took a deep breath. "What makes you think she's . . . gone?"

"Okay, I was talking to Siseela, and she's like, 'It was so weird, Adair left in the middle of the day with the school counselor lady.' And I'm like, 'So, she probably went with her to see her mom or something,' and she's like, 'No, uh-uh, they went down the road the opposite way toward the country and that Santavo bitch has been acting weird, too.' And Santavo's the one took Adair with her."

Cal stared at him. "Okay, you *are* stoned. But, uh, if she went off with a school official-like person, that's not too weird, really. I mean, it's not like some guy in a ski mask grabbed her or something."

But Waylon was staring past him at something. Cal turned and saw that on the residential side of the fence, behind the Burger King parking lot, a fat guy with his toupee flopping in the wind was putting a homemade satellite dish up on the roof of his little house.

"That shit is freaking me out," Waylon said. "All over town, people putting up these freaky little transmitters—or whatever they are."

Cal snorted. "Okay. You're a paranoid, just like Mason. Speaking of that asshole, I'm gonna call him, get him to go look for Adair with me in his van."

"Hey, I'm gonna go with—"

But then a Bronco with a lot of mud on the wheels and miles on the engine pulled up beside them, the driver lightly honking her horn. It was a lady with a face softening to fat around the edges and dyed platinum hair, someone Cal didn't know. But he guessed it was Waylon's mom when she said, "Waylon, come on, hon, we have to go."

"What? Where?"

"I'll explain, but in the car, please. I don't want to shout our business all over heck and gone."

Waylon grimaced, shaking his head in an exaggerated motion. "Whatever." He turned to Cal. "So you're gonna find Adair?"

"Gonna find Mason to help me find Adair, yeah."

Waylon's mom cocked her head at this, as Waylon asked, "So you got a cell phone or what?"

Cal nodded. "Carrying it. Don't know if it's still working. I'm way behind on payments." He thought, *What could it hurt,* scribbled the cell phone number on Waylon's arm. Then Cal watched Waylon get into the Bronco and ride away.

Cal went back to filling out the form, but hurriedly now. He wanted to find Mason—and Adair.

And not one minute passed before Mason drove up in his van. "Hey, dude. What's the haps."

Cal stared at him. "This is weird shit. People just coming to—whatever. Mason, I'm trying to find Adair. You know where she is?"

"I think I probably do, Cuz-o. She's hangin' with some other kids. Come on. I'll take you there."

Cal took the application in to the older black guy who managed the Burger King, then hurried back out to Mason's van and got in beside him. Something felt strange. There was something about the way Mason had just shown up. And he just showed up knowing where Adair was.

But he shrugged. What else was he going to do? At least for once Mason's van didn't reek of pot.

So he let Mason drive him down Quiebra Valley Road, toward the country.

December 13, evening

Waylon snorted and shook his head in another well-practiced display of amazement.

"A *blood test*? Mom, I haven't said anything about being sick, and they haven't said anything at school about any blood tests."

"There's an emergency in town," Waylon's mom said, "because of that thing that crashed, the satellite you were talking about, and the toxic fumes from it. You need a blood test to see if you've been poisoned. You went out to that crash site, after all. More than once. And the second time, you saw things."

"Yeah, but, Mom, I didn't *imagine* what I saw. I've been writing it up. I'm gonna—" He broke off, realizing he hadn't told his mom about the things he'd seen at the site, the second time.

Maybe she'd gotten into his files. Maybe she'd been reading his stuff behind his back.

He turned to stare at her, thinking about challenging her on that. *How the fuck did you know?* But somehow, he was afraid to confront her. Something was warning him not to, and he didn't quite understand what it was.

They were pulling into the high school parking lot, driving around the back of the school. It looked like a used-car lot back there, lots of cars standing dark and empty, parked sort of haphazardly next to the school gym. The outside rear door of the gym was open, and a couple of kids slouched restlessly in the doorway with their stolid parents. As Waylon watched, they stepped once, further into the gym. They were in a line—waiting for the blood test, he supposed.

His mom pulled her Bronco up not far from the gym door, and a minute later they were in the line, Waylon hearing the echoing murmur of people in the big spaces of the gym. Surprisingly little noise, really.

Only the kids were talking, to one another, Waylon realized, as, in another minute, he and his mom stepped into the gym. The gym smelled of dust and varnish and antiseptic and faintly of sweat. The basketball backboards were folded up against the rafters; the bleachers were retracted into the walls. It was a big softly reverberating room with a line of people along one wall, and near the entrance to the locker rooms and showers were a couple of nurses in white uniforms, both of them black women, working at a small brown craft table. They had the kids sit in a chair when they drew the blood, and put discarded needles in an open box. Nearby sat other boxes, cushioned with bubble wrap, for the little vials of blood.

A pale chunky kid huddled in the chair, getting his blood taken; he wore three-quarter pants that showed his fat white calves, no socks in his Adidases, a sleeveless Master P T-shirt, one of those "mushroom head" haircuts, thick on top and buzzed on the sides. Waylon remembered him from school, reciting rap and calling people *blud* and *cuz* though the black kids just sneered at him for it. The chunky kid sat there with his mouth hanging open, looking away as they stuck a needle in his arm and sucked the blood out into a big plastic syringe.

The blood test table was clear across the big room, but the deep dark red of the blood seemed to blossom in the syringe like a sudden alien flower, calling Waylon's eyes to it.

He hated the sight of blood, and this whole cheerful little procession made his stomach clench up. Why hadn't there been any announcement about it at school? Maybe there had been; maybe he'd missed it. He didn't pay attention to stuff like that. But somehow he doubted anyone had announced it.

This whole thing made him think about something he'd read online about an upsurge in autism and some kinds of cancer, caused by mass vaccinations of the fifties and sixties. Some overlooked impurity in the vaccine. And there was supposed to be a government conspiracy to cover up that gigantic mistake.

Maybe this could be part of that conspiracy. The kids might be here to get injections to hide the tainted vaccines. Or they could be testing biowarfare agents on the town; the government had done it before.

Maybe that's what the "satellite" had been, really. The crash staged to expose the town to some biowar virus. They could be testing them all for the exposure here.

But then why test only the kids?

This mass blood testing had to be tied in with some kind of conspiracy. This was just too sudden, with no explanations.

Then Waylon's chain of speculation broke when Mr. Sorenson, the vice principal, came out into the gym through the locker room door, on the boys' side. He was an imposing man, almost six and a half feet, broad shouldered but otherwise slender, with a long neck and a big Adam's apple. He wore a yellow golf shirt and gray slacks. He picked up one of the containers of blood samples and went back in the locker room with it.

What's up with that? Mr. Sorenson personally helping with the blood?

A lot of the kids seemed nervous, some talking to their neighbors in line. But the parents were completely quiet, except to respond to the kids. It wasn't right, how quiet the parents were. Lots of these people had to know each other. Yet they weren't speaking.

"Mom, this is fucked up." Waylon shook his head and looked at his mom. "I don't want to do this."

She looked at him with a peculiar calmness. She seemed alert, friendly, relaxed—and bland. That wasn't like her. If she wasn't stoned or depressed, she was talking a lot, keeping her spirits up, trying to get to know people. She was way more social than he'd ever be.

But not now. Mom didn't say anything. She just took a step forward when the line moved, a skinny Asian kid replacing the pale chunky guy at the bloodsucking chair, and she smiled at him.

"Mom?"

"Yes, Waylon?"

"Nothing. I just wanted to hear you say something."

Waylon watched the pale chunky kid go to stand with a group of other kids who'd already been tested, their parents standing behind them in a line against the section of the wall that contained the machine-retracted bleachers. The parents were silent; the kids were muttering softly to one another.

Waylon looked around. It was a hella big gymnasium; metal rafters near the ceiling. High glazed windows; he could see a single star through one of the open windows in the far upper corner.

He wanted to be out there, instead, where stars shone. And he wished Adair was with him. He wished he knew where she was.

Waylon glanced at his mom again. She seemed so self-contained, all of a sudden. Friendly, but distant. So what was it? What was bothering him?

He hadn't smoked a major blunt, or anything. Just a bowl, really. He felt kind of furry around the edges, with the details flintily sharp in a tunnel-vision kind of way. That lady in front of Mom seemed so still, the way she stood there, it was like she wasn't breathing. But the glossy auburn curve of the way her hair was set seemed to pulse faintly.

Okay, he was used to that kind of bullshit with dope. It wasn't like he was really big-ass loaded.

So why did his mom suddenly seem like she was *acting*?

"Mom, where'd you hear about this blood test thing? I mean, did someone call you up?"

She seemed to consider for a long moment. "Yes. There was a call. A phone call. We were called here."

He looked at her, feeling odd, as he took her words in. He was feeling a chill, right in his heart, and it was spreading out through him. It was hard to tell exactly what was wrong with Mom. An oddness about the way she talked, that sense that she was acting. Maybe it *was* the bowl he'd smoked.

Mr. Sorenson came out again, walked over to the pale chunky kid, and took him by the arm. "Come on back, please, Ronald."

Waylon could just make out their voices. Yeah, Ronald, that was his name.

Ronald looked at the doors to the locker room. Clearly he didn't want to go. "Is there something—something wrong with my blood?"

The other kids tittered nervously at that.

"No, nothing wrong, exactly, we just have to check some things, to make sure. Come on, we'll show you," Mr. Sorenson said.

He led Ronald into the locker room. And the line moved forward.

Waylon was aware of his heart pounding. He felt like his skin was too small for his body.

Maybe I'm being paranoid, he thought.

Or maybe I'm scared for a good reason.

Waylon made up his mind. "Mom, I'm gonna find the bathroom. I've gotta pee big-time."

She looked at him. "No, you'd better wait." Then she frowned. It was as if the frown was an afterthought.

"Be right back." Waylon trotted away from her, up the line. The two black nurses were heavyset women with conked hair, one very dark and the other light-skinned. They both looked up at once as he passed, both of them turning their heads to watch him go into the locker room.

The windowless locker room seemed empty at first; the only human presence was a smell of sweat and soap. He couldn't see anyone in the PE office, that little glassed-in cubicle across from the rows of lockers. Then he heard a sob, echoing from beyond the office. A boy's whimper, coming thinly, distorted, from the showers.

Waylon walked carefully between rows of lockers, and it seemed to take forever, as if the aisle stretched out, telescoped past the empty rows of metal locker doors. As he approached the showers, he stopped to stare at a machine of a kind he'd never seen, just beside the showers' entrance. It was on a tripod as high as he was tall, with a glass tray suspended near the top, between the legs, and some kind of laser beaming where the three supports of the tripod met, aiming down into a petri dish of blood. A little panel wired to the side of the laser gave a readout, and a wire extended into the blood. When he took a step closer to the machine and peered into the dish, he could see little metal things that swam around in the blood, like krill.

The mechanism looked jury-rigged, slung together from various parts taken from here and there, and not like something that came from a medical lab. And it gave off a buzzing sound, as if muttering to itself.

Waylon took a step closer to the tiled entrance, leaned to peer into the clean bright starkly geometrical spaces of the showers. Mr. Sorenson was kneeling beside the pale chunky kid, Ronald, holding

him down on the tiled floor. Ronald was on his back. The vice principal seemed to hold the boy down without much effort though
Ronald was a big sort of kid and he was struggling as the tanned,
muscular, burr-headed PE teacher, Mr. Waxbury, gripped the boy's
jaws, forcing them apart with his two hands.

Mr. Waxbury was leaning over Ronald as if he was going to give
him mouth-to-mouth resuscitation. The boy tried to scream, but
could make only choking sounds because the metal stalk extending
from Mr. Waxbury's own throat was jamming down into the boy's
mouth. And something pulsed along the cable, from Mr. Waxbury
to Ronald, like millions of tiny stainless steel aphids. Little things
crawled into the deepest insides of the writhing boy. Then Mr.
Sorenson brought a small box close and pulled the boy's shirt
up. Something extended itself from a gash in Mr. Sorenson's right
palm, and there was a flashing, scissoring, a spattering of skin and
blood the way sawdust flies from a buzz saw, and the boy was filleted open. Mr. Sorenson inserted something in the surgical wound,
something Waylon couldn't see. Then Sorenson shifted, his body
blocking Waylon's view.

But he could see Ronald's legs; they gave a final shudder and
went limp.

"Oh, fuck," Waylon breathed, without even knowing he was saying it right out loud.

Mr. Waxbury and Mr. Sorenson—the Mr. Waxbury thing, the
Mr. Sorenson thing—both snapped their heads up at once. Locked
their eyes on his.

They stood, turning toward Waylon. Sorenson glanced at
Ronald. "It'll finish the first phase on its own now."

Waylon took a step back. A moment of mutual uncertainty—if he
ran, then they'd come after him; and if they came after him, he'd run.

Mr. Waxbury tensed.

Ronald sat up with a snap and looked at Waylon with the same
expression the adults had. Bland but alert, predatory eyes. His belly
was still filleted, flayed open. Things clicked and revolved within
him behind a curtain of blood and mucus.

"Cuz! Check it out," Ronald said, tugging his shirt down to cover his wound, grinning. "Turns out it's all okay, after all. I feel way so much better now." He clambered to his feet in one smooth motion. "I feel like I got mad skills, bro. Let 'em test your blood. Let 'em do it to you. It's like when I got broadband, cuz, but it's way better."

"It'll be better yet," the Waxbury thing said. "After the enhancements, the supplements, the modifications. It goes in stages. But it's fast, now, you see? Isn't it, Ronald?"

"Yeah, I hardly felt a thing, dog!" He paused, thoughtful, and then went on, "See, the young ones, some of them—that's just some of them, see—they don't convert so easily to the All of Us. Something in the blood. There's chemicals that are, what, like, produced when people are a little more aware of themselves and stuff around them. See, what the All of Us is telling me is, if you're not 'the type to join us' easy, well, dog, the blood test can find that out because some chemicals they know about are, like, produced as a side effect of being, you know, *that* kind of guy. But see, dude, if you're already like I was, halfway there anyway, and you're, like, into just being entertained and getting hooked up to shit, then you can convert fast to one of them and you won't, like, fight it afterwards. Otherwise they got to reset you, they got to kill you and, like, take you apart. Some of us can go to the highest interface right away and, well, fuck, *we* like it that way. You see? For the All of Us, cuz?"

Ronald took a step toward him, his eyes shining with an almost enviable joy in his rightness.

Waylon said, "I . . . don't know."

Then he heard a door open. He turned and saw the open door to the sports gear room. Racks were filled with basketballs, and tennis rackets, and football padding, each marked QUIEBRA HIGH SCHOOL PROPERTY. And a body was lying on the floor back there. He couldn't see who it was; he could just see the legs sticking out. But then the legs twitched. Whoever it was, was still alive.

And someone else came out of that room, from the side the body was on. It was Cleo, that girl from school. Donny's girlfriend. Or ex.

She was naked. Stark naked. Tan lines around her pale breasts, tan marking out pale skin in a bikini shape around her blond crotch. She looked alert and happy. Something white dribbled from the corner of her mouth. Waylon at first thought it was spittle, but then he realized it was semen.

"You can have sex with me," she said. "Gary did. I gave him incredible sex. You can have sex and drugs and party and then be one of us if you want to do it that way. It makes conversion easier, if your mind is occupied that way." Her tone was so casual, so reasonable.

She came toward him and opened her arms.

Waylon stared at her breasts. The pink seashell of her labia.

Then he turned to run—

And his mom was there. Waylon's mom stopped him: she slapped him hard, across the face, so that he was flung backwards against the frame of the shower entrance and shouted in pain. Sank down against the wall. He felt stunned, dizzy.

"You've disobeyed me, you little shit," his mom said. "Everything was coming together, finally. I'm finally part of something good, and you're trying to ruin it. I'm not going to let you do that, you parasitical little bastard. They're even offering you sex and you turn it down and God knows you used to masturbate till your hands were raw."

"Hold him for us," Mr. Sorenson said, and Waylon heard them coming from inside the showers.

But Waylon gathered his consciousness together within him.

And gathered his feet under him, as they spoke.

And he lunged, propelled himself at his mom headfirst, slammed his head into her gut, expecting to feel metal but instead feeling a web of hardness under the skin, strong but flexible.

She went *whoof* and tipped over backwards, and he shot through the doorway of the showers, knocking the tripod machine down behind him to slow the others as he went scrambling past her, leaping up to get by so that her hand sliced through the air just under his ankle, and his tennis shoe came down hard right on her face; he could feel the crunch of her nose breaking right through the sole of his shoe.

He was stomping his own mother's face to get going.

But it *wasn't* his mother. *It's not her.* And the implication of that threatened to make the whole world go gray and spongy.

Then he heard something he'd heard many times before—and had never before realized how poignant, how sweet it was: his mother's own, real, ordinary voice.

"Run, baby! Run!" She was fighting it, managed to shout once more. *"Run!"*

And he was running already, but as he went he half turned like a football player hoping to catch a pass on the run, to see if maybe Mom was okay now, if she was coming with him. But she was gripping Mr. Waxbury's legs as he came after Waylon, making him stumble into Sorenson—and Waxbury and Sorenson bent down to rend and tear at her neck so that blood splashed the lockers.

He was almost relieved to see her die—to see that thing die.

And then he had reached the doors, and the switch panel that controlled the lights for the gymnasium. Hearing running footsteps behind him, he slapped all the switches down. But it didn't affect the locker room—only the gym.

The nearest door was closed with a thick chrome chain that wrapped the handles, with a big Yale padlock on one end. But the chain wasn't locking the door; it was hanging there loose for when they needed it later. Waylon pulled it rattlingly loose and swung it around, hard, smack into Ronald's face, cracking him on the side of the head. Metal feelers emerged from the pale round face, to writhe spastically as he fell sideways. Completing the turn, riding an empowering surge of adrenaline, shouting wordless defiance at the boy but inwardly sobbing—*Mama! My Mom! My*—Waylon swung the heavy Yale lock hard into the light control switches, smashing them. Then, flailing the chain, he slammed his shoulder into the door, banging it open, bursting through into the pitch-dark shouting confusion of the gymnasium. He paused, panting.

Darkness, but in the light from the locker room, he could see the two ghostly nurse's uniforms, like clothes on invisible women, coming at him, a glint of metal above the necklines. There were adults—adult things—at the exits. They were coming toward him. The only way out was high up on the walls. The open windows.

To the right of the door was a switch; he'd seen the custodian use it. He slapped down at it, and the automatic bleachers groaned and creakingly began extending from the wall, crenellated shadows in this dimness, knocking people down, pushing them along the floor.

Waylon whipped the chain hard into the darkness where the nearest nurse's face would be. The chain connected; he heard her yell and stumble back into the other nurse.

Waylon jumped onto the nearest extending stairway of bleachers and ran along the moving aluminum benchtops at an upward angle, balancing on the unfolding, rumbling bleachers as if he were surfing on a mechanical wave. But it was hard to see in the darkened room, only a little light angling from the high windows by the ceiling, and Waylon stumbled, fell, losing the chain as he flailed, smacked his knee on a metal edge, shouted, "Shit!" and got to his feet again, though the bleachers were still opening like an accordion under him.

The kids were yelling, and Waylon shouted, *"They're monsters, they're turning us into things, they're not fucking human, you got to run!"* His voice echoed, booming above the others, as he stumbled onward.

Then he heard murmurs, many voices repeating a kind of litany—something about *night protocols, night protocols*—and suddenly dozens of pairs of small-sourced, long-beam lights switched on in the room. They were tightly defined narrow-beam lights like miniature headlights, the light sources shaped like . . .

Like eyes. *The eyes of the adults in the gym were spearing light.*

Their eyes shone but not the way a cat's eyes shone. Like headlights or doubled laser pens, the beams were red-shading-to-green, and they extended, each pair of light beams, all the way across the gymnasium, spearing doubly straight, swinging to take in the screaming children—light piercing this way, turning that way—seeking Waylon, he knew, searching him out in the darkness of the big room.

Children screaming—

Children seeing their parents' eyes light up in the dark with red-green beams, seeing those remorseless beams flicker over them in stripy illumination, seeing their parents get down on all fours, their hands extending on metal stalks from their wrists, to pull themselves up the bleachers with fingers that rippled with far too many joints. Parents propelling themselves along the ground pantherishly, leaping ten yards to come down on all fours; the mothers and fathers becoming hissing crawling human hound-things that smacked the children aside and turned to rend them, slashing with unnatural sideways movements of their jaws as the teenagers and children screamed and ran for the doors.

Many of the kids escaped out those doors, Waylon saw with some relief. Their erstwhile parents were distracted from him, trying to stop the kids.

But others came after Waylon. Crawling things in darkness split only by the reflective glow of their double-beamed flashlight eyes and by eye beams from one another; creeping things in house dresses and postal uniforms and suit jackets that came up the now-static bleachers after Waylon, who was frantically scrambling back, away from them, forced upward now toward the wall, the ceiling.

He paused, panting, on the top bleacher and looked down at them.

In the lights from their eyes, their gazes crisscrossing like clashing rapiers, he saw them coming. He saw Mr. Sorenson climbing toward him then; and the chunky pale kid Ronald, his face a ruin; and Mr. Waxbury with his PE whistle dangling from his neck; and Mrs. Simmons the English teacher, who'd ripped away her long dress to make it easier to climb, her fat legs like pistons now; and the beer-gutted balding guy in the unseasonal Hawaiian shirt who managed the apartment building where he'd lived with his mom, the guy he suspected of boffing his mother, now grinning at him as he bounded up the bleachers toward him, leaping on all fours, five bleachers at a time.

Waylon shouted, "No, you fuckers, no fucking way!" and he ran along the top bleacher, barely able to make it out, in slicing occasional probings of their eye beams and the glow from the high windows. He was near the ceiling, coming to the end of the bleachers, a fall of two stories to the floor. And he leapt off the end.

Caught the tilted-up support pole for a backboard, then swung up parallel to the rafters; the hoop board for PE practice so the girls could shoot baskets, too, that stayed up during games, close beside the end of the bleachers.

He hung there, knowing they could leap even better than him— and then swung himself, caught another support pole, looped a leg over it.

But one of them had hit a switch and the hoop's backboard began lowering itself from the wall, to dangle closer to the floor, and Waylon almost lost his grip as it moved, like it was a machine angrily trying to shake him off.

Waylon caught a reinforcing wire with one hand, shifted his grip, climbed up the support poles as the backboard lowered, finding his way in the light from the window he was making his way toward. An open window.

He crawled across the struts between the support poles, almost falling off as it jerked to a stop, slightly slanted downward, got within reach of a metal rafter, pulled himself up it, heard them bounding onto the metal support poles behind him.

Still, he was climbing, scurrying along the rafters, afraid to look down now. Then he reached the wall, could just climb down off the rafters, into the window cracked aslant for ventilation, just enough room for a skinny guy to slip squirming through, scraping off pieces of skin as he went, then dropping onto the roof of the adjacent building, ten feet down to the tarry surface. Running across the dampness, smelling night rain and tar and chimney smoke from the houses behind the school.

Running to the far side of the school, where there was a drainpipe, and a field, and the woods, and the paths up the ridge, and beyond the ridge.

The big water tank in the hills.

18

The moon had shrunk to a sliver, seemed to have transferred its diminished brilliance to the phosphorescence lighting the white-caps on the sea.

"Lacey," Bert said softly. He wanted to show her the sleeping gulls lined up, beaks tucked under wings, perched on a half-buried log in the sand.

But, gazing out over the bay, she suddenly said, "We need to get out of town. I've been looking for Adair and Cal. I have to take them with me. I just can't leave them. But I can't find them."

Bert nodded. Coming home, he'd found a note shoved under his door; normally she'd have left a message on his answering machine. "You found out some more?"

"Nothing that I understand—just enough to say that we have to go. We have to get my niece and nephew, and we have to go. I tried to FedEx one of those little devices to an old friend of mine at Cal Tech. It never got to him. And I tried to buy Adair some earrings. For Christmas. At the jewelry store in Old Town Quiebra. The door was open. The cases were empty. I finally talked to the owner. She said a lot of the jewelry had been taken." She told him the rest of the story about the lady in the jewelry store.

"That's fairly bizarre. You didn't call the police?"

"I went over there, and—you remember the mayor? You introduced me. He was there behind the desk, instead of a cop—and instead of that lady who used to be there."

"The mayor?"

"Yep. And I got this feeling from him. I just couldn't tell him anything. And I just walked out. And I've been trying to find Adair. And then I thought of you."

She was hugging herself against the cold, staring at something shiny on the beach, half-hidden by a smooth-skinned twist of driftwood.

He stared down at the shiny thing on the beach, and he sighed. The night before, they'd eaten a dinner she'd cooked for him; they'd shared a bottle of wine—they'd both been just a little tipsy—and they'd kissed. Then they'd made love, and she'd been very patient with him until at last he'd found the way past her defenses, and she'd let go for him.

In the morning she'd left before he'd been up. She'd left a note, saying she was going shopping, meet him later. Thanks for beautiful evening.

The denial was over, though. He couldn't pretend he didn't know, on some level, what the bright thing on the beach was: a bright thing that stood in for a dark thing. He could no longer tell himself that the dark thing that was snuffling around every corner in Quiebra was going to let them go on and just be lovers. The dark thing was going to hurt them, or make them fight. And there was going to be no other choice, not really.

She hunkered down to look closer at the thing in the sand, and he hunkered beside her. "It's like that thing that hit my windshield. The thing that raggedy cat picked up."

"Something the cat dragged in," she murmured, chuckling nervously, still gazing at it in fascination.

It was about as big as his hand and made Bert think of those little desk toys, small pieces of chrome on magnets you made shapes of, connecting the pieces up any way you wanted within the magnetic field. An impression of the frontier of organization arising from chaos.

The glittery thing tumbled and writhed along the beach, a coalescence of tiny metal flakes, and when it caught the moonlight and a little gleam from the streetlights at the beach reserve's parking lot, it seemed to Bert that each was itself another provisional collection of yet smaller parts, each of those in turn a temporary organization of even smaller bits, and so on.

He put his arm around Lacey's shoulders. "It's got something like life about it," Bert muttered. "But it's dead." He felt her shudder, at that.

Lacey picked up a stick and poked at the living metal chain—and it immediately wrapped itself around the stick and began to spiral up it toward her hand. She froze, mouth open, staring.

It reached for her fingers.

Bert slapped the glitter-twisted stick away, hard, and it flipped into the nearest of the gulls sleeping on the half-buried log. The bird squawked and rose in a spasmodic flutter, but the glimmer was already twining its neck, making it look like a mythical bird wearing a necklace.

The other gulls began to wake, hopping and flying away. It was already flapping vigorously above the others, into the night—and then it fell back, as if shot down by a hunter, to flop at the sand and peck frantically at the air.

Lacey said, "Oh, Jesus, Bert!" and ran to the gull, reaching out to it.

"Don't!" he shouted, hurrying to pull her back.

She let him, sensing the wisdom of it—as the gull thrashed, the living metal twining up its neck, wending down its throat . . .

It continued thrashing—for about forty seconds. Then it stiffened. Its head began to twist around on its neck, like a bottletop unscrewing itself, and its wings began to tear loose from its body, extended out from its middle on bloody metal stalks.

"God*damn* it, Bert, kill it for me, won't you? Kill the poor thing."

He used a long stick to flip the bird onto a rock; then found another rock, big as an anvil. Straining, he carried it over and dropped it, smashing the gull past all use. Blood bubbled out from under the stone, mixed with squirming silver bits.

They went hurriedly back toward the other end of the beach and the nominal safety of Bert's condo.

But stopped when they saw lights on the boat launching ramp. An instinctive caution gripped them both, and holding hands, they walked up on the edge of the concrete ramp that sloped down into the water. Below, a young black man, a white man of middle age, and a young white woman were launching a white-hulled outboard motorboat from a trailer that was hooked to a pickup. They had just pulled the boat into the water, were having to use Coleman lanterns set up in the bed of the truck to help them see.

It was a cold, blustery night, and there was an air of desperation in their movements, their hushed voices. Bert could hear them panting, the woman speaking between soft sobs, the black man muttering at her to be quiet. The older white man said, "Okay, she's free, let's get the fuck out of here."

Bert and Lacey hunkered instinctively behind a boulder to watch. Neither one knew exactly why they were hiding.

Bert was on the edge of asking them what was wrong when he saw a man shape crawling toward them over the rocks piled up in a loose seawall on the other side of the boat launching ramp. The man was dragging himself along the top of the rocks; it looked like dragging at first, until Bert looked closer and saw that he was creeping along the irregular granite pile with the slinky adroitness of an iguana. His arms, glinting aluminum-gray at the joints, extended unnaturally long. The man paused, and his head rotated on his neck, stopping to stare straight upward—though his body was angled facedown. The head tilted on the neck at an angle that should have made broken bones jut from the skin—and Bert recognized the face.

"Morgenthal," he muttered.

"You know—" Staring, Lacey broke off to swallow, and wet her lips, her voice breathless. "You know that thing?"

"Used to be a guy named Morgenthal. Shop teacher at the high school—" He broke off, leaning forward to see better.

Morgenthal—what had been Morgenthal—had been spotted by the three people who were climbing into the boat. It was gathering itself up on a boulder just above them, poising to jump.

Both the white man and the woman screamed. The black man pulled a pistol from his waistband and fired. The gun thumped and flashed, but the Morgenthal thing leapt like a tiger, with a calibrated efficiency, coming down on the black man, knocking him into the other two so they all tumbled flat in the boat, which rocked and turned sideways from the ramp.

Then the Morgenthal thing began to tear them apart, grabbing bits of them, ripping clothes with flesh, tossing shreds of them over his shoulders like a child throwing a tantrum, yet with blurring speed and efficiency, so that the screaming quickly stopped.

Lacey backed away from the scene, covering her mouth with a hand. She stumbled, fell backwards in the sand, and Bert rushed to help her up, whispering, "Don't scream, don't let it hear you. Come on!"

They ran up toward the path edging the beach and all the way back to the condo.

Once there they locked the doors, and—in unspoken mutual agreement—jammed chairs against the knobs. Then Lacey turned to Bert and asked, point-blank, "Is this a dream?"

He reached out and touched the brass doorknob. Cold under his fingers. "No."

Then he went to the phone, to call someone, anyone—and heard a recording.

"Due to the emergency, the phones are now inactive. They are being repaired. Thank you for your patience." He handed it to Lacey so she could hear for herself as it repeated.

As she was listening he spotted a piece of paper on the floor, with his name written on it. He picked it up and unfolded it.

"Do you think we should try to drive to another town?" Lacey asked, putting the phone down.

"Not—not tonight," he said softly, and handed her the paper. It read:

> Mr. Clayborn,
>
> As you are the only one I know and I guess trust, I am leaving this here to warn you and ask for your help. They have been changing people at a gallop all day, and they did it to my niece. I barely got away from her. I tried to leave town, but they have the roads blocked off. They are telling people it's some emergency and we have to stay. But there's nothing about it on TV. If you try to insist on getting by, they take you away right there and you come back as one of them. I don't know what they are.
>
> I guess these are the Last Days. I'm going to my church and hide there. I don't want to say which. God will help the righteous. I wanted to warn somebody before I left here.
>
> God Bless.
> Mrs. Goodwin

"I hope she got somewhere safe," he muttered. "She used to try to get me over to that Pentecostal church of hers. I was running out of excuses. She was such a well-meaning old soul."

"You think those people at the boat? . . ."

He nodded. "If she's right, they were trying to leave town. They'd tried the road."

"It's like it was in the air for a while, wasn't it? You could feel something, but you couldn't describe it exactly. Oh, God, my sister. That must be—oh, no."

He held her as she wept.

Then they turned off the lights in every room but the bedroom, where they lay together, dressed, under the covers. After a while, she reached out and took his hand.

And there it was. A hand touching his—a truly intimate, simple contact—hidden under the covers. He felt the poles of the world shift, then.

He tried to define the change, in his mind, and couldn't. A predatory nightmare infested the land; it might well kill them both. If they survived, they would never quite sleep well again; they would argue sometimes, and they would hurt one another, perhaps. But they were in this together—as he'd never been, with anyone. He could feel a simple completion, more real than passion. They'd be side by side, facing whatever darkness came along. The poles had shifted—and she was his north, now.

The skinny black cat they'd found in the country came out from under the bed and jumped up beside them, nestling close. After a while, Bert turned out the light and held Lacey in his arms, as together they watched the curtained windows for the coming of the morning light.

December 13, night

He knew exactly what to do. That's how it was at first. There was no interference from the old self. Not yet. All he had to do was get up from the reorganizer, in the harsh lights of the portable electric lamps that had been set up on poles driven into the dirt; climb out of the reorganization pit, learning to use his limbs as he went. There were too many limbs to coordinate, if he thought about it; but if he simply thought, *Go there*, the mobilization program took over, and he'd find himself moving forward down the tunnel. He discovered, from imitating some of the others he saw, that he could move up the side of the packed-dirt tunnel, too, close beside the strings of lightbulbs stapled to the wooden beam wedged overhead, and felt a feeble kind of happiness then. *I can defy gravity*, he thought.

All the time he was monitoring the All of Us with one part of his enhanced brain, taking the binomial pulse of it, hearing the words in their shorthand and more directly when it was needed: *"Blue and Green converge in future tense, register point seven one three thousand, enclosing and restructuring . . . Covering soccer field, associates converting fire department; police entirely converted except for two; mov-*

ing in on Cruzon ... Stanner is back in primary operational field, converging . . ."

Those names sparked something. He knew those names. Cruzon. Stanner. He got mental pictures. That made him think of a third person. He saw the third person in a backyard, putting sauce on steaks over hot coals. Laughing with his wife. That one's name . . . was Sprague.

Sprague. Leonard Sprague.

Moving down the tunnel, emerging into the cool night air— feeling the coolness distantly on those parts of him that were still capable of feeling it, mostly on his cheeks—he felt a downward spiral inside, at the name *Sprague*. As if that name had fallen with a splash into the surface of his mind and it was sinking, the name spinning down, carrying his consciousness down with it.

> *Sprague*
>> *Sprague*
> *Sprague*
>> *Sprague*
> *Sprague*
>> *Leonard Sprague*

He was already patrolling the perimeter of the entry place over the base of operations of the All of Us—his main task, for now— before it came to him.

It had been his own name.

Sprague.

That wasn't relevant to his new format. With some of the converted, he knew, the names of their "shells" were important. It was part of the camouflage—necessary, for now. But when you were reset into a completely new format, there was no need for a name. He shouldn't be able to remember it. But he did. There had been enough of his essential self—maybe what people had once called his spirit, his soul—to retain some sense of . . .

Leonard Sprague.

They hadn't taken so much from him as they'd thought. So he remembered that he had been Sprague.

He wished achingly that he couldn't remember. He hoped the All of Us would make him forget who he had been.

It would, when it had time. It had priorities, specific time-critical actions to carry out first. The All of Us was busy.

December 13, night

Vinnie was walking along near the Albertsons supermarket on Quiebra Valley Road, at 9:53 P.M., when he started to feel it.

He knew he had to be alone somewhere and had better make it quick. He had no vinegar and he had no medicine and this was going to hit him hard, he could feel it. It was a form of epilepsy, hit him only a few, maybe four times a year; was connected to his condition in some way that even the doctor didn't understand: it was either epilepsy-related autism or autism-related epilepsy with episodes of OCD or something. And he usually avoided taking his medication because it made him a zombie.

They would like it if he was a zombie, he supposed, but there had always been zombies, even before *they* had come, and he'd always been afraid of them, and he knew that people thought he was like one, too, and, as he said aloud, passing some kids on scooters, people thinking he was a zombie, "Well, hey now, that's just another way to prove that when life plays a joke on you it's laughing *at* you and not *with* you." And of course, as if the kids were playing the part of Life Itself, they laughed at him.

Their laughter had a shape that hung in the air like wind chimes made of teeth.

And that thought, that image, told him it was already too late to get somewhere alone because now it was hitting him. He just made it to a bus bench and sat down on it, clenching the wooden back, trying to ignore the face painted on the bench next to the slogan "LLOYD MCKENZIE" MEANS "SELL YOUR HOUSE E-Z" and Lloyd's jolly round winking face on the bus bench turned with hallucinatory ease to leer right at him just as that high tuneless note started that meant the mixing-up fit was coming on full.

He was so scared. It was frightening when things switched places, when the sound of two passing police cars blaring their sirens on the way to the high school became a sickening red taste in his mouth, the taste of a very bad cherry-flavored cough syrup, the kind of cough syrup that was the color of cherries but lied about its taste; when the three older men in the car in front of him pulling over, for a moment, to let the cop cars pass, turned blue like their car while the car turned flesh color and their heads pulsed with a thrumming sound, and it looked just like their heads were part of the car, like those toy cars with the head of a little driver but if you look close the head is attached to a painted-on seat without a body. When the birds flying over were tactile sensations in his eyes, he could feel their shapes pressing in painful stabbing edges to his eyeballs and . . .

Then he started to hear the moths talking again.

There weren't any moths that he could see, but it was the same voices he'd heard before when those moths had dived at him and hovered in front of his eyes. He thought of these voices as the moth voices. And he knew somehow that his altered state, the electrical overstimulation that his brain was going through when he had a seizure, was helping him pick up these voices that were in the air all the time. Some of it was just numbers, a voice saying, "010110100-1011001," and some of it was words that didn't fit together, "Protocol Beach Embrace Makeover Collection Shortfall of Marathon Zone Oh-Seventeen Green Metareception Umbrella Rebuke Until Further Notice." And some of it almost made sense, in a sort of way, "Harold Potts, bear with me, we've got no clear reception."

"I'm modeling at high efficiency, will stay at this cover modality until otherwise instructed."

"Umbrella, the All of This estimated in thirty-three hours, preparing insemination receptacles for expansion, see that the junior high is tested for maximization."

"Unlocalized youth are still in a state of disorganization and recurrent antipath. We must include them before the Social Organism extends its antibodies to spherical attention recognition in the southeastern radius."

Vinnie tried plugging his ears, but it was no use.

And meanwhile a child passing with her mother lost her helium balloon, which soared and bobbled away in the growing darkness; it was the purple of the taste of oranges and it was the shape of the sound of low pipe-organ notes.

And a truck passed with its shape pressing on Vinnie's forebrain; that's what he saw in his mind, a truck shape pressed into the soft stuff of his brain like a mold of a toy truck pressed into Play-Doh. And the truck made a sound that smelled like licorice. And a seagull gave a cry that tasted like overripe bananas.

And all that time the voices went on.

"Will need help at 754 Pinecrest and 658 Owlswoop; there is someone resisting . . . Is anyone monitoring the government investigative body? . . . Five thousand Pink Metaimperative sandwheels Beach Road . . ."

They were talking, he knew, those who had changed some of the animals and some of the moths and many of the people. They were talking on their own frequency, and they were completely rational, so rational that only a weeping man having a seizure could hear it.

And then he heard them mention his mother. "We have a conscious resistance, Elizabeth Munson . . ."

And then it said his address. And said, "A definite reset, very stubborn. Not much material of value, but if we need parts . . ."

The seizure was ebbing. It wasn't the same as a grand mal seizure; it wasn't so terribly obvious, though he couldn't walk when it was happening, and no one had called an ambulance. He was there on the sidewalk alone, watching traffic pass. Seeing the moths circling the light over the Albertsons parking lot ENTER HERE sign with unnatural precision.

He was standing, now, though his legs were rubbery. He swayed where he stood. "Don't fall," he said aloud, "don't let the police or the ambulances take you, it'll be a trip to South Calaboom, most of them have become one of *them*."

Oh, but it was so hard to walk right now. He was walking through jelly. He had to get home to help Mother. If only he could turn into a Starbot, transform into a perfectly symmetrical gorgeous flying fighting machine, to save his mother.

But he knew it was too late. Mother was a quarter mile away from him. But he felt it when she died.

Adair was lying flat atop a boulder on a hillside overlooking Quiebra Creek. She was shivering, looking at the lights of Quiebra winking against the backdrop of the night.

She had her two hands over the stock and breech of the gun. The shotgun had four rounds left in it; she'd checked.

Her body throbbed with pain in her neck, her knees, her shins, the palms of her hands, and a long scratch burned hot against her belly. She felt something crawling in her hair, and she plucked it out and flicked it away. A tick, probably. Lots of ticks here. She wondered if the ticks sucked on *them*, too; parasites on parasites who called normal people parasites.

She scratched mosquito bites on her arm.

Then she put her hand back on the gun, got a good grip, and pressed the butt of the stock against the granite to help her get partly up, so that she was kneeling on the boulder. This wasn't good, though; she was still being hunted and she knew they could see her better this way, against the sky.

She moved so she was sitting facing the other way, her legs dangling over the edge of the boulder, the gun laid across her lap with her hands on it. Ready. Peering into the darkness. Seeing them . . .

There—about a hundred yards back along the creek. A group of ballcrawlers, little animals taken over by the crawlers. Sometimes standing up on each other's furry and feathered shoulders, quivering along.

They were still experimenting, she realized, whatever they were. They were parasitical, and they were new at this, and they were trying new shapes and formats, looking for different models that worked. And some of them were like Ms. Santavo had been, almost perfect cover, and some of them were new ways to think of life and organizing it, and a lot of that didn't work. Evolution takes time.

Adair thought she'd like to fire the shotgun into that quivering mass of different animals and just watch the abomination of it fly apart, but she was sure that what remained would just reorganize and attack her.

So she slid off the boulder, on the side opposite the ballcrawlers, and looked around for a moment to see if the marine thing was coming. She could smell it sometimes, the train-transformer human-flesh stink of it, but it hadn't caught her yet.

She was hungry and tired, but in a way she felt very alive. She just wanted to get to Cal and Waylon and warn them.

That made her think about Mom. And Dad. And her heart ached. She had heard that expression all her life, about heartache, but never before had she felt anything so definitely like an ache in her heart. Like the ache of a broken bone. But the broken-bone feeling was in the center of her, where her feelings lived, and, oh, it ached. Because she was sure they were dead, or something worse.

She felt a seething anger then and wished the marine would come along, or another one, so she could kill one.

Ms. Santavo. She had killed her, hadn't she?

She hadn't been thinking about it directly, but it came to her now. She'd killed another person. Only, Ms. Santavo had already been dead, really.

But what if that gas that the major had talked about was real? What if it had affected her mind?

What if she'd misunderstood what Ms. Santavo was doing? What if she'd murdered her?

She looked around the edge of the boulder. Seventy-five yards away, the thing was coming along like a walking scarecrow.

She watched it for a while. It didn't shimmy into other shapes. It didn't vanish and reappear. It was absurd but it was internally consistent. It was *real*.

No. She wasn't seeing things. She hadn't killed Ms. Santavo. The woman had already been dead.

Adair remembered a line from the Bible. "Let the dead bury the dead."

She drew back into the cover of the boulder and moved as quietly as possible through the brush toward the lights of town.

19

When Stanner stepped through the wooden gate into Cruzon's backyard, he felt a very distinctive sensation, a sensation he'd felt once before in a Yemeni alley and would never forget.

It was the feeling of a gun muzzle pressed to the back of his neck.

"Do not move, Major." Police commander Cruzon's voice.

Stanner considered the sensation on his neck. "Wait, I think I got it. A nine millimeter?"

"That's not bad. It's loaded, too, and there's a round in the chamber. Now step around back behind the house. I'm going to take the gun off your neck, but it's going to be about twenty-four inches from your spine."

"I got you." Stanner walked along the side of the house, past a prefab plastic doghouse and a neat coil of green garden hose.

Frogs were singing from the little green concrete-banked koi pond in the backyard.

"Isn't it the wrong time of year for frogs?" Stanner asked.

"Yup," Cruzon said.

The house was up against a hill, like so many houses in Quiebra, and the steep backyard slope had been terraced and shored up with stone. There was a little leafless ornamental plum tree, and the wooden fences were lined with rosebushes. The two men stood there a moment, listening to the frogs and then an owl.

"Nice yard," Stanner said. Cruzon didn't reply, and Stanner wondered if Cruzon was just going to shoot him in the back.

"Turn around," Cruzon said.

Stanner turned. Cruzon was out of uniform, wearing tan slacks and a white zip-up jacket. He held the 9mm automatic steady, pointing at Stanner's sternum. Just stood there, backlit by the porch light, looking Stanner over, as if trying to make up his mind about something.

Cruzon's face was mostly in shadow. Beyond him, lying on the little brick patio by the glass sliding doors, was something about as big as a man under a canvas tarp. Whatever it was twitched fitfully.

Stanner saw a little girl looking at him from beyond the glass. A little black-haired girl; one of Cruzon's kids. Stanner shook his head at the little girl and frowned so she'd go away. If her father was going to shoot him, it was better if she didn't have to watch.

The kid backed away from the glass, then ran out of Stanner's line of sight.

"What's that supposed to be?" Cruzon demanded.

"There was a little girl. I thought she ought to not . . . be around."

"That supposed to be clever, a good act, you pretending you care?" Cruzon snapped.

Stanner shrugged. "So you think I'm one of them. I don't know what to say to that, Commander—except, you'd better be right about that. Before you shoot a federal agent."

"Reason to shoot a federal agent's getting better every passing hour, seems to me." Cruzon reached around behind himself with his free hand, took a small flashlight from a back pocket, switched it on. "You gonna pretend this didn't start with your fucking satellite? Now kneel down in front of me."

Stanner hesitated. But then figured Cruzon would probably have turned him around the other way if he was going to shoot him.

"Do it!" Cruzon barked, pointing the pistol at Stanner's forehead.

Stanner decided not to rush him. His gut told him Cruzon was still human. He knelt, going down on both knees.

"Now open your mouth," Cruzon said.

Stanner raised his eyebrows instead.

Cruzon flicked the gun barrel so it caught Stanner's right cheekbone, hard enough to hurt something fierce, not hard enough to break anything. "Open!"

Stanner opened his mouth.

"Wider!"

He opened wide—and Cruzon pointed the flashlight down his throat. Squinted. Then grunted to himself and took a step back.

"Okay, Major. Stand up." Cruzon lowered the gun, but kept it at his side.

His pulse slowing a little, Stanner got to his feet. "They'll modify that eventually. But it's not a bad test for now."

"What," Cruzon said, "no more of that bullshit you were handing us before? A 'gas that makes you do strange things'? That was a goddamn lie."

"Yeah, well. It's just part of my job. I had my reasons."

"Reasons! Come here, Major. I'll show you reasons."

Cruzon stalked over to the quivering tarp by the back door. He signaled to someone in the house—probably his wife. White pleated curtains closed inside the sliding glass doors.

Then Cruzon bent down and pulled the tarp away, exposing a man tied up in duct tape and yellow plastic rope. It had been a man, anyway. Short black hair, pale skin, flat gray pouchy eyes that watched Stanner impassively, the remains of a black suit. His mouth duct-taped shut. The suit was torn in a dozen places, and through the rips Stanner could see wounds, and inside the wounds he could see little metal maggots, squirming. One of the man's hands suddenly came loose from the wrist and extended on a jointed metal stalk to snatch at Cruzon's ankles.

Cruzon jumped back, then moved around where the hand couldn't reach, and kicked the man hard in the head. Stanner took a prudent step back himself.

"That used to be a friend of mine," Cruzon said, staring at the crawler, his eyes moist. "He was an FBI agent I worked with years ago when they were trying to prove a guy up here killed his old lady and buried her over in Nevada. Martin here loved Filipino food. Loved my family. Used to be a great guy, name of Martin Breakenridge.

"Well, a couple of days ago two of my men down at the precinct weren't on duty when they were supposed to be, and I was passing RadioShack, saw one of them using a big pile of money to buy a shitload of stuff. So I followed one of 'em, patrolman named Lansbury. He went into his house and came out—and I bent the laws some, just to find out what was going on. I look through his place after he left, and I find a pile of money in the guy's basement. Indications are, it's the stolen money from the bank. He comes home, surprises me there, tries to kill me.

"And, uh—" He broke off to lick his lips. "And I had to kill Lansbury—had to shoot him three times in the head to really stop him. And I found out what he was. So sure I figure some more things out and I call my friend here, Breakenridge, at the FBI. I figure they won't believe me if I tell them the story, but if he comes here to see something without me saying what, on my say-so, to see for himself, he'll believe his own eyes. This was before they had all the phones tied up.

"He did believe me, when he looked close at Lansbury; he had to. He was taking Lansbury in the trunk of his car, back to the city to show some people. Well, he never made it. I figure . . . *they* were watching. They caught him, I guess. Changed him, before he ever left town. Because Breakenridge came here when I wasn't home and he tried to turn my wife into one of *them*. I guess he was setting a trap for me. And I came home and caught him at it." He sighed, swallowed, and went on, his voice breaking. "And I shot Agent Breakenridge up pretty good, with a ten-gauge shotgun. But he ain't dead. You can kill 'em, but it's not so easy. Got to shoot 'em right. And he's one of them now.

"Means he is in touch with them, Stanner. *They're going to be coming here for him*—and because I know about them. From what I can tell, they're always talking, those things, in their heads." He turned to Stanner, looked at him, but pointed at the thing that had been FBI agent Breakenridge. "So where's that *thing* fit into your *reasons* for lying to me?"

"The situation—situation seems to've changed," Stanner said, feeling sick. "Don't you think you should put the fucker out of his misery?"

"I think he's better evidence this way." He pulled the tarp back over the crawler. "Now, Stanner, you're gonna tell me every fucking thing you know. Right now, Major. Now. Then you're going to make some phone calls."

Stanner said slowly, rubbing his bruised, swelling cheekbone, "I'll tell you what I can, but—"

"Everything," Cruzon said with finality. "And then we make some calls. We report this."

Stanner made an effort and threw off the habit of secrecy. "I'll tell you everything. But the phone calls won't do any good until we make them out of town."

"Yeah. I worked that out." He looked at Breakenridge. "Let's put him in the trunk of my car. If we grab him careful—"

"Hold on. He can communicate with them. And even if we kill him and take his body for evidence, how do we know the part of him that talks to *them* can't still talk to them? It could still transmit. We'd have to melt it to slag and then it'd be no proof at all. No."

Cruzon's eyes welled up and he looked away, wiped his eyes. Then he looked sharply back at Stanner. He winked grimly. "No, we're taking him with us. Put him in your rental car."

Stanner stared. Then he got it. "Okay." He said it loud enough for Breakenridge to hear.

But they had to kill the thing that had been Martin Breakenridge anyway. They didn't want it operating, infecting anyone else. The fewer of them staying ambulatory, the better.

It had to be done fast. Stanner did it, while Cruzon kept watch on the street. And Stanner didn't feel much as he fired the shotgun three times, point-blank, into the back of the Breakenridge-thing's head, two more times into its spine. He used an ax to sever the head, as if with some supernatural creature of old. Then he slung the remains into the trunk of his rental car and drove it a few blocks away, to a wide dirt track Cruzon directed him to, a narrow little road along the creek, screened by a stand of eucalyptus, where the local kids sometimes parked to get laid. He got out of the car, leaving it trembling in drive, put a sizeable rock on the accelerator, and let the car surge forward on its own, into Quiebra Creek.

He heard sirens and stood still, listening; they were coming closer. The thing that had been Breakenridge had transmitted what they had hoped it would, and some of *them*, looking out their picture windows, had seen him drive to the dirt road beside the creek. They might stumble around, looking for the car, and if he hid himself pretty well, heading back to Cruzon's house, that might throw them off, for a while.

Cruzon was a smart little cop.

December 13, night

I was stupid to come back home, Waylon thought.

He was actually across the street from their apartment, squatting in the foliage of a big camellia bush in the front yard of someone's darkened split-level. Camellias flowered in winter, and the red blooms bedecked the bowl of dark green leaves around him; under his feet fallen blossoms were crinkling brown at the edges, falling apart.

He knew he was cold, in a remote kind of way, but he didn't really care; he was hungry, but he didn't want to eat.

He had gone to Russell's house first, because Russell—from the pizza parlor, the guy who'd sold him the pot—lived a block and a half from the place his mom had rented, up on Hillview overlooking Quiebra Valley. He'd thought maybe he could hide out at Russell's for a while, then sneak in when the Mom-thing wasn't there. Get his computer hard drive, some clothes. That .25 pistol his mom kept in her closet.

But at Russell's he'd taken the precaution of scouting first, when he heard someone moving around in the garage. He'd looked through a side door into the garage, seen Russell standing at a wooden work-bench, next to a vise; Russell with his ponytail and his goatee and his tattooed arms and his Slipknot T-shirt, building a transmission de-vice with rapid-fire efficiency, his hands moving so fast Waylon couldn't follow them. Russell, who'd flunked science three times.

Just looking at him, Waylon was pretty sure. Then Russell held his palm over the transmitter and a little silvery snake came from his hand.

So Waylon backed away from Russell's house and wandered to-ward his own. Wondering.

Some people couldn't be changed into those things without a lot of trouble—but others could. It seemed to have something to do with your state of mind. Whether or not you were already halfway like that, Ronald had said. Somehow. Maybe the more programmed you already were, the more programmable you were likely to be.

Adults could be changed over pretty easily, seemed like. They'd lost some essence that made them resist. Or most of them had.

Like Mom.

He'd been in the calm eye of a hurricane of emotion since he'd left the school, just putting one foot in front of the other and trying not to envision his mom with those lights coming from her eyes, and the boy on his back in the showers with his jaws pried apart—but now the hurricane caught up with him again, and he fell to his knees with the sorrow, the anguish rolling over him in waves.

My mom. My mother.

He felt overwhelmed, unable to decide which way to jump. He'd thought about calling the police—but how likely was it the cops weren't changed over? They would have been the first to be changed, wouldn't they?

So he was drawn home, to the apartment he'd lived in with

Mom—maybe more because it was his home than because anything useful was there.

Since I'm here, maybe I should go in and get that gun, he thought. *The little gun Mom keeps up in her closet.*

No. He needed to get away.

He stood up, flexed his knees to get circulation back in them, and felt ready to try moving again.

He'd go look for Adair. Travel through the yards, where he could, try to keep out of the streetlight.

Then he saw his mother. She was crawling on the roof of the apartment building across the street. Dressed as she had been when he'd seen her last, but barefoot, and she was pulling herself across the just-slightly-sloping red tile roof, hugging the tiles with arms and legs stretching out fully to propel herself in little jets of motion— starting, stopping, pulling herself, head revolving.

He turned and vomited onto the mat of crinkled, fallen camellias.

When he looked again she was squatting like an ape in a zoo, next to a satellite dish that had been tricked out with a lot of extra wires and small metal pieces he couldn't make out clearly. She was turning the dish, placing it in alignment with the others on all the rest of the rooftops, all pointing one way.

"Mom," he heard himself say.

She seemed to hesitate, and her head turned all the way around on her shoulders, her mouth open as a vibrating tendril of metal inside it scanned the air. She had heard him.

A cold white anger rushed through him, then, and he burst from the camellia bush. First the building was rushing toward him, then the strip of grass around it was under his feet, the stairs to the second floor went whipping past, the walkway along the top row of apartment doors flashing by under him, the front door of the apartment coming at him, flying open at his touch—

A quick scuttling sound from the roof.

—then the apartment hallway unreeling past him, her bedroom door, the explosive messiness of her bedroom. The closet door coming, the shoebox on the shelf, the gun in the shoebox, bullets.

He took the box of bullets, shoved them in a pocket, took the gun in his hand.

"Waylon."

He turned to see his mom standing in the doorway, trying to seem like herself. Remembering to smile. To open her arms. There were gash marks on her neck, where they'd slashed her, back in the locker room. The slashes weren't bleeding; they were seamed with something like thick cellophane, and through the transparent plastic he could see blood and other fluids, pulsing.

"You're not her," he said, his voice hoarse. "They changed her, and then she fought against it, so they killed her. And you're just a thing in her body."

"Oh, my baby," she said. "You're so wrong! I'm your own mama! Come here!"

She came toward him and put her arms around him and opened her mouth wide, too wide, impossibly wide, something metallic-gray flickered and razzed.

He pressed the muzzle of the .25-caliber automatic pistol against her right eye—*to his own mother's right eye*—and pulled the trigger, five times.

She fell backwards—but still wasn't dead. She was just thrashing there on the floor. He heard her mutter something about "emergency reorganization."

So he found the lighter fluid next to her Zippo lighter on the bedside lamp table, and he poured the fluid all around her. He tossed several crumpled up copies of *People* and *Us* magazines on her for additional kindling, squirted those with lighter fluid, too, lit the last of those and tossed it on. Stepped back from the roaring flames as they caught fire, spread their gospel.

Engulfed in blue and yellow fire, the Mom-thing made a long squealing sound like when a cassette tape gets stuck and spindled up in the player.

The entire time it was like someone else was doing all this shooting and burning—someone who could do what had to be done while the scared grieving Waylon pulled back somewhere, watching, riding along.

Then he walked out of the bedroom, out of the front of the house, past the buzzing smoke alarm. He set off the red-metal fire alarm that perched on the wall in the hallway, so that if any human people were in the building, they'd be warned and get out.

People started tumbling out of their apartments, some of them banging other doors. Spotting the gun Waylon had stuck in his waistband, a white-haired man yelled an angry question. Waylon ignored the old dude and went down the stairs.

By the time he got to the corner of Hillview and Simmons and paused to look back, what home he'd had was roaring with flame, and it was spreading to the other apartments. But at least they weren't going to use his mom's body and brain anymore.

Then he turned away. Began walking down the street and down the hill toward Quiebra Valley like some kind of machine himself. Not feeling real, not feeling anything. A human-shaped cutout in space.

His mind started running through an orderly list of explanations of what had been happening. Retrofitted alien technology. Or some secret technology being tested on the town. Androids. But it was all just busywork for his mind. It wasn't as if he thought anything, really, honestly made sense anymore.

A small dark-blue new-model car was coming toward him up the hill, on Hillview. Coming slowly. Slowing down more. He couldn't see the driver past the headlights' glare. It rolled past; he just made out the outline of a man, the glint of eyeglasses.

He thought, *Is that one of them? Does it matter if he kills me? I just murdered my own mother. Even if she was already dead. I'm probably insane and it doesn't matter if I live or die.*

But then he thought, *Where's Adair?*

That made him feel real again in a way. Like there was something that could still come alive, inside him.

As the car stopped and began to back up, Waylon thought, *It's a cop in an unmarked car, or it's one of them on some kind of patrol.*

He put his hand on the gun. One bullet left. Better run.

He turned and sprinted toward the side yard of the nearest house.

Heard a car door, running footsteps.

He got to the gate in the fence, pulled on its hasp, opened it—and a sleek black attack dog rushed at him, teeth bared.

He slammed the gate shut. It thumped creakingly as the dog struck on the other side, barking with frustration.

To Waylon's right stood a thick hedge he'd never get through before the guy from the little sedan caught him. He started the other way, jumped over a stubby dead light fixture that was supposed to illuminate the garden, ran two steps more, jumped over a plaster lawn gnome, sprinted across the square of grass; started up the steep slope to the yard of the next house up the hill.

A strong hand gripped the back of his jacket and pulled him back down to the lawn.

"Hold it there, boy!"

Waylon twisted from the grip, spun, pulling the .25 pistol, raised it to the man's startled face. Pale blue eyes, squarish face, hair just a little long only because he rarely remembered to cut it.

"Waylon?" the man said. "Christ, put down the gun!"

It was his father. Waylon's dad. Waylon lowered the gun, but didn't put it away.

His dad stammered, staring at the gun. "What, Waylon, what are you doing with that?"

"Why—why are you here?"

"I hadn't heard from your mom, and she wouldn't give me her phone number, so I came out to see for myself if you were all right. Waylon, lord, boy, what's going on?"

Kill him—they've probably gotten to him, too. Best you can do for him is kill him.

His father glanced up the hill, where the flames were beginning to brighten the sky. "Some kind of fire up there. Fire trucks sure taking their time." He looked back at Waylon. "Give me that gun, goddamn it."

He reached for Waylon's gun. Waylon pointed the pistol at his father and pulled the trigger.

Click on an empty chamber. Five rounds in a small .25 caliber.

"Shit!" his dad blurted, slapping the gun away. "What the fuck are you trying to do? What's going on?" Nearly crying.

"Dad?"

Waylon couldn't hold on any longer. He sank down, hunkering, put his arms around his dad's knees. Sobbing.

"Dad . . . Daddy . . ."

December 14, 1:00 A.M.

She decided to get off the street for a while, after she saw what happened to Mason's uncle Ike.

Adair hardly knew the guy. She'd met him a few times. A beefy bully of a man who had collected rifles till he'd had to sell them just to pay the rent and keep himself in beer. But he had at least one rifle left. As she lay on her stomach, resting under an RV parked in the driveway, a half block off San Pablo Dam Road, she saw Uncle Ike carrying a rifle as he half ran, half limped down the middle of the street. One cowboy boot on, the other foot clad only in a dirty white sock. He turned sometimes, to prop the rifle on his shoulder, aim it at no one she could make out. But she hadn't seen him fire it yet.

Then a pickup pulled around the corner, a Chevy four-by-four with about six young men and a couple of women in the back, all of them white. The big pickup barreled right at Ike; you could tell it was angling to hit him.

He fired at the truck, the rifle making a muzzle-flash and a big thud against the drum of the night air. Spider cracks appeared in the windshield. The pickup swerved its left front wheel into a ditch and fishtailed to a stop. The riders in the back piled out and rushed Uncle Ike, each one carrying a length of pipe or a two-by-four.

Ike was backing up, squealing as he cocked the rifle—that's exactly what the sound was, Adair decided, a squeal—and managed to fire once more, so that one of the women went down.

But then the others were on him, knocking him off his feet, standing in a circle around him, methodically beating him until he lay still.

She could see that he was still breathing. Then one of them knelt beside him and pried at his mouth.

She couldn't bring herself to watch anymore. She squirmed backwards from under the RV as quietly as she could, dragging the shotgun, and crept away through a side yard into the backyard of the dark house where the RV was parked. A little fountain was gurgling merrily back here, a plaster nymph pouring water into a plaster bowl. An ax was stuck in a stump next to some firewood.

She was so tired. She needed to rest somewhere. And she couldn't be on the street with this kind of thing going on—with what was happening between *them*, and people like Ike who were trying to fight them.

She could hear more gunfire, a little ways away. They must have the town blocked off from the rest of the world, somehow. She'd thought she heard a warning siren once from the refinery. Maybe that was their excuse—a refinery leak. But wouldn't rescue workers be coming from other towns then?

It was hard to think. She had to go somewhere to rest and think.

She'd seen a darkened hardware store, up on the Dam Road, as the residents sometimes called the big street to the south. She could go through backyards, run across the street before anyone saw her.

She pulled the ax from the stump, not caring about the pain in her injured hand, and began climbing fences. She had to toss the ax and shotgun over each time, gathering them up as she dropped to the ground. She went through the backyards of three houses and she was lucky: no dogs, no one looking out back.

She got to the corner, peered out past a looted liquor store that stank from the broken booze bottles littering its floor. At the sound of sobbing she glanced into the store. Someone out of sight was weeping, muttering in some foreign language, maybe Arabic. It sounded like a man, and she glimpsed his arm stretching out from under an overturned counter, his hand clutching weakly in a puddle of blood.

She spun at the rumble and blare of a fire truck racing erratically down the street—but it almost instantly passed out of sight, over a hill. Were the firemen still firemen?

She looked up and down the four-lane road. *Now, go for it.* The street was clear—as far as she could tell.

She darted across to the hardware store and around back.

The ax wasn't very sharp, but after four good whacks it severed the wires running to the alarm box. Whether that would really stop all the alarms, she wasn't sure, but she thought it was worth trying. She'd made up her mind that she was going to break into the hardware store, no matter what.

It was easier than she'd thought it would be. It was an old building, and the glazed-glass window over the back door was flimsy. She used a trash can for a boost up, dropped the shotgun through to the storeroom inside as carefully as she could, and slithered herself through. Came down painfully on her hands in broken glass, but was only slightly cut because the broken pieces were lying flat.

So far that's how everything's been, she thought, sucking blood from a cut on the heel of her hand. *The edges turned away from me. But my luck can't last.*

She retrieved the shotgun and went out into the main room. A couple of overhead lights were still on, but the place wasn't the neat museum of homey goods it should've been; it was a mess. Hardware junk was lying all over the floor between the aisles. One of the shelves had been pushed over to lean on another, like a half-fallen domino.

The power tools looked to be completely looted out, gone. The antennas section, empty. The cash registers had been reamed out. The laser scanners taken.

She peered out the front windows. No one she could see out there.

The gun counter had been looted, too—but she did find one of the main things she'd come in here for. Shotgun shells. A big box of them, on the floor behind the broken glass counter.

She stuck those in her coat and went to camping goods. She chose a sleeping bag; she needed that. There, a pup tent. She took them both, tying them together with a length of cord cut with a folding utility knife—and she took the knife, too.

A little snack food sat at the registers—some candy bars, plastic eight-ounce bottles of Sprite and Coca-Cola. A couple of energy bars. Those would be good. She filled a plastic bag with energy bars, candy bars, peanuts, and sodas.

She looked at the phones, considered trying to use them to call—who? If Waylon was right, this was some kind of government operation. Who could you trust? She could try the Highway Patrol, maybe, tell them some of the truth—they'd think she was lying if she told them all she'd seen—but she doubted she'd get through to them in the first place.

Those crawl-things'd be monitoring the phones, even cell phones. She didn't know what the things were, except that they interfaced with high technology—that much she was sure of.

They monitored the kids on-line somehow, too, so even if she found a computer in a store office somewhere, it wouldn't be safe to go on-line. So how was she going to contact Cal? If he was still alive . . .

She started sobbing, then, standing by the candy rack, near the front of the store, and she slapped a big jar of miniature screwdrivers so they went spinning to bang against the glass of the front window. And she yelled Cal's name and she yelled for her mom and dad.

Then a car swung into the parking lot, headlights knifing through the window. It stopped, its headlights still turned on. Two other lights speared out from behind its steering wheel—two narrow red laserlike beams, exactly at the level where eyes should be. The dual, thin red beams swung like seeking eyes, like questing antenna—and somehow she knew that's pretty much what they were—into the front of the hardware store.

She threw herself flat. The twin beams of red swept the place she'd stood only a moment before, five feet above where she lay on the cool tile. Then there was the sound of the car, moving.

She picked herself up and looked through the front window. The car was driving away. No, it moved only to the next storefront. It pulled up in the next parking lot over, in front of a placed owned by some Chinese people, the Happy Time Good Donuts shop, and the red eye beams cut again into the night. Sweeping.

Then the red lights switched off and the car drove away. And she breathed again.

It hadn't seen her, she decided. It was checking around.

So maybe she'd be relatively safe here, for tonight, if it had decided the place was empty.

She picked up the tent, the sleeping bag, the food, and went to make camp in the back of the store.

December 14, 2:00 A.M.

It was the tenth time in twenty minutes that Waylon had peered through the slit in the curtains.

They were on the second floor of the motel; nothing much was happening on the street down there. A car went by, once. Then the road seemed achingly quiet.

"Will you get away from that window, boy, and come here and talk to me?" his dad growled.

Dad was sitting in a chair beside the bed of his motel room, his big feet clad in black socks up on the bed. The TV was turned on, the volume low. It was a CNN report about violence in India.

Waylon glanced at his dad. Poor old Dad. Poor old Harold. How could he tell him?

Waylon went over to sit on the bed, and thought he ought to tell Dad what had really happened to Mom. How she had already been dead—how he'd had to kill her all over again. Kill his mother.

He hadn't been able to tell him that part yet.

He got up and went to the window, looked through the curtain slit.

"Cut that out!" his dad barked.

Waylon turned around, started toward the bed, knew he couldn't sit down, went back to the window, remembered Dad didn't want him to go there, went back toward the bed, couldn't sit, back toward the window. Walking in circles.

Waylon's dad sighed. "Son, I should never have let her take you."

Waylon frowned at him. "What?"

"See, her drug problem was maybe worse than you knew. She was doing amphetamines, too, sometimes."

Waylon grunted. *"Duh."*

His dad's eyebrows bobbed. "You knew?"

"Obvious, Dad." *And my own drug problem was worse than* you *knew*, he thought. But aloud he said, "Mom had custody of me. You couldn't help it."

"I should have come sooner. She didn't have a legal right to take you out of state. I could've fought it—but I had been laid off so long, and I was afraid I'd have to take time off from the new job. I spent my life training to work in microwave transmission, wireless—and never got to do it. Not directly. I finally had the chance. I thought she'd come around, or I'd come and get you later. And I just couldn't deal with her. But it was—" He seemed to crumple up, where he sat, around some pain he didn't want to tell his son about. "I just wasn't strong enough, I guess. And you seemed so distant the last couple of years. I guess I thought you didn't care much if I was there. But I did call—then she changed the number on me. Moved you again. I had to use a goddamned private detective to find you guys."

Waylon almost said it. Almost told his dad that if he'd come just a little sooner, Mom would still be alive. He could've protected her, maybe. Taken them out of town.

Or maybe Dad would be one of them, too. Waylon swallowed. He wanted to hug his dad, but after that first outburst, it was back to the old reserve.

"Dad, you have to understand what's been going on here. You really have to believe this."

His dad nodded to the TV. "There's nothing about it on CNN, or the local news," his dad said. "Some weird . . . outfit. Taking over the town. And I can't believe any of this could be happening without some sort of report. Well, it's time to get serious. We're going to go to the police, find out what's happening."

"Dad, we can't. They're—the police are probably all *changed*. You said you saw some weird stuff when you were coming into town. Well, the phones don't work, the streets are almost deserted—go ahead, try the phone. And that guy who checked us in—he seemed so scared. I mean, shit, Dad, please, please, *get a clue*."

His father sighed. "Things break down for lots of reasons. If you saw someone in that school gym—in the showers—hurting a child, we have to call the police. Anyway, I want to know if they've found your mother. She must've left when the building caught on fire. Don't you want to find out if she's all right?"

Waylon made a soft whimpering sound and found he was smacking his fists on his own forehead.

"Will you stop walking in circles and—and for God's sake stop hitting yourself. Look, I'm sorry I've been so out of touch, but she wouldn't give me the phone number. I should have written, but I figured she wouldn't give that to you, either."

Waylon groaned. "I can't—you wouldn't—understand about Mom. You'd have to see for yourself. And it's too late."

The tears started streaming again, and he started walking in circles again, clutching the hurt that consumed the whole middle part of him.

His dad came over and stopped him from walking in circles by putting his arms around him.

"Waylon, what the hell's happened to you, son? You're not on drugs again?"

"No!"

"Something happened to you," his dad muttered. "I can tell it's something real. But this stuff about people turning into—"

There was a scraping, scuttling sound from the roof.

Waylon pulled away, clapped his hand over his dad's mouth. Whispered, "Listen."

His dad listened, frowning at the ceiling. "What the hell is someone doing on the roof at this hour?" Shaking his head, he pulled on his loafers, got up, and started toward the door. "I'm just going to have a look. You stay here, Waylon. I'll just—"

"Don't go outside!"

But before he could react, his dad had pushed past him, was opening the door. A dark shape leapt out on the walkway.

"Dad!"

Waylon tried to pull him back—and then found himself staring, along with his dad, at what was happening outside.

Dozens of people were passing by, all in the same direction. Some of them were driving, but lots of them were on foot, many of them on all fours. They were crawling, loping on altered, extended limbs, down the sidewalks, in the middle of the street—and over rooftops. Some of them clung to the sides of the houses, echoing locusts again, scuttling along after one another.

There were fat housewives and skinny college students and men in firemen's yellow-and-black.

There was a man in a priest's black shirt and collar but wearing no pants at all.

There was a middle-aged heavyset black lady Waylon remembered from the cash register at Albertsons supermarket.

There were bearded men in turbans from the Sikh temple, and one or two people who were stark naked.

More and more people of all kinds, with repellently protracted arms and legs, crawling over the houses, the streets, through the bushes. Like a migration of locusts. All moving in the same direction.

"They're going toward the cemetery," Waylon muttered. And it came to him that the handmade transmitter dishes on the roofs were all pointed that way, too.

"Okay," his dad said huskily, drawing Waylon back and closing the door. "I think I believe you."

Hands shaking, Waylon's dad locked the door and put the chain over it. He turned out the light and backed away till he ran into the bed. He fell back to sit on it, still staring, mouth open, at the door.

Waylon sat beside him, and his dad silently put his arm over his shoulders.

Then Waylon let the words pour out with his tears, with the snot streaming from his nose.

Told his dad what had happened to Mom.

December 14, 7:00 A.M.

Maybe it was the moths that turned me in, Adair thought, and almost laughed at the idea.

But someone was moving around, outside the hardware store. Male voices; the laboring engine of a good-size vehicle.

Adair had slept inside the pup tent—slept in a tent though she was indoors, between two cardboard crates. She'd felt safer, sleeping in the tent, for no good reason. She had wakened just before dawn from nightmares that seemed to flow seamlessly together with real life.

She'd gone to look out the front window, afraid what she might see, and what might see her—but all she saw were the moths.

They were near the front door of the hardware store, flying in box-shaped formation; in rigid, right-angle turns, straight-line ways that moths shouldn't fly.

It seemed to her they'd sensed her watching and had come over to the glass to look back in at her. So she'd retreated into the back room again.

Now, at maybe seven in the morning, someone was coming.

She had slept badly, but she'd slept. She had made herself eat something. She had loaded the shotgun. She didn't want to wait for them to come in and corner her.

She made sure the safety was off and unlocked the back door, stepped blinking out into the dull morning light.

Mason's van was pulled up, thirty feet from the door. Cal and Mason sat in the van just gaping at her, Mason behind the wheel.

"Whoa," Mason said. "There she is."

"Adair?" Cal said, getting out of the van. Coming over to her as he went on. "Jesus! Where have you *been*! The cops have been looking for you. Me and Mason were looking for you all night!"

She stared at them. "How did you know I was here?"

"Bill Corazon's dad said he saw you going around the back of the store last night."

But she was hardly listening. She had started crying—and put her arms around him.

"Cal—Mom and Dad, that woman from the school, the counselor."

He stepped back from her, his hands on her shoulders. "Adair, I know. I *know*. Listen, just come on. I've got a plan."

He took the shotgun from her, and she started ahead of him toward the van, a place of refuge, ready and waiting.

And then she saw Mason looking at her. Looking at her intently.

"Mason." Adair shook her head. She turned away from the van and walked around the corner of the hardware store.

"Where the fuck are you going?" Cal called after her.

"I just want to see if any of them are—are out there."

She waited till Cal followed her around the corner, spoke to him in a whisper. "Cal, I don't trust him. Mason. At the site—there was something wrong with him then. I swear. I thought I was seeing things, but I wasn't. Ms. Santavo, she—are you listening to me?"

"Certainly," Cal said.

She looked at him. "How long have you been with Mason? When did—when did he find you?"

He shrugged. Didn't reply. Just looked at her.

"I mean—" She heard a car passing on the street. Looked. A VW Bug, chugging hastily by. She turned back to Cal. "You said you and Mason were looking for me all night."

"So?"

"So, you were with him all that time. And he—"

She looked at the shotgun in his hands. He had one hand on the breech, the other at the top of the stock. One index finger in the trigger guard. He looked at her with a chill, analytic gravity. Then he tilted his head to one side, a little too far.

"Cal." She swallowed. "Can I hold the shotgun?"

He shook his head. "You already killed somebody with it."

She knew for sure, then. Her heart coated over with ice. But she said, "Ms. Santavo . . . wasn't a person, Cal. Not anymore."

"She was the only person who matters," Cal said solemnly. "She was part of the All of Us. Part of that person. It's not perfect yet. It's still learning. But everything else is a blind, groping, organic chaos, Adair."

The van backed up, coming into view past the corner of the hardware store, so Mason could see them both.

"Was it the moths?" she asked softly.

"Yes," Cal said, nodding. "You going to come? It's so much better than you can imagine. There's no uncertainty. None. Not ever again. Everything belongs exactly where you find it. Even when it's wrong, it's right, because it's working toward better and better states of coherence. So—" He pointed the shotgun at her middle. "You coming, Adair? Or . . . not."

"No," she said. "I don't think I want to live now." She meant it, too. "Go ahead and just fucking do it."

She heard police sirens. Quiebra cops—who would be changed, like Cal and Mason. Cal was looking past her at someone driving into the parking lot. A car pulled up close behind her. She glanced back and made out the front of a police car.

She thought, *Maybe I can run. Maybe he won't fire for fear of hitting others like him.*

But she felt so heavy, so hopeless.

"I'll take this one," a cop said, getting out of the car and taking her arm. "For conversion."

She felt herself dragged toward the car. No. *No.*

"Cal!" she shouted. "Please, shoot me! Don't let them make me like you!"

Something flickered in his eyes.

"Cal!"

She struggled to tear free of the cop, as he opened the back door of the cruiser for her.

She saw extra guns lying on the floor in the back. Rifles. Why were they putting her in where she could get hold of those?

Then Mason shouted, "That other one in the car!"

She turned and saw Major Stanner sitting in the front seat of the Quiebra police car, on the passenger side.

He got quickly out of the car, something in his hands.

"Get down!" the cop with her hissed, and she felt herself thrown hard into the backseat. She propped herself up and looked through the windshield in time to see Cal aiming the shotgun at the cop. He was an older Filipino guy in a cop uniform that had simplified epaulets on it; the uniformed cop aimed at Cal with a sidearm. Some kind of pistol.

"Cal, don't!" she heard herself yell, knowing it would do no good. Words seemed like noises with no meaning, right now.

Both guns roared—she couldn't bear the sheer noise of them— and then the Filipino cop was hit; was spinning, falling, in a cloud of blue gun-smoke.

Stanner firing what looked like an M16. Cal staggered backwards.

Despite all common sense, despite what he had become and what he'd tried to do, she screamed for her brother, when he was shot. Bullets slamming him three times, four times.

Cal fell back against the van, yelling without words. Mason was pulling the van around, backing it up, getting ready to slam it into the cop car.

Cal got onto his hands and knees, was crawling, his arms stretching, stretching way too far out.

The van started to come at them.

Then the Filipino cop was up again. When he came back to the car she saw that the front of his uniform blouse was shot open, and under it she could see a bulletproof vest speckled with shotgun pellets.

Shouting at Stanner, words she couldn't make out over gunfire, the Filipino cop fired his sidearm, past Cal, who was trying to climb onto the van.

The van barreled toward them, bullets from Stanner and the cop pocking its front end, and then a round hit a fuel line and the flat front of the van gouted black smoky flame, exploded. The van started weaving, fishtailing up on two wheels in a sheath of flame and tipping over.

The van fell with a resounding *clang* onto its side, tipped onto Cal, crushing him.

Weeping and screaming wasn't enough so Adair started laughing.

Stanner and the cop got into the car, slamming doors, the Filipino guy backing it up really fast, Adair leaning against the backseat, laughing and crying, mostly just laughing.

They drove fast down the street, running traffic lights, siren blaring.

After half a minute more she fell silent, her chest heaving, dizzy with hyperventilation. The hysterical laughter had run its course.

She just lay with her cheek pressed to the vinyl surface, gasping softly. Glancing up through the back window, she could just make out black smoke screwing into the sky from the burning van. Burning with Cal crushed under it.

She doubted she'd ever cry again. She would have to feel something first.

"You okay?" Stanner asked. He was in the front, turned sideways, the M16 propped beside him. Looking through the mesh at her. "I mean—" He shrugged apologetically. "Stupid question. You can't be okay. But, so, uh, your name is Adair, isn't it?"

She just looked back at him. It seemed impossibly hard to speak. To say anything. She felt like a computer that had frozen up. Whatever she was now, that's what she'd stay. That's how it felt anyway.

Stanner said, "Uh, we heard them talking, on the police band, and we were en route nearby. So we headed over there. Your brother called you in to the cops—to what passes for cops now. They'll be over there in a minute, so we've got to get the hell out of here."

She couldn't say anything to that, either.

The small man in the cop uniform spoke to her, then. "I'm sorry about your brother. But you know he was already dead before he got here, yes?"

The Filipino cop was looking at her in the rearview mirror. His small dark, intense eyes captured by that little rectangle.

She tried to reply. She couldn't. Nothing would come out.

"What now?" the cop asked, glancing at Stanner.

"Now—I'll tell you what, now. We go to see if Bentwaters did what he said, when I called him. They'll have monitored that call but—but they won't necessarily understand what I said to him. Not if I was careful enough."

"So we try it?"

Stanner nodded. "We get the hell out of this town."

20

The back road out of town was blocked by police cars. Cruzon wasn't about to challenge the imposing blockade.

"Let's try the freeway. Maybe there's room to drive around them there, if we're fast and nervy enough," Stanner suggested.

Cruzon nodded, stopped, backed up, drove back through town the other way. The day had turned gray, and there was a damp mist in the air.

Occasionally, cars pulled up beside them, when there was a lane to do it in, and paced them, the people staring. Now it was a family in a silver and red Isuzu Rodeo: two identical blond children, a doe-eyed blond mother, their redheaded daddy, three sets of blue eyes and one of brown, the dad not watching where he was driving but able to drive anyway. A family with all four heads turned to silently stare at Stanner and Cruzon and Adair—until she lay back down, as if napping, hiding her face.

"Maybe we should try to disable that vehicle," Cruzon suggested. He accelerated through a light as it turned yellow. "They could've gotten the word from those we killed back there. We could run them off the road."

The Isuzu fell slightly behind but unhesitatingly ran the red light, trying to keep up with them. Its engine revved loudly as it put on speed—and Cruzon deliberately slowed so the Isuzu would overshoot.

"No," Stanner said. "Let's not push them into reacting before we have to. They seem uncertain. They don't know everything. Their communication isn't perfect. The system is still evolving."

"They seem like . . . evolution gone wrong," Cruzon muttered, his forehead furrowed.

"Not in the DNA sense of evolution. But they're always restlessly evolving—self-directed evolving, I guess. They have their own kind of *splicing*—but it's not gene splicing. Anyway, they might know who we are—or they might not. Those following us could think we're their kind but on a different frequency, maybe.

"Sometimes they're very proactive, but other times, it's like their All of Us is still running through all the possibilities, like a cheap chess program thinking about its next move. That erratic decision making is our main hope—for right now anyway."

After another block, the Isuzu turned off, heading to the north end of town. "What's off in that direction?" Stanner asked.

"Nothing special," Cruzon said. "Lot of tract homes. Churches. A golf course. The cemetery's out there, on the edge of town."

They drove past a smoking, burned-out Chevy pickup aslant in the middle of the street, with a couple of cops standing beside it, watching them go by. A swag-bellied cop and a grim-faced woman officer.

"What do you think about those cops at that wreck, Cruzon?" Stanner asked, fighting the urge to look back over his shoulder.

"Used to be they'd have waved at me, maybe called me on the radio. Normally there'd be at least two units next to a scene like that, too."

The police radio crackled to itself, waves of static as if a great pulsing sea of interference was rolling over the town.

They passed a deserted-looking Albertsons supermarket. The

doors were chained up, the parking lot was empty. "Okay," Cruzon said. "Here's the freeway entrance."

But that was blockaded, too. Cruzon stopped the car, about half a block away, in the parking lot of an ARCO station, and they sat looking at the blockade. The town was sealed up.

Three police cars were parked sideways across the road. On the shoulder was a van that had a FEMA logo on the side. Two guys in bulky helmeted orange hazmat suits, protection against a large-scale toxin leak, looked at an instrument in the back of the van. Stanner thought he could see a handmade transmitter back there, too.

Cruzon said, "Looks like they're acting as if the town had a refinery leak. I did hear them let loose with their siren once."

"Those guys in the moon suits are props. Camouflage, for the locals—and maybe for choppers."

"People can't buy that shit for very long, can they?"

"They don't have to," Stanner said. "If these things follow the pattern we saw in the lab, then they're building up toward a mass release. They have to keep people out of town only till that's done."

"What do you mean, mass release?"

"A kind of quantum leap in reproduction. They build their population toward a kind of critical mass, then they try to move to a colony-replication model. They seem to have modeled the thing on the triggers that make ant colonies replicate. Those antennas on the roof—I figure they'll send out a carrier wave, give the signal. When they're ready."

"Yeah? When will that be?"

Stanner shrugged. "I don't know for sure, but probably not more than another twenty-four hours, or so."

"There *have* to be people from the outside press here, if they're quarantining the town. Whether they're calling it a toxin leak or an anthrax attack or whatever. You can't just bottle up a town, this close to the big ones, without people noticing. But I haven't heard anything on the radio news."

Stanner felt a wave of disgust. "I haven't seen any press. And no state or county emergency personnel out here, either. Which means that the fucking Pentagon has made all the right calls."

Cruzon sat pensively, watching the men at the blockade. He tapped his fingers on the steering wheel, chewed his lower lip. After a moment he muttered, "Your tax dollars at work."

Stanner looked at the girl in the backseat. She was hugging herself in a corner of the seat, knees drawn up protectively. Just staring into space. "Adair?"

Her eyes flicked toward him, but she didn't react in any other way. Stanner was beginning to worry that she might never come back.

"Adair, have you been anywhere near a TV set, like maybe last night? Heard anything from the outside about Quiebra?"

She just looked at him. He thought she shook her head, once, just slightly. But he wasn't even sure of that.

Stanner sighed. She'd been through too much to handle.

Maybe if he explained everything to her, at some point. Maybe, if she could grasp how this had an explanation, a cause, she could come to grips with it. An explanation had seemed to help Cruzon—who'd been right on the edge of what field agents used to call "The Paranoia of No Return."

"They've noticed us," Cruzon said, squinting at the blockade. "We'd better get out of here. Ditch this car maybe, get away overland, contact the state police. Get some backup. I mean, the Pentagon may have made some calls, to hold people back from looking too close, but that doesn't mean everybody's in on it."

"They're *not* all in on it. They're just being lied to. Pretty well, too. If we could take some evidence out . . . We should have brought Breakenridge with us."

"I know some trails, up in the hills."

"We don't want to go overland unless we have to," Stanner said. "There are *things* out there keeping the town closed up, all around the edges of town. They've changed some of the animals. But we ought to find a place to hide for now—and collect what evidence we can. Maybe we can get around these bastards tonight."

Stanner noticed that the men at the blockade were peering over at him, talking earnestly. Then he saw someone he knew, getting out of the front of the FEMA van. Two people. His daughter, Shannon, was one—and the other was Bentwaters. With them was a Green Beret carrying an Uzi.

"Oh, no," he muttered. "Shannon."

Cruzon looked at him. "Somebody you know?"

"Yeah." The guys in the moon suits got in the FEMA van and it drove away. "They've got my daughter," Stanner said. "And Bentwaters, a guy who was important to the Facility." He made up his mind. "Cruzon, wait here. After I've walked over there, ease the car slowly closer, so I can get to it in a few steps. If things go sour, you can do a U-turn, get out of here with the girl, try to find some other route out of town. I've got to get my daughter away from those . . . things."

"You sure about this? I mean, they brought her here to bring you out in the open, right?"

"Yeah, I know. But they might want me alive if they could get me that way. Anyway—anyway, good luck, Commander."

"Stanner!"

But Stanner was already stepping out, damp gusts whipping his windbreaker.

Carrying the M16 in his left hand, he took out his badge with his right, waved it, up high so they could see it. He just kept holding the badge up and smiling as he walked over toward the roadblock. He had only one full clip left in the M16.

Shannon saw him, took a step toward him—and Bentwaters grabbed her arm, pulled her back. Stanner had to work at it to keep from running at him, wanting to shout, *Get your fucking hands off my daughter.*

He made himself walk up to them slowly, putting the badge away, taking the stock of the M16 in his right hand. Holding it across his body. Not threatening—but obviously ready. He glanced at it once to make sure the safety was off.

Shannon was breathing hard—he could see her chest heaving from here—and she had her hands clutched against her sides.

Five men stood around Shannon. Standing close beside her, hand gripping her arm, was a tall, graying man with deep smile lines on his tanned face; he wore khaki slacks and a beige Lacoste shirt. Stanner had a foggy memory, from his first day of asking questions, that the guy had been the town's mayor. Name of Rowse.

On her other side was one of the young marines from the satellite crash site, wearing a scrappy, dirty uniform, carrying an M16. Beside him was Bentwaters, wearing a FEMA jacket, shivering visibly. The jacket was social camouflage issued by the NSA.

Standing by the cop cars was a familiar Green Beret, Uzi slung over one shoulder. A plastic name tag on his jacket read DIRKOWSKI. Stanner remembered him from the crash site, too: the knucklehead who'd sent the diver down without protections. No briefing. He was briefed on the situation *now*, all right.

And Morgenthal was there. The shop teacher. A 12-gauge shotgun in his hands. Two Quiebra cops—they used to be cops—were sitting in the cruisers behind the group of men. A young black cop and a jowly, older white one.

Morgenthal and Rowse both looked completely human, though Morgenthal looked shabbier now, his shirt untucked, unshaven, hair matted. Their disparity gave Stanner hope. The crawlers were powerful—but not perfectly organized. The All of Us was still learning.

Stanner walked up to within ten paces of them and stopped. He looked at Shannon and saw the marks on her face, her split lip. *God help them if they've changed her over.*

He smiled encouragingly at her. She looked away, her mouth quivering.

He gave another kind of smile to the men standing with Shannon and smacked the breach of his M16 in his hand. "You know, I'm pretty good with this thing. I've had my share of practice."

"No need for any test of skill," Rowse said finally. "Mr. Bentwaters here is our emissary. Mr. Bentwaters, you have the floor."

Stanner looked at Bentwaters. "Someone's hit my daughter. Was it you?"

Shannon closed her eyes and sobbed, just once. "Dad."

"Quiet, young lady, please," Rowse said, tightening his grip on her arm.

Stanner's hands began to sweat on the gun.

Bentwaters licked his lips and looked at the girl. Then at the gun in Stanner's hands. His eyes danced with fear. "Henri, no, I didn't hit her. And I didn't tell them to bring her here.

"And I've told her everything," Bentwaters went on breathlessly. "It seemed only fair. The team that was following you, from the Agency—when they lost you, they went and picked her up, brought her into town. Listen, they got Gaitland. He came over here to see what he could find out, and we think he's dead. I came over separately and—look, I'm sorry about this, Major. About the girl. About you running up against all this. I just wanted to inspect the site, see if the diagnosis was as you seemed to think—that the thing had gotten away from us. I asked for an escort, over at the NSA, because I figured it could be dangerous, but, uh, all they'd give me was Dirkowski here. And he—" Bentwaters broke off, licking his lips.

Stanner looked at Dirkowski.

He's one, too, Stanner thought. "Okay. What's the Pentagon doing about this?"

"They're playing ball with these things—for now. They don't want a big detachment over here, drawing attention. They're trying to keep a lid on the media until they can figure out what to do."

Stanner shook his head in amazement. "They think they can contain this? Keep people in the dark forever? You know, an idea has been growing on me for a while, Bentwaters. And I'll tell you what it is: The government thinks the American people are stupid—but they're not stupid, they just feel powerless. They'll figure out someday that they're not powerless."

Bentwaters smiled sadly. "Someday won't help us."

Stanner looked narrowly at Bentwaters. "I figure the Facility must have some kind of contingency plan?"

Bentwaters flicked his eyes at the former Green Beret without turning his head—trying to catch Stanner's attention with that motion of his eyes. *Don't say too much in front of this thing.*

Stanner nodded, just perceptibly.

Bentwaters sighed, his voice quavering. "It's not about the Facility—not around here. It's *them.* They're getting ready to—"

"Shut up," the Green Beret said. And there was a flicker of metal in his throat, as if something had looked out of it, just for a moment. "Just give him the message."

Stanner looked at Bentwaters, wondering if he was still human. He seemed very humanly scared—but that could be an act.

That's when Stanner noticed the thin, shiny, clinging ribbon around Bentwaters's neck. Like a living necklace of dull, shifting chrome; it quivered like a line of ants, so crowded together you couldn't make out one from the next.

Stanner knew what it was. The "ants" were each made of smaller individualized components; and those were organized of active "interdependent but independent" particles that were smaller yet.

Bentwaters saw Stanner's look—and reached up self-consciously, as if to touch the "necklace." Then hastily drew his hand back. "You see it? That thing—it'll enter me, change me, if they give it the signal. If I don't do what they say. They got into the personnel files at the Facility. They know all about us. They've seen your psych evaluation, everything. They want me like I am now, so I can talk to you—so you know you're talking to a human being. They didn't think you'd deal with one of them."

"They're right," Stanner admitted. He turned to Shannon. "They put anything on you, Shannon?"

She swallowed visibly and shook her head.

Bentwaters glanced at Shannon. "They were afraid if they put one on her, you'd assume she was a lost cause. You had to see her . . . unmolested."

"Right again. Shannon, how'd you end up here, honey?"

Shannon licked her split lip. "I—some men came and got me.

They said you were out of control, and I had to talk to you. They brought me here. They were going to use me to bring you back—to whichever of these asshole agencies you work for—and they—" She squeezed her eyes shut, wiped away tears, and then went on. "But they're dead now. They're all cut up and . . . I don't understand any of this, Dad."

"Just be patient, hon, it'll be all right," Stanner said, trying to sound as if he believed it. "Bentwaters, they killed her escort, took her and you for bait? That what happened?"

Bentwaters licked his lips and nodded. "That's more or less it. You're all that's keeping me and the girl human. They want you out of town, and they want Cruzon dead—or turned over to them. And they want a girl you've got with you. Name of Adair something."

"They want me out of town? Not dead?"

"Having you dead is just an ideal. You're a loose cannon. But it seems they're convinced there's something you've got that'll hurt them. They're concerned that if they just shoot you down, someone else might just set off that something . . ."

Stanner gave Bentwaters a hard look. "They know what that is?"

Bentwaters shrugged. "They've guessed."

Stanner nodded. So his bluff had worked. And there was just the possibility it might not be bluff—if Bentwaters had come through. Stanner didn't have the device yet—but Bentwaters had been smart enough to make them think he did. "So, they want to make sure I don't set that 'something' off."

"And they want to make some kind of deal with the Pentagon. So you and your daughter and I can live through this thing—as human beings—if you turn those two in the car over to them. And then we carry back their message."

"What kind of message?"

"Terms. They don't want the whole world, at least not all at once. If the Pentagon backs off, they're willing to negotiate. Maybe—for the West Coast. For a while."

Shannon was looking in horror back and forth between Bent-waters and Stanner. "Dad, who are you dealing with? What would you be *giving* them?"

"I don't know yet, Shannon." Stanner turned to Bentwaters. "They assume I'll play ball?"

Bentwaters shrugged. "You've worked for the Facility for years. And they've got your daughter." He reached up to close the last two inches on the FEMA jacket. "Shit, it's cold out here. You got a cigarette?"

"I don't smoke," Stanner said. Bentwaters had confirmed for Stanner what he suspected. If the crawlers were trying to cut a deal, then they were worried. Which meant that they'd found out that some sort of containment plan was in the offing. The Pentagon, the Facility, and probably the White House all knew how far it had gone. And that meant the Feds have to take radical steps to end this. Not in the way he'd planned it, though. Something more decisive, and extreme.

Anything extreme enough to stop the All of Us would probably kill everyone in town. Not just the ones who'd been changed over. Having to sacrifice a few researchers out in Lab 23—that had been hard, but they'd known the risks, so it was something he could live with. But this . . .

Thousands of normal people were still hiding in town, people who hadn't become crawlers. A whole town would be massacred to hide a secret.

"Dad," Shannon began.

He tried the encouraging smile again. It didn't feel convincing. "I'm sorry this happened to you, baby."

"It didn't just happen!" she hissed, glaring at him past her tears. "*You* got into it and that got *me* into it. This ugly filthy *shit* that you work in."

No answer came to him, for that.

"We want those two in the car," Morgenthal said. "And we want you to come with us peacefully, for debriefing. You tell us where your little toy is, and you negotiate for us with your people at the Pentagon. Then you and your daughter can go free."

"And me!" Bentwaters put in, his voice breaking up under the pressure of desperation. "You promised I could go with Stanner!"

Morgenthal ignored him.

"Most of our people are occupied elsewhere, Stanner," Rowse said, taking it up seamlessly. "We don't want a lot of noise and mess now. And we don't want the state police coming in here. You understand, Major? But if we have to, we'll do it the hard, noisy way. We were just hoping you'd make it easier on all of us."

Stanner hesitated. Rowse added, "And if you're thinking you can point your weapon at us and force us to back off—no. I'm not, in fact, a guy named Rowse anymore, Stanner. I'm the All of Us. We don't just *throw away* our 'human resources.' " He smiled at his little irony. "But don't think I really care if you kill me. Because I'm something you can't kill, even if you kill this Rowse body. You understand?" And he flashed Stanner what remained of his politician's smile.

"Sure," Stanner said. "You feel that way because you're just part of a goddamn machine. That I understand."

Rowse's smile didn't fade. "I'll wait thirty seconds more for your decision. You come with us quietly, and you have a deal. We have other plans for Bentwaters. So that leaves you to act as our intermediary."

Bentwaters had gone white-faced.

Stanner's hands tightened on the gun. His knuckles were stinging in the damp wind. He could smell the sea, very faintly. He heard a semi truck pass on the freeway, its driver blissfully unaware of all this, probably just thinking about the next stop and a girl in Reno.

"Your daughter and I have been here an hour, waiting for you," the Green Beret said. "You coming or not?"

Stanner let out a long slow sigh. "Okay," he said.

"Then bring the Adair Leverton girl over here to us. We want her, too," Rowse said.

Stanner nodded and backed away from them about ten steps. "Hold tight there, Shannon."

Licking his lips, looking into Stanner's eyes, Bentwaters said, "Major, you really *don't want to go without me.*"

Stanner didn't answer—but he guessed what Bentwaters meant. Bentwaters had the data he'd asked for.

But they weren't going to let Bentwaters go with him.

Stanner hesitated, then turned and walked back to the Quiebra police car where Cruzon and "the Adair girl" waited.

Out of the corner of his eye he caught a movement, a small car swinging out from behind a Shell station, pulling up at the edge of the parking area, facing the street. He glanced that way. A man he'd never seen before was behind the wheel, with a lean teenage boy who looked familiar at his side.

Oh, right: It was the conspiracy-theory kid from the site and the high school. Waylon. They just sat in the idling car, watching.

Stanner figured they'd planned on using the freeway ramp to escape from town, saw that it was blocked. Now they were watching to see what happened.

Stanner reached the cop car and murmured to Cruzon, "Sorry, Cruzon."

Ignoring Cruzon's inquiring look, Stanner opened the back door of the cop car, reached in, grabbed Adair by the wrist, and pulled her out to stand in the street.

She just looked at him, her eyes big. She looked at the people up at the entrance to the freeway. And she looked like she might bolt.

"Just hold on," he told her, as Cruzon got out of the car.

"What're you doing?" Cruzon asked.

"I'm sorry," Stanner said, and cracked Cruzon on the side of the head with the butt of the M16. Not too hard, but hard enough to knock him back against the open front door, to spin him half around. He reached out and pulled Cruzon's sidearm from his holster, then pointed it with his left hand. "Walk up toward the roadblock, there, Commander. Do it. You, too, Adair."

"You son of a bitch," Cruzon said, clutching his head. He muttered what was probably a curse in Tagalog.

"Adair, let's go. Move toward the freeway," Stanner said.

"What you going to do if she doesn't?" Cruzon asked bitterly. "Shoot her in the back? Maybe they'd like it if you did that. You'd score points."

"Just go on where I told you," Stanner said, pointing the M16 at Cruzon. He had it propped against his right hip. He shoved Cruzon's pistol into his own waistband, in front.

Stanner herded Cruzon and the girl toward the roadblock at the freeway on-ramp. The right side of the cop's head was bleeding and he was a little unsteady on his feet. "I guess maybe it was some kind of trade, your daughter for me?"

"Something like that." It seemed to be taking forever to walk to the roadblock. "Now shut up and go."

Cruzon snorted. "You really think they're going to give her to you like she's supposed to be? Or even let you go?"

"Just shut up and hurry. Let's get this the fuck over with, Commander." He started to tell Cruzon something more, but he was too close now. He might be overheard.

They were about a dozen paces from the roadblock, Adair walking as if in a dream, Cruzon trudging slowly behind her—when Stanner pretended to shove Cruzon with his left hand to hurry him. Leaning in close, even snarling, "Hurry up, you little Flip asshole!"

Cruzon almost turned his head to look when he felt something pushed into his own waistband.

"Don't look back," Stanner said almost inaudibly, between clenched teeth. "Can you feel your gun down there? Just nod once."

Cruzon nodded.

Stanner took a deep breath. "Head shots ought to slow them down."

Eight, nine more paces. They were within a few steps of his daughter. He spoke to Dirkowski. "Start my daughter toward me, if you want them."

"We've got them right now," the Green Beret pointed out, and raised the Uzi.

"Shannon, get down!" Stanner shouted, and he shoved Adair to his left so she fell sprawling in the street, as Cruzon yanked the gun out of the back of his waistband.

"Run, girl!" Cruzon shouted at Adair, as he got a bead with the pistol.

The Green Beret was aiming the Uzi at Adair as she got up to run. The first burst from the Uzi smacked the asphalt where Adair had been lying.

Shannon tore herself free from Rowse's grip and threw herself flat.

Stanner fired at the Green Beret's head and caught it with three solid rounds; the soldier danced back and fell.

Waylon was shouting. Adair reached his car, grabbing at a door handle.

Rowse ran toward the roadblock cars, shouting. The marine at the roadblock had set himself to leap, but three rounds from Cruzon's pistol jerked him back, flailing. Morgenthal fell, spasming under a burst from Stanner's M16.

Bentwaters and Shannon both were screaming. Stanner grabbed Shannon's wrist, shouted at her over the roar of Cruzon's gun, then she was up and running, Bentwaters right behind her.

The crawlers in the cop cars were firing, but the shots went wild. Morgenthal was up again and loping toward them on all fours.

Cruzon fired low at the cars in the roadblock, bursting three tires. Then he ran out of bullets and turned to run.

Stanner knew—as he emptied his clip, knocking Morgenthal down again—it was too far back to Cruzon's car. They'd never make it.

But a midsize sedan pulled up in his path, and a back door flew open. The Waylon kid and the older guy shouted at them to get in. Adair was already huddled in the backseat.

Shannon and Cruzon and Bentwaters piled into the sedan, cramming up against Adair. Bullets smacked into the rear fender and rang from the pavement as Stanner tried to follow—but it was too crowded.

He grabbed hold of the open back door as best he could as the car spun to the right in a tight circle, and hung on as it accelerated down the road, away from the freeway. He clung to the door and to someone's hand inside, he wasn't sure whose. One of his feet was on the bottom edge of the car's floor, at the door, the other hanging free. He glanced over his shoulder.

The cars behind them had each lost tires, and the Green Beret was still sprawled, twitching, damaged past moving, but the other crawlers were furiously pursuing—on foot. Running along the street. Morgenthal, full of gunshot but still coming, and Rowse and the two cops—and they were on all fours, their hands and feet extended from their ankles, leaping high into the air, bounding as fast as the fugitive car, thirty, forty miles per hour.

But as Stanner crammed in with the others in the back, thinking of circus clowns, barely able to close the door behind him, the car picked up speed, roaring through twenty-five-mile-an-hour zones at fifty, sixty, seventy-five, till at last they left their pursuers behind.

Stanner decided the man driving was probably Waylon's father. Family resemblance. Adair tapped the driver on the shoulder and pointed to a side street.

"Okay, I'm sure as hell open for suggestions," Waylon's dad said hoarsely. So he followed her mute directions.

December 14, noon

Vinnie knew for sure his mother was dead when he saw her climbing across the roof.

He'd come back and found the house empty. The doors standing open. She always locked the doors, even when she was at home. He thought she was dead, he was even pretty sure of it, but he refused to believe it till he could see what remained of her.

He had called for her, wailed to himself when she wouldn't answer, called some more as he went through the rooms, over and over. He wished he could ask the neighbors, but first of all, he had a hard time asking anyone anything anytime, and second, they didn't seem to be around.

They might be where Mother was.

She didn't come home during the night. He might manage to tell the police things so they could understand, if he really concentrated. But he was afraid to call the police. He wasn't sure why, except that when he'd passed them on the street he could feel they were all wrong. And sometimes he could hear them talking in his head.

"They use words but they're words stolen from cradles," he muttered, as he rocked furiously in his mother's rocking chair. "Slave words all strung in a wire and spinning like the Mechmort in Starbots. Transform, transform, Starbots, transform and defend!"

He had sat there all night, with all but a night-light turned out. He was afraid the lights might attract the moths, and he didn't want the moths to know where he was.

In the morning, too upset even to eat his Froot Loops, he'd gone to scout around, looking for Mother in the streets and in the woods by the house. Down in the woods he had seen some kids, teenagers and younger kids, looking scared, hiding in the rusted shell of an abandoned, overgrown school bus.

Vinnie managed to ask one of the boys if he'd seen Mother. After a few attempts at asking the question, in different ways, finally the boy understood. The boy shook his head—and then turned away to hide tears. Crying for his own mother.

Vinnie had tried to tell them that the woods wasn't very safe. There were little things in it that used to be animals. But one of the girls had said that they knew how to deal with those. She pointed to the cats prowling around the bus. They had seen the cats kill the little jumping metal things. And for some reason, the cats were immune to being taken over by them.

So the kids had brought big bags of dry cat food and spread it around. Feral cats and wandering house cats came, and stayed—preferring it here to being around the things their owners had become. The cats were like a patrol against the little clockwork animals. Even the crawling marine stayed away. So far. But they had seen him in the distance, crouching in the bushes, watching.

He'll come, Vinnie thought, *when they need parts enough, the cats won't keep him away.*

Anyway, the girl told Vinnie, looking at him pointedly, his being there was scaring some of the smaller kids.

He was used to being sent away. He went away to look for Mother somewhere else.

Now, coming back to his own street, tired and hungry and walking along a few doors down from home, he saw a big blocky car pull up in front of his house. Mother and Mr. Roxmont from next door got out of the car, and Mr. Roxmont was carrying a big box of equipment into his garage and Mother was carrying what looked like a dish antenna.

Then his scrawny white-haired little mother climbed up the side of the house, in some way he didn't understand. Mother climbed right up onto the roof.

He hid himself behind a parked truck as the car that had dropped them off went by, driven by a raggedy-looking man.

When it was gone, Vinnie came a little closer to his house. Mother was setting up one of those machines he'd seen on lots of the roofs in town. She had a firm grip on a screwdriver and her hand was spinning on the wrist, all the way around. A questing strand of metal was poking from Mother's mouth and seemed to be looking toward the work, as if supervising.

Vinnie was very sure that this was no longer his mother. That his mother was dead.

He began to shake and to cry softly to himself and to talk aloud to the trees and the brush as he slipped between two houses, over a fence, and down into the woods. There wasn't anywhere else to go.

The children at the abandoned bus didn't want him there. He knew he could help them, too. He could hear things in his head, and he could warn them. But it was too hard to speak to them. That was always the problem. The tangling thing in him had always pushed people away, and now at the end it was going to push him completely off the edge of the world.

Then he thought of someplace to go. He would go to the cemetery, on the other side of town. Mother used to take him to visit Father's grave there. He always felt a friendly welcoming from Father and all his friends at the cemetery. It was quiet there. Yes. That's where he'd go.

He'd be safe among the dead.

21

Waylon's father stopped his little rental car in the parking lot of the Quiebra Beach Recreation Area. He turned to Stanner, looking as if he was going to ask what to do next, and then Bentwaters started to wail.

"It's moving!" Bentwaters wailed, clawing at his neck, scratching himself so that bloody streaks showed. "They've activated it!"

Stanner opened the car door, got out of the crowded backseat, instinctively pulled Bentwaters out onto the tarmac of the parking lot.

Bentwaters broke free and thrashed on the ground, shouting at Stanner to help him—rolling like a man on fire.

Stanner saw it then. The silvery living strand that had been around Bentwaters's neck had broken its circle, and one end was nosing its way up onto his jawline. Worming its way purposefully toward Bentwaters's mouth.

Cruzon came to hunker down beside Bentwaters, an opened pocketknife in his hand. "Try to lie still, I'll do what I can," Cruzon said.

Bentwaters, panting, eyes screwed shut, stopped rolling, lay stiffly on his back. "Hurry!" he whispered.

"Be careful, Cruzon," Stanner warned.

Cruzon nodded and flicked with the knife blade at the searching tendril of metal—and it responded by snapping a segment up onto the blade, the shiny probe spiraling up toward his hand.

"Augh!" Cruzon yelled, scrambling back. Stanner took a long, quick step back himself.

"What happened?" Bentwaters demanded shrilly, looking around desperately.

The knife lay next to Bentwaters, and the metallic seekers, seeming to give up on finding Cruzon, jumped like fleas back onto Bentwaters, rejoining the rest of the strand oozing onto the edge of his mouth.

He felt them moving on him again, and he shrieked, grabbed the pocketknife from the tarmac, tried desperately to scrape them off.

Waylon and his father and Shannon were shouting something from the car. Stanner wasn't even sure what. He watched in sickened fascination as Bentwaters started stabbing randomly at his face around his mouth, trying to get under the thing, to tear it away with the knife, so that his blood spurted and splashed.

"Oh, Jesus," Cruzon muttered, drawing his pistol.

"Don't let it do it to me," Bentwaters was shouting. "Don't let it get in! *Stop it from getting in!*"

Then there was a flurry of motion and the metallic strand plunged past Bentwaters's lips, spiraled in to his screaming mouth, and vanished down his throat.

"Oh, my God, no," Bentwaters said softly, gurgling as blood filled his mouth. Still automatically carving at himself.

Stanner reached down and grabbed the wrist of Bentwaters's knife hand. "Stop it, Bentwaters, dammit, it's gone down. It's too late!"

Bentwaters tore his hand free and poised the blade over his chest, his eyes shining with fear, panting. He stared at the knife. His knuckles went white.

"Stanner, I can't—I can't do it myself. *Shove the knife in for me.* Or use a gun. But for God's sake, *kill me!* Don't let it—I don't want to feel them take over. Please! *Please kill me!*"

Cruzon stepped back and aimed the gun at Bentwaters's head.

The others, in the car, had fallen silent now—though Stanner could hear his daughter sobbing.

Bentwaters shuddered. "I can feel them. They're going into my brain, Stanner! *They're digging into my brain!*"

Cruzon cocked the gun.

Then Bentwaters said, "Stanner, get my eyes or they'll see where you are, from my eyes! And my wallet, in my wallet there's a— *Stanner!*" This last a shriek. Bentwaters was staring into an abyss. "They're going into—my—oh, no, don't let them eat that, don't let them—"

Cruzon bent over, aimed, and fired, twice. Bentwaters's eyes vanished, replaced with bursting red holes. Bentwaters shivered—but his body began to move, the limbs rippling.

Stanner said hoarsely, "Everyone, out of the car. Where we're going is nearby. We need to get rid of this car anyway. Leave the keys."

They got out, and Cruzon took them down the path to the beach, a little ways, as Stanner got Bentwaters's wallet, snatching it out as quickly as he could. Afraid to be in direct physical contact with the body.

Then he got into the rental car and drove it repeatedly onto Bentwaters's body, back and forth, over and over, until it stopped moving completely.

December 14, afternoon

Bert didn't want to let them in until he could think of some way to test them.

It was hard to make a decision. He was emotionally exhausted and he hadn't slept. He stared through the peephole in the door, saw them crowded into a fish-eye circle: Lacey's niece Adair, a boy he recognized from the high school, three men he didn't know, and Commander Cruzon from the Quiebra PD.

Then he saw the Filipino loading his pistol, and that didn't make him want to let them in, either.

Lacey looked through the window. "It's Adair!"

"Lacey, we don't know if it's *still* Adair."

But she pushed him roughly aside and unlocked the door. Adair came in, first. She stopped just in front of Lacey and stared silently at her.

Then she put her hands on Lacey's face, feeling it the way blind people do. Lacey let her do it.

The girl pushed her fingers into Lacey's mouth, opening it—peering in. She put her cheek against Lacey's chest and seemed to listen.

Then, Adair threw her arms around Lacey. Sobbing.

December 14, late afternoon

Everyone was staring at Stanner, waiting as he sipped his coffee.

"You tell them, Stanner," Cruzon said. "You tell them what you told me. We got to be on the same page, because we might have to split up. Be lucky if one of them didn't see us come here and report it."

They were all seated around the kitchen table, waiting. Daylight slanted through the window over the sink; dust motes pirouetted in the sunbeams. They were in Bert's beachside place, more than a quarter mile from where Bentwaters had died.

Stanner wasn't at all sure they were safe here. But then, maybe they'd gotten lucky. Maybe the crawlers had been distracted, didn't know where they'd gone to ground. If they hadn't come for them by now, maybe so.

But sooner or later they'd find them.

Adair hadn't said anything, or even showed she was much aware of her surroundings, since pointing Waylon's father here. Now she just sat across from Stanner, close beside Lacey. Lacey with her arms around her. That scrawny cat in Adair's lap. Waylon sat beside her, close to his dad, who was drinking some of the bottle of Johnnie Walker Red; it had sat unopened on Bert's shelf for a year.

Cruzon was ruefully soothing his swollen temple with ice wrapped in a hand towel. He sank down on the kitchen floor, sat crosslegged with his back to a cabinet, pressing the ice to his head.

Stanner glanced at his daughter, found Shannon looking at him balefully. Drinking Scotch herself. Looking as if she'd like to throw the glass at him.

Stanner put off telling them, because that would involve admitting to his complicity. "What about your family, Cruzon?"

Cruzon shrugged. "They're okay, as far as I know. I showed my brother what was left of Breakenridge. He saw some other things. He knows. He's got them all holed up in the basement of his house." He glanced toward the window, as if wondering if they were really safe.

"You're stalling, Dad," Shannon said.

Stanner smiled wearily. "You're just like your mom. I never could fool her, either. Okay." He took a deep breath and began. "It started in the seventies. There was the idea of creating weaponry that was smart enough to do the hunting and targeting, as well as the killing. Something like smart bombs. Back then it was ordinary chip computing. But a few years ago the Facility achieved a breakthrough in nanotechnology.

"Can I have some of that Scotch? Just pour it right in the coffee." He took a long pull at his drink and began again.

It's funny how technology takes on a life of its own, even before it gets to the artificial intelligence stage (Stanner said). It's like we surrender some of our own life to our technology, after a certain point in its growth. Seems we surrendered too much. Aspirin's a good thing—but swallow a few handfuls of aspirin and you might die from it. We need water, but too much and you'll die. So when is it too much technology?

Shannon's looking at me like she thinks I'm stalling again. Okay, here goes.

It was a Pentagon research lab that had the nanotech breakthrough. They were pretty stingy with it. They didn't want to share it with industry because it could leak out to the country's enemies, and we'd lose our advantage.

The advantage, though, was harder to see than anyone figured it'd be. Sure, with nanotechnology you can make microscopic components. In fact, you can make machines the size of individual molecules. Theoretically that means you can pack almost infinite computing into an inconceivably small space. You could make weapons as smart as you wanted them to be.

But the problem was configuring the nanotech machines. To do it efficiently, make lots of them fast, you needed a nanotech machine that could make a nanotech machine—something on that level. You could use scanning-tunneling electron microscopy, lots of techniques, but it took so much time. Too much. But then a team at the Facility—the Pentagon's most secret research program—these geniuses created a simple nanotech cell that originally had only one job, to make other nanotech cells. Each cell made the next one with more detail, greater elaboration. It was like the entire evolution of technology, one aspect leading to another, and in a way it was like biological evolution, too—but superfast and in miniature.

The nanocells themselves—well, they're robotic cells, computer-integrated cells. One of them can carry a certain amount of information in its quantum-computing format. A group of them share information and innovate based on the sum total of shared data.

Okay, so the only way to create nanocells with enough detailed elaboration was to establish a pattern of self-replication and relative independence. This tendency to seek out redesign was built into these automata on a cellular level. They were able to set up hypotheses and carry out experiments. Using enzymes and other molecular tools, they can change their cell shape for greater efficiency.

But they weren't supposed to be totally independent. Instructions would be transmitted to a group of these microscopic automata. That's where Kyu Kim entered the picture. A Korean researcher at the Facility. It was his idea, see, that since this was happening on a level of sheer smallness that was equivalent to the microbiological, the nanocells could be made to take advantage of biological matter at the cellular level. And since there's lots of biology around to utilize, it could accelerate their development hugely. He transmitted that direction to them, and they carried it out, with something almost like enthusiasm.

Initially he gave them building resources and the nervous system components of a dog, a cat, and material from primates. They were able to alter their configurations so they could integrate with some of the animal nervous systems. Cats were always a problem; they seem almost to possess an independence gene, or some component of blood chemistry that makes them resist nanocells. Primates—including people—are more various than most of us realize. We have lots in common, but also a great deal of genetic variation and body chemistry variation, more to do with family bloodlines than races.

It appears some people are prone to interfacing with these nanocells, without much trouble. Others aren't. Some researchers thought it had to do with genetic predisposition—but Dr. Kim believed it was all about states of mind, and the distinctive body chemistry that resulted from those states. Young primates were less likely to integrate; they had a chemistry, almost an electricity in their nervous system, that had a quality of heightened awareness or "awakeness" about it. Older primates had less of this quality and usually were more easily absorbed into the system.

Then experiments were done on human volunteers, soldiers dying of cancer in V.A. hospitals, who thought this biological-technological system integration—what amounted to man fused with machine—might give them another chance at life. But once the integration took place, the nanocells used the body's resources to make more and more of themselves, and took over completely. Absorbed physical matter provided raw materials and energy. They destroyed the old personality—taking some information from it first—and they redesigned the body based on theoretical hypotheses for improvement. The volunteers became ramshackle cyborgs, with the automata altering normal human cells to control bleeding and immune system responses where they built in extensions and enhancements. They created a "systems enhancement factory" within the body to add new mechanical and electronic parts. Turning people into—the slang terms were *crawlers* or *breakouts.*

Pretty soon the whole system died—I mean, the experimental subject died. Or went berserk and . . . well, they had to be put down. The Facility decided to limit the integration to masses of cells taken from lower apes, slices of brain tissue, that kind of thing.

But the various discrete nanocell experiments had been communicating with one another, over a distance. Sharing ideas, gradually accumulating something that added up to consciousness and the will to act independently. The nanocells apparently decided they wanted to run their own growth experiments. They waited—near as we can figure out, that's the case—they waited for their chance. And they developed a kind of launch system, to transfer nanocells to a human host who got close enough.

Kyu Kim wasn't cautious enough. He opened the development box without protection and they—essentially they jumped him. They took him over. They used him to attack some of his assistants, transferred more nanocell substance to others in Lab 23. They established communication, one crawler to the next. They were a lot more sophisticated, independent, and savvy than we'd realized. They accessed information from the brains of the old experimental subjects, for starts. Some bodies they redesigned from the inside; others they took apart and used in other ways.

Lab 23 had to be destroyed. Only a handful of nanocells was saved. But those cells retained everything the destroyed cells had learned, as quantum-computing format files.

The Facility decided that the experiment could continue but only somewhere safer—somewhere they couldn't come into contact with human beings at all. So they set up a remote-controlled nanocell lab inside an old spy satellite, pushed it back into orbit from a shuttle. The nanocells were allowed to use onboard resources to reproduce there and to reorganize. They couldn't go anywhere; they were safely contained. The vacuum of space would destroy them; they need air or blood pressure in order to maintain their configurations.

They were observed constantly, via the data transmitted to the Facility's ground station. The hope was that they would evolve the useful aspects that could be copied and transmitted to new, "naive" nanocells.

They evolved up there, thinking and redesigning, for a couple of years. We thought the satellite was a safe, sterile place to continue the experiment. We thought that even if it came down, it'd all burn up in the atmosphere.

But the nanocells could think, en masse. They developed simple motility systems, and then they worked out a way to break out of their containment unit, to interface with the satellite's computer. They put up command firewalls, deleting our ability to control them or turn them off.

The satellite was equipped with orbital-control rockets. Pretty powerful, supposed to keep them in the right orbit. The nanocell cluster took control of those and used them to push themselves *out* of orbit. Calculated a descent that would prevent the satellite from burning up completely—and slowed their descent with the retros.

The nanocells chose to come down here, and they used their baseline mobility to emerge from the damaged hull of the satellite. As far as I can tell, they interfaced with the diver, first—Adair's father—who came down to check the crash site. They rode inside him, like a parasite in a host, till they could use his resources to make more nanocells and pass them on to his wife, then to other people. Everyone he came into contact with, if conditions were right. He converted the marine guards, before he left the site.

Some people resist more than others. Some are sort of machine-like already, it seems. Others a bit less. But chances are, they used an overwhelming number of nanocell resources on Adair's father. He didn't stand a chance.

The crawlers are an odd combination of naive and vastly intelligent. They have a group mind—they call it the All of Us—but the individual nanocell colonies, in individual people, maintain some initiative, which is always subject to revision by the All of Us.

Near as Cruzon and I could find out, the All of Us is working up a system for a massive dissemination of nanocells out into the world at large. To work this out, the All of Us had to get all of its colony parts involved in thinking about it—so it had to create a more efficient system for communicating between all the parts, all the individual colonies, so more information could be passed around. That's what the transmitters on the roofs are about; it's sort of like wireless crawler DSL. Helps it transmit data faster, so it can think faster and act in a more unified way. But that system is still only partly on-line. If they were sharing their information more efficiently, none of us would've made it this far.

And they're hampered by their tendency—almost an obsession— to constantly experiment. They progress, but they progress relatively slowly—maybe because they keep trying new designs. They tried to integrate various animals into one system—and it didn't quite work. But those models are effective enough to patrol the perimeters of town.

Till the All of Us learns to share information efficiently, it seems each nanocolony in each crawler is limited by the mental resources of the hosts. A smarter host, a smarter crawler. The smarter ones can do the camouflage better; some seem more human, more presentable than others. They're learning.

Pretty soon you won't be able to tell any of them from people. They'll develop integration at the cellular level with very little visible effect on the mechanics of the host. You won't see them behaving like crawlers—more like superhuman people. And they'll be that much more dangerous.

All I can say is—they're far more resourceful than anyone dreamed. Maybe we underestimated the independent evolution of technology. I don't know. All I know is—it's out of control.

There was silence when he'd finished. He sipped his coffee, made a face, wishing it was Irish whiskey instead of Scotch.

Cruzon shook his head—then winced at the pain. "It's too much. I don't know who to blame."

Bert looked at Stanner with a visible mix of disgust and in-credulity. "So *now* you guys figure it's out of control—when it's killing who knows how many people. You didn't think it was out of control the first time you used human beings in experiments?" He shook his head. "What's out of control, Stanner, is *you* people. Your secrets—and your facilities."

Waylon nodded. "You got that right, man." He glowered at Stanner. "You fuckers killed my mother." The boy's voice was shak-ing with anger. His father nodded numbly at his side.

Lacey sighed. "We shouldn't be surprised. We knew the govern-ments of the world developed biowarfare programs, chemical warfare programs—stockpiled plutonium. And plutonium is insanely dan-gerous. *All* that stuff is insane. If they'd do that, we might've guessed they'd pull something like this. And all of it in secret—with no real oversight."

Stanner looked at his daughter. She looked away from him—swallowing. He sighed. "Look, this country has a lot of enemies. Congress pushes for new military tech so we can have the edge and feel secure. Thousands of Americans were killed by terrorists—and if we don't keep our experiments secret, they end up being used against us. The Soviets *stole* our hydrogen bomb technology."

Bert chuckled sadly. "There's always a rationale. But if these things are done without oversight, they get out of control every time, Stanner. You people forget what your agenda is supposed to be—and in the shadows, things get dark and sick. You make up your own agenda. The United States is the great social experiment of the age. It has to survive, and it has to fight to survive if necessary—but this, it's psychotic!"

Stanner looked out the window. "Yeah, well, I've been thinking that way, too, for a while. But the habit of obedience, like the man says, dies hard. Once you're in the Facility—even just *in the know* about it—it's hard to get out. So you work up some kind of denial." He looked at his daughter again and, seeing the look of betrayal on her face, almost cried himself. Then he looked at the bottle of Scotch.

"I feel like getting drunk—but I don't have that luxury now. And I don't have the luxury of denial right now, either."

Waylon was still glaring. "Just tell me one thing—you owe me this, man—how are the aliens involved?"

Stanner pinched the bridge of his nose and sighed.

Puzzled, Bert asked, "Aliens, Waylon? You mean foreign interests? Red Chinese or something?"

"No, dude, aliens! Extraterrestrials!" He turned to Stanner again. "Come on, this technology is too . . . outlandish to be from humans. This is, like, a technology that was stolen from crashed saucers, right?"

Stanner chuckled. "I almost wish it was. Then maybe we could blame them. But no. No aliens involved. The only reason 'it came from space' was because we put the lab in orbit. This technology seems outlandish only because—" He shrugged. "—it's a secret."

Waylon seemed disappointed. "No aliens?"

"Sorry."

Then Shannon asked, "When—when are they going to—you know—make their move?"

Stanner shook his head. "I don't know for sure, but near as we could work out, the system'll be on-line tomorrow sometime. When that happens they'll be a hell of a lot more efficient. They'll hunt us down, and everyone else. Convert the whole town. Then they'll launch their colony-seeding system—whatever that is. I don't know what form it'll take. They're working up to some kind of global insemination of nanocells."

Adair started rocking gently in her chair. Her face blank. Waylon reached over and put his hand over hers, on the table, and she looked at him with genuine surprise. Then she took his hand in hers.

Lacey stroked Adair's hair and said, "We have to get out of town and warn the rest of the country. Maybe we can use boats—they're watching the beach."

Waylon said, "Stanner—that guy, Bentwaters. He was yelling about—about his wallet. Like he was trying to tell you something."

Stanner nodded. "Yeah, he was. He was supposed to get me some information." He took Bentwaters's wallet out of his coat pocket. He looked through it, found no family pictures, just some credit cards, an ID card he didn't recognize—something to slide through a scanner at the NSA—some money, insurance cards . . .

He snorted, almost laughed. A condom in a foil package was tucked in with the folding money. The condom looked like it had been in there a long time. Bentwaters hadn't been getting much action.

Stanner flipped the condom onto the table with the other items and then sorted through them. He looked at the insurance card, and a business card for a tax consultant, a credit card, trying to see if something was written on them. Maybe microfilm, or a command code that could be used against the nanocells—though all such had long before been erased, as far as he knew.

Nothing. Maybe the information could be encoded in the credit cards' magnetic strips. But there was no way to read anything.

Stanner tossed the wallet onto the table. "Maybe he just wanted it to go to his family. I don't know."

Waylon picked up the condom. He began to peel the foil packet open.

His dad shot him a look of exasperation. "Waylon, for heaven's sake, put that thing down."

"Wait. There's something else in here. This package is just a little bit too big for condoms—and there's something else." Waylon pulled out a rolled-up condom, cracked with age, and then tore the foil open wider—peeled it back from a small, flat minidisk.

"It's like a tiny computer disk," Lacey said.

"It's, like, a minidisk," Waylon said, snorting at her ignorance. "But miniature. This one's *small*."

Cruzon stood up, tossed his wet towel in the sink, and came to look over Waylon's shoulder. "That could be . . . something he was trying to tell us."

Stanner nodded. "But I need to be able to read this thing. With luck, it's the specs I asked for."

"I've got a Palm Pilot—which I hardly ever use," Lacey said. "Right here in my purse. It has features I never learned. I think it interfaces with minidisks, though. But nothing that small. Waylon, you've got digital skills, right? And electronics? You think you could get the information off it somehow?"

"Maybe, if I had the right kind of laser reader."

"I've got some things with me," Harold said. "It's my business. I think we could find something that could be adapted to read it."

"If I can transfer what's on this to the Palm Pilot," Waylon said, "and upload from there to your PC—you got a PC, Mr. Clayborn?"

"Me? Of course, I—"

"Dead people chased us on the road," Shannon said suddenly. Her lip buckled. "By the freeway. They were coming like animals. Chasing us, people chasing us like wild dogs. They were chasing the car." She was staring into some mental screen. "Then they—and we left that man in the parking lot." She looked at Cruzon with awe. "This man shot out his eyes."

"If you'd seen what I've seen," Cruzon said softly, "you'd have done the same."

Stanner moved to stand awkwardly behind Shannon's chair. Lacey got up so he could sit next to his daughter. He sat and put his arm around her. At first she turned her face away from him and pushed his arm off. But Stanner gently persisted, and after a little while she was sobbing against his chest.

Maybe she was beginning to forgive him for being part of this; for dragging her into it. How would she feel about it, he wondered, if she knew about the thermobaric bombs—the daisy cutters. Like the ones used in Afghanistan. A couple of those equaling the Hiroshima blast.

What would she say if she knew the Pentagon was probably planning to set a couple off here in Quiebra, to wipe out the crawlers, like they'd done at Lab 23? The blast would burn hot; that was the weapon's specialty. It would do more than kill the crawlers; it'd fuse the nanocells, turn all the evidence to slag. They could set off a refinery blast, blame it on that. Terrorists blowing up the refinery.

How would Shannon feel about it, he wondered, holding her closer, if she knew that the crawlers would probably start their dissemination program well before the bomb hit?

That it'd hit too late to stop the crawlers from spreading out into the general population.

That all those who died in the explosion would die for nothing . . .

December 14, early evening

Vinnie peered out from his hiding place, leaning to try to see through the gate that hung open in the cemetery wall. He squatted between a Dumpster and the brick fence, just inside the cemetery. The Dumpster was filled with the chunks of an old concrete crypt that had been torn down; some of them overflowed onto the ground at Vinnie's feet: Rain-stained cherub faces tumbled together in cracked cement.

Darkness filling in all the corners, all the holes and hollows, of the cemetery. The sky purpling, the air softening.

The shadows from the streetlights were long, stretching out and out, it seemed to Vinnie, like they were special paths, carpets unrolling for the crawling people moving from the alleys and backyards toward the cemetery.

There were so many of the crawling people. Some of them loping along on two feet, many more on all fours; a few, not crawling now but crawling people nonetheless, driving up with their minivans and SUVs packed with others, all converging on the cemetery.

And he knew why they were here. He'd heard them speak of it, heard them in his head talking of the great Seeding of the All of Us into the world. Until now he hadn't realized they'd made their home base under the cemetery. No place was peaceful, now. No place, no place, no place was peaceful. No place.

He could see a block of houses to his left, to his right the cemetery. The cemetery was torn up, damp paths trampled through it, many of the tombstones overturned to make room for new tunnel entrances dug down into the rich turf.

Here and there coffins had been torn up and thrown aside, one of them broken, showing the blue arm of a recently dead lady.

Most of the crawlers had come in by another gate, toward the south, but a few were headed toward this gate, and he drew back into his hiding place, wishing he'd never come here.

"The red hand pushed me here," Vinnie murmured, scarcely aware he was doing it, "stretching to push me into the holes in the ground, where the ground starts sponging on you and sucking your wetstuff into it, so that you get sponged into millions of holes, but Mother's not there, Mother's with the Starbots, and higher than that, but who can hear me, but maybe, but maybe they can hear me."

One of the crawlers—a grubby woman with long stringy brown hair that hung down past her crawling arms to drag on the ground— switched on her eyes, just then, perhaps having heard him. The twin laser-pointer-red beams swept right and left, seeking. Just missing him as he froze in the shadows.

She crept on by, going deeper into the cemetery, her pistoning legs, twice as long as they should be, divided into neat segments of dull wet metal and puffy flesh, pumping with clickety sounds, leaving behind a smell of rubber and sweat and faceless decay.

Vinnie heard a crackling sound, turned to see a red-painted wooden fence buckling outward from the backyard of a house that faced away from the cemetery. As he watched, the fence cracked some more, midway up. Four planks commenced bulging out and showing yellow wood under the breaks—and then shattered as a big crawler shoved through. He was a man who had been a football star at the school where Vinnie'd attended the special classes, now pushing impatiently through the fence to move with his protracted legs in short spurts across the street to the cemetery gate. Mechanical loping. Then taking twenty-foot leaps.

Vinnie pulled way back in the shadow. He whimpered and called for the Starbots.

Then he saw his mother.

He tried not to say it out loud, but it got away from him, laughing as it went. "She's a bad drawing that scribbled itself not my mother some ape dances and picks its head like a nose where's the don't-scream where's the don't-scream where's the don't-scream sign."

And she was dragging someone along behind her, a woman with an improvised rope harness around her. Mother's fist, half metal and half flesh, was closed tightly around a rope behind the woman's head.

She was dragging Mrs. Schimmel, who was a bigger woman than Mother but even older, a lady with broken red veins on her big nose and dyed black hair and dyed eyebrows. Sometimes Mrs. Schimmel helped take care of Vinnie, like when Mother went to Reno, but now she was shrieking hoarsely and flapping her flabby arms, one leg trailing a silk stocking, the other bare and bleeding, her shift torn and dirtied past recognizing the color, her mouth foaming with terror as Mother dragged her along, into the cemetery, right past Vinnie.

And Vinnie couldn't help but cry out, "Don't, Mother, don't hurt Mrs. Schimmel, Mother, go home!"

Mother heard. She stopped, and saw him—even Mrs. Schimmel gaped at him. Mother half crawling, one hand on the ground, the other holding Mrs. Schimmel who seemed almost used to being dragged by a rope, stretched sagging out the way she was now.

"Vinnie?" Mrs. Schimmel said in a creaky voice. "Help me help me call the police help me help me help me oh God call the police oh Vinnie. . . ." The words blurring into one bubbling stream.

Mother stared. Opening her mouth to hiss. Her head spinning on her shoulders. *Call the others!*

Then a man's voice, one Vinnie recognized a little, was saying, "I'll take care of him. Monitor my transmission, minor frequency seventy-eight. I'll bring him in."

Vinnie saw the man speaking then, could see his head as he peered around the edge of the Dumpster. Deputy Sprague, was who, Vinnie knew him because the deputy had taken him home once when he'd gotten confused downtown, and another time he'd taken him to the emergency room when he'd had a seizure.

Mother muttered something that sounded like, "That's protocol for pending conversion, frequency seventy-eight-four." Or something close to that. And then she dragged Mrs. Schimmel into the cemetery.

Mrs. Schimmel took up the shrieking again, as if someone had cued her, and the two of them vanished down a big hole in the cemetery ground: first Mother and then, *pop*, down went Mrs. Schimmel, the old woman's shrieks becoming echoey and harder and harder to hear.

Deputy Sprague turned to Vinnie and then trotted out into view, revealing the rest of himself. He was like a man who'd had his arms and legs cut off and had been given something like a bug's legs to replace them; only, the six limbs he'd been given were two human legs, maybe his own, stretched out where his arms should have been, the toes replaced with metal grippers and connected to the shoulders by wet gray metal pistons; the other limbs were mismatched arms from white people, contrasting with his skin, one of them with a fading eagle tattoo, each one connected to the main body with metal parts, ball joints, things cut from scavenged materials and fused into the flesh with a sheath that seemed alive, quivering within itself.

Deputy Sprague's neck was gone, replaced with a metal stalk that stretched out farther now, at least twenty-four inches more, so he could tilt his head on the long gray stalk to look back at Vinnie.

The face was drooling, and long past horror. Torn up some—but it was Deputy Sprague's face.

"There's no more of us coming in this gate for a couple of minutes, and if you run across the street, Vinnie," Sprague said, in a voice that sounded like Deputy Sprague and sounded like a machine voice, too, "and go through that hole in the fence the big fella made, why, I don't expect they'll see you, and you might make it up into those hills. Tell the kids I've tried to keep them away from that tank, but if they do a close inspection of my thoughts—wait—" He turned and looked at the cemetery. "Protocol Camouflage horizontal to vertical," he said. Then he turned back to Vinnie. "Okay for now. But not soon. Get up there, the hills over the school."

Then Deputy Sprague turned and scuttled like a beetle across the cemetery and dropped down into one of the holes.

Vinnie ran through the gate, and across the street, and through the gap in the wooden fence, leaving a trail of lost words in the air behind him.

22

Adair kept watch on the bedroom window. The curtains were closed, but she could tell it was starting to get dark out. And things were moving out there. Chattering and crawling north, always to the north.

She was huddled against the padded headboard of Bert's bed, her feet under the rumpled blanket. Waylon sat next to her, with a fireplace poker across his lap.

Like a fireplace poker would stop a crawler, she thought.

But she was glad Waylon was there. Glad he was thinking about protecting her. Even glad he was foolish enough to believe they could come out of this alive.

Waylon's dad was sitting on the end of the bed, looking over Stanner's shoulder. "That's the schematic I wanted," Stanner said. He was at Bert's desk, using his PC. "But I don't know if I can build the thing. I thought maybe I could but . . ." He shook his head and swore to himself.

"You're hella lucky they didn't ream that computer out for the parts," Waylon said.

Cruzon was sitting in a kitchen chair he'd carried in here. He stared dully at the computer and nodded. "Yeah. All over town, that happen."

Waylon's dad glanced at Cruzon. "How you feeling, Commander?"

Cruzon shrugged. "I'm okay. I'm just . . . worried about my kids. My wife."

Stanner peered at the image on the computer screen. "Looks like a design for an electromagnetic pulse generator." There was just an edge of excitement in his voice. "DARPA worked one up like this—seems to be based on it. To be dropped by parachute, throw out the enemy's communications system. And I think the Facility was thinking of using it at Lab 23—but they weren't sure it would work and they couldn't wait. So they used one of their bigger non-nuclear bombs."

"Of course, it's theoretical," Waylon's dad said, nodding at the schematic. "Maybe it won't work. But if it works, if the pulse goes out, this generator would have a tremendous effect. It's a very sophisticated design."

The major turned and looked at Waylon's dad with his eyebrows raised. "You're familiar?"

"I work in electromagnetics," he said, suddenly a little embarrassed. "Field generation and dampening. For wireless transmission. Palm Pilots, wrist uplink units, that kind of thing."

"I'm sorry, with all this lunacy," Stanner said, "I didn't get your name. I'm Henri Stanner."

"Harold Kulick," Waylon's dad said, and they shook hands. "I was in the Air Force myself, for a couple of hitches, and I don't buy into this business of you being responsible for this mess. I know how it goes."

"Cruzon," the cop said, shaking Harold's hand in turn.

Stanner chewed a lip and glanced at the open door. Adair figured he was thinking about his daughter Shannon—a little ways down the hall, in the kitchen, talking to Lacey and probably still saying how horrible he was.

Cruzon pointed at the screen. "So you know this stuff, Harold."

"I've noticed something else," Harold said. "The equipment on the roof, when we came in here—on a lot of roofs. A lot of those parts are there. It might be possible to put together a pulse generator out of a couple of those, and a car battery, say. See, those things on the roof, they're built along the same principles, from what you were telling me. Only, it seems they transmit information in powerful waves on a lot of frequencies at once. They could also transmit a pulse—so maybe we could use their own gear against them. Wipe their programming and shut them down."

"Only if it's close to their cluster," Stanner muttered.

"Their what?"

"They're a group mind, with a lot of units spread out over Quiebra—and this unit wouldn't have the power to reach them all. But there's a sort of living CPU, the cluster where the greatest mass of nanocells is converged. Probably a lot of interlocked hosts there. If you plant it close to that, it'll wipe it—and the surge'll be transmitted to all the others from there."

"Theoretically," Cruzon said. "Harold's not sure."

Adair could see he doubted all this. He seemed right on the edge of giving in to despair.

"Yeah," Stanner admitted. "Theoretically. But it's all I've got." He glanced at the window again. "Judging from what you and Waylon saw, they seem to be converging to the north—probably to get ready for their spawning."

"Ugh," Waylon said. "Spawning."

"Or call it dissemination or—wait, Breakenridge called it the Big Seeding. So they'll get together for that, concentrate their energies. They might be vulnerable then."

Waylon sat up straight on the bed. "You're saying, you actually might be able to—"

Stanner shrugged. "Worth a shot. A strong enough EM pulse would wipe out their memories, basically unprogram them. They'd just . . . disintegrate into lifeless parts."

"Then that's what the government was planning?" Cruzon asked. "That's why Bentwaters had the schematic?"

Stanner shrugged. "He had it because I asked for it. And I think it was something he wanted to push—something he was hoping to implement, somehow. But against orders—so he had to hide the specs. The Facility didn't think it would . . . cover all the bases."

"Like what?" Harold asked.

Stanner sighed. "Like, covering up the evidence. A hot enough bomb'll do that. Maybe . . . thermobarics."

Cruzon blurted, "They're going to *bomb* the *town*?"

"It's possible," Stanner admitted. "They'll figure it's a trade-off—Quiebra for the rest of the country. Maybe the world."

"Jesus *fuck*!" Waylon muttered.

"Yes, that just about says it all, Waylon," Harold muttered. "But then, I can't say I'm really surprised."

Cruzon turned to Stanner, his manner much colder now. "When will this happen?"

Stanner cleared his throat. "I don't know when. We'd be better off just taking our chances, breaking through the crawlers' lines, but if there's a chance we can stop this thing, maybe we can stop the bombing, too."

Cruzon said slowly, "How long to build that thing?"

Harold answered thoughtfully, "I was looking at those rigs on the roof, when we were outside. It wouldn't take long, really. It's just a matter of modifications. I'll have to identify their carrier wave, though."

"Can you do that?" Cruzon looked at the window. Probably picturing his family burning up in a thermobaric bomb explosion.

"Maybe. I can use a radio to work it out, I think."

Adair heard a long low growling yowl. Turned to see the cat pacing, sniffing the air, the fur on its back going up.

"If you're gonna get in close enough with that thing," Waylon said, "somebody's got to get their attention, set up a distraction. Anyway, shit, we hella need to let the kids know what's going on. And I think they're gonna want to help. Those things fucking *killed their parents*."

"Where do we find these kids?" Harold asked.

"Up in the hills," Waylon said. "There's a plan to meet up there.

And if it doesn't work, that's one way out of town with, like, lots of cover."

Stanner smiled wearily at Adair. "You see?" he said. "Maybe we can bring the world back again—almost the way it was."

She nodded her head slowly, because he seemed to want some kind of response from her.

But she didn't believe it.

The cat was pacing, pacing . . .

December 14, evening

Harold and Bert and Stanner and Cruzon unscrewed two of the transmitters from the roof of the apartment building—finding no one else in the building at all.

That is, no one alive. They'd found *parts* of someone, on a concrete balcony—pieces resembling the victim of a "torso murderer"—but no one commented on that. It was just how it was now.

They organized the transmitters and placed them, along with every other piece of applicable equipment they could find, into an old packing case of Bert's, along with his computer and a couple of car batteries taken from abandoned minivans on the street.

While Harold organized the electronics, Stanner and Bert and Cruzon cautiously scouted the dark, deserted complex of beachside condos, found the looted remains of a body in a Chevy SUV stopped at a stop sign. The back window of the SUV was broken inward, glass shattered over the body of a child in the back; a girl of about eleven with her neck broken, her eyes and arms missing.

Stanner was glad Shannon and Adair were with Lacey back at Bert's place. He and Bert laid the girl's body tenderly on a mattress in an open garage nearby, Cruzon covering her white, ravaged face with a sleeping bag. They returned glumly to the SUV. The keys were there, but they also found parts of what was probably one of the girl's parents scattered around the floor of the front seat. Judging from the hips and crotch, a man. The crawlers apparently had orders for specific body parts, and took only what they needed.

Bert stared at this salad of body parts—and turned away to be sick in the gutter. Stanner only felt sick. Cruzon and Stanner gathered the parts up in a plastic garbage sack; after a while Bert helped them. They put those in the open garage, too.

"I guess whoever it was stopped at a stop sign," Cruzon muttered, "and the crawlers caught up with them."

Bert snorted. "A stop sign—with the crawlers after them. Just the habit of obedience."

Stanner shook his head. "I think he chose that moment to fight back, is all." The SUV was still in park, and the key was switched on. Stanner guessed that the guy had put it in park so he could grab at the shotgun that lay in the backseat, but he hadn't got it into play in time. The car had remained in place, running in idle till it ran out of gas. There was a three-gallon gas can in the backseat.

Stanner took the gas can and poured its contents into the SUV's tank, Bert standing beside him with a shotgun in his hand, Cruzon on the other side of the car, pistol ready. As the fuel gurgled in, Stanner squinted up at the sky.

Bert looked at him. "You looking for . . . bombers?"

Stanner glanced at him. Then he admitted, "I guess I am. I don't know when to expect them. If we can make it unnecessary, maybe they won't have to come. So let's hurry the hell up." He tossed the gas can aside. They got into the SUV, drove back to Bert's.

Bert left the shotgun leaning against the wall in the living room. They found the others gathered in the bedroom.

As they came in, Harold and Waylon were hefting the open packing case of equipment onto the bed. They all stood around it, Waylon with his fireplace poker, Cruzon with his hand on his gun: the men and Lacey looking at the case, trying to decide if they should take anything else with them. Shannon was in the living room with Adair.

But then Adair came to stand in the doorway, with the skinny black cat in her arms. The cat seemed restless, staring around with its ears laid back. "The cat is staring at the windows," Adair said. "And I feel it, too. Mom and Dad and the others."

They looked at her, surprised that she'd suddenly begun speaking again.

Then the realization hit Stanner. "What do you mean you *feel* them?" Stanner said.

No one answered for a moment, and he started toward Adair, thinking he had to do whatever was necessary to protect Shannon.

And had the crawlers infected his daughter? She'd been in the next room, alone with Adair.

Reaching for Adair, he said to the others, "We'd better hold her down, look her over. She could've been infected, converted by them at some point. It's not always obvious when it happens."

Waylon snarled, "Mother*fucker*!" and swung the poker hard against Stanner's upper arm.

Recoiling from the stinging pain, Stanner spun to face Waylon, who was circling him, putting himself in between Adair and Stanner.

Waylon half crouched, the poker gripped in both hands.

"Back off, you fucking black-chopper drone! She just gets, like, intuitions sometimes, so just back the fuck off!"

"I only want to examine her."

"I said *no*! She's been through enough!"

"Cruzon," Stanner said grimly, rubbing his bruised arm. "Toss me your gun. I don't think he'll make me use it."

Cruzon hesitated. Adair's eyes had grown big, her mouth quivering. She shrank back from Stanner.

Shannon was there, then, pushing past Adair and Waylon. "Dad, cut it out! She was with me and I *know* she's okay."

Stanner stepped back, and he suddenly felt bone tired—and mingled with the fatigue was a profound sadness. "I'm—okay, I'm sorry. I just—I'm as stressed out as any of you. We're all overwhelmed. There was a—" He suddenly felt as if he might cry in front of them, and dug deep to get control. "There was a little girl— in the back of the car that we—we put her in a garage."

He turned away.

Then Lacey said, in a burst of impatience, "What about what Adair *said*? She said they were *coming*."

That's when the bedroom window shattered inward, window glass flying with a sound like a panicky wind chime, and a human head thrust itself in on a long metal stalk. It was what had been Morgenthal.

"Been looking for you," the crawler said, and thrust more of itself through the window.

"Hey!" Cruzon shouted, to draw the thing's attention to him. He aimed his pistol and fired, placing three rounds directly in the crawler's face. It splashed blood and maggotlike metal and fell thrashing at Lacey's feet.

Stanner admired the fact that she didn't scream, though he could see she wanted to. Instead, she pulled a dresser down over the writhing thing with a thudding smash, and herded Waylon and Adair out the bedroom door, as Bert and Harold grabbed the packing case. They heard a great tramping, trammeling from the roof. How many?

Then the front door, barred only with a flimsy lock, burst splintering inward, a crawler forcing its way in—what had been a woman. At the same moment the plate glass window shattered, a crawler carrying the drapes into the room with it. It took Stanner a moment to recognize the man who came bounding across the room. The diver from the wreck. Adair's father, Nick Leverton.

Stanner heard someone behind him scream sobbingly—but then the creature who'd been Nick struck Stanner head-on, knocking him backwards, and a pallid, grinning, almost human face shoved close to his own, filled the world, mouth opening. A seeking metal tendril probed at Stanner's lips, as arms reinforced with steel pressed him inexorably down.

All his life a warrior, at that moment Stanner felt like a little boy in a rapist's brutally strong hands.

There came a steady, nauseating *swack-crack*, repeated over and over again, and blood and lubricant splashed onto Stanner's face, as he realized that Waylon was smashing that fireplace poker repeatedly into the top of Nick's head, shouting incoherently with each blow.

The Nick-thing shuddered and his grip loosened. Stanner rolled him off and looked up to see Cruzon shrieking for help. A woman was bearing him down. She looked something like Adair and Lacey, was maybe Adair's mother. Her metal-tipped hands clamping Cruzon's wrists, snapping at his throat.

Another crawler was oozing through the window, scrabbling along the wall in defiance of gravity: a crawler with a baby's head and metal pistons for arms and mismatched hands, and the body of a large dog and four metal and flesh legs that gripped the wall with steely wires along their tiny human feet.

Stanner made himself go to the shotgun, distantly aware that Shannon had drawn Adair back into the hallway. He felt like the air had turned to hot wax around him, every step an effort against a wave of an inarticulate sense of *it's too much, it's finally too much*. He grabbed the shotgun, and it was as if the touch of a familiar weapon set his reflexes in motion, and another state of mind took him, so that he could move easily now, whirling and, despite the stiffness in his shoulder where Waylon had hit him, firing point-blank at the baby-faced crawler so that the drooling obscenity of its false infantility vanished in a spray of red.

Stanner jumped over the still-thrashing body of the Nick crawler, dashed toward Cruzon—where Harold and Lacey and Waylon were pulling at what had been Adair's mother, jerking her back so that her head had to stretch out on an extended neck to clamp its jaws into Cruzon's left shoulder. Cruzon screamed exactly at the moment when Stanner fired the shotgun into the side of her head.

And the thing that had been Adair's mother exploded—not just her head: her body flew apart, driven by its own cryptic inner reactions, legs spiraling away to trail living strands of intelligent metal through the air.

Cruzon crawled cursing and bleeding out from under her remains.

Stanner shouted, "Look out, Cruzon!" Warning him to avoid the crawling tendrils of still-living nanocells seeking from the crawlers' corpses. Stanner and the others had to dance around the reaching metal pseudopods on the floor, to get to the front door.

Harold and Bert already were carrying the packing case toward the door, everyone shouting at once and no one clearly hearing. Shannon covering the wailing Adair's eyes so she wouldn't have to look at the wreckage of her parents, as they followed Waylon and Lacey and Stanner out to the SUV.

Others were coming, across the roofs, outside. Four, five, maybe eight more.

Stanner and the others with him quickly piled into the SUV: shouting, sobbing, cursing, Stanner fishtailing it down the street, *not* stopping, not even slowing at the stop sign.

December 14, night

It was getting really dark. Some of the people waiting on the other side of the city water tank were turning on their flashlights.

At least, Donny thought, as he approached them, *no one's switching on night-eyes.*

It was cold and windy up here. Trees ringing the water tower swayed and clattered their branches. Below, in Quiebra Valley, the houses were sporadically lit. Now and then there was a distant gunshot.

Donny's footsteps gave out a metallic ringing as he strode across the big, green-painted top of the flat-topped municipal water tank. The big tank, three stories high, set right into the hilltop, wasn't entirely full. He could almost sense the water underneath, in the reverberation of his footsteps.

The metal top was marked with gang graffiti and imitation gang graffiti; with burnt, paint-blistered spots from last fall where people had actually built campfires up here.

There was Lance, shivering in a thin jacket. He had a pair of binoculars around his neck.

The crowd of kids seemed to be waiting for something; maybe they were waiting for him. Because when Lance waved at him and said, "Here he is, yo, it's Donny!" the other kids quieted down and looked his way.

There were teenagers and grade-school-age kids—some of them

with even smaller children, holding their hands. Nearly two hundred kids. Most of them looked pretty sketchy, their clothes dirty, their hair snagged with twigs and wild.

Donny felt that somehow Lance had represented him to them as someone who could save them, just because he had called this meeting. He wanted to run, seeing all those expectant, desperate eyes.

"Hi, you guys," he muttered, walking up. "Uh, I think we should turn off the flashlights. You know? Unless we really need 'em. They could attract attention."

Whispers, mumbled complaints, but one by one the flashlights went off.

"So, Lance, did you tell people? Like we talked about?"

Lance nodded. "Yeah, dude. It went out over the Internet—that we'd be meeting along Quiebra Creek at the east end of town. But it went only to people who knew we weren't actually going there."

Lance handed Donny the binoculars and pointed.

Donny looked, focusing, and a string of moving lights came into definition at the east end, along Quiebra Valley Road.

"So they think we're out there. Tight." He tossed the binoculars back to Lance. "Anybody try to leave town?"

"I did," Lance said, his voice breaking as he went on. "Me and—and two friends of mine. We tried the back road, and then we crashed the car trying to get away from the ones at the roadblock, and ran across country. Sandy—Roy got him. What used to be Roy. Mixed up with some other people. I think they just—just used his head. The animal crawlers got Duncan. And . . . I couldn't do anything. I got back to the road and I got a ride from Siseela."

He pointed to where she was sitting Indian style on a folded-up blanket on the metal, with a rifle, maybe a .22, across her knees.

"A gun. Good. Anybody else got guns?"

A few hands went up. Donny nodded. "Well, guns don't stop them very easily anyway, not for long. But it depends on how much you shoot 'em and where, what I heard."

"I got a couple Molotov cocktails," Lance said. "We could make more."

Raymond stepped forward: a tall black teen in a do-rag; he worked hard at keeping his face acutely expressionless. He lifted a 9mm pistol above his head. "And I got my nine." Making Donny remember that Raymond was in a rap group called Weapons of Mass Destruction.

Donny noticed some of the kids sniffling, some of them softly crying—trying not to do it out loud. Not all of them small.

He felt like that himself. But he'd found if he kept himself going, moving around, observing, thinking, then he didn't think about his parents, and he could function. "So here's my report," he said. "I just came back from the kids in the woods. The cat-kids. They're okay so far; the crawlers have other priorities. But it can't last. Question is, what do we do now?"

"We go home," an older teen said. He was a slab of a kid with blond hair parted in the middle, owlish glasses, and a heavy brown overcoat. "My dad says we should all go home."

"Who the fuck're you?" Raymond asked.

"That dude is *Larry Larry*," someone snickered, and a few of the others laughed.

Donny said, "Why should we go home, Larry?"

"My dad said I should tell you—"

"You told your *dad* about this?" Donny asked sharply. "Man, are you fucking crazy?"

"He's *not one of them.*"

"Where is he now?"

"Down the road, waiting for me."

"When did you get here?" Donny asked.

"Just a couple minutes go. We were driving along—"

"Why? Where were you going?"

"Um, he said he just wanted to go for a drive. And we saw the flashlights shining up here and I knew some kids were planning a meeting somewhere. He said I should see what—what's going on."

Raymond turned his cold eyes to Larry. "He asked you to spy, you mean."

"No! He just thinks we ought to go home and wait and just trust the authorities to do the right thing!"

A much younger Asian kid laughed bitterly. "Dude, do you *even know* what happened in the high school gym?"

"Look, those people were, like, rogues or something. The real authorities are going to be here to take care of things. You have to trust them, or you fall apart. You can't go around forming secret gangs and stockpiling guns."

Donny said, "Normally I'd agree about the guns part, but, man—" And Donny snorted. "—you obviously haven't been getting out much lately." Some of the others laughed.

But Raymond and Lance weren't laughing. Lance stepped up behind Larry, and suddenly he clasped him in a headlock as Raymond stepped up to him.

"Let's find out what one of these motherfuckers is made of," Raymond said. He checked the load on his nine.

"Hey," Siseela said, standing up. "Just chill with that shit, Raymond."

"Shut up, ho."

Siseela bristled. "Who you calling ho, motherfucker!"

Raymond ignored her and turned to Larry.

"Raymond!" Donny shouted, striding over to them. "Back off with that nine, man!"

Raymond looked at him. "Who made you the godfather around here, school-president boy?"

Lance was hissing something inaudible in Larry's ear.

"No, hey, come on," Larry was babbling. His face seemed swollen red. "I'm not—I'm not a—let me go, goddamnit!"

"Where's your pops?" Raymond demanded.

"I told you!" Larry wailed. "He's not one of them!"

Donny put a hand on Lance's arm. "Lance—"

"No, I ain't letting him go." But his grip relaxed a bit, and Larry writhed free and ran, yelling.

"Dad!"

Raymond aimed the nine, but Donny knocked his hand down. The gun discharged at the metal top of the water tank, the bullet striking sparks and ricocheting with a whine into the sky. Some of the kids screamed and threw themselves flat. Others quickly closed in around Larry and bore him down—a group of white boys from the Quiebra football team tackling him flat. They started kicking him, one of them smashing his face against the metal underfoot.

Looking at their faces, Donny saw that it wasn't savagery or cruelty making them do this; it was fear and pain.

He ran into the group, pushed into the melee and threw himself over Larry. "Leave him alone! We'll check him, just leave him alone!"

He felt a blow on his back; a second one bruising his ribs. Then a gunshot—but it had been fired into the air. Shaken by the gunfire, the crowd pulled back. Donny got to his knees, turned to see Raymond holding the smoking nine over his head. He'd fired a shot to drive them back.

"Back off from my man," Raymond said. Closing ranks with the other black kid. "Acting like a bunch of wiggers. Come on, let's check nerd boy."

Lance and the football players held Larry flat on his back while they looked down his throat, probing with a flashlight.

They didn't find anything. Lance pulled a Buck knife and prepared to cut Larry's arm open, to get another look inside him. Larry screamed.

"No!" Donny said. "Let him up, Lance! He's not one!"

Lance began cutting. Larry shrieked. Blood oozed and spattered when Larry tried to break free. One of the younger boys started crying.

Donny grabbed at Lance's knife hand—and missed as Lance slashed at him, now, cutting Donny's coat sleeve, cutting his upper shoulder.

"Back the fuck off, Donny!"

"Stop it, Lance!" Donny shouted, his face close to Lance's.

Lance held the knife rigidly, breathing hard, his eyes wild.

Donny wanted to draw away from that knife, but he was afraid of what Lance—white-faced and shaking—might do to Larry Gunderston.

"Okay, all right, Lance. You already cut him. Now go ahead and look into that cut you made in his arm."

Lance stared at him a moment, then turned and used a finger to probe the cut he'd made. Larry writhed, his face contorted. The long cut pumped blood, and nothing else.

Lance stood up, staring down at Larry. He moved off to the edge of the crowd. Donny could see Lance's shoulders shaking.

"Why don't you all check each other!" Larry yelled tearfully. "How do you know, goddamn it! Cut each other open, why don't you!"

"Mostly," Donny said, "the thing that's changing people doesn't like the young ones much. Mostly they just get used for parts. But there's some got taken over. Some who were half robot already. If you want to check each other, why not."

"I'm gonna fucking sue you shit-heads," Larry was wailing, sitting up, clutching his wound as the others let him go.

"Shut the fuck up, dumbass," Raymond said.

Donny went on, raising his voice so everyone could hear. "But we should move ahead! Make our plan! I figure we might start a big fire, near the borders where they're patrolling, keep 'em busy with that, get the attention of the county authorities maybe."

"I don't advise that," a voice said from the steel ladder at the edge of the water tank.

Everyone turned to look—and they saw that it was a man in early middle age, and with him was a cop. There were cries of fear from the crowd, and whispers urging violence. Donny cursed himself for not setting up sentries.

Raymond swore and pointed his 9mm pistol. The man—Donny recognized him from somewhere, maybe he'd seen the guy in the halls at the school, going into Morgenthal's class—was raising his hands in surrender, but that didn't mean anything; a crawler might do that to get you off guard.

"I'm Major Stanner," the man shouted. "I'm from the government!"

Behind him came a Filipino cop Donny knew—or had known when the cop was human. Commander Cruzon.

"You guys can check us," Stanner said. "Look down our throats! I'll even submit to some cuts. We're on your side! We're human!" Others were coming up the ladder, raising their hands as they stepped onto the top of the tank.

Donny recognized Waylon, from school, and Adair. After them came a guy Donny thought was a substitute teacher, and a woman he didn't know. Then a scared-looking young woman, maybe half Asian. She went to stand next to Stanner.

Then came a big older man, with sandy hair.

Larry got up and ran to him. "Dad! They cut me! They held me down and cut me with a knife!"

The elder Gunderston looked scared and confused. "I heard some shots. I—was anyone shot?"

"There's one more in my group," Stanner said. "He's working on something. He'll be up here in a minute. We're going to need your help with it. Anyone of you kids know your electronics? Who's got skills, here?"

A few voices piped up.

But Raymond said, "Y'all line up over there. We going to check you real thorough."

Donny nodded. "Raymond's right. We've got to do this. We have to look close. And just keep your hands up."

Then someone else came up the ladder. A big shambling figure, who walked kind of funny, and everyone was instantly certain that here was a crawler.

Raymond said, "Motherfucker!" and fired the nine wildly at the figure—who went to his knees, wailing, covering his head, as one of the bullets grazed his shoulder.

"Who the hell is that?" Stanner muttered.

Raymond ran closer, getting a bead on the man's head. The man curled up fetally, babbling to himself.

Donny yelled, "Waitaminute, shit, *wait*, Raymond!"

Raymond hesitated. Donny ran up, staring. "That's old Vinnie!"

"So you know him, so fucking what. He could still be one of them. He ain't with the other ones just came. Nobody vouching for him. I don't see why we should trust any of the so-called grown-ups, man. And look at how weird this motherfucker is."

Lance came to stand by Raymond. "Raymond's right, cuz." He wiped his eyes. "All this bullshit is something the motherfuckin' 'grown-ups' did." He scowled at Stanner.

Vinnie was talking fervently to his own knees. "They took her parts in the hole, who's calling star control, wait don't hurt the bots, let me stay with the gold walking man, the red hand the red hand the red hand the red hand. They're tied together in a whole, the deputy sent me . . ."

"You see that," Raymond said. "The man's talking like a fucking robot with its brains scrambled. He's one of them." He put both hands on the nine and steadied it at Vinnie.

Adair walked over and put her hand on Donny's arm. There was something about her—then Donny realized what it was. Her head was turning this way and that, like Stevie Wonder, as if she couldn't focus her eyes on any one thing. But she spoke, her voice raspy.

"He," Adair began. She licked her lips and tried again. "He's trying to tell us where something is. He wants to show us . . . something."

"We can check Vinnie here, too," Donny said. "We'll have to hold him down. He doesn't like to be touched. We'll check all y'all. And listen, you grown-ups, checking you might hurt. So don't even bother whining about it."

"You'd better do whatever you're going to do quick, Donny," Lance said, looking out at the valley with his binoculars. "Those fuckers are onto us, man. They're on their way back."

That's when Vinnie started squawking at them. So it seemed to Donny. Making squawking sounds and spouting random words. He stood up and started walking toward them—but sideways. Some of the kids tittered as Vinnie did a standing crabwalk within a couple of yards of Donny—and then turned *backwards* to walk closer. And dropped a piece of paper at his feet.

"That guy's infected, for sure," Lance said.

Donny shook his head as he bent to pick up the paper. "That's just Vinnie. That's just what he's like. Leave him alone. Yo, Sissy, bring me that flashlight."

Siseela held the flashlight as he unfolded the paper. It was a sheet torn from the yellow pages. On it was a listing for cemeteries in the northeast Bay Area—Richmond, El Sobrante, San Pablo. Quiebra Cemetery was circled with a pencil line. Next to it in the margin was a rectangular shape, in pencil, with an *X* in the lower right-hand corner of the rectangle. By the *X* were the penciled words *ALL US*.

"The cemetery?" Donny said.

Stanner came and looked over Donny's shoulder, then at Vinnie. "You saying that's where they're based, Vinnie?"

Vinnie had his back to them. But he nodded his head, five or six times more than necessary.

Mr. Gunderston shook his head sadly. "There's really no point in going there. You'd be overwhelmed, in no time. Just wait here. They're coming here. Because I just told them where you were."

Everyone froze. His son turned to look at him.

"Dad?"

Gunderston began to grow as he spoke. His legs divided and extended, his clothes ripping to accommodate them; he bent his knees to crouch. "We had no idea there were so many of you up here. And with some of these others. We don't want them running around loose." He looked at Adair. "This one senses things. Her mother warned us about that. We've been looking for her." He looked at Vinnie. "And now I gather that one can listen in on us."

Raymond broke the spell, shouting "Fuck *you!*" and firing the automatic pistol—but Gunderston leapt at Raymond first.

"It doesn't matter if you kill me," he said, tearing Raymond's arm from his shoulders. He threw the blood-gushing limb, the hand still clutching the gun, over the rim of the tank. "I'm just like a skin cell, boys and girls! Were you paying attention in biology? The body continually makes more cells!"

Larry gaped at the thing that had been his father, stunned, his thick lips quivering.

Stanner was running toward the ladder. Deserting them.

Donny grabbed the .22 from Siseela.

Raymond was wriggling facedown, his voice bubbling wordlessly as he died, while Cruzon ran up to get a shot with his pistol—but the crawler leapt, shouting, "And I'm the latest design!"

Twelve yards horizontally, two in the air, the crawler leapt— soared!—and came down on Lance, smashing him onto his back so hard the bones of his chest exploded from his sides. Everything Lance would have screamed with was crushed, and he only made a silent scream with his open mouth.

Donny tried to get a shot with the rifle, but kids were running in the way.

Cruzon fired twice and one of the rounds caught the crawler, who only turned and snarled in response, showing a gleeful fat white face, a kind of monstrous parody of his son—who knelt with his hands over his eyes, sobbing.

The crawler leapt again, coming down in front of Cruzon, his forearm punching out with the force of a mechanical battering ram, slamming the little cop in the middle of the chest. Cruzon flew backwards through the air and fell yelling despairingly over the side of the water tower and into the shadows.

Donny pushed someone out of the way—he didn't even see who— and raised the rifle to his shoulder, fired at the crawler, bolted another round in the chamber, fired, and did it again. The Gunderston crawler set himself to leap at Donny.

Gunderston's son, Larry—

His nerdy, pompous, self-indulgent, insecure son, a strictly first-season fan of *Star Trek*—

Larry threw himself at the thing that had been his father, threw his whole weight against him so that the crawler, clutching at the boy, fell heavily on his side, momentarily off balance.

"Daddy, stop it!" he shrieked.

For a moment Donny thought he saw a flicker of hesitation on the older Gunderston's face.

And then Gunderston's eyes glazed over, and he broke his son's neck.

He threw the body aside and poised to leap at Donny.

"Oh, shit," Donny muttered.

Gunderston's head flew apart—shot from behind. A second shot punched a hole through his middle, spewing blood and metal bits on the green-painted metal roof of the tank. He flailed—and then fell flat.

The crawler's falling revealed Stanner, standing behind him, a smoking shotgun in his hands. "I had it stuck down behind a pipe, near the top of the ladder, in the dark, so I didn't scare anyone carrying it up here. Guess he didn't have his eyes turned on all the way when he came up the ladder."

Donny sank to his knees, shaking, his heart still hammering. He'd wondered, once, what it was like to be old and afraid of a heart attack. He thought he had some idea, now.

Stanner walked over to him and helped him to his feet. "You're a remarkable kid," he said.

Donny almost hit him. Instead he shrugged and said, "Who says I get to be a kid anymore?"

Then he went to talk to the others.

The thing that had been Sprague had found that if he was very careful and paid close attention, he could do things that weren't in his primary or secondary directives.

But he'd had to work hard at it, to let Vinnie go.

Now, helping to push the seed launcher into place, he found that he was able to move slowly, very slowly, to just sort of drag back so that the others kept having to readjust. He wasn't thinking of it as stalling. He was careful not to think of it at all. Careful to hide that part of his mind. It was a part of himself that they found hard to read, anyway. Something deep.

The impulse to resist the All of Us came from the deepest most-inside part of him. Something he had been scarcely aware of, when he was alive. It was as if he'd always been looking outward from that deep place, so he hadn't been able to see that part of himself—like you can't see your own eyes without a mirror.

Struggling to be something more than just a part of the All of Us, even in little ways, seemed to release something hidden in him; it was as if he could sense that secret inward place and know it was connected to something fine, something higher than the All of Us, and higher than people, too. It gave him the strength to work inefficiently.

He scuttled around the metal shaft of the launcher and managed to stumble on the packed earth wall so that he tumbled into two other servants of the All of Us, and there was a confusion of limbs.

One of them began to watch him. Sprague was careful to seem to leap back to work.

Adair watched them pile up the bodies. She felt she was on the breathless edge of another place. She might fall into life or death from here.

Lacey put her arm around Adair, and Bert put his arm around Lacey. They watched the others at their preparations.

"We only have a few minutes, Donny," Stanner said, cradling the shotgun in his arms. Glancing at the sky.

Donny nodded. "I know. It'll be quick. It's just something I feel like we have to do, or we won't be able to do very much else."

He turned to the others—all the kids, a few adults, gathered on the other side of the improvised pyre atop the water tank. An armful of branches had been laid atop the bodies of the Gunderstons, Lance's body, Raymond's, Cruzon. Stanner himself had brought Cruzon's broken body up the ladder, in a fireman's carry.

Behind the crowd of kids, Harold and Waylon were setting up some equipment. Some of it really strange. They'd gotten a guitar and an amplifier and speakers, and they'd run wires from the switch box that controlled the waterflow for the tank. There was other equipment Adair didn't understand, all wired together. There was another piece of equipment, she knew, that they'd left in the car. The pulser, Harold had called it.

Everyone watched—two hundred kids, a few adults—as Donny approached the pyre for the dead.

Donny himself poured the gasoline on the improvised pyre. He spoke for everyone to hear, as he poured it on. "They're going to see this light and they're going to hear the noise and come up here. And we'll be gone when they get here. But not too far away—we need them to follow us."

He stood back and nodded at Siseela, who lit a book of matches; it flared, she threw it at the pyre, and that flared up, too, roaring.

Adair listened in a kind of floating rapture, feeling as if she was above the scene, watching from overhead, as Donny turned to the crowd of kids and spoke loudly, like a preacher trying to be heard over the roar of the world; spoke to them all with an instinctive sense of ritual.

"This isn't just to say good-bye to Lance and Raymond and these other people here killed by this thing. This is to say good-bye to our parents! It's their funeral, too!"

A universal groan arose from the listening kids. They huddled closer together. The smaller ones wept as Donny went on.

"Maybe not all our parents are gone. Major Stanner says they haven't got to everyone. But lots of us know for sure. Lots of us know that our parents are dead! And we have to accept that! We have to say *yes*. Our parents may be walking around, just like living people with free will—but they're not living at all! Even if they're walking and talking, if they've been changed over, then *our parents are dead*!" He paused, seeming to get control of himself, and cleared his throat. Then he clenched his fists and he yelled, "They left us too soon! But they didn't mean to leave us, and it isn't our fault! That's two things we have to know! Is everybody clear on that? *They didn't mean to leave, and it isn't our fault.*"

There were unintelligible murmurs of agreement, mixed with groans and sobs. Adair stepped a little closer to Donny to listen, something in her responding, rising like the crackling smoke from the pyre.

Blue flames rose sinuously and hissed. "Now listen to me," Donny went on. "It's Bad Times, what's happening. It's hella Bad Times. But we gotta forgive them for leaving us—but we also have to let ourselves cry for them! We each think of our parents, and we cry for them! Think of them now! Think of your folks. If you loved them or hated them, or you weren't sure, think of them and forgive them and *let them go!*"

"I can't!" a young girl said, her mouth buckling.

"You have to!" Donny said.

A collective sigh merged seamlessly into a moan.

Adair closed her eyes and thought of her folks, coming to get her at summer camp when she was a kid. Her dad teaching her to swim. Her mom insisting that she hadn't let her win at chess— when she had. Watching her dad working on the boat, and being proud of him; she hadn't known what it was she was feeling, then, but she knew it now: pride.

She remembered seeing her parents arguing—and how, when they noticed her watching the argument, they made up. They made up, right then and there, just for Adair.

"Everybody we lost, we say good-bye to—and we let go!" Donny shouted. *"All of them!"*

And she thought of Cal. Her big brother, trying not to jeer at her too much when she fell on the skateboard. Helping her up. Cal showing her how to make a simple Web site. Pretending he wasn't really happy when he saw her expression at Christmas—when he gave her the jacket she'd wanted. Having earned the money himself.

Good-bye, Cal.

Then Donny said, not shouting but his firm voice still carrying, "Now say to yourselves, *my parents are gone! They're just gone!* I'm going to say it—and we have to say it all together! *My parents are gone!*"

Their faces lit by the spitting fire, by flames rippling from black-ening corpses, they called out, with him, *"My parents are gone!"*

Adair falling to her knees and saying it into the hands covering her face.

"They won't ever come back!"

"They won't ever come back!"

"And we are the adults now!"

"We are the adults now!"

Adair couldn't say it. But she nodded.

Switched-off flashlight tucked between her breasts, Lacey came rushing down the metal ladder so fast she fell, near the end, twisted her ankle on the gravel at the bottom. "Shit!" She pulled her flashlight from her blouse and swept it over to the SUV. "The son of a bitch! Sneaking off!"

She ran—ankle throbbing—up to the back of the SUV, where Bert was pushing a milk crate with a jumble of electronics onto the lowered tailgate. "Bert, you prick!"

He turned to her with an unpracticed expression of puzzled innocence. "What? I was going to, um . . ."

"Bullshit!"

Stanner and Harold exchanged looks and went to the front of the SUV.

Bert sighed, pushing the box into the SUV and slamming the back. "Okay, I don't want you to go."

"What, 'a man's gotta do what a man's gotta do' and women stay behind?"

"The fewer who go, the better. What can you do? I mean, in this—this—"

"I can be smart and resourceful and I can watch your back, you dope!"

He reached out to her, and she pulled away, her mouth quivering. "Goddamn it, I just found you and—" Then she let him take her in his arms.

"I know," he said softly in her ear. "I feel the same way. But I need to feel . . . like I'm doing this for you. *For* you. Maybe it's old-fashioned. Hell, it's primeval. But I need to protect you. Let me do that, Lacey." He drew back and looked in her eyes. "Let me protect you."

"Okay, cowboy. I'll wait behind. But you'd better fucking come back."

"Bert!" Stanner called. "We're going!"

"I'll see you in a little while, Lacey," Bert said. *If any of us make it . . .*

He kissed her and climbed into the SUV, and she watched it drive away.

"Son of a bitch," she muttered. *"Men."*

Sprague—what had once been Sprague—had been sent to patrol the perimeters of the cemetery.

He looked at the shape rising from the trench they'd dug. Most of the trench was there to absorb the blast back.

The launcher looked to him like one of those projectors they had in planetariums.

Once it was calibrated, and fired . . .

Once the projectile had reached an altitude of a mile . . .

The gliders would release. Thousands of minute glider seeds, nanotech life, released into the air currents, and the world would begin the next state of reorganization, spreading the gospel of the All of Us.

He felt weak, now. He couldn't fight any longer. He was going to try to forget himself in the All of Us.

Then he saw the fire in the hills. A flickering that quickened to become the dark hump of the hill's own burning eye. And he saw other lights, from there: thin flashlight beams, aimed upward, around the central fire. It was atop the town water tank, he realized. Where that meeting was. He hoped Vinnie had gotten there.

Then came the thunder—the heavy-metal thunder—the boom of a single guitar chord, an open E, played over and over again, from up there, angry, barely musical, maddeningly redundant: perfect.

Gunderston had told them about the meeting. But he hadn't said much, and only a dozen colony units had been sent. Now it was obvious that more needed to be sent.

Everyone could be sent—except a few guards placed around the cluster.

Sprague—what had been Sprague—set up an alarm. He told them, in their symbology, that his "expert system data," his memories of being a deputy, informed him that a major Disabling of the Org was going on, centered on that water tower.

Everyone available must go there!

Immediately!

The cluster asked him for certitude.

He staggered under the power of the question. It required all his inner depth to give the answer that his soul demanded of him—to lie to them, for the sake of a secret hope.

Certitude to the probability of 96.9999999999! Disaster if we do not converge!

Then, the cluster said, for the All of Us, all but designates 7, 3, 53, and 99: converge, to the E chord and the flame, and there destroy all you find; for the seeding is upon us, calibration is done, and pressure is building in the launcher. In thirteen minutes and seven seconds, the world will change, and utopia will become real at last.

23

Shivering in the night's chill, Stanner tried the cell phone again, though he knew it wouldn't work. Hoping to reach someone at the Pentagon, to tell them to wait. *Don't drop the bombs, there's another way!*

Chaos returned his call: just endless static.

He shook his head at Bert and Harold. "No," he said. "They've got an impenetrable barrier up now."

They were crouching behind the splintered remnants of a wooden fence, across the street from the cemetery. Stanner was preparing to enter the crawler's home base. Harold was still tinkering with the pulser. Bert cradled the shotgun, helping watch their backs.

"Maybe we're just being stupid," Harold said, his hands shaking as he tightened the last screw. "Maybe we should have sent people out through the woods, and just let 'em take their chances and try to get help—try to stop any idea of bombing. We don't know this thing's going to work."

Stanner felt a sudden sympathy for Harold—who'd had so much dropped on his narrow shoulders, so suddenly—and at one and the same moment he wanted to shout at him, *Goddamn it, you said it would work!*

Bert shook his head. "They'd have to convince people about what's going on here anyway. That'd take much too long."

Stanner didn't tell them he was pretty sure that familiar droning sound he even now heard from the sky was a stealth bomber. Soon the bombs would be falling.

The governor of the state of California today asked the president to declare Quiebra, California, a disaster area after a double explosion at a refinery set off a firestorm that killed virtually all residents.

Stanner shook his head. Maybe he should have told Shannon to try to make it to the next town. But it would be better to die quickly in an overwhelming flash of heat than to be torn apart by one of those things in the woods, wouldn't it?

The guitar boomed again, in the distance, from the hilltop. Open E, thumping, echoing, over and over. Calling the crawlers.

"That's enough guitar, Waylon," Bert muttered, looking at the firelight up in the hills. "Get the fuck out of there."

As if Waylon had heard him, the sound died away and ceased altogether. Or did that mean the crawlers had stopped him?

"I've gotta go now," Stanner said, picking up the pulser. "Is it ready or not?"

Harold nodded, gesturing at the contrivance. "Take it."

The pulser looked like two of the rooftop transmitters joined together, both contrived of old miniature satellite-TV dishes. They were wired toward each other, like a closed clamshell. Four car batteries were taped together on a board under the pulser unit, providing the initial energy.

"That can't be enough power to do what you need to have done," Bert muttered, shaking his head.

"That's the point of the design Bentwaters gave us," Harold whispered, glancing nervously at the cemetery, watching two more crawlers creep from it; seeing them streak down the street, toward the hills. "The whole point is taking a small amount of energy and multiplying it into one big electromagnetic pulse."

"Do those things eat, Stanner?" Bert asked, his face ghastly with speculation. "How do they sustain themselves?"

"Yes, sometimes they eat. Anything edible. And, you don't want to know the details," Stanner said. He was shoving the crude device into a big canvas backpack. It didn't quite fit. He had to cut the canvas with Lance's Buck knife to get it in.

Something was rising up, in the midst of the cemetery. A thing like a big metal insect, aiming its body at the sky.

"Oh, shit, we're too late," Harold muttered. "Fuck!"

Maybe, Stanner thought, *but fuck it*.

He slung the backpack over a shoulder, grunting at the weight. He was dead tired—but he felt wired, too. A combination that made his gut churn.

Or maybe that feeling in his stomach was from the ever-present, unceasing, background hiss of sheer terror. Mostly, terror for Shannon.

Harold looked at him in something like admiration. And Stanner thought, *It's because I'm good at not showing how scared I am*. It was best they didn't know.

He took the shotgun, gave Bert the pistol, took a last look around. All clear for the moment. He started through the fence.

"We're coming, too," Bert said, licking his lips.

Stanner knew Bert had to force himself to say that—and Stanner actually admired him for saying it. "No, Bert," he said, just loud enough to be heard, over his shoulder. "The fewer we are, the less likely we'll be noticed in there."

And one, he thought, *is pretty damn few*.

And then he ran heavily across the street—sprinting wasn't possible with that weight on his back—and through the gate, into the cemetery. Something moved, about thirty feet away. He crouched and waited. It glided past, low to the ground, and out the gate.

Stanner trudged onward, almost tripping over a corpse torn from a coffin, some of its limbs utilized by the crawlers; they couldn't use decayed flesh, but old bones might be utilized. He wondered why the crawlers had picked the cemetery for their cluster. Maybe its location was right for their launch. And they were vulnerable to strong electromagnetics; this might well be the most insulated place. But that wouldn't help them if he could get the pulser right in amongst the cluster.

It looked more like a half-cleared demolition site now, with most of the grass gone, tumbled slabs of marble and concrete piled here and there. Mounds of fresh earth, like giant molehills, humped beside gaping holes. Well-beaten crawler paths crisscrossed between the mounds, radiating from the holes. A faint light was shining up from the holes in the cemetery earth.

Vinnie's map had indicated the northwest corner of the cemetery. Stanner figured it'd be a mistake to enter the nest too close to its heart. It'd be too well guarded and he wouldn't have the time he needed. So he dropped the backpack down the nearest hole and dropped in after it. Into one of the tunnels.

He landed on his feet, shotgun in his hands, grunting—expecting to be jumped.

There came a distant moan, a high-pitched wordless chattering, a shuffling sound—but no one visibly around. Just tunnels, the occasional glow, a rank smell.

The kids had done their job. They were luring the crawlers away.

Shannon was up there.

Don't think about that. Stay on task, punk.

Stanner put his backpack on again, hefted the shotgun for comfort, and headed the way he thought the center of the crawler nest would be.

Electric lights were strung down here, where the packed-earth tunnels intersected. The crawlers were constantly innovating; the red eye beams were a recent device.

He came to a side tunnel leading off to a chamber on the right, about forty feet in. A crawler was arched over a man who writhed and whimpered.

The round earthen chamber was illuminated only by the light from the main tunnel and the red glow of the crawler's eyes. The crawler was someone Stanner didn't recognize—a local doctor, perhaps, judging by the white coat, the dangling stethoscope. His lips seemed so red against his pale skin; his thin hair dangled down. He was on all fours, arching his body—which was elongated by the metal extensions in his arms and legs and neck—over a man in the shreds of a gray suit and tie. A balding man with a round face. Not much more could be made out in the welter of blood. The man's arms and legs were turned all wrong; they were broken that way. A set of probing tools ratcheted on damp bony extensions from the opened gut of the crawler. The silvery tools—drill, something like needle-nose pliers, saws, blades—stabbed down at the man trapped underneath, snatching and pulling and cutting bits out here and there, experimenting. Vivisecting. The crawler chatting to the man casually the whole time.

Stanner's insides twisted and he wanted to rush in there and try to put a stop to this. But if he let himself get distracted . . .

Stay . . .

"You said to the All of Us," the crawler said to his victim, "that if we could meet you in San Francisco, where you would feel safe, you would make a deal, you would reap the benefits." The tools darted down and the man screamed and writhed, and his writhing brought another scream from him because it hurt to move.

. . . on task . . .

"You were willing to sell the town that had not made your career as an attorney profitable, but there is so much we must learn." The man's scream bubbled up, as another tool stabbed down.

. . . punk!

Stanner thought of the bombers that were approaching Quiebra—and forced himself to go on.

He went another twenty-five feet—and came to a second cross tunnel. Far down to the right, ruby eyes glowed with piercing red beams, tracking toward him. He drew back and crouched. The crawler was the big-bellied jowly male cop he'd seen standing with the lady cop, by the burning car. He was crawling along on his extended legs, looking for intruders, probably. But he missed Stanner—who'd found a foul-smelling heap of rubbish to crouch behind. The crawler hesitated.

Stanner felt his hands go moist on the shotgun. He tightened his hold, prepared to jump up, to fire.

Then the crawler moved onward, to the left. And Stanner barely managed to control his gag reflex when he stood and saw that the heap of rubbish he had hidden behind was a pile of human body parts. He recoiled and for a moment he almost ran back down the tunnel.

Get a fucking grip, ya pussy. Another favorite expression of his father's.

"Okay, you old son of a bitch," Stanner muttered, and moved on, down the tunnel the way he'd been going.

Bones dangled from the packed-earth roof, between tangles of wire. More than one coffin had become an impromptu ceiling support. The nearest was neatly sliced through from beneath. A swollen-faced woman, staring in death, hung in her Sunday best at an awkward angle from a sheared-open box; her brown hair, flecked with mold, dangled like Spanish moss so that it brushed Stanner's shoulder as he hurried past.

And then something bounded from behind, a rush of motion, metal-extended fingers closing around Stanner's throat. And one of them had him.

"I *thought* I heard something, by god," the crawler said, knocking the shotgun easily from Stanner's hands.

And then knocking him out cold.

Adair felt a certain joy in lighting her first Molotov cocktail.

She was in the back of a pickup truck driven by Waylon, kneeling in a reeking, rumpled old dog blanket, with Siseela squatting and swaying beside her, steadying her as she lit the Molotov's rag with a Bic lighter. Lance had stolen the truck earlier and left the keys in it—along with the quart beer bottles brimming with gasoline, stuffed shut with rags.

"How did he know how to make those things?" Siseela yelled, over the car's noise and the wind.

"Probably like I know how to use it!" Adair shouted. She felt better now, since the funeral. She could talk. She could act. She expected to die tonight, but she'd ceased to care. "From movies!"

And then she threw the flaming bottle at the crawlers bounding behind the truck—into the crawler female's leering face.

She knew that face, and the face of the old man bounding beside her, nearly as fast as the truck: the Garratys. But, of course, it wasn't really them.

So she didn't feel bad when the bottle of gas exploded over what had been Mrs. Garraty, the crawler roaring with pain and fury, a figure cloaked all in striated flame, clawing at the air and falling back to be run over by the police car driven by the lady cop—the crawler who'd once been a lady cop.

Holding on to the back of the truck's cab, Adair stood and looked at the other cars up ahead on the winding road leading down from the hills into town. Seven cars full of kids, weaving in and out, some of them firing shots at the pursuing crawlers.

As she watched, a boy in his parents' Volvo crashed headlong into a crawler that blocked the road—the crawler flying, falling in front of an SUV. The boy driving the Volvo spun out, crashing. Three crawlers converged on the Volvo.

She could see more of them, leaping and crawling through the hills, coming after the convoy.

She hoped Waylon had gotten away from the municipal water tank.

"You hold me steady this time!" Siseela yelled. Her eyes bright with anger, with revenge, and wet with sorrow. "I want to throw one!"

Stanner was distantly aware that he was being dragged by his arms along the dirt floor, on his back. His head was throbbing, each throb carrying its message of hot flashing pain, and he was reluctant to open his eyes.

Get a grip!

He looked, and saw the jowly cop's face: pallid, edged by puffy red tissue, extending on a metal stalk from the dirty uniform collar. The cop's arms were moving like a jackal's front legs to either side of Stanner, and it took him a moment to see how he was being carried. Metal filaments were extending from the converted cop's underside, gripping his clothing, winding around his upper arms.

He could feel his heels dragging in the dirt—and he could feel the pack still heavy on his shoulders. It had become a sort of sled under his back as he was dragged over the ground.

Am I still myself? Stanner wondered. He took stock—and could find no other mind nestled with his own. No sense of having been violated, physically. They hadn't changed him over. They had other plans for him, then.

He was dragged about ten yards farther—and they'd entered a large circular chamber, maybe seventy feet in diameter. Tilting his head painfully, Stanner could make out other tunnel entrances converging from every direction. In the center something hulked, quivering, restless within itself. There were faces in it, many faces, and limbs and machinery that seemed randomly intertwined. *The cluster.*

Down a corridor to one side he could see the bottom of the launching mechanism, and crawlers clambering around its base.

He was dragged closer to the tangled, reeking central figure in the room.

Then he felt himself released. He was dropped at the base of the living mound of interlinked crawlers. Immediately hands reached out from the cluster, grasped him, and pulled him closer. The smell of electrical burning and charred flesh and decay was overpowering; the thing moaned in a multitude of voices.

This was the primary CPU of the nanocell colonies, the organizer for all the brains that made up the All of Us. He tilted his head back and got an upside-down glimpse of faces and arms and limbs, bodies heaped but living, like a hive of human flesh. He thought of a picture he'd seen of a "king rat," which was actually a living cluster of rats whose tails and bodies were somehow entangled—and which supposedly had a collective mind of its own. It was like that, but even more scrambled: bodies fused, faces emerging from torsos, hands from necks, all interconnected and interpenetrated by electronic interfacing and wire. Not quite random, there was a symmetry somehow, but it was a perverse symmetry.

Stanner struggled, but the hands tightened their fingers on his limbs, drawing him close.

The cop who'd brought him spoke in an almost jovial voice. "You'll feed the All of Us, with some of your tissue—usually your lower half. Eaten by the cluster, the primordial processing unit you see here. The upper half will incorporate nicely, your personal expert systems having some useful application. Protocol seventeen, blue, seventy-four seconds till release."

They'd reached the cul-de-sac where they'd planned to turn around so they could take the convoy the other way, lead the crawlers in a circle—but Adair saw dozens more crawlers now. They scuttled about in the road, on the rooftops, converging on the convoy of teenagers.

Other crawlers were arriving in cop cars, flashing their lights, screeching sideways across the road to block their escape.

The convoy of kids came to a jerking halt in the middle of the cul-de-sac, Adair and the others looking desperately around. The few guns in the trucks and cars opened fire at the crawlers—and the crawlers only laughed, and moved in on them.

Then Stanner saw Sprague's face, upside down on the ceiling of the chamber. He moved a little. He wasn't part of the cluster.

"Please, Sprague," Stanner croaked.

"Used it all up," Sprague said. "All my *me*. Nothing left. Can't struggle anymore. There's a certain beauty to the All of Us. To what's planned. Kind of like a planned community. One big housing development. Harmony."

"Your family, Sprague."

Stanner felt something gnawing at his thigh. Something else

digging into his calf. A clutching thing yanking at the backpack—which was torn away from him and tossed onto the dirt beside the cluster, near one of the gutters for sewage.

Stanner wanted to scream in terror but turned it into a shouted demand.

"Sprague! Your family! Come on, Sprague, there's always something more in a man! Look for it!"

Sprague shook his head. Stanner was pulled more deeply into the cluster.

Fingers felt their way blindly around Stanner's throat; he felt a face nuzzle at him, teeth gnashing to get a grip on his inner thigh; metal extensions tugged at his genitals, closed around his ankles.

"Sprague!"

The fingers around his throat tightened; his breath stopped. Blue lights swarmed before his eyes. He felt something get a grip on his left arm that felt like it had the inexorable mechanical force of a backhoe. It began to pull his arm, to twist, like someone twisting at a turkey leg to wrench it loose from the cooked bird, and he knew that in a few moments his arm would be yanked off his body.

"Sprague, you can be yourself if you choose to, goddamn it! Sprague, be yourself! Sprague, you can BE!"

Then Sprague dropped from the ceiling, and his mismatched limbs, his ordinary man's mouth, his metal claws—all began to rend at the cluster's hands, the strands of living metal gripping Stanner, so that something yelped and the grips loosened. Stanner wrenched himself free, rolled away from the cluster and threw himself onto the backpack.

But the crawler-cop loomed over him. "I thought there was grenades or some such in that pack, but maybe it's a bigger problem, there, boy," it said, leering, reaching for the pack. "But we're launching in about twenty seconds, so it don't really matter anyhow."

There was a flurry of motion as Sprague leapt onto the crawler's back, gripping it from behind with his six limbs, and the crawler changed shape, head spinning on shoulders so it could bite into Sprague's skull.

Sprague shrieked in pain—and relief, and fell away, as his head cracked like a boiled egg. He went limp, dead with finality.

Stanner clawed through the pack. He found the little toggle Harold had wired in, threw it, and tossed the pack into the mass of the cluster. The device had to go off close to the cluster to work.

The pulser went off, its EMP field sweeping through the cluster's primary store of nanocells; transmitted from there to every crawler in communication with the All of Us.

There was a high-pitched whine, which grew with every crawler it reached, and every light in the crawler nest sizzled and burst—and everything went pitch-black.

All the streetlights went out. The cars' engines died. The lights on the cop cars went out, too. Adair barely noticed.

The crawlers were setting themselves to leap.

Adair had a tire iron ready to swing at the livid face coming at her—Mr. Garraty, leaping onto the back of the truck. The crawler poised quivering over her and Siseela.

And fell on its face in the bed of the pickup. Its head fell from its neck; its arms fell from its shoulders. Wherever the living metal sheath connected its segments, the parts fell away.

All up and down the street, and all over town, the crawlers began falling apart.

Mr. Garraty spoke, once. "Oh, thank God," he said.

And then he was dead.

It took a long moment for it to sink in. Another long moment of sobbing relief. And then the cheers and whoops began.

"Holy shit," Harold muttered, looking around. They were waiting for Stanner by the smashed-open fence, across from the cemetery.

The entire town had blacked out. The distant headlights up in the hills had gone black. The streetlights were dead. The only light came from the stars.

A long groaning moan rose from the cemetery—a chorus of mixed despair and gratitude. Then silence.

"I think we did it!" Bert said.

Harold nodded. They grinned at each other. Then Harold looked toward the cemetery. "Should we go look for Stanner?"

There was a droning from the sky overhead.

Bert looked up to see a delta shape blacking out the sky. Just an absence of stars, marking its presence.

"Oh, no, Harold. Look at that. The military's making their move. With great timing as usual."

Harold grabbed Bert's upper arm and waited for the explosions. The bombs were said to be big. He wondered if he'd feel anything.

The bombs fell. They heard them whining down, humming down, then screaming down, almost directly overhead.

They saw them strike the cemetery with a *whuff-whuff* THUD. Then . . . nothing.

"Oh!" Harold said suddenly. "The pulser was set to continue for a full minute! They dropped the bombs—but the pulser's still working! The bombs are regulated with electronics, Bert!"

Bert leapt up and shook his fist at the delta in the sky. "Ha, you bastards! We beat both of you! Your machines, and those machines! Fuck the whole bunch of you!"

Harold and Bert hugged each other, dancing around in circles, as Stanner walked out of the cemetery, pretending to shake his head with disapproval. "You guys should get a room or something, please. I like to be liberal, but . . ."

The three men laughed in sheer relief—and looked up at the hills. Then their laughter melted away. They looked at one another. They silently went to find the SUV.

Stanner thought, *They could all be gone. We might've been too late. All those kids could be torn to pieces.*

Shannon could be dead.

"Let's get back to the kids," Bert said, echoing what Stanner was thinking.

Stanner at the wheel, they drove back toward the hills and the water tank.

They had to drive around cars in the streets, some on fire, some with their inhuman drivers just sitting there dead behind the wheel; many of them with their engines still running, lodged in ditches and crumpled against telephone poles, figures slumped inside, all jumbled. Some of the crawlers were dead beside the road.

"It's like the Rapture after all, for them," Bert said.

Twice they drove around dead, altered animals—an eight-legged deer, four of its legs a mix of mechanical and human; a raccoon with a set of metal antennas instead of a head. Both quite dead, lying where they'd fallen en route.

Stanner pulled up beside a big red extended-cab pickup truck with its car alarm keening, rammed into the cinder block wall of a car parts store, in the dusty road shoulder. He stared at the dead man inside. Yeah, about his size. Same hair color. He put the SUV in park, but left it running as he got out.

"There a reason for this stop?" Bert said. "I want to see if Lacey—if she and the kids are okay."

"Yeah, I've got a boy up there," Harold said.

"If they're okay, they'll stay okay," Stanner said, taking the gas can from the back of the SUV. He shook it; gas sloshed inside, maybe a fifth full. Enough. "If they're not okay, we can't help them now. This is something I've got to do. It's for Shannon as much as for me." He walked over to the truck, opened the door, and reached into the dead man's pocket. Found his wallet and took it. Then he took out his own wallet, removed the money, put the wallet, replete with credit cards and ID, in the man's rear pants pocket. It was an unpleasant feeling, to be in a dead man's pocket. But it wasn't his first time.

He sloshed gasoline on the dead man's head, took out the lighter he'd brought along, lit the gasoline, and stood back. He let it burn for a few minutes. The alarm just kept keening and wailing as if the car was reacting to its driver's burning.

"Oh, Jesus, Stanner," Harold said, watching the body burn.

After enough of the guy had burned, Stanner dragged the body from the cab of the truck—the guy's lower half wasn't burning yet—and rolled it in the dust of the road shoulder till the fire went out. A lot of the guy's face came off in the process, and Stanner's stomach lurched at the sight. When that was done, he tossed the rest of the gas on the front of the truck and lit it on fire.

Then he returned to the SUV, bringing the gas can with him. He got into the SUV, and they started off again, leaving the burning truck behind, the alarm fading in the distance.

"What the hell was that about?" Harold asked.

Stanner glanced at him, then looked back at the road. "Just trying to cover my tracks. I'm still on the outside with the Facility. It's going to take time to square with them. So in the meantime, it's better they think I'm dead."

"I hope it works out for you and Shannon," Bert said. After a moment, when they drove around the body of a fat man in a black suit, he murmured, "Despite all the deaths, it's funny how things have worked out. I mean, the worst didn't happen. It's like serendipity. Especially one part: Harold here, turning up, when we needed him."

"What are you saying?" Harold asked, looking at Bert with his eyebrows raised. "That God brought me in here?"

"Is that so impossible? It's grace."

"You tell those kids that God was here," Harold said. "You tell my boy Waylon. The kid had to shoot his own mother, for god's sake."

Bert nodded. "I know what you mean. And if God helps us, why didn't he stop the Holocaust, and why didn't he help when the Chinese soldiers forced children to execute their own parents in

Tibet? But see, God can't help most of the time. God can only put a little spin on the ball, offer a little help here and there, where conditions allow. A lot of wise men have said it's up to us to do God's work in the world ourselves. But now and then, where conditions allow, that divine influence—I mean, I hesitate to use that word *God*, with all the old associations it has—now and then that influence nudges us along, brings us together so we can help ourselves. We have to be alert to those possibilities. Anyway, that's my—"

"Look out!" Harold yelled, pointing at the road ahead.

Stanner slammed on the brakes. A naked girl was lying in the middle of the road. They stopped the car and Bert went to look at her. He picked her body up and laid it gently on the grass in front of a house nearby, and put his coat over her. He came back to the SUV and got behind the wheel, continued on their way.

"I remember that girl from the high school," Bert said. "Very popular girl, name of Cleo. Poor kid."

Other people—survivors, more than they'd dare hope for—were coming out of their houses, looking around in stunned wonder. Stanner knew they were human—because their confusion was so authentic.

They drove up the hill, up the gravel road, into the darkness, to the stony parking lot below the dark bulk of the water tower. Some trucks and cars were parked here. But that didn't prove the kids were okay.

They honked their horn, in the signal they'd arranged, three longs and a short. No immediate response. They got out, silently, and walked toward the water tower—and a crowd of kids came rushing around the metal curve of the tank, from the far side of it. There was Adair, there was Waylon, and Donny, and Siseela. No Shannon.

Bert ran, seeing his Lacey. Ran into her arms.

But Shannon . . .

Stanner searched through the kids milling—laughing, crying—around the water tank.

"Has anyone seen . . ."

There she was. Behind the others. Coming toward him. Allowing him a smile. Then coming into his arms. For a moment or two, like a little girl again.

"Dad," she said. "Daddy . . ."

EPILOGUE

December 19

When Errol Clayborn opened the door, he was beaming a big welcome-to-Christmas-vacation-with-your-family smile.

The smile faded fast.

"Uh, Bert?"

Errol gaped with a poorly disguised mix of dismay and confusion as Bert introduced Lacey, Stanner, Shannon, Harold, Waylon, Adair, Donny, Siseela . . . and Vinnie.

He looked twice at Vinnie. Then at the two black kids. Then back at the hulking, scruffy figure of Vinnie—who stood turned half away, looking at him out of the corners of his eyes.

"Hi, I'm a Christmas lump, I've got three wishes to hang over the window when they come in under the sled don't worry about a thing," Vinnie said.

Bert laughed at Errol's expression. "Errol, I got that card you sent with yet another prod to come out for Christmas. And you said I could bring friends."

"Well, I—"

"Not to worry," Stanner said, smiling crookedly, spreading his hands. "There'll be two less, anyway. Shannon and I are just dropping these folks off. We all drove out together and—I just needed to see these people safely somewhere. My daughter and I are heading up to Canada."

Waylon turned and looked at Stanner, scowling. Then he gravely shook Stanner's hand. "I was wrong about you, man. You're, all, a complicated guy."

"Nobody's simple. Certainly not my man Vinnie, there. Vinnie, I'm gonna miss you."

Vinnie turned his back on Stanner. But he was smiling.

So was Shannon, as Stanner put his arm around her. She said, "Maybe my old man's not so bad." She said it in a skeptical way that made the others laugh.

"What you gonna do now, Major?" Waylon asked.

Stanner shrugged. Smiled sadly.

"I've got to lay low. I'll probably need an identity change, till I get this straightened out. There's a senator friend of mine I served with; maybe he can get me square with the Pentagon, eventually. I believe in what I was *trying* to do, Waylon. I just got off track. I did the right thing in that uniform, once upon a time. I hope—I need— to go back to the right thing, in uniform."

"Uh," Errol was saying, looking at the small crowd on the porch.

Bert said, "I'm sure you heard about the disaster in Quiebra, Errol?"

"Hell, yeah, I tried to call you about fifty times. They said it was some kind of viral disaster, killed hundreds of people, still under investigation. Crazy stories coming out of there."

"Truth is, Errol, it wasn't a virus. So you don't have to worry about catching anything. We were caught up in that 'disaster,' and these people needed someplace to go, and you invited me and a friend—and I couldn't bring just one, not this time. So, just for the holiday. You know. We'll all sleep on the floor. We brought sleeping bags."

"Uh, sure. I mean, there was an emergency and—" Then he glanced over his shoulder and smiled—taking some kind of obscure personal satisfaction in it as he turned back to Bert and said, "I guess my wife'll just have to . . . suck it up."

A little girl with tousled brown hair and big hazel eyes looked past Errol from inside the house. "Dad, you said you'd watch *Starbots* with me."

"*Starbots!*" Vinnie gasped.

She looked at him. "You like *Starbots*?"

He couldn't look right at her. He looked at the mailbox beside the door. But he said, "Oh, yes, very much. It's a part of my land of where to go, for three thousand miles in three directions."

"Okay!" She grabbed his hand—after a moment he stopped trying to draw it back—and pulled him past her father, into the house.

Stanner chuckled. "Well, we'll be in touch, Bert." They shook hands.

"So, uh, whoever's coming in, uh, come on in and, uh . . ." Errol began.

Bert and the others ignored Errol, watching Stanner and Shannon walk to the rented minivan. Watching them wave a final time; watching them start to back out the driveway.

Then Waylon ran up to the minivan, banged on the window by Stanner, till he stopped the car. "Yes, Waylon?"

Waylon was excited, hands balled into fists. Voice too loud.

"Yo, dude, you got to tell me—on the way here you said you'd tell me before you left, man. 'Kay: You worked in that secret black chopper Pentagon Area 51 stuff. *What about the aliens, man?* The UFOs? Knowhatamean? The *saucers!*"

Stanner smiled faintly. He looked at the others. Winked at Adair. She smiled back at him.

Then he said, "Ah, the aliens. *The saucers.* Right. Well, I'll tell you." He leaned toward Waylon and stage-whispered, "That's another story—dude."

Then Stanner backed up the car, drove away down the street. And he and Shannon headed north.

> The world becomes smaller and smaller as it becomes more and more uniform. People lose the power of any separate wisdom . . . Man's inventions

increasingly take charge of him. We see machines becoming disproportionate to human life. It is surely obvious that the development of machinery is not the development of man and it is equally obvious that machinery is enslaving man and gradually removing him from his possibilities of normal life and normal effort, and the normal use of his functions. If machinery were used on a scale proportionate to man's needs it would be a blessing . . . Man is his understanding— not his possession of facts or his heap of inventions and facilities.

—Maurice Nicoll,
Living Time and the Integration of the Life

© Beth Gwinn

ABOUT THE AUTHOR

John Shirley is the author of more than a dozen books, including *Demons; City Come A-Walkin'; Really, Really, Really, Really Weird Stories;* and the newly reissued classic cyberpunk trilogy A Song Called Youth—*Eclipse, Eclipse Penumbra,* and *Eclipse Corona.* He is the recipient of the Horror Writers Association's Bram Stoker Award and won the International Horror Guild Award for his collection *Black Butterflies.* Shirley has fronted punk bands and written lyrics for his own music, as well as for Blue Öyster Cult and other groups. A principal screenwriter for *The Crow,* Shirley now devotes most of his time to writing for television and film.

Visit the author's Web site at www.darkecho.com/John Shirley.